THE QUEEN'S FAVOURITE

ROBERT DUDLEY, EARL OF LEICESTER

THE TUDOR COURT
BOOK ONE

LAURA DOWERS

Blue Laurel
Press

ISBN (Paperback): 978-1-912968-44-2

ISBN (eBOOK): 978-1-912968-06-0

For my beloved mother who started it all!

THE QUEEN'S FAVOURITE

'Droit et Loyal'

"I am now passing into another world and must leave you to your fortunes and to the Queen's graces, but beware of the gypsy, for he will be too hard for you all. You know not the beast so well as I do."
- THOMAS RADCLIFFE, EARL OF SUSSEX, ON HIS DEATHBED

"I am a Dudley in blood… and do acknowledge… that my chiefest honour is to be a Dudley, and truly am glad to have cause to set forth the nobility of that blood whereof I am descended."
- SIR PHILIP SIDNEY

CHAPTER ONE

1542

Robert Dudley was bored. Bored with the lesson, bored with Master Cheke droning on about Seneca, Suetonius and other Romans long dead. He was bored with sitting still for hour upon hour.

Robert sighed and ran his fingers through his thick, dark hair. If only the rest of his classmates felt as bored as he, they could perhaps mutiny. His elder brother Ambrose sat beside him, his chin cradled in one hand, the other idly brushing away the wood shavings he had made by carving his name in the desk with his penknife. Behind were their younger brothers, Henry and Guildford, playing cards beneath their desk. Robert knew he could count on his brothers to be with him, but he doubted the others would dare. Prince Edward and Jane Grey were sitting, all attention, at the front of the class and wouldn't dream of absconding, while Jane's sisters, the tall and pretty Catherine and the hunch-backed dwarf Mary, sitting at the back where no one paid her any mind, were too unadventurous to even try.

But maybe Elizabeth would join him. She was sitting in front of Robert, head bent, scribbling furiously. She too was paying little heed to Master Cheke, not because of boredom, but because she had learnt this lesson months before in private study and had now moved on to the Ancient Greeks.

'Master Robert!'

Robert jerked his attention back to his tutor. 'Yes, Master Cheke?' he said, his lips broadening into a grin.

Charming though his smile was, it had little effect upon the aged scholar. Cheke sighed as he leant on a pile of books. 'Master Robert, I realise study of the Classics holds little interest for such an energetic boy as yourself, but your parents have arranged for you to be educated with the children of His Majesty the king, and you would do well to follow their example and attend to your books instead of gazing around the room like a moonstruck calf. Do you comprehend me, young sir?'

Robert bent his head in answer and dipped the tip of his quill into the inkpot, grinning as he heard Elizabeth snigger. Master Cheke, satisfied that Robert was behaving, turned his back and searched through another pile of books heaped on a chest by the wall. Robert stole a look out of the window and saw with joy it had finally stopped raining. He leaned forward and hissed at Elizabeth. When she turned her frowning face to him, he jerked his head towards the door. Her frown deepened disapprovingly and she shook her head. He glared at her, his black eyes insisting. She poked her tongue out at him and turned back to her work.

Undeterred, Robert eased his backside from the stool and edged around the desk. Ambrose opened bleary eyes to see what his brother was up to and watched in amusement as Robert grabbed Elizabeth's wrist, plucked the quill from between her fingers and tugged her from her stool. She grimaced but allowed herself to be led from the schoolroom.

Ambrose's gaze wandered over to Master Cheke, who was wholly unaware his star pupil and the mischief-maker had absconded. He closed his eyes, wondering how long it would take the tutor to realise.

'I wanted to work,' Elizabeth protested as Robert pulled her along the corridors of the palace, dodging servants and the ever-constant parasites of any royal palace, those hoping to gain favour or a position in the household.

Robert ignored her complaint, giving her arm a vicious extra tug. He burst out of a door into the small courtyard, high walls on either side plunging him into shadow. The air was fresh and cool after the rain. Elizabeth came tumbling out after him, slipping on the rain-washed cobbles.

'Let go of me,' she said, twisting her wrist and breaking free of his grasp. 'Where are we going?'

'To the stables, of course.' Free of Elizabeth's reluctance and certain she would follow, Robert broke into a run.

Elizabeth hitched her skirts up to her bony knees and shouted, 'Wait for me!'

But Robert couldn't wait, and with his longer legs taking great strides, reached the stable yard before her. Curving his body around the door, he breathed in the aroma of straw and animal, too long absent from his nostrils. He moved along the stalls, murmuring greetings to the horses as they pressed their noses into his outstretched palm.

Horseshoes hanging from nails on the back of the stable door clattered, signalling Elizabeth's arrival. 'I told you to wait.'

He smiled, not looking up. 'See how they've missed me, Bess?'

'Stupid beasts.' Elizabeth snatched an apple from a

3

bulging sack leaning against the wall. She rubbed it against her bodice before snapping off a bite.

'Don't call them that,' he scolded. 'You'd miss me if you didn't see me for a week.'

'No, I wouldn't.' She stomped past him, halting only when Robert prised the apple from her hand, and flung herself on a bale of hay.

Robert held the apple to the mouth of Phoebe, his favourite horse, who munched at it contentedly. 'You're in a foul mood today. I wouldn't have bothered bringing you if I'd known you would be such a bore.'

'You're a pig,' Elizabeth spat. 'Speak so to me again and—'

'You'll what?' he dared her.

'I'll... I'll...'

'Banish me to the Tower, cut off my—'

Robert broke off, horrified at what he had been about to say.

'Cut off your head,' she finished for him, her eyes wide and wet.

'Bess!' he breathed in apology and hurried over to the hay bale where she sat. He put his arm around her shoulder.

'Katherine,' she croaked in explanation.

'I know.' He shook his head, angry at himself. 'I shouldn't have said that. I'm such an ass.'

'Why is my father doing this to her?' Elizabeth asked, wiping her eyes.

'Don't you know?' Robert was surprised.

He thought everyone knew about Queen Katherine, the pretty girl who had caught the lustful eye of the ageing king and married him, letting him believe he was the first to enjoy her body. Katherine had had all the daring reck-lessness of youth, and secure in the king's love, had taken one of his gentlemen, a Thomas Culpeper, to her bed. She and her lover had been discovered. The king's anger and humiliation were too great; there could be no forgiveness for such betrayal. Culpeper had already gone to the block for his crime. Katherine was now in the Tower, waiting her turn to die.

'I heard some of my women talking,' Elizabeth said, 'but they shut up when they saw me. How has Katherine offended my father, Robin?'

Robert withdrew his arm. 'Father said I wasn't to talk about it.'

She grabbed his hand and held it tight. 'Rob, if you know, tell me, please.'

He considered for a moment, then reluctantly agreed. 'Katherine bedded Thomas Culpeper.'

Elizabeth frowned. 'What does bedded mean?'

He stared at her. 'Don't tell me you don't know? You're supposed to be the clever one.'

'Don't laugh at me.' Her pale cheeks had flushed red.

'I suppose I could tell you,' he said, toying with her.

She slapped his hand hard. 'Tell me.'

Proud to know something she didn't, Robert gloatingly told her what bedded meant, leaving no detail out, and laughed even harder when she clamped her hands over her ears and told him to shut up, to stop lying, that it wasn't true, that her parents had never done such a disgusting thing.

'It is true, Bess. And you'll have to do it when you marry.'

'I won't. I'm not going to marry. Not ever.'

She sounded so certain that Robert didn't bother to argue. He was disappointed at how this little adventure of his was turning out. This wasn't what he had planned at all when he had dragged her to the stables. He had wanted Elizabeth to ride out with him, to feel the cool air sting his face and thrill to the strength of the horse beneath him, to laugh together at having fooled Master Cheke and leaving the others to remain hunched over their books. There seemed little hope of having such fun now, and he wished he had come alone.

He looked towards the stable door at the sound of footsteps. A moment later, a woman appeared in the aperture.

'There you are!' the woman declared and Robert recognised Elizabeth's governess, Katherine Ashley.

'Kat,' Elizabeth gulped guiltily. 'What are you doing here?'

'Looking for you, young miss,' Mistress Ashley retorted. 'I have had Master Cheke complaining to me that you disappeared from his schoolroom.' Her top lip curled as she looked at Robert. 'I might have known he would have something to do with it.'

Robert stuck his tongue out at her.

'Do that again, my lad,' Mistress Ashley shook her finger at him, 'and I'll have you up before your father before you can shake a stick.'

'He wouldn't care, you old hag,' Robert muttered.

The governess took a quick step towards him. 'What did you say?'

'He didn't say anything, Kat.' Elizabeth jumped down from the hay bale and, moving swiftly, slid her hand into Mistress Ashley's. 'Come, let us go. I'll see you tomorrow,' she mouthed at Robert, pushing her governess out of the stable door.

'Fooling in the stable with a courtier's son,' Robert heard Mistress Ashley say as Elizabeth led her away. 'Whatever would people say?'

He slouched to the door and watched them go, indignation growing in him at her words. How dare she scorn him for being a courtier's son, as if there was something laughable in being so? At least he was legitimate, which was more than could be said of Elizabeth.

And besides, he wouldn't be a mere courtier's son forever, not with his father's ambitions for his family. Let Mistress Ashley look down her nose at him when the Dudley family were among the greatest in the land.

Robert moved back to Phoebe's stall, lifting her saddle from its post. Phoebe whinnied and stamped, like him, impatient to be outside. 'There now, my lovely,' he said, kissing her neck and holding his cheek against the warm flesh. 'You know we can do it, don't you?'

CHAPTER TWO

THREE YEARS LATER

The greyhound nudged its slim, silky body around Robert's legs, trying to get comfortable. There wasn't much room on the window seat, so the dog used a long, trim thigh to rest its chin, and thumped its tail in pleasure whenever fingers tickled behind its ears.

Robert was reading, tilting the book towards the window to make use of the setting sun. Its orange light bled through the glass, picking up on strands of dark brown hair among the black and giving a golden glow to his tawny skin. His interest in the book was desultory and his gaze wandered towards the window, flickering over the hedges and flowers of the gardens and down to the river. The river was crammed with vessels; large boats carrying cargo, wherries ferrying their passengers, but it was a barge painted in blue and yellow, the family colours, that his eyes picked out and which he craned his neck to see.

Robert watched as the barge banged against the river steps and a figure climbed over the gunwale before it was even secured. He recognised the hurrying shape of his father and wondered what had brought him back from the court in such haste. Looking back to the boat, he saw a woman, who could only be his mother, taking the hand of a boy who helped her out.

The greyhound lifted its head, ears pricked as the hall door opened and banged against the wall. It thrust its wet nose against its master's hand as Robert's father called.

'Be still, Rollo,' Robert said, closing his book, keeping his eyes on the door.

A moment later the door opened and his father strode in. He pointed his finger at Robert. 'I've been calling you!'

'I didn't hear you,' Robert lied.

'Didn't want to hear, more like,' John growled, flinging himself into a chair. 'Have you been idling in here all day?'

'No, Father, not all day.'

'Huh. You're in one of your facetious moods, I see.'

Robert smiled, looking back to the door at the sound of swishing skirts dragging rushes across the floor.

'Thank you for waiting, John,' Jane muttered as she entered, pushing a fat white cat from a chair and sitting down. The cat immediately jumped onto her lap and submitted to her vigorous caresses.

John pointed again at Robert. 'I wanted to find him.'

'I could have told you where he would be,' Jane said. 'Lounging around with his dog.'

'Then it's about time he stopped lounging around, don't you think, Jane?' John gave his wife a meaningful glance.

Jane held his gaze for a long moment, then nodded and said, 'Tell him.'

'Tell me what?' Robert asked worriedly.

John turned to face him. 'I've secured a position for you at Hunsdon, where you will join the prince's household as one of his companions.'

'You're sending me away?' Robert said, a tremble in his voice.

Jane held out her hand to him. He hurried over and

took it. 'My darling,' she said, 'you knew you would have to leave sometime. After all, both Jack and Ambrose have been gone for a while now.'

'I know, Mother,' he nodded, biting down on his bottom lip. 'I just thought I could stay here with you.'

John let out a snort of exasperation. 'For God's sake, do you have any idea how long we've been trying to arrange this appointment for you? Months, Rob, that's how long. And you stand there, whining like a girl—'

'I'm not,' Robert shouted at him. 'I'll go, and gladly, if that's what you want.'

'It should be what *you* want, you fool,' John said, shaking his head. 'Don't you want to be a friend of the prince?'

Robert shrugged as if it was of no consequence. 'It's been years since I've seen him. I might not like him.'

'Oh, you'll like him,' John assured him. 'And you'll serve him well, or you'll have me to answer to.'

'John, don't talk to him like that.' Jane widened her eyes at him, an instruction to calm down. 'We've surprised Rob with this, that's all. He knows how important it is he does well at Hunsdon.'

Robert didn't know, and he didn't feel like pretending he did. 'Why is it important?' he asked his father.

John sighed, his temper abating. 'The king is not well. He is so unwell, in fact, I cannot see him living much longer. When Henry dies, Edward will be king, and the closer you are to him now, the closer I hope you will be in the future. You understand?

'Yes, Father,' Robert said, 'I understand.'

'Good. You'll be leaving in a few days' time, so you can start packing what you want to take. One chest only.'

Rollo nuzzled Robert's hand. 'I can take Rollo, can't I?'

John studied the dog. 'Best leave him here.'

'I won't go without Rollo,' Robert declared, the

thought of being parted from his dog even more terrible than leaving home.

John jumped up, crossed to Robert in one stride, and cuffed him about the ear. 'You will do as you are told,' he roared.

Jane rose and stood between her husband and her son. 'Enough.' She pushed John away, and he moved back to his chair. She turned to Robert, who was rubbing his reddened ear, his chin dimpling as tears threatened to fall. Jane put her arms around him and he pressed his head against her breast.

'We'll take care of Rollo,' she promised, smoothing his hair. 'And when you're settled, we'll see about sending him to you. How does that sound?'

Robert nodded and sniffed. He pulled away as his father walked out of the room. 'He's angry with me.'

'That will pass,' Jane said soothingly. 'He's already sorry he hit you. You'll see. He'll apologise to you later. You must understand, Rob, your father is working so very hard at court. It's not easy keeping the king's favour. It takes its toll.'

'I don't want to disappoint him.'

'And you won't, my darling. The prince will like you and you will become great friends.' Jane pulled him back to her bosom and held him tight. 'You must be friends with the prince, Rob. Our family's future may depend upon it.'

HUNSDON PALACE

Prince Edward closed his book with a loud bang. 'I've had enough of studying for today.' He turned to his friend sitting beside him. 'What say you to some target practice, Barnaby?'

Barnaby Fitzpatrick shrugged. 'If you please, Edward.'

'You don't mind, do you, Master Buckley?' Edward asked his tutor, already getting to his feet.

William Buckley threw down his quill. 'It doesn't seem to matter if I do, does it?' He puffed out his cheeks and shook his head at his pupils. 'Oh, go on, get out. Lessons are over for today.'

All the other boys in the schoolroom chorused a hurrah and closed their own books with alacrity.

'Now, Master Buckley, you mustn't sulk,' Edward chided.

'I'm not sulking,' Buckley said. 'I'm merely wondering how I am to explain your lack of education to your father's secretary when he demands a report on your progress.'

'Oh, that's easy,' Edward said. 'All you have to say is that I am progressing well and exceed all your expectations.'

The boys laughed, and Buckley, despite himself, joined in. Thomas Cobden, hearing horses, pressed his nose to the window. 'Is this the new boy, do you think?'

Edward joined him at the window. 'Yes, that's him. Robert Dudley. He used to study with me and my sister years ago. They were always running off together. Master Cheke would get quite annoyed.'

'I can sympathise,' Buckley muttered wryly.

Henry Sidney moved to the door. 'Are we going out to shoot or not?' he asked impatiently.

'We're going out to shoot,' Edward declared. 'Come on.'

The boys rushed out of the schoolroom, shouting goodbyes to Buckley, and hurtled along corridors and down stairs to burst out into the courtyard where Robert stood with his trunk, the coach that had brought him already trundling away. He took a step back at the gaggle of boys.

'Robert Dudley,' Edward greeted him, looking him up

and down. 'I thought I had seen the back of you years ago.'

Robert bowed. 'I hope it does not displease you to have me here, Your Grace.'

'Oh, let's have none of that,' Barnaby said, pushing Edward out of the way and holding out his hand to Robert. 'I'm Barnaby Fitzpatrick. Very pleased to meet you.'

Robert took his hand and wrung it. 'Robert Dudley.'

'And this is Henry Sidney, Thomas Cobden, Christopher Kempe.'

One by one, the boys shook hands. Only Edward held back, watching his friends greet the newcomer.

'We are going to the butts, Robert,' he said, his tone implying the new boy wasn't welcome.

Barnaby shot Edward a disapproving look. 'And you're invited,' he told Robert pointedly.

Edward said nothing but turned on his heel and walked towards the gardens. Barnaby gave Robert a wide grin, clapped him on the shoulder, and hurried to catch up with the prince.

'Don't mind him,' Henry Sidney said, gesturing for Robert to walk alongside him. 'He must always be the centre of attention. But you probably know what he's like.'

'We studied together,' Robert said, 'but I was more Elizabeth's friend than his.'

'Is that so? I've never met his sister. Edward is very fond of her and talks of her often, but she lives at Hatfield and never comes here.'

'That's a pity. I would have liked to see her again.' Robert looked around, taking in the gardens and the house. 'What's it like here?'

Henry smiled. 'Don't worry, you'll like it. It's not as stuffy as you might think, and there's always something to do.'

'Are pets allowed?' Robert asked.

Henry made a face. 'None of us have any. There are the hunting birds, but I don't suppose they count. Why?'

'I had to leave my dog, Rollo, behind at home. Father wouldn't let me bring him.'

'Well, don't let it bother you. A dog's not worth getting upset over.'

'Rollo's not just any dog,' Robert snapped. 'He's *my* dog and he'll pine without me there.'

Henry, startled by the outburst, opened his mouth to apologise for his lack of sympathy, but before he could speak, the prince called out, 'Don't dawdle, you two,' and Henry waved to show they had heard.

'We'd best not keep him waiting. Come on. And don't worry. We'll see what we can do about Rollo, eh?'

He grinned at Robert and Robert smiled gratefully back.

CHAPTER THREE

1546

John Dudley studied the king as the last of September's daylight faded. Henry was certainly ill. His body, already corpulent, had swelled like a bellows over the past month. The small eyes were bloodshot and yellowed, sunk into the flesh that rose in mounds of clammy pinkness, the contours of the cheekbones long since buried.

A fat, trembling hand laid down a knave of hearts. 'Can you match that, John?'

John scanned the cards he held. 'No, Your Majesty, I fear I cannot.'

Henry chuckled. 'Then come on. Pay up.'

John sent four gold coins spinning across the table to clink against the king's winning pile. He dealt them each another hand.

'How does your son, John?' Henry asked, picking up the cards and fanning them out in his hand. 'The one with the prince?'

'You mean Robert, Your Majesty,' John said, laying down a card. 'I had a letter from him only this morning. He is doing well. The prince enjoys his company and Robert hopes he is of great service to him.'

'Ah, now,' Henry waggled a fat finger at him, 'service is a trait that runs in your family, John. Your boy serves my son well, you serve me well, and…' the little mouth pursed and expelled a puff of sour breath, 'your father served my father well.'

'So I understand, Your Majesty.' John felt Henry's eyes upon him but he kept his own firmly upon the cards.

'I think much about the past, John,' Henry continued. 'Too much, my Fool says, but I cannot seem to help it. I did a foolish thing when I allowed your father to be executed. But my council persuaded me to it.'

John wondered what Henry meant by telling him this. He didn't want to hear of Henry's anguish, an anguish probably only recently felt now the king found himself nearer the grave, or have painful memories raked up. He wished the king would stop talking, but Henry was oblivious to John's distress and continued.

'My father was a mean man. He loved money more than anything and he used your father to extract all the money he could from his subjects.' Henry reached for his goblet and raised it to his lips. The wine spilled over his trembling lips and soaked into his beard. 'I was persuaded it would show the love I had for my people to… to…,' he floundered for the right words.

'To offer my father up as a sacrifice?' John suggested, his voice brittle.

Henry groaned. 'You are still angry.'

'He was my father, Your Majesty.'

'But you must have been very young when he died.'

'Old enough to remember his execution. I remember everything. The jeers, the shouts and the foul names my father was called. He tried to speak, but the mob drowned out his words. And then came the kneeling, the wait while the axe was raised and then the bl....' His voice broke and he willed himself to be strong. 'The blood.'

Henry's piggy eyes grew moist. He blinked and tears fell down his cheeks. 'I hoped you had forgiven me.'

John watched in horror as the trickle of tears turned to sobs that made Henry's massive body shudder. He was so shocked by the sight that he couldn't move, could not go to the king and offer comfort as he knew he should. A kind of pleasure flowed through him that the king should feel such remorse, and yet aghast that it was he who had reduced the king to a blubbering mess.

Someone brushed past him. The crying had roused Will Somers, who had been dozing in a corner of the room, and the loyal Fool now took the king's hand and pumped it up and down playfully, trying to summon up a smile or a laugh. He turned a scowling countenance to John and mouthed a question: What did you do?

John shook his head and moved to the king's other side, sinking to his knees, wincing as he felt his knee bones crack. 'I do forgive you, Your Majesty,' he lied. The king's bloodshot eyes opened and stared at him. 'As you said, it was not of your doing. Others persuaded you to it.'

Henry's hand clutched John's. 'I was, I was. I...'He broke off as his brow creased, and he turned his face away in embarrassment. 'But you weary me with all this, John.' He pushed John's hand away and wiped his fingers across his eyes.

John scrambled to his feet. 'It is late. I will let you get to your bed, Your Majesty.' He called for Henry's Gentlemen. As they fussed around the stumbling mountain of flesh, John bid them all goodnight and hurried to his rooms.

'John?' a sleep-heavy voice mumbled from the bed as he entered and closed the door behind him.

'Yes, it's me.'

Jane sat up, blinking as John lit a candle. 'You're very late.' She noticed his expression. 'What's wrong?'

He sank onto the bed and gave a deep sigh. 'I made

17

the king weep tonight, Jane. He sobbed right in front of me.'

She grabbed his hand and dug her nails into his palm. 'What in Heaven did you say to him?'

'Sheath your claws, vixen. It wasn't my fault. He spoke of my father. Can you believe he actually expected me to have forgiven him for cutting off my father's head? He said it hadn't been his idea, but that his council had made him do it. He said he was sorry and wept. And then,' John sighed again, 'he realised what a fool he was making of himself and grew embarrassed. I thought he would have my head then and there for seeing him in such a state, but he just wanted to be rid of me.'

'Oh, John, are you in disgrace?'

'No, I don't think so. In the morning, he will pretend we never had such a conversation.' He began untying his jerkin. 'I'm still his John, his good fellow, someone to while away the time with.'

'Thank God for that,' Jane said, watching him as he undressed. 'Though I wish He would take that old monster to his bosom sooner rather than later.'

John rounded on her. 'Hold your tongue, Jane. I've told you before, do not speak of the king so. You will forget yourself one day and say it in company, and then where would you be? You'd be in prison, that's where, or worse.'

Jane gave him a sulky look. 'Yes, very well, John. You can stop glaring at me. Anne Seymour was here earlier,' she continued as he rolled off his hose, 'snooping about. Whatever possessed Edward Seymour to marry that woman?'

'He must like shrews. What did she want?'

'To find out what you were up to. She hates it that the king prefers your company to her husband's and wanted to find out what it is you do that Henry likes so much.'

'Did you satisfy her curiosity?'

'What could I tell her?' She flipped the bedclothes back for him to climb in. 'The king likes you because you are clever and interesting and charming. Edward Seymour has all the charm of horse manure.'

John laughed at that and settled back against the pillows. 'I need you to be friends with Anne Seymour, my love. I know it isn't easy, but I can't have her pouring poison into Edward's ear about us.'

'You don't need him,' Jane said, lifting his arm so she could nestle against him.

'I do need him,' he said, squeezing her hip. 'He's the prince's uncle. When Henry dies and the prince becomes king, Seymour will be his closest adviser. And I need to be Seymour's closest adviser. You understand, don't you?'

'Of course I do,' Jane sighed. 'And don't worry, I'll do what I have to. I would just find it easier to be friendly with Anne Seymour if she wasn't such a miserable old cow.'

Rollo had persisted in poking his head through the coach window throughout the journey, forcing the leather curtain to bunch up around his neck like a bizarre headdress. For the last few miles, the greyhound had been standing on the toes of Mary Dudley, who had long since given up trying to persuade the animal to sit down, its tail banging against her brother Jack's legs.

The coach came to a stop in the courtyard of Hunsdon Palace, and Mary opened the door, not waiting for the driver to jump down and do it for her. Rollo bounded down and ran over to the figure standing in the entrance porch, barking joyfully.

'Hello, Rob,' Mary called, smiling as Robert gave Rollo a hug. 'We're here at last.'

Robert grinned up at her, his face screwing up in pleasure as Rollo licked him. 'I've been waiting all morning for you. How have you been, boy? Has Mary been looking after you?'

'He's been spoilt rotten,' Jack said. He and Robert embraced. 'Good to see you, brother.'

'And you.' Robert's tone was earnest. 'It seems ages since I was home. Come in. There's food and wine for you.'

He led them into the hall and pointed at a food-laden table. Jack tucked in hungrily, Mary more modestly, and Robert fed slices of pork to Rollo, laughing as the dog's tongue flicked over his fingers.

'You've missed him,' Mary observed.

'So very much,' Robert admitted, giving Rollo a kiss between his eyes. 'It's not bad here, but it's not like being at Ely Place. How is it at home?'

Jack's face darkened. 'Things are a little tricky for Father at the moment. He's been banished from court.'

'What?' Robert cried. 'Why?'

'He had an argument with the bishop of Winchester in the council chamber. Father struck him about the face, and the bishop made such a fuss about the blow that the king felt compelled to banish Father.'

'But that sounds serious,' Robert said, alarmed.

Jack held up his hands. 'Stop your worrying, Rob. It's a little hiccough, that's all. Father said the king found it all rather amusing. He's sure he'll be back at court this time tomorrow.'

'You're certain?'

'He's sure, so I'm sure. Hallo, who's this?'

Henry Sidney had entered the hall, and Robert introduced him to his brother and sister.

'Good day, Master Jack, Mistress Mary, and this,' Henry bent down to the greyhound and held out his hand, 'must be the magnificent Rollo.' Rollo sniffed Henry's fingers gingerly, then gave them a lick.

'Magnificent?' Mary asked, raising her eyebrows.

'Yes,' Henry said with mock seriousness. 'Apparently, there has never been nor ever will be a dog quite like Rollo.'

Mary giggled, her cheeks flushing a delicate pink.

Robert threw a chunk of bread at his friend. 'Don't talk rubbish, Henry. Why don't you try to amuse my sister without being vulgar while I talk to my brother?'

Henry was more than amenable to such an idea, and Robert jerked his head at Jack to move closer. 'Is Father really all right? You're not just saying that so I don't worry?'

'He's fine, Rob, really,' Jack said. 'In fact, he seemed quite happy to have some time away from court. It's given him a chance to talk business with Edward Seymour away from eavesdroppers.'

Robert frowned. 'What has Father to do with Edward Seymour that he doesn't want anyone knowing?'

Jack shrugged. 'I couldn't say, but you know Father. He's always about something. He and Seymour have become very friendly.' He gave a little laugh. 'Mother doesn't like it. It means she has to be civil to Seymour's wife, who is, and I quote, a devil-whipped bitch.'

Robert laughed at that, though there was a sadness in his manner, too. Looking to cheer his brother up, Jack turned around to study Henry and Mary.

'Rob,' he said in a low voice, 'is it my imagination or is Mary blushing?'

'I do believe she is, Jack,' Robert said, his mouth turning up in amusement.

'Has your good-looking friend turned our sister's head?'

'I can't think how. He is such a clod. Hey, Henry,' he called. 'What are you saying to my sister to make her blush so?'

Mary's eyes widened at him, and the pink circles in her cheeks deepened to a crimson. Henry, though, seemed not to mind the question.

'None of your business. And may I say, Mistress Mary,' he said, taking her hand and pressing his lips to her fingers, 'that I had not expected Robert to have such a delightful sister? Who would have thought that dullard could be related to someone as lovely as you?'

Mary giggled and dropped her gaze to her lap, but didn't withdraw her hand.

'Careful, Mary,' Jack said, reaching for a jug of wine, 'or you'll end up marrying that rascal.'

CHAPTER FOUR

BANKSIDE

John Dudley pressed two pennies into the pit master's hand, one for himself, one for Edward Seymour, and climbed the few steps into the cock-fighting enclosure.

'Why couldn't we go straight back to court?' Seymour asked, leaning on the wooden barrier and gazing down into the ring of blood-stained sawdust. 'The king's forgiven your offence. We could be in our rooms right now having dinner.'

'First things first,' John said, his eyes on the activity in the ring. Two men had entered carrying wooden cages with wings poking through the bars. There was a squawking as the cages were set down on the ground. 'I need you to fill me in on what I've missed before I walk back into court. Where do we stand?'

Seymour rubbed his hands together to warm them. 'We're still strong with the king. He's been asking after you, laughing about that incident with Bishop Gardiner, which hasn't gone down too well with the bishop, I can tell you.'

'Stephen Gardiner's hurt feelings don't concern me,' John said. 'What of the Howards?'

'The duke of Norfolk has returned to his country estate, so he's out of the picture. There is talk of his son joining him, but he's lingering around the court a little too much for my liking.'

John grunted. 'There's no need to worry too much about Surrey's influence. The king is long past his reckless youth, so he doesn't wink at the foolish scrapes Surrey gets into as he used. What else?'

Seymour cleared his throat. 'I believe I've persuaded the king to consider changing his will.'

John turned to stare at him. 'You've done what? And you leave telling me that till last?'

Seymour shrugged as if it was nothing, but his pursed lips and raised eyebrows told a different story. He pretended interest in the birds as they were removed from their cages.

'Tell me,' John hissed.

'Not here.' Seymour looked around uneasily.

'Are you serious? This is the best place to tell me. No one here gives a damn about the king's will.'

Reluctantly, Seymour moved closer and put his mouth next to John's ear. 'I've dined with the king every day since your banishment, and it soon became clear to me that he's frightened.'

'Of what?'

'Of what will happen when he's no longer here. He fears for the prince.'

A cheer erupted from the spectators as the cocks began to fight.

'Henry's worried about the Catholic faction at court,' Seymour continued. 'He wants the prince to enjoy the same privileges he has enjoyed since marrying the Boleyn bitch, but he's concerned that if the Catholics get their hands on the prince, they'll force him to return to Rome.'

'They would certainly try,' John agreed. 'But what does that have to do with—?'

'I've seen the king's will. Paget showed it to me.'

John's mouth dropped open. 'The king's secretary showed you the king's will? Why would he do that? He's a Catholic.'

'Aye, but a Catholic who will bend with the prevailing wind. He's seen the way things are, John. He knows the Protestants at court have the king's favour and he's eager to ally with us. Anyway, Henry's will states that if he dies before the prince has reached his majority, then a council of regency will rule until Edward is of age. As well as you and me, that council of regency will have a lot of Catholics on it. Paget, naturally. Wriothesley.'

'The Howards?'

Seymour nodded.

John grimaced. 'That's unfortunate. If we want to neuter the Catholic faction at court, we will have to begin with the Howards.'

'I agree, but how?'

One of the cocks drew blood, and the spectators roared encouragement. John watched the birds, his eyes narrowing. 'We have to discredit them with the king. Make him believe the Howards are a danger to him, or at least a nuisance he would be well rid of.'

'Any ideas how we can do that?'

'Not yet,' John said, leaning over the barrier and shouting encouragement to the bird he had wagered would win the fight.

'Well then,' Seymour sighed. 'I suppose we shall to keep our eyes and ears open.'

John straightened and grinned at his friend. 'Oh, mine are always open, Ned.'

Anne Seymour pressed her nose against the window pane. 'There's William Hampton again, disappearing into the bushes with that young girl from Frances Woolley's little group. I told his wife about his secret trysts, but she didn't seem to care. And there's Knollys's boy walking that damned dog again, the one that bites my skirts whenever I pass. You said you would talk to him about the dog. Have you?'

Her husband, to whom the enquiry was directed, did not look up from his desk. 'Not yet, my dear.'

'When will you?'

'When I have a moment.'

She made a noise of irritation. 'I shall have to speak to him about it myself, I see I shall.'

Edward Seymour scratched his signature across a document. 'Perhaps that would be best, my love.'

Anne's dull eyes widened. This was not the reply she had expected. 'I see.' She gathered up her skirts and stomped past him, disappearing through a doorway into the small antechamber beyond.

Seymour was considering whether to follow her and make amends when the main door to his study was flung open and John Dudley strode into the room. He dropped into the chair by Seymour's desk and laughed.

'Oh, Ned. He's done it. He's only gone and bloody done it.'

'Who? Done what? What are you grinning like an idiot for?'

John's eyes glinted in the early morning sunshine. Its unforgiving light caught too the grey hairs upon his head, the creases at the corners of his mouth and yet, Seymour thought with not a little resentment, he was still hand-some. His own mirror, when he bothered to look into it, showed a prematurely aged man with tired eyes and sagging jowls.

John drew a deep breath and began. 'I refer, my dear Ned, to Henry Howard, earl of Surrey. That reckless young man has made the mistake we've been hoping for.'

'What has he done?'

'He has had a portrait painted.'

Seymour's eyebrows raised sceptically. 'A portrait?'

John held up a finger, his lips twitching in amusement. 'Not just any old portrait. Included in it are some rather dangerous motifs.'

'Such as? Oh, get on with it. Tell me.'

John grew serious. 'Henry Howard has had himself painted standing beneath an arch with statues on either side. At the feet of the statues are two shields, and this is where it gets interesting. These shields have symbols and devices upon them that should only be borne upon the arms of the kings of England. Not only that, but Howard has had himself painted leaning upon a broken pillar.' He paused for effect.

'So?' Seymour cried desperately.

'A broken pillar,' John said, 'which could be said to symbolise a broken house.'

Seymour stared at John thoughtfully. 'The broken house being the House of Tudor?'

'Why not?' John shrugged. 'Couple that with the shields and what you have is treason.'

'Will the king think so?'

'If we're clever about it. If we choose our moment carefully.'

'Today?'

John shook his head. 'A little patience, Edward. I'll decide when.' He slapped his hands on his thighs and rose with a sigh. 'Will you dine with me?'

Seymour nodded, watching John as he left. He didn't

hear the door behind him open nor did he hear his wife until she said his name.

'Did you hear that?' he asked in reply.

'Every word,' she said. 'Is he right about this portrait?'

'I expect so. John usually is.'

'And if he is right, and the king does take offence, what will happen?'

'If the king is offended enough, then arrest, trial, imprisonment, or…'

'Or?'

Seymour looked up at his wife. 'Execution.'

He had wondered before he said the dread word whether she would flinch or shudder, but Anne Seymour had a strong stomach. She did neither. Her eyes narrowed as she considered.

'So, that would rid us of the son, but what of the father? What of the duke of Norfolk?'

'I don't know. John said nothing of him.'

'Edward,' Anne said in a tone that made Seymour instantly wary, 'you don't think you're letting John Dudley take the lead rather too often, do you?'

'No,' he said, a little too quickly. 'I don't.' Anne raised a dark eyebrow at him. 'Why? Do you?'

She looked away and played with the keys hanging from her girdle. 'I would just prefer it if you made some of the decisions. To anyone who doesn't know you, I imagine it looks as if John Dudley tells you what to do and you do it.'

'I hardly think that's fair, my dear.'

'Do you not?' she said. 'And yet it is he who talks with the king whenever he wants to.'

'The king enjoys his company more than mine,' Seymour protested.

'You are the king's brother-in-law. You are uncle to his

son. How can Henry not value your company more than John Dudley?'

Seymour picked up his quill and dipped it in the ink pot, trying to pretend his wife didn't know what she was talking about.

It was a week later and dinner in the Great Hall was ending. John rushed to Seymour's side, smacked him on the shoulder and jerked his head at him to follow.

Seymour jumped up to do as he was told, spilling wine over his hose in his hurry, and caught up with John in the corridor. 'What is it?'

John's brow furrowed. 'It's time to tell the king about that portrait. His mood is ripe for talk of treachery.'

'How do we go about it? Do we—'

'It's already in hand, Ned. I've had my secretary write up a witness statement about the portrait. I'll fetch it from my rooms and then we'll go to the king.'

'What witness? Is this something else you haven't told me about?'

'Stop being so paranoid, will you? There is no witness, I've made one up.'

'You've done what?' Edward cried.

'We have to have something to present to the king as evidence of Surrey's treachery. Paget told me about the portrait, but Paget isn't about to sign his name to anything that deals with treason. He's not a fool.'

Seymour grabbed John's arm. 'Are you sure we should do this?'

'Good God,' John cried, shrugging him off and throwing open the door to his apartments, 'where are your balls, man? Or has your wife robbed you of those along with your brains?'

'Watch your mouth, John,' Seymour growled.

John looked about the room, then spied a roll of paper on the desk by the window. 'This is it. Come on.'

The two men hurried through the corridors of the palace until they reached the king's private apartments. The guards on the doors let them through at once.

Henry was sitting by the window, one fat bandaged leg propped up on a footstool, a book held up to the light. 'John,' he halloed, taking off his spectacles, 'back so soon?'

'Necessity compels me, Your Majesty.' John stepped up to him and held out the roll of paper. 'I have here a statement that I fear will distress you greatly, Your Majesty. It is a deposition given by a reliable witness regarding the actions of the earl of Surrey.'

Henry took the paper. The fleshy neck and drooping cheeks flushed and the little, yellowed eyes bulged from their sockets as he read. When he finished, he screwed the paper up. 'I'll have his head for this.'

Seymour stepped forward. 'Shall I make out a warrant for the earl of Surrey's arrest, Your Majesty?'

Too hasty, you fool, John thought. *Give him time.*

Henry's eyes narrowed. 'You'd like that, wouldn't you, Brother Seymour? Get him out of the way, eh? I know you have no liking for the Howards.'

Before Seymour could splutter a protest, John interjected. 'With respect, Your Majesty, you yourself have no reason to love them. Twice have they hurt your generous heart with women of that family, and so rumour has it, would have tried to do so again.'

Seymour and Henry stared at him in utter surprise.

'What are you talking about?' Henry growled.

John swallowed down the lump in his throat. 'It is rumoured about the court that the earl of Surrey entreated his sister to...,' he paused for effect, 'to make herself available for your bed.'

He'd said enough. Henry's face turned purple and he

struggled out of his chair. 'I will have his head,' he growled. 'To sully his own sister's honour. To impugn mine! Has there ever been such a rogue? Am I to be continually plagued by these Howards?'

'I beg you, sire, put an end to their malicious plots,' Seymour said. 'If they are not wary of threatening you so, they may also consider threatening the prince.'

'Yes, yes, you're right.' Henry clutched at him and dragged him close. John saw Seymour's nose wrinkle as the king's sour breath washed over him. 'The father too, then. I will have them both sent to the Tower.'

John slid a sideways glance at Seymour, his mouth curving into a smile.

Prince Edward and his companions were invited to court for Christmas, and Robert looked forward to the change of scene and the entertainments he would attend. But a few hours at court made him soon wish he had remained at Hunsdon.

The arrest of the Howards had created a hushed, anxious atmosphere. Everyone at court seemed to be living on nerves. People whispered that if the foremost peers of the realm could be arrested on a charge of treason for nothing more than having a portrait painted, then no one was safe. The king grew ever more irascible and unpredictable, and even Prince Edward emerged from an interview with his father pale and shaking.

Another dinner in the Great Hall came around, where his father talked in whispers with Edward Seymour and his mother in earnest with Queen Katherine. Robert leant against the wall and looked on.

'You look as fed up as I feel,' Henry Sidney observed, smacking him on the shoulder by way of a hello. 'Hardly fun and games all this, is it? Look at Edward up there next to his father. He still looks scared to death. I wonder what happened at his audience with the king. But tell me,' Henry raised his eyebrows at Robert in pretended astonishment. 'Is that… I do believe it is… could it be…?'

'You know damn well it's Elizabeth beside him,' Robert said, finding no amusement in Henry's mockery. He knew he talked about Elizabeth rather too often at Hunsdon for the boys often ribbed him for it. He had seen her sitting with her father and brother as soon as the dinner had begun. Noticed too that she ate very little and that her pale brown eyes darted often from one person to another.

'She's looking this way,' Henry said.

'Is she?' Robert said nonchalantly.

'Why don't you go over to her?'

'Because she's with the king and queen, you idiot. I can't just go over there and say hello.'

Henry grinned. 'Go on. I dare you.'

'Shut up, Henry.'

'You're scared.'

'I am not.'

'Prove it, then.'

'All right, I will,' Robert declared before he could stop himself. He made his way to the top table, approaching it from the side, hoping the king wouldn't notice him.

'Robin!' Elizabeth halloed loudly, dashing his hopes.

Robert's cheeks reddened as all eyes at the table turned towards him. He bowed. 'My lady.'

'It's about time you came over,' Elizabeth chided.

'I wasn't sure I should, but Henry dared me.'

Elizabeth bid him sit down beside her. 'Well, I'm very grateful to Henry, whoever he is. How have you been, Robin?'

'I've been very well, Bess. And you?'

She grimaced. 'I sometimes get terrible headaches and then I'm in bed for days, but mostly I'm well. But tell me,

Robin,' she lowered her voice, 'how do you think my father looks?'

Robert peered around her and cast a surreptitious glance at the king. The flabby cheeks shone with perspiration and the hand shook as it lifted a cup of wine to the pink lips. 'I don't know. A trifle hot, perhaps.'

'Don't lie to me,' she said earnestly.

Robert sighed. 'In truth, I do not think he is very well, Bess.'

'No, nor do I.' She bit her lip, her pointy teeth turning the thin skin white. 'I'm worried, Rob. What if he were to die?'

'Then Edward would be king.'

'Edward, king! Look at him. Does he look like he can rule?' Elizabeth dropped her gaze to her hands lying in her lap. 'Oh, Rob, I'm frightened. What will become of me when my father is gone?'

Robert reached for her hand. 'I'm sure my father will look out for you, Bess.'

She smiled sadly. 'You are so foolish, Rob. It will be my brother's uncle who will take matters into his own hands. You can be sure of that.'

Robert drew himself up. 'You don't understand how important my father is, Bess. It was he who discovered the Howards' treason, and what's more, he and Seymour…' He broke off, realising he should not have spoken of matters he had overheard in the privacy of his father's apartments.

'What?' Elizabeth grabbed his wrist, her nails digging into his flesh. 'What is it you know?'

'I don't know anything. Let me go, Bess, you're hurting me.'

She looked into his face for a long moment, then pushed him away. 'What could you know?' she sneered, looking much older than her thirteen years. 'You can leave me now.'

Robert was too relieved to have been released from her presence to be hurt by her accusation of ignorance. He hurried back to Henry.

'What's the matter?' Henry asked. 'You scurried away from her like a frightened cat. Were you arguing?'

'Don't be stupid.'

'It looked like you were.'

'Well, we weren't. It's just that Elizabeth thinks she knows everything and she doesn't.'

'And you do?'

Robert snatched a goblet of wine from a passing servant and downed the lot in one gulp. Wiping his mouth with his sleeve, he said, 'I know a damn sight more than Elizabeth.'

CHAPTER FIVE

1547

TOWER HILL

Birds circled overhead, black bodies against the grey sky, and dogs sniffed around the feet of the spectators, hoping for scraps of food. They lifted their legs and urinated against the upright wooden posts of the scaffold while the crowd swelled and the stench of unwashed bodies grew denser. They shouted and laughed in expectation of the morning's entertainment.

A crow swooped, perched on a wooden post, and cawed loudly in John Dudley's ear. 'Accursed thing,' he said, flapping his arm at the bird to make it move away. It cawed again in indignation and retreated to a further post.

'Never mind the bird,' Seymour said. 'Enjoy the show.'

John closed his eyes as his stomach turned over.

'What's the matter with you?' Seymour demanded irritably. 'We both worked hard to get Henry Howard to the scaffold and now you baulk at this.' He gestured at the block that stood in the centre of the wooden platform.

John couldn't explain to Seymour why he wasn't able to share in his enjoyment at seeing their enemy's downfall.

His friend couldn't possibly understand how this scene brought back memories of the execution of his father. He pulled his cloak tighter.

'Here he comes,' Seymour said a moment later, gesturing towards a channel opening up in the crowd. There were guards in front of and behind the prisoner, their halberds glinting in the sunlight.

Henry Howard had lost weight since his trial, and his skin had the grey pallor of a man who had not seen daylight for some time. But though his appearance had changed, Henry Howard had lost none of his arrogance. He walked tall through the crowd, head held high as cries of 'God bless you' mingled with those of 'Traitor'.

As Howard drew near, he met both Seymour's and John's eye unflinchingly, passing them without a word. His footsteps were heavy on the steep wooden stairs, thudding in John's ears like a knell, and he shuffled through the straw laid down to soak up his blood to stand before the block.

The executioner, his face obscured to hide his identity, knelt and asked for forgiveness. Henry Howard gave it, along with a gold coin, as a priest standing behind him read from the Bible. The executioner offered a blindfold, but Howard glanced at it disdainfully and shook his head. He lifted his chin a little higher and looked out over the crowd.

John knew Howard would make a speech and he waited anxiously for his words. It was the custom to praise the king for his mercy to protect the fortunes, and some-times lives, of those the prisoner left behind, but this was Henry Howard and John couldn't predict what the reckless young man would say. He watched as Howard took a few deep breaths, his exhalations turning to smoke in the cold January air.

'Good people,' he began without any trace of fear in

his voice, 'you come here to see me die, for I have been accused of treason. I tell you now, I have never been guilty of treason. I lay no blame for this injustice upon the king. He is the most kind and goodly prince beneath Heaven. No, I do not blame the king but his advisers, those who spit venom upon their enemies and seek their removal for their own benefit and advancement. I confess I have been rash and caused much offence, but none so great that I deserve to stand here awaiting the axe upon my neck. God knows my heart and will judge me fairly. Good people, I beg you, pray for me.'

Most of the crowd made the sign of the cross and a murmur of prayer bubbled up as Howard knelt and set his neck upon the curved block of wood. His bloodshot eyes, bulging from their sockets with strain, locked on John's. 'May you suffer,' he hissed as the axe descended.

John shut his eyes, bile rising in his throat. When he opened them, dark red blood was trickling over the edges of the platform and the crowd was roaring. He had to get away. Without saying a word to Seymour, he pushed his way through the crowd. It wasn't until he had left Tower Hill and entered into the twisting streets around the Tower that he slowed down. His heart was banging in his chest and he was having trouble catching his breath. He stopped and leaned against a wall. Seymour found him there a few minutes later, eyes closed, head tilted back, breathing deeply.

'Why did you hurry away? What's the matter with you?'

John shook his head, cursing himself for letting Seymour see him so upset. 'I felt sick. It was the crowd. The stench.'

The excuse seemed to satisfy Seymour, who rubbed his hands together with relish. 'Well, that's the son gone. His father's turn will come.'

John stroked his throat. It felt rough, dry. 'By Christ, I could do with a drink.'

Seymour pointed at a tavern door a little way down the street and they made their way there. Once inside, Seymour headed for a table in the corner and ordered two cups of sack from the potboy who had hurried over when he spied men of quality. He came back with a jug and two cups, the only two in the place that weren't chipped.

'This will put some colour in your cheeks,' Seymour said, pouring out the wine. 'I never knew you were so squeamish.'

John took the cup without replying. The wine warmed his throat. It felt good, calming, and he gestured for a refill.

'There's something I wanted to talk to you about,' Seymour said, topping up his own cup after refilling John's. 'I think you'll be pleased.'

'About what?'

'About the king's will.' Seymour looked around, leant a little closer and lowered his voice. 'Paget has rewritten the will to exclude Gardiner and the other Catholics from the regency council.'

John almost dropped his cup in his astonishment. 'On whose instructions?'

'On mine.'

'Does the king know you've done this?'

'No.'

John banged his fist on the table. 'Which means it's not signed and of no bloody use. By all that's holy, Edward, why didn't you consult me before taking such a dangerous step?'

Seymour's face darkened. 'I don't answer to you, John.'

'You do realise we've just had a man executed for having a portrait painted, don't you?' John demanded. 'Bearing that minor misdemeanour in mind, how do you think the king would react if he knew you'd changed his bloody will?'

'He won't find out,' Seymour said, snatching up his cup. 'He never asks to see his will. And as for it not being signed...'

'Yes?' John prompted.

'Signatures can be forged, if need be.'

John sighed and shook his head. 'In future, Ned, we discuss everything before taking such a step. I can't have you going off and doing things on your own.'

'Why? Because you're the only one who has the brains to act?'

'Because I don't have a wife who makes me do stupid things,' John shot back, and he knew he had touched a nerve because Seymour's cheeks coloured. 'I'm right, aren't I? It was Anne who said you should change the will?'

'She suggested it,' Seymour admitted unhappily.

John reached across the table and grabbed his friend's wrist. 'No more acting alone, Ned. Agreed?'

Seymour held his gaze for a long moment, then nodded. 'Whatever you say, John.'

'He said what?' Anne Seymour's reaction was exactly what her husband had expected it would be: incredulous, indignant, furious.

'He said I should have consulted him,' Seymour shrugged.

'Who does John Dudley think he is? And I expect you just sat there and said nothing, like always.'

'I suppose I did.'

She gave a snort of disgust, her skirts dragging the rushes around as she paced the floor. 'Why shouldn't you make a decision on your own? You don't answer to him.

My God, I wish I had been there. I would have put him in his place. Did you tell him I told you not to involve him?'

'Of course I didn't,' Seymour spat. 'I can just imagine what he would have said to that.'

'Oh yes, I know what the Dudleys think of me,' she said with a proud nod of her head. 'They think I rule you. Just because Jane Dudley is content to trot around after her husband, she thinks all women should do the same.'

There were moments when Seymour wished his wife was like Jane Dudley: demure, soft-spoken, yielding. 'The pity is,' he said, rubbing his hand across his forehead where an ache had begun, 'I need him so much.'

Anne stopped her pacing. 'But do you really need him, Edward?'

'While the king is still alive, I'm afraid I do, Anne.'

'Well then, we have only to wait. When the king dies, you must seize your chance, and to hell with John Dudley.'

CHAPTER SIX

Katherine Parr sank gratefully into the chair the page had brought for her and held a handkerchief to her sore eyes. It had all happened so suddenly, this decline of her husband's, and it upset her more than she would have believed possible. All the pain Henry had caused her, those dreadful months when he had suspected her of trying to rule him over religion, those terrifying days when she knew he had ordered her arrest and was in danger of losing her life, didn't seem to matter now he was about to die.

'Honestly, Kate,' Jane Dudley shook her head in wonder, 'I wouldn't dare say this to anyone else, but think what a relief it will be when he's gone.'

'Oh, Jane, how can you talk so?' Katherine said, blowing her nose. 'He is the king. I am his wife.'

Jane opened her mouth to explain that she would not have agreed to be Henry's wife for the world, not when he got through them so quickly, but closed it again as the floorboards vibrated beneath her feet. She turned to see Thomas Cranmer half-walking, half-running along the corridor, his loose, fleshy face unusually pink and moist.

'My lady,' he said, bowing to Katherine, 'why are you sitting out here?'

A fresh assault of tears answered his question. Jane leant close to Cranmer and murmured, 'The king didn't want her near him. Have you been sent for, archbishop?'

'I have,' he said, straightening the purple sash around his neck. 'I received a message from Edward Seymour to attend the king without delay. Do excuse me, my lady.' He stepped past Jane and tapped on the bedchamber door.

Jane tried to see into the room as the door opened, but Seymour grabbed Cranmer's arm and dragged him inside, closing the door before she had a chance.

Katherine grabbed Jane's hand. 'If Archbishop Cranmer has been sent for, then my husband must be very ill.'

'Kate,' Jane said as patiently as she could manage, 'the king is going to die. 'Tis but a matter of time.'

'But what will I do when he is gone?'

Jane laughed and bent down to look her in the eye. 'Why, my dear, you rejoice.'

Katherine stared at her for a moment in horror, then landed a stinging blow upon Jane's cheek.

Jane cried out, her hand flying to her face. 'Why did you do that? I meant only to relieve your suffering.'

'Oh, no, you meant what you said. You forget how long I've known you. You're not like your husband. You always speak your mind.' Katherine blew her nose noisily into her handkerchief.

Jane's top lip curled up in disgust, all patience with her friend gone. She stared at the bedchamber door, wishing she knew what was happening inside so she could send word to John. She pressed her ear to the wood but could hear nothing.

. . .

'Not long now,' Seymour whispered, glancing towards the bed where the king lay, blankets domed over the enormous body.

Cranmer peered at the king. His face seemed thinner, for the flabby cheeks had fallen away from the long-hidden bones, and there were hollows in the cheeks where pink, plump flesh had been only a week before. His eyes were closed, his breath ragged.

Gathering up the skirts of his vestments, Cranmer knelt beside the bed. With great gentleness, he lifted the king's hand into his own. 'Your Majesty,' he said softly, 'can you hear me?' Henry's eyelids fluttered but remained shut. Cranmer closed his own eyes and prayed.

Seymour's hand pressed against his jerkin as he watched Cranmer, feeling for the key tucked inside, the key to the box that held the king's will. His heart beat faster at the thought of the coming hours, what he had to do, who he had to trust. He hated having to involve others in his plans, but it couldn't be helped. He needed Anthony Browne and William Paget, for Paget kept the chest containing the king's will and Browne, as Master of the Horse, had access to the stables.

Panic suddenly struck Seymour. His entire plan depended upon him getting away from court quickly. Would the horses be ready? Browne had promised they would be, but what if they weren't? *No, I have to trust Browne will keep his word*, he chided himself. If only there wasn't all this waiting. And if only Jane Dudley wasn't right outside the door. If she got wind of what he was up to, she would go straight to her husband and then he really would have problems.

Henry suddenly drew a long, painful breath, breaking into Seymour's thoughts, and opened his eyes. Seymour saw the king's fingers grip Cranmer's hand with a strength that made the archbishop wince.

Cranmer leant closer, his face inches from the king's, and asked the question that concerned him most. 'Your Majesty, am I to continue with the reform of the church?'

The little mouth puckered like a fish gasping for air. No sound came forth and the beady eyes looked into Cranmer's with fear.

'Am I to continue, Your Majesty?' Cranmer pleaded. 'Say I am and your soul will be saved.'

Henry's hand tightened around Cranmer's, then slackened and fell upon the blanket. The small eyes closed and the king breathed no more.

'He squeezed my hand,' Cranmer gasped. 'He squeezed it. That meant yes.' He turned, his eyes seeking Seymour's. 'The king meant yes. He wants me to continue.'

Seymour gripped the foot of the bed, his knuckles turning white. 'Is he dead?'

Cranmer put his ear to Henry's mouth and listened. After a moment, he nodded at Seymour. 'The king is dead.'

'God bless his soul,' Seymour breathed.

'Amen.' Cranmer pointed at the door. 'Should I bring the queen in?'

Seymour shook his head. 'Not just yet.' He licked his dry lips. 'Can I trust you, Cranmer?'

'I am a man of the Church,' Cranmer said, affronted.

'Then I can trust you because we want the same thing. The same thing the king wanted. To continue in the Reformed faith. I cannot countenance a return to Rome, and neither can you. But the prince, Cranmer, is just a boy. Wrongly advised, he may turn back to Rome.'

'My lord, the prince is a good Protestant.'

'And it will be our duty to ensure he stays so.'

Cranmer frowned. 'What are you proposing, my lord?'

'That I become the prince's chief adviser. I am his

uncle. We share the same blood. It should be me. But I need time, Cranmer. I need the king's death to remain just between you and me for the time being.'

'You want me to pretend the king is still alive?'

'You need pretend nothing. No one will come in here. All you need do is stay in here until I have the prince.'

'I don't know,' Cranmer shook his head. 'It seems wrong to be speaking like this. The king has only just died. His body is not even cold.'

'You reprove me, Cranmer, for my lack of loyalty. But don't you realise? I am being loyal. I want to protect King Henry's realm and his son. I can do nothing more to prove my loyalty than that.'

'There is truth in your words, my lord, and so I will not argue with you. Do what you must. It is not my concern.'

'You will keep the death of the king to yourself? Please. A few hours, Cranmer, that is all I need.'

'I will pray alone when you are gone, my lord. I daresay I will be praying for several hours for the king's soul.'

Seymour breathed a sigh of relief. 'I will leave for Hunsdon at once.'

'And my lord?' Cranmer called as Seymour grabbed the handle of the door.

'Yes?'

'Be kind to the prince. He will need your sympathy.'

'It sounds as if you doubt I would give it,' Seymour said tersely.

Cranmer gave him a steely look, but made no answer. Seymour's lip curled in anger as he yanked open the door and hurried out.

CHAPTER SEVEN

Edward grunted in his sleep and kicked Robert beneath the bedclothes, raking toenails down his calf. Suppressing the urge to kick back, Robert turned over, slamming his head into the pillow.

How he hated these nights when it was his turn to sleep with the prince. He tugged at the blankets Edward had pulled over to his side of the bed and opened one bleary eye to stare at the wooden shutters covering the window. No sunlight bled through the shutters, so it was still night. Still time to try to get some sleep. He closed his eyes, but opened them a moment later. He could have sworn he had heard horses' hooves, but that was absurd. Who would come to Hunsdon at this time of night?

There came a loud banging on the hall's front door and Robert sat bolt upright in bed, wide awake now. He heard a murmur of voices below and then the sound of someone running up the staircase. Footsteps hurried along the corridor, coming to a stop just outside the door.

Robert heard the latch lift and the hinges squeal as the

door opened. He tried to see into the darkness as someone whispered, 'Bring a light.'

A small flame flared a moment later, and in its light, Robert saw Edward Seymour standing in the doorway.

'What are you doing here?' he cried.

Seymour didn't answer. Instead, his gaze moved beyond Robert to the boy propping himself up on his elbow.

'Who's there?' the prince asked, his speech thick with sleep.

'It's me, Edward,' Seymour answered, bringing the candle nearer his face.

The prince narrowed his eyes at him. 'Uncle?'

'You must get up.' Seymour grabbed the blankets and pulled them off of the two boys.

'But it's cold,' Edward protested, reaching to pull the blankets back over himself.

Seymour held them fast. 'You must, Edward. You, Dudley, help the prince to dress.' He hurried from the room.

Robert climbed out of the bed, grabbed his hose, and pulled them on. Sensing no movement from behind, he turned to Edward. The prince sat unmoving, goosebumps pimpling his legs. 'Aren't you going to get dressed?' Robert asked.

Edward shook his head, his bottom lip thrust out in a pout. 'I don't understand.'

'Neither do I, but your uncle meant what he said. And if he comes back and you're still sitting there...'

'I'm not afraid of my uncle.'

Robert pulled on his jerkin, then sat back down on the bed. 'I wonder why he's come here.'

Edward threw himself back on the bed. 'I don't care. I'm not going anywhere.'

Seymour reappeared in the doorway. He had heard his

nephew's last words and his face was grim. 'You must do as I say, Edward.' He crossed to the bed and grabbed the boy's thin arm, yanking him upright. 'I will tell you why later, when things are...,' he struggled to find the right word, 'when they are better. Now, please, get dressed.'

Seymour waited until Edward obeyed, then he left the room once more, and Robert heard him barking orders in the hall below. He finished dressing, trying to hurry Edward along by throwing his clothes across the end of the bed and fetching his shoes.

'What's this all about?' Henry Sidney said in a hushed voice as he tiptoed in. 'Why are we going to Hatfield?'

'Hatfield?' Edward cried, looking from Henry to Robert in astonishment. 'Is that what he said?'

Henry nodded.

'Why is he taking you to Elizabeth?' Robert wondered. 'Is she ill?'

'I don't know,' Edward said, his expression anxious.

'It may be nothing,' Henry said, shaking his head at Robert not to worry the prince.

'Don't talk nonsense, Henry,' Edward snapped. 'This isn't normal, is it? I don't get ordered out of bed and dragged miles away in the middle of the night for nothing.'

'He's right, Henry,' Robert said. 'Seymour is up to something. And I mean to find out what.'

Winter had made the road to Hatfield crisp and hard, and riding in the dead of night ensured the journey was not without peril, with many a horse stumbling and nearly throwing its rider. It was a cold and miserable party that drew rein outside the red brick palace as the new day dawned.

A guard darted out from the entrance porch and

pressed the tip of his halberd against the breast of Seymour's horse. 'Identify yourself,' he demanded.

Seymour's arm tightened around the prince, who sat before him on the saddle. 'I am Edward Seymour, earl of Hertford, and I have here Prince Edward to see his sister, the Lady Elizabeth.'

Satisfied, but more than a little surprised, the guard lowered his weapon and called for the hall door to be opened. Seymour dismounted and pulled his nephew from the saddle. Cold and weary, the boy made no protest as he was pushed inside the house.

Boys appeared from the stable yard, pulling on jackets and shaking straw from their hair. Robert thrust his reins into the hand of one boy and hurried into the house, trying to keep Seymour and Edward in his sights, but having difficulty because of the number of people milling about in the hall as the servants realised Hatfield had visitors. He was just in time to see a door to a small chamber closing upon them. He was wondering where he could find some ink and paper to write to his father when someone called his name. Looking around, he saw Elizabeth on the stairs, clad only in her nightdress and a thin shawl around her shoulders.

'Robin? What is it?' she asked, her red hair falling about her face. 'Why are you here?'

'Edward Seymour's brought us, your brother and all the companions. I have no idea why. Seymour wouldn't tell us. But Bess, can you get me some paper? I need to get word to my father. I need to tell him what Seymour's done.'

'Dudley!'

Robert jumped at the call of his name. Seymour was standing in the doorway of the small chamber he had taken Edward into, light flooding over the floor. He glanced from Robert to Elizabeth and back again. 'Do not detain the lady. Lady Elizabeth, would you come in here?'

Elizabeth obeyed, pulling her shawl tighter as her bare feet slapped upon the brick floor. She slipped past Seymour and disappeared inside. Robert heard the prince call out her name as Seymour closed the door, his eyes never leaving Robert's.

The new arrivals had disrupted the routine of the household. Elizabeth's lessons were cancelled, and the servants wandered around the house, their duties neglected as they gossiped. The prince's companions were given rooms with extra beds crammed in to accommodate them all, and the boys resumed their sleep, filling the silence of the house with snores.

All but one slept. When he was certain the other boys were fast asleep, Robert lifted the latch of the bedchamber and peered out. The corridor was empty. Stepping out into the hallway, he tiptoed across the floorboards to Elizabeth's rooms, having discovered their location from a pageboy whose eyes glinted at the coins Robert pressed into his palm. Reaching the door, he knocked softly. A few seconds passed, then he heard murmurings from within, and then a voice through the wood asking, 'Who is it?'

He recognised the voice. 'It's Robert Dudley, Mistress Ashley.'

A moment later, the door opened, and Katherine Ashley jerked her head at him to enter. He hurried inside and saw Elizabeth standing by the bed. Her eyes bore signs of weeping and her thin lips pursed and puckered in barely suppressed agitation.

'What's happened?' he asked.

'It's the king, Master Dudley,' Mistress Ashley said with a heavy sigh. 'He's dead.'

A sob burst from Elizabeth, and she buried her face in her hands. Mistress Ashley hurried over to her and pulled her charge into an embrace. 'Look what you've done,' she scolded Robert. 'She had settled before you came.'

'It's not his fault.' Elizabeth pulled herself away from Mistress Ashley and wiped her cheeks savagely. She held out her hand to him.

Robert hurried to take it. He squeezed the thin, bony fingers. 'I can't believe it.'

Elizabeth sniffed and pulled her hand out of his. She climbed into her bed, pulling the bedcovers up to her chin. 'My brother's pissing himself. He's terrified that he's the king now.'

'My lady, you mind your language,' Mistress Ashley chided, not too harshly. 'Your brother is only nine years old. He has not your courage.' She turned to Robert. 'What do you want? 'Tis not seemly for you to be here at this hour.'

'I need ink and paper,' Robert explained.

'Oh yes, I forgot, you asked before.' Elizabeth told Mistress Ashley to provide him with both and watched as her governess opened a chest beneath the window and took out two sheets of paper, a stoppered ink pot and a goose quill. She handed them to Robert.

Robert hitched himself up on the bed. Setting the paper and ink down, he smoothed out the blankets to make a flat space. He pushed Elizabeth's feet away, leant forward on his elbows, and dipped the quill in the ink.

'What are you writing?' Elizabeth asked, squinting at the page.

'I'm telling my father that Seymour has brought your brother here. I don't know why he's done it, but I'm sure he's done it in secret.'

'Seymour said it was so we could be a comfort to each other.'

'You believe that?'

'We are a comfort to each other. Edward needs me and I need him.'

'If that is so, why are you not together now? Or did his tears not last as long as yours?'

'I grew tired,' Elizabeth shrugged, her expression registering sudden doubt. 'Seymour said he would look after my brother.'

'Oh, you can be sure he will. Now,' Robert surveyed his letter, 'not my neatest hand, but I doubt Father will scold me for that.'

Elizabeth kicked at him beneath the sheets for him to move as she nudged herself down the bed. 'What can your father do? Seymour has every right to be with Edward. He is his uncle.'

'My father likes to be kept informed.' Robert folded the letter and tucked it into his doublet. He studied her face. 'Are you all right?'

'Oh, at last, you ask.'

'My lady will be well enough,' Mistress Ashley said, crossing the room quickly and smoothing Elizabeth's hair. 'Now, Master Dudley, you must go.'

'I'll see you later today,' he promised Elizabeth, jumping off the bed and heading for the door. He paused and looked back at her. 'I am sorry about your father, Bess.'

Elizabeth gave him a weak smile as Mistress Ashley pushed him out of the door. And into Edward Seymour.

'What were you doing in there?' Seymour demanded.

'I was just paying the Lady Elizabeth a visit,' Robert said. 'A good thing I did. She's very upset and needed to see a friendly face. I know now why you've brought us here. The king is dead.'

Seymour's eyes narrowed. His hand shot up and grabbed Robert's jaw, his fingertips digging into the skin.

'Don't go behind my back, ferreting out information to send to your father or I'll have you replaced before you can blink.' He shoved Robert away. 'Now, get back to your room.'

Robert rubbed his cheeks where Seymour's fingers had dug in. He hurried back to his chamber and closed the door, falling back against it and letting out a shuddering breath. He squeezed his doublet, heard the crinkle of the letter he had stowed there, and felt a tingle of satisfaction that his father would know of what had happened this night, despite Seymour's threats.

CHAPTER EIGHT

John Dudley barely glanced up from his desk as the door opened, and his wife entered. 'How is the queen?' he asked.

'Crying in her room.' Jane yawned, peering through the lead-glass window at the grey sky. The sight did not cheer her, and she turned to her husband. His desk was piled high with papers, and it seemed to her he had imprisoned himself behind them. She moved to stand behind him and slid her arms around his waist, pressing her cheek against his. 'I think you need to rest, John.'

'I can't. There's too much to do here, and I need to be on hand should the king call for me.' He scribbled his name at the bottom of a paper and reached for another.

'I don't expect the king will call for you if he is as bad as everyone seems to think. Besides, Cranmer knows where we are and will send word if you're wanted.'

John shifted around in his chair to face her. 'Cranmer will send word? Do you mean he's here in the palace?'

'He's in the king's bedchamber.'

'But who sent for Cranmer? Was it the king?'

'How would I know?' Jane cried. 'Edward Seymour, I

suppose. He was the only other man in there once Katherine came out. Why? What does it matter?'

'It matters, Jane, because if Cranmer has been summoned, then it means the king must be near dying. Didn't Seymour say anything to you when Cranmer arrived?'

'No, he just shut the door in my face once he got Cranmer inside and didn't even look at me when he came out.'

'Seymour came out? Cranmer's alone with the king?'

'Yes. What is it, John? Why are you looking at me like that?'

John grabbed her hand. 'When did Seymour leave?'

'Hours ago. Does it matter?'

'For Christ's sake, Jane, of course it matters.' He rose from the desk and snatched up his sword from the chest by the wall, buckling it on around his waist.

There came a knock on the door. Jane opened it to find a pageboy standing outside.

The boy held out his hand. 'Letter for Lord Dudley.'

Jane grabbed it and closed the door without a word. She peered at the handwriting. 'It's from Robert,' she said, passing it to John. She watched as he read it, seeing his face turn pale. 'What is it, John?'

John stared at her. 'The king is dead, Jane. Seymour arrived at Hunsdon in the middle of the night, packed up the prince's household and made them ride to Hatfield Palace.'

'My God,' Jane cried. 'He has the prince and the Lady Elizabeth under his control. Oh, what did I say, John? I said you couldn't trust him.'

John screwed up Robert's letter and tossed it aside. He yanked open the door and ran along the corridor, bursting into the king's bedchamber. Cranmer, kneeling by the bedside, started in surprise and kept his eyes on John as he drew near to the dead king.

'I should have been told of this,' John said as he looked down on the king, lying motionless and grey in the early morning light. 'Why wasn't I told, Cranmer?'

'It is not my place to inform the court, my lord,' Cranmer said testily. 'I assumed Edward Seymour would tell you when he thought fit.'

'When he thought fit, archbishop? I should have been told at once.'

'That you were not is no fault of mine.'

'It may become your fault. Do you know what he did instead of informing me, Cranmer?' John asked, and he knew his voice had become hard, threatening even, judging by the change of expression upon the archbishop's face. 'He rode to Hunsdon to take possession of the prince, and now he has both him and the Lady Elizabeth at Hatfield.'

Cranmer swallowed uneasily. 'What of it? He is the prince's uncle. Perhaps he thought to offer comfort to the boy. As to the Lady Elizabeth—'

'I never took you for a fool, Cranmer,' John said. 'We both know what this means. Seymour is getting ready to set himself up as Lord Protector.'

'And what if he is?' Cranmer countered. 'Why should he not be Lord Protector? The prince is too young to rule alone and, as the boy's uncle, Seymour is the natural choice.'

'The king stipulated in his will that a council of regency would rule until the prince was old enough to rule alone. Not a Protector. He knew what could happen if a Protector had the rule of a country.'

'You allude, I think, to the protectorship of Richard of Gloucester.'

'You're bloody right I do,' John said, gripping the

bedpost in his anger. 'King Richard killed his nephews to get the throne.'

'And you think Seymour would do the same?' Cranmer gave a little, uncertain laugh. 'Seymour has no royal blood that gives him a claim to the throne, nor, I believe, the evil nature you seem to think he has. What does it say for your friendship that you should think so vilely of him?'

John jerked his head at the dead king. 'Get back to your prayers, Cranmer. We're going to need them.'

A few hours' sleep, a little food in his belly and a calm appraisal of the situation, and John felt ready to deal with Edward Seymour.

His first act had been to announce the death of King Henry to the court; his second to summon the executors of the king's will to the council chamber. That was where he now sat, at the table's head, watching as each member entered. John studied the faces of Sir Anthony Denny, Sir Anthony Browne, Sir William Paget and Cranmer carefully as they took their places at the long table. They were, all of them, close to Seymour.

'Where is my lord Wriothesley?' he asked as everyone settled into their chairs.

'He is still at the House of Commons, I believe, my lord,' Cranmer replied in a somewhat cool tone that suggested to John he had not forgotten their last meeting.

'Then I'm sure he'll join us in due course,' John said. 'And what of Edward Seymour? Any news from him?' He saw Denny and Browne exchange glances and realised his suspicions were correct. They had allied with Seymour.

'I have not heard from my lord Seymour,' Browne prevaricated.

'Nor I,' Denny added.

'Indeed?' John nodded. 'Ah, here comes Wriothesley.'

'Damn cold out there,' the Lord Chancellor declared as he strode in, the red tip of his long nose testament to the cold weather. 'There's ice on the river and the boatman took an eternity to row me back here.' He sank into a chair at the opposite end of the table with an exaggerated sigh and looked around. 'I've had a very tedious morning at the House of Commons and would like to get this business over with as few interruptions as possible. So, I have informed the Commons of the death of King Henry and disclosed the contents of his will. The crucial point of which is that Prince Edward succeeds him to the throne. The prince is being brought to London by his uncle, Edward Seymour, and they will arrive at the Tower later this afternoon. So, we had all better be there to welcome him.'

'To welcome the prince or to welcome Seymour?' John asked.

Wriothesley frowned at him. 'The prince, obviously.'

John gave him a playful smile and waved him on.

'While we are all here,' Wriothesley continued, 'we may as well discuss the fact that the prince is in his minority and cannot rule alone. We must therefore consider a regency.'

'The queen?' Cuthbert Tunstall, a small man with wide, watchful eyes, suggested. 'She has acted as regent before.'

'For mere months, Tunstall,' Wriothesley said. 'The prince is but nine years old, almost seven years away from his majority. We cannot trust the governance of the country to a woman for so long, and we do not need to. King Henry foresaw he might die while the prince was still a child and in his will suggested a council of regency.'

There was a long moment of silence, then Cranmer spoke. 'From the way you phrase it, Sir Thomas, are we to assume that King Henry anticipated there might be problems with such a council?'

'He realised it might be unmanageable,' Wriothesley nodded.

'So,' Browne said, his expression all innocence, 'if not the queen as regent and possibly not a council of regency, only a Protectorship remains.'

'Personally, I favour a council of regency,' Wriothesley said.

'I disagree, Wriothesley,' Denny shook his head. 'A Protector would serve the country much better.'

'I agree,' Browne said.

'And I,' Cranmer nodded sagely.

'And I think we need look no further for a Protector than Edward Seymour,' Denny said, catching the eye of each of his allies around the table, who all nodded back.

John saw Wriothesley glowering and realised that Seymour must have swayed all the counsellors, barring himself and Wriothesley, to his side some time before. How had he not noticed the game Seymour had been playing?

'Oh, that reminds me,' Paget said. He was a poor actor; there was no truth in his sudden recollection. 'King Henry had begun to make arrangements to bestow titles on several members here present in recognition of their services to him, which I'm sure Edward Seymour would feel duty bound to honour were he to assume the office of Protector. If, however, a council of regency were to rule, those elevations might have to be reconsidered, as I think it would appear self-serving to bestow those titles upon ourselves.'

'Let us take a vote,' Browne declared, licking his lips at the prospect of new honours. 'What say you, gentlemen, to Seymour as Protector?'

All, saving John and Wriothesley, said, 'Aye.'

'Well then,' Denny said, his long face broadening with

a grin, 'if that's decided, we had better make our way to the Tower.' He rose and led his fellow counsellors out of the council chamber. John rose too and made to follow.

'What do you make of that, Dudley?' Wriothesley said, halting him.

John turned around to see Wriothesley lounging in his chair, left leg hooked over the arm, one elegant finger tapping against the table. 'Make of it?'

'Seymour's bought our fellow counsellors with the promise of titles. Henry didn't make any such provision in his will.'

'No, I don't expect he did,' John agreed.

'You didn't say aye to Seymour having the Protectorship. That surprised me. Did you not want another title to add to your bag?'

John bridled. 'I can't be bought, Thomas.'

Wriothesley laughed, a high, girlish laugh that made John want to hit him. 'Every man can be bought, John. You just like to think you're more costly than most. But you know what I think? I think Seymour's done all this without involving you.'

John sighed in annoyance. 'There was no point in my voting. If I said nay, I would have been outvoted.'

'You can stomach Seymour as Lord Protector, then?'

'I don't see we have any choice. As you said, all the others are with Seymour. If we cannot prevent him becoming Protector but can gain by agreeing...,' John shrugged. 'Why not go along with it? It is the best we can hope for, at present.'

Wriothesley grunted. 'Aye, there's sense in that.'

'So,' John gestured at the door, 'shall we go to the Tower to greet our new king?'

With a great sigh, Wriothesley shoved away from the table and jerked his wiry frame erect. 'I suppose we must, but you'll have to stop me from spitting in Seymour's eye.'

John laughed, patting him on the shoulder as he passed. *You'll have to wait your turn*, he thought.

1547

WHITEHALL PALACE

'Excuse me, sir, but do you mind if I sit here?'

Robert looked up at the pageboy standing before him, holding a wooden cup in one hand and a platter of meat in the other. He was wearing livery, and the badge sewn on his sleeve showed he worked for Edward Seymour.

The boy shuffled his feet uneasily. 'I wouldn't normally ask, only the Pages Chamber is full.'

Pages were not supposed to eat in the Great Hall with courtiers, but most of the diners had departed and the servants were already disassembling the trestle tables and stacking them against the walls. Robert nodded, and the boy clambered onto the bench, muttering his thanks.

'You serve the earl of Hertford?' Robert asked, and the boy nodded, his mouth full of food. 'How do you like him?'

'He's all right,' the boy shrugged. 'He has a foul temper, but it's not him you have to worry about. It's his wife. It's best to be invisible when she's around.'

Robert grinned. 'I've heard my father say something similar.'

'Oh yes? Who's your father?'

'John Dudley,' Robert said proudly.

Perhaps the boy had been too long at court because he didn't seem as impressed as Robert had expected. Instead, the boy nodded and said, 'Your father was with my lord earlier. He was furious.'

'Why was my father angry with your master?'

The boy wiped his mouth on his sleeve and leaned closer. 'I know little about it, but I gathered Thomas Wriothesley has been placed under house arrest on my lord's orders. Your father demanded to know why.'

'And did your master tell him?'

'Something to do with Wriothesley sending his clerks to do work he should have been doing himself.'

Robert frowned. 'That doesn't sound very terrible.'

'Aye, that's what your father said. My lord swore at him, reminded him he was the Lord Protector and warned him not to forget his place.'

Colour flooded Robert's cheeks. 'He said that to my father?'

The boy nodded and continued eating.

'I don't understand,' Robert said. 'Thomas Wriothesley is Keeper of the Great Seal. All official documents have to have the Great Seal on them. How can Seymour expect to manage without him?'

This was beyond the boy's knowledge and interest and he shrugged, digging out slivers of meat from between his teeth with a fingernail.

'What happened after my father left?' Robert asked.

'My lord instructed one of his secretaries to not delay writing up the charges against Thomas Wriothesley. But that's all I know. My lord's brother turned up complaining again that he was being left out of things, and I knew a quarrel would blow up, so I got out of the way.'

'Do the brothers fight much?'

'They're always arguing, and I heard they drew swords on each other once.' The boy licked his greasy fingers clean. 'I should get back. Thanks for letting me sit here.'

Robert watched the boy hurry from the hall, thinking over what he had learnt. It was only when the servants stood at the side of the table that Robert realised he was holding them up and rose from the bench. As he did so, he saw his father enter the hall.

'Still eating, Robert?' John said, not stopping as he passed. 'You should be twice the size you are, the amount you eat. I expect most of the food bills for the household are down to you.'

He seemed to be in a good mood, which Robert found surprising considering what he had just been told of his father's encounter with Seymour. Robert hurried to catch him up. 'Father, I was just talking with one of Seymour's pages and he said you two had had a quarrel.'

John stopped so abruptly that Robert careered into him. 'Who is it you've been talking to? I won't have gossip, especially when it's about me. Tell me his name.'

'I don't know his name.'

'But you'll recognise him?'

'Father, surely the page is not important?' Robert said, not wishing to get the boy into trouble. 'Would you like to know what he told me?'

'Very well,' John said. 'What did he tell you, my little spy?'

'He said that after you left, Thomas Seymour turned up and he and his brother began arguing. The page said it happens a lot, that they can't stand one another. That they've drawn swords on each other.'

'Have they really?' John's eyebrow rose in surprise. 'Well, all right, so they quarrel. What of it?'

'I...,' Robert floundered, 'I don't know. I just thought it might be useful to you to know.'

John smiled and patted Robert's shoulder. 'All information is useful. Thank you, Rob. Now, putting gossip to one side, tell me. Does the king talk about Seymour to you?'

'Sometimes. He's quite glad he has Seymour looking after things for him...'

'But?'

'But I don't think he likes him very much. He said his uncle is very grim, and he much prefers his Uncle Thomas who makes him laugh.'

'I bet he does,' John said with a smile. 'All right. Off you go, back to the king.'

Robert nodded and walked away.

'And Rob?'

He turned back. 'Yes, Father?'

'Keep talking to pageboys for me.'

Robert grinned. 'Yes, Father, I will.'

Despite his casual dismissal of Robert's information, John had thought hard about what he had learnt of the relationship between the Seymour brothers.

Edward Seymour was becoming more unreasonable by the day, and more obviously paranoid, treating the council with great suspicion. He had known Wriothesley was his enemy and had got rid of him with ease, no one speaking up to defend the Lord Chancellor. Seymour also knew he couldn't rely on John's support any longer, and John knew it was only a matter of time before a way would be sought to get rid of him, too. He would not allow that to happen, and Robert's information about the Seymour brothers' argument had shown him how he might prevent it.

John peered around the corner of the corridor. Further along at a window embrasure, two legs were sticking out. The occasion was perfect. John headed down the corridor and tripped over the outstretched limbs.

'What the devil!' Thomas Seymour roared as he jumped up to face the clumsy oaf who had dislodged him. 'Oh, it's you, Dudley.'

John made a face. 'Those damn long legs of yours, Thomas.'

Thomas chuckled. 'You'll have to forgive me. I was somewhat distracted.' He gestured with his eyes to the woman curled up in the window seat, her cheeks flushed and dimpled.

'I should be going,' she said, setting her feet on the floor and smoothing out the creases in her skirts. She skipped away, her heels clicking against the floorboards.

'In the corridor, Thomas?' John frowned.

'Don't be so disapproving, you old dog,' Thomas said, thumping John on the shoulder. 'A man must find his pleasure where he may. Anyway, sit down and talk to me, now you've scared my delightful little wanton away.'

'Very well, I shall sit, and you can tell me why you weren't at the council meeting today.'

Thomas's expression darkened. 'What council meeting?'

John's eyebrows rose with innocence. 'I thought your brother would have told you about it.'

'He did not, blast him,' Thomas snarled. 'Ned's determined to leave me out of everything.'

'I'm sure he simply forgot to mention it.'

Thomas shook his head. 'You don't know him like I do. I know what he's about.'

'And what is that?'

'He wants the boy all to himself, that's what. But, blast it, Dudley, I'm his uncle too and I will have something.'

'Well, if there's anything I can do, Tom, just ask,' John said. 'And don't worry. I'll let you know when the council meets again.'

'Thank you,' Thomas said grudgingly and stood. 'I think I'll pay a visit to my nephew. See how he is.'

John rose too. 'I'm sure he'll be very pleased to see you. From what I hear, you're much his favourite uncle.'

'Really?' Thomas's face relaxed into an amiable smile. 'Who told you that?'

John tapped his nose. 'Oh, a little bird.'

Thomas nodded. 'You'll let me know about the next meeting?'

'You can count on me.'

Thomas thumped him on the arm gratefully and departed. John watched him go with the sense of a job well begun. He had a feeling causing trouble between the two brothers was going to be easier than he had expected.

Edward Seymour fixed his expression into one of patience and waited for his brother to stop talking. He looked around the table, wondering which one of them had told Thomas about this meeting. Paget, Browne? No, they had no time for Thomas. Cranmer, perhaps? No, he looked more bored than usual and didn't seem to be paying any attention to Thomas. There was Parr, brother to the former queen, Katherine, who had once been in love with Thomas and might be still, for all Seymour knew. Parr may have told him,... but no, of course, John Dudley! He was hiding it well, but Seymour could see the tiniest upturn of his lips beneath the thin moustache.

'And I say, my lords,' Thomas concluded, 'as the king's favourite uncle, and as my brother already has the Protectorship, I should have the Governorship of the King's Person.'

All heads turned towards Seymour. His insides churned with indignation and fury. It was ludicrous. There could be no worse person to govern the king than Thomas. What would Thomas teach young Edward? How to gamble? How to swear? How to whore?

Seymour didn't trust himself to speak. He would lose his temper, he knew, if he gave his brother an answer or pretended to consider the idea at all. So he rose, pushed back his chair and strode out of the council chamber, leaving the counsellors and Thomas to stare after him, open-mouthed.

'Thomas never ceases to amaze me,' John said, pouring himself wine from a jug on the windowsill. 'To demand that he be made Governor of the King's Person! And to not even do it in private, just you and he, but to demand it in the presence of the entire council.'

'I'd like to know how he found out about the council meeting in the first place.' Seymour kicked at a log in the hearth, wishing it were Thomas. 'My brother is insufferable. That he should act this way towards me.'

'He is an envious man, Ned, and will not be content until he has eclipsed you entirely.'

'Did you hear him? "I am the king's favourite uncle". I mean, where does he get such nonsense?'

'Oh, that's just Thomas's fancy. I'm sure the king loves him, but no more than he loves you, never fear.'

'I don't fear that, John,' Seymour snapped. 'I fear Thomas pushing his way into council matters he should stay out of.'

'He will keep on if you don't give Thomas something to do.' John paused, as if considering. 'I do have a suggestion, if you'd care to hear it.'

'What?' Seymour looked at him warily.

John shrugged. 'He could have my position of Lord Admiral. I would expect some recompense for relinquishing the post, of course.'

'What would you want?'

'Well, I rather have a fancy for an earldom. I was thinking Warwick would do very nicely.'

Seymour considered quickly. The earldom of Warwick

was not so very much to give away if it meant Thomas would be kept quiet. He nodded. 'It's yours.'

'Thank you,' John got to his feet. 'It's late and my wife expects me. I shall bid you good night, Ned.'

'Good night, John.'

As he stared down into the flickering flames of the fire, Seymour had the uneasy feeling he had missed something of importance in his conversation with John Dudley.

John fell onto his bed and laughed aloud.

Jane rubbed her eyes and frowned at her husband. 'What are you laughing at?'

John rolled over onto his front. 'It's done, Jane.'

'What's done?'

'I've sown the seeds of discord between Edward and Thomas Seymour and received the earldom of Warwick as my reward.'

'I'm glad,' she said, settling back into her pillow and closing her eyes.

He nudged himself up the bed next to her, his boots becoming entangled in the bedclothes. 'Show me how glad you are,' he said, pulling at the laces on her nightgown.

She giggled and slapped his hand away. 'What made you think of setting those two against each other?'

'Rob. He found out they argue a great deal and he thought I could use that information.'

'He's already thinking like a courtier. He gets that from you.'

John pulled his boots off. 'He's ambitious. That's a good thing.'

'Gets above himself at times. Do you know, I heard him telling Guildford how one of the boys could be a king one day? He heard us talking about you asking for

Warwick and he was telling the children about Warwick the Kingmaker and how that could be you.'

John smiled. 'Was he?'

'I beg you, don't encourage him too much, John.'

'Rob would make a fine king,' he protested. 'Although I suppose you would rather Guildford wore a crown.'

'He has a better temper.'

'Only because you indulge him, you foolish woman,' he said, climbing into bed and holding out his right arm.

She moved into his embrace and began pulling playfully at the hairs on his chest. 'John, do you think it's wise to do what you're doing? Pitting the Seymour brothers against each other.'

'I'm just doing what I have to for the protection of our family. And anyway, I think the brothers would destroy each other before long without my interference.'

'Well, I suppose you know what you're about. Just be careful.'

He squeezed her gently. 'I always am, Jane. I'm damned if I'll go the same way as Wriothesley. I'll have Seymour's head before he has mine, I promise you. Don't worry.'

CHAPTER NINE

Thomas Seymour leaned against the tree trunk and wondered how much longer he would have to wait. The grass beneath his feet was wet and was seeping into his leather shoes, and he had to pull his cloak tighter to keep out the night chill.

A latch lifted nearby, hinges squealed and a voice in the darkness called softly, 'Tom, are you there?'

'I'm here,' he said, pushing away from the tree.

Katherine Parr emerged from the shadow of the doorway. She wore a dressing-gown over her nightdress, and dark brown hair curtained her face. She pressed herself against him. 'I've kept you waiting.'

''Tis shameful,' he said, kissing her forehead. 'You know how impatient I am for you.'

'I almost wrote to you and told you not to come. I'm sure this isn't right.'

'For Christ's sake, Kate,' he cried, holding her at arm's length, 'you were mine before King Henry ever looked at you. But I was sent out of the country so he could marry you without a rival compelling you to refuse him. Was that right?'

'Don't be angry with me, Tom,' she said, putting her fingers to his lips to quiet him. 'I'm thinking of the children. Of Elizabeth and Edward. What will they say?'

'They'll be happy for us, I'm sure. In fact, why should we delay any longer? The old goat is dead. There's nothing to stop us from marrying. So, I'll see the king in the morning and ask him for permission to marry you.'

'But what if he says no?'

Thomas made a noise of annoyance. 'Then I won't bother asking for permission. We'll marry and tell him once it's done.'

'Do you think we could?' Her voice was eager, excited.

He smiled down at her, basking in her admiration for his daring. 'What say you, Kate? Will you take the risk?'

'Oh, Tom, I so want to be married to you.'

As she laid her head against his chest, his gaze raked over the façade of the splendid house that would soon be his. Something caught his eye. He squinted into the darkness and realised what the something was. It was Elizabeth, looking out from her window. Looking down at him! He had a small moment of panic at what she must have seen, but then relaxed. What did it matter if a twelve-year-old girl saw his wooing?

He angled Katherine's head back and forced his lips onto hers. She moaned and pulled her mouth from his so she could place fervent kisses upon his neck. Thomas kept his eyes on the figure at the window. A shiver of excitement ran through him as Elizabeth continued to watch.

Robert's head ached. The sermon had been going on for hours, a long time to be sitting on a hard, wooden pew in a chilly chapel, forbidden to talk and only to listen. It was a relief when the sermon ended and Robert and his fellow companions followed the king out of the chapel.

'It's not over yet,' Henry Sidney said to Robert with a sigh. 'We've now got to spend hours discussing the sermon we've just spent hours listening to.'

'Don't remind me. My head's killing me and my arse is numb. I could do with some fresh air. What about sneaking off and having a ride?'

Henry made a face. 'We'd need an excuse.'

'I know. Think of one, will you? I can't take any more today. Hey!' he cried as Thomas Seymour rudely shoved the boys out of his way and hurried after the king. 'Where did he spring from? Come on. Let's see what's he up to.'

They quickened their step and heard Seymour call out to the king using his Christian name. Robert saw Edward stop and turn in surprise just as he reached his privy chambers. Edward did not look pleased at being shouted at.

'Edward,' Thomas said again, clamping his arm around the young man's shoulder. 'A fine sermon, don't you think?'

'Very fine, Uncle,' Edward said, pulling away from the embrace. 'I didn't see you in the chapel.'

'Oh, I was at the back,' Thomas said, and Robert knew he was lying. Robert had had plenty of time to look around the chapel during the sermon, and Thomas had not been there. 'I've got something for you.' Thomas delved into his jerkin and pulled out a leather pouch. He thrust it into Edward's hand. 'There's ten pounds in there.'

Edward's cheeks flushed. 'Thank you, Uncle,' he said, tucking the purse away as he avoided the eyes of his companions.

'Not at all, my boy. Can't see you going short, can I?' Thomas stroked his beard thoughtfully. 'And now, Edward, there is something I wanted to ask you. It's rather delicate. I don't know—'

'You are free to speak to me on any subject, Uncle,' Edward assured him.

'It's about your stepmother, my boy. She has a fancy to marry again, and she's worried about what you might think. You know how women are once they get an idea into their pretty heads. She thinks you might object to her taking a husband.'

Edward squatted to stroke his pet dog that had waddled into the room. 'My father's been gone such a short time, Uncle.'

'And your stepmother feels his absence keenly, but she is a woman who needs a man about her.'

'Is she unhappy?'

'Yes, I rather think she is.'

'I don't want her to be unhappy. She's been so kind to me. I'll ask Uncle Edward what he thinks.'

'No, don't do that,' Thomas said, a little too quickly. 'I mean, it's nothing to bother him with. Good God,' he laughed, 'can't you make a decision without having to run to him?'

'Of course I can,' Edward cried. He took a deep breath. 'Very well, Uncle. You can tell my stepmother she may marry again.'

Thomas clapped his hands and laughed. 'Nephew, you are kindness itself. I knew you would say that. But I must be honest with you. I confess I have stretched the truth of this matter a little. You see,' he said, rubbing his beard, 'your stepmother has already married.'

'She has?' Edward cried, his voice high with indignation. 'Without my permission?'

'But you've just given it, haven't you?'

'But she didn't know I would. Who has she married?'

Thomas chuckled. 'Me, my boy. Isn't that the best news you could have?' Before Edward could reply, Thomas thumped him on the back and left, shouting a goodbye over his shoulder that resounded along the corridor.

Robert kept his eyes on Edward, sure the young king

would not be happy with how his uncle had manipulated him. Edward swore under his breath and kicked at a stool, sending it crashing against the wall and making his dog yelp in alarm.

Yet something else I must tell my father, Robert thought as he bent to set the stool back on its feet.

CHAPTER TEN

Thomas Seymour stormed into the hall and bellowed, 'Kate, where are you?'

Katherine appeared on the upstairs landing. 'Must you shout, Tom?'

He took the stairs two at a time, striding past her into the bedchamber. Unbuckling his sword belt, he threw it across the room, where it landed with a clatter on the floor. Sprawling across the bed, he listened to Katherine's footsteps as she followed him into the room.

'What's he done now?' she asked quietly, knowing who it was who was most likely to have upset her husband.

Thomas clasped his hands beneath his head and stared up at the tester. 'He won't let me have the jewels.'

'But they're the queen of England's jewels,' she protested. 'They're mine.'

'Ned says as you are no longer queen, you have no right to them.'

Katherine came to stand by the bed, her hand gripping the carved bedpost. 'Then we must appeal to the king.'

'I already have. He said the Protector knew best.'

'Edward said that? After all you've done for him?'

Thomas's jaw hardened. 'I'm going to need more money, Kate. My nephew's getting greedier by the day.'

'It's getting expensive, Tom.'

'I know, but the money isn't just to give to Edward. I need it to pay Fowler.'

'And who is Fowler?'

'One of his attendants. Fowler's working for me now, passing on the money to Edward. He also says very pleasant and encouraging things about me to him.'

'Not pleasant enough, it seems.'

'Fowler does what he can.' Thomas closed his eyes.

Katherine smiled and, hitching up her skirts, climbed onto the bed. 'Husband,' she said, tugging at his beard, 'you are very serious today.'

'I'm tired.'

She slid her hand beneath his shirt. 'Too tired for this?'

His lips twitched in weary amusement as he looked at her, the shy yet passionate woman he had married. In the sunlight streaming through the windows, her skin seemed dry and thin, and the corners of her eyes and mouth had deep lines around them. Why hadn't he noticed before how old Katherine had become? He placed her hand on his codpiece, an instruction, and she obediently untied the laces.

There was the sound of running feet and the door, only half closed, was pushed open.

'Elizabeth,' Katherine cried, pushing away from the bed and pressing her hands to her flaming cheeks.

'God damn you, girl,' Thomas roared, 'don't you know how to knock?'

How despicably like her brother she looks, he thought. She had the same supercilious expression, the same arrogance. Only the colour of her eyes was different. Edward's were blue and pale, like his dear sweet mother's. Elizabeth's were black, like the Boleyn whore, and to

Thomas, were just as knowing. Could she really be only thirteen?

'You can't talk to me like that,' Elizabeth hissed, her fingers tightening around the book she had come to show her stepmother. 'I am the Princess Elizabeth.'

'You're the *Lady* Elizabeth,' he corrected. 'No bastard can be a princess. And even bastards should learn some manners.'

Elizabeth's arm shot up and her book flew at him, striking him on the chin. The anger that had been bubbling away all day boiled over. He lunged forward and grabbed her arms. As she pounded futilely against his chest, he pulled her towards the bed.

'Tom, please,' Katharine said. 'She's only a child.'

'She's a witch, and she needs chastising.'

Elizabeth screamed as he forced her face down over his legs and clamped her wrists together with one large, powerful hand. With the other, he grabbed the hem of her skirts and yanked them up over her waist.

'Tom, no,' Katherine cried in alarm.

'By God's Death, stop kicking, you little devil.' He brought his hand down hard across Elizabeth's pale buttocks and she cried out in pain. The imprint of his hand showed red on the smooth white skin. The sight of it urged him on, smacking her again and again until his hand stung. At last, he let go of her and Elizabeth slid to the ground. He shoved at her with his foot. 'Get out of my sight.'

Elizabeth, sobbing and pulling her skirts down, stumbled from the room.

Katherine turned on him, her face white with shock. 'Tom, how could you?'

'I will be master in my own house,' he panted. 'I won't have an insolent chit of a girl behaving like that.'

'She meant no harm—'

'Say nothing more,' he warned her, tearing off his jerkin and throwing it to the floor. He forced her back onto the bed and covered her body with his own. 'I will have obedience, Kate, from her and from you.'

On her knees in the hallway, Elizabeth tried to catch her breath, tugging strands of hair from her tear-dampened face. When she heard groans from the bedroom, she turned back to the open door, hoping they were cries of pain, that somehow, she had hurt him. But what she saw made her breath catch in her throat.

Katharine lay beneath Thomas, her eyes tightly closed, her body jolting with each thrust he made into her. He gasped and grunted, his face twisting grotesquely. She remembered a conversation from years before, when Robert Dudley had laughed at her ignorance and explained the carnal act to her. What he had described was an act of love, of mutual desire and pleasure. Surely, he couldn't have meant this!

Robert shuffled the pack of cards and yawned. It was tiresome having no company. Henry Sidney had been ill in bed with a head cold for two days, Barnaby Fitzpatrick had been shipped off to France on a diplomatic mission and the king was busy translating a Latin text into English. Or was it an English text into Latin? Robert couldn't remember.

He looked out of the window and saw John Fowler idly kicking gravel from the path onto the lawn. The young man had piqued Robert's interest when he suddenly began flashing his money around. He had always previously protested poverty whenever the companions had wanted to play at cards, but lately, he had been positively eager to gamble. Eager to learn where this new wealth was coming from, Robert unhooked the latch and leant out of the window.

'John,' he hallooed, 'come in and play cards with me.'

Fowler grinned and hurried into the room. Dragging over a stool to Robert, he placed his money bag on the table. It looked very full.

'What do you want to play?' Robert asked.

'Whatever you like.'

Robert dealt the cards. 'You're a sly devil, John. When you first came here, you said you were terrible at cards and yet look at all the money you've won since you've been at court. You had us all fooled.'

'I wasn't pretending,' Fowler protested earnestly. 'I didn't get this money from cards. Thomas Seymour gives it to me.'

'Why does Seymour give you money?'

'Because I'm useful to him. I speak to the king on his behalf and sometimes pass on money from him.'

'Does the Protector know you do this?'

'Good heavens, no.'

'But surely the king has mentioned it to him?'

'The king is most eager to keep the money from Thomas Seymour a secret because he knows the Protector would put a stop to it. To tell the truth, Rob, the king is growing mightily tired of the Protector.'

'You're very well informed, John,' Robert said, admiringly. 'To have the confidence of the king and his uncle. Thomas Seymour must think very highly of you.'

Fowler preened. 'I flatter myself he does. He wouldn't entrust me with his plans else.'

Robert's heartbeat quickened. 'And what plans are they?'

'Why, to have the king all to himself.'

'All to himself, eh? And how does he expect to do that?'

'He has a key to the Privy Chamber—' Fowler broke

79

off and clumsily changed the order of cards in his hand. 'That is, I don't really know. Whose play is it?'

Robert plucked a card from his hand and laid down a knave. 'Mine, I think.'

John Dudley tapped his quill thoughtfully against his chin. 'So, he's got a key, has he?'

'I think,' Robert began tentatively, not wanting to sound foolish, 'he plans to abduct the king, Father.'

'I think you're right. The man must be out of his mind if he thinks he can get away with such a foolish endeavour.'

'Perhaps the death of his wife has made him foolish,' Jane suggested.

John gave her a look of disbelief. 'You really think he loved Katherine?'

'He cared for her, I'm sure of it. And he lost the child she bore him, too, remember? He was very upset, by all accounts.'

'Maybe,' John conceded, 'but even so. To contemplate abducting the king. It beggars belief.'

'What are we going to do about it, Father?' Robert asked.

'I'm thinking.'

'We could put more guards in the corridors to the Privy Chamber.'

'We could,' John nodded.

'But?' Robert prompted when his father said nothing more.

'But,' John said, 'I wonder whether it might not be better to allow Thomas to carry out his plan.'

'You're not serious, Father,' Robert cried. 'We can't allow the king to be taken prisoner.'

John smiled. 'I wasn't thinking of letting it get quite

that far, Rob. Just allowing Thomas to make the attempt should be enough to be sure of a treason charge.'

Robert grinned, understanding. 'How can I help, Father?'

'Anything Thomas tries will be at night. So, instead of increasing the number of guards, we reduce them. We might even leave one door open. Now, the king sleeps with his dog on the bed, doesn't he? And the little monster always barks at anyone who comes in the room, yes?'

'Always,' Robert nodded.

'So, you lock the dog outside the king's bedroom. Just outside, mind, in the next room. Thomas will find it easy to get into the king's apartments and he'll get cocky. He'll get to just outside the bedchamber and then the dog will bark and the whole corridor will be roused and we'll catch him red-handed. And that,' John patted Robert's face playfully, 'will be the end of dear Uncle Tom.'

CHAPTER ELEVEN

'Goodnight, Your Majesty.'

Robert bowed to the small, thin figure beneath the bedclothes. He looked about him, at Henry Sidney climbing into a pallet bed on the floor, at the dog sniffing around the edges of the room. He pulled the hangings together, enclosing the king in his bed. Robert moved to the dog, and placing his foot behind its hind legs, gently nudged the animal towards the door.

Pulling the door shut, he locked it. The dog seemed unperturbed to be away from his master, but Robert knew it would soon scratch at the door if it wasn't given somewhere soft to sleep. So he untied his cloak and threw it on the floor, bunching it up to make a bed. He whistled softly, and the dog trotted over. Grasping the sturdy little body, he lifted it onto the makeshift bed.

The dog turned around three times and then dropped, curling up and resting his head on his paws, perfectly content. Satisfied, Robert moved into the corridor and locked the door behind him, making sure the Yeoman Warder guarding the door saw him do it.

His room was a little way down the corridor. He made

his way to it, laid down on his bed without undressing, and waited.

Thomas had run across the gardens, almost slipping on the dewy grass, holding his sword against his hip to stop it jangling. Now, he was at the door, waiting for Fowler to let him into the palace. How long he had been standing there? Cold was creeping up his legs and his nose was frozen, and he wondered if it was these sensations that led him to doubting whether he could go through with his plan. *Good God, Tom*, he said to himself, *you're kidnapping a king.* But that thought put a smile on his face. He was proud of the audacity of his plan.

He jumped as he heard the heavy bolt of the door draw back. A moment later, the door opened, and Fowler stuck his head out, his eyes widening as he saw Thomas.

'What?' Thomas asked with a roguish smile. 'Did you think I wouldn't come?'

Fowler took a deep breath and gestured Thomas inside. He followed Fowler to the king's apartments. Thomas suddenly halted.

'What's wrong?' Fowler asked in a whisper.

'There's only one guard,' Thomas said, pointing. 'There's usually two.'

'So?' Fowler shrugged. 'It just makes it easier, doesn't it?'

Thomas hesitated, then nodded. 'Yes, I suppose it does.'

Pushing the small sense of unease to the back of his mind, he strode down the corridor, Fowler close at his heels. The guard turned his head at their approach, but Thomas nodded at him and he looked away. Inserting his key into the lock, Thomas and Fowler stepped into the dark of the antechamber and closed the door.

Thomas's heart was beating almost painfully in his chest and he heard the rushing of blood in his ears. Another noise broke through, loud and jarring. The dog had awoken and was barking furiously at the intruders. The noise seemed to emanate from everywhere, and Thomas stretched out his arms to find the source. His hand came into contact with something hairy and warm. Sharp teeth bit down, piercing the flesh of his hand.

Pain made him foolish. Thomas pulled out a pistol he had tucked into his belt and shot blindly, the report deafening in the little room. The shot found its target. The dog gave an ear-splitting whine of pain and there came a sound of tiny claws scrabbling against wood.

Thomas probed inside his purse, trying to find the key to the inner room. His bloodied fingers closed around it and he thrust it into the lock, cursing as he heard shouts from the corridor.

'They're coming,' Fowler squealed, tugging at his cloak.

Thomas shook him off and opened the inner door. A cry of alarm came from Fowler, but he didn't look back. His eyes were on the bed, the box that held his prize. But before it stood a boy with his sword drawn, its tip towards him.

It was all so absurd, Thomas suddenly realised. How could he have hoped to succeed? He threw back his head and laughed, even as hands grabbed him and forced him to his knees.

'Is the king hurt?' someone shouted from the corridor.

'The king is unharmed,' Henry Sidney shouted back, his voice shaking with fear. He kept his sword up.

'What's that on the floor?' the voice asked from the antechamber.

'The king's spaniel,' the guard from the door answered. 'It's been shot.'

A cry of anger and pain came from the bed. The

curtains were wrenched apart and the young king stumbled out, tears streaming down his red cheeks. He flew past Thomas into the other room.

'Bring some light here,' the voice yelled.

'What's happened here?' a new voice asked, and Thomas's heart sank. *Please, God, don't let it be him.*

'An attempt has been made to abduct the king, Lord Protector,' the guard said.

'By whom?'

'By Thomas Seymour.'

Edward Seymour hurried into the room, a candle in his hand, and stared down at his brother.

'Yes, it's me,' Thomas snarled. 'God's Blood, but how this must please you, Ned.'

John Dudley strode in, Robert at his elbow, and Thomas saw the barely suppressed smile break upon his face.

John touched Seymour on the arm. 'Ned, this must be difficult for you, so please go back to your rooms. My son, Robert, will see to the king.'

'But what of my brother?' Seymour asked, staring at Thomas.

'He will be removed.'

'Yes, yes, of course. He can come with me.'

'No, Ned,' John said. 'Your brother must be placed under arrest.'

Seymour frowned at John. 'This is a misunderstanding, John, a prank of his. You know what my brother's like, the jests he plays. He can come with me to my rooms and tell me there what this is all about.'

'He must be arrested. You know he must.' John steered Seymour out of the room, gesturing at the guard to take Thomas away.

Robert stepped back as his father passed. The king was curled on the floor, cradling the dead dog in his arms, its

85

blood staining the front of his nightshirt. Robert knelt and put his arm around the boy's shoulder.

'Your Majesty,' he said softly, 'you had best come back to bed.'

'He killed him,' the king sobbed. 'Why did he have to kill him?'

'I don't know. It was a wicked thing to do.'

'I'll kill him. I'll have his head cut off. I trusted him.'

'We have all been deceived by your uncle.' He pulled the boy to his feet. The nightshirt clung to the small body and Robert felt blood on his hands. 'We must wash you, Your Majesty.'

'We must bury my dog, Rob.'

'I'll see to it first thing in the morning. And if it will make you feel better, I have a bitch at home that whelped weeks ago. The pups are old enough to be separated from her now. I'll bring you one tomorrow. Shall you like that, Your Majesty?'

'Yes,' Edward sniffed. 'I would. Not that another dog could replace...'

Robert ushered him back to the bedchamber as the boy continued sobbing, and with the aid of Henry Sidney, stripped and washed him down.

And if Henry wondered why Robert was fully dressed at such an hour, he made no mention of it.

CHAPTER TWELVE

1549

Secretary William Cecil watched his master read the report he had just delivered. He almost felt sorry for him. It couldn't be easy reading of a brother's treachery.

'I can't—,' Seymour began, but the words caught in his throat. He swallowed hard. 'I can't believe my brother capable of this. Kidnapping. Piracy. Counterfeiting. Proposing marriage with the late king's daughters. Cecil, this can't all be true.'

'Your brother has confessed it, Your Grace.'

Seymour shook his head. Pointing to a section of the report, he asked, 'What is all this with the Lady Elizabeth?'

Cecil hesitated before answering. He liked Elizabeth. She was his ideal of royalty: intelligent, charismatic and, most importantly, a Protestant. He was not eager to smear her character, for he believed there was great promise in her, but there was no denying she had endangered her reputation by her wanton behaviour while in the care of her stepmother. It would be best for her if all the blame could be laid on Thomas Seymour.

'There is evidence your brother behaved most inappropriately with her during his marriage to the late Queen

Katherine. Apparently, he visited her in her bedchamber and played with her in bed. There is also an incident where he cut her dress to pieces while his wife held Elizabeth down. But I'm sure it was all just high spirits. Your brother is notorious for his jests.'

'It says here she bore him a child.'

'That is but a rumour, and one the Lady Elizabeth denies most vehemently. If you read further, she has demanded of Sir Robert Tyrwhitt that a proclamation be made publicly clearing her name of the slander.'

'She demands?'

Cecil inclined his head in a sympathetic gesture. 'She does, Your Grace.'

Seymour shoved the report away and sank back into his chair. 'Thomas will be tried and found guilty, but that will not matter. The king will show mercy.'

Cecil cleared his throat. 'It is my understanding, Your Grace, that the king is not kindly disposed towards his uncle.'

'He's angry at the moment, Cecil, that's all. Thomas killing his dog has upset him greatly.'

'And yet, it has been some little time since that regrettable incident, if I may say, and the king does not show any signs of forgiveness.'

'What do you know of it?' Seymour glared at him. 'Who have you been talking to?'

'No one, Your Grace,' Cecil lied smoothly. He had, in fact, been talking to John Dudley, who had been talking to his son Robert, who, in his turn, had been talking with the king. Cecil's information was accurate. The king intended no mercy towards Uncle Thomas.

'I'll talk to the king,' Seymour said with a wave of his hand. 'I don't doubt Thomas will have to endure some little time in the Tower, but nothing more. And anyway, a spell in there will do him some good. Knock some sense into him. Yes, I shall talk to the king.'

Cecil gave a tight smile and said nothing.

Edward Seymour stood at his study window. Below him were the gardens, intricate, beautiful, but he wasn't looking at them. Instead, he saw himself and Thomas as young boys playing Hoodman Blind while their sister Jane looked on. There had been no rivalry then, no jealousy, no ambition. What had happened to those children?

A shiver ran through him as he thought of that other child, his nephew, the king. He had talked with him, expecting mercy. Instead, he had discovered Edward Tudor was every inch his father's son.

There came a knock at the door, and Seymour heard his name called. With dismay, he recognised the voice of John Dudley. 'Yes, what is it?'

John entered, closing the door behind him. 'I've just come from the council chamber. We've been discussing Thomas Seymour and—'

'How dare you discuss anything without me?' Seymour snapped.

John eyed him coolly. 'You were aware we were meeting, Ned. Business must continue, even if members choose to absent themselves.'

'I am the Lord Protector, John, not a member of the council. Nothing is discussed without me.'

'We did think that perhaps it would be kinder not to involve you.'

'Kinder? I've never known the council to be kind.' Seymour fell into his chair and began sorting through the papers on his desk as if John wasn't there, as if he could will him away.

'I have the warrant here.' John held up a paper. 'Will you sign it or do you want me to take it to the king?'

'What warrant?'

'Don't be obtuse. The warrant for Thomas's execution.'

Seymour gave a mirthless laugh. 'For God's sake, John, I know Thomas has to be punished—'

'Punished?'

'—but aren't you taking this just a little too far?'

'Thomas has been tried and found guilty of thirty-three separate treasons. There is only one punishment.'

'You would have the king execute his own uncle?'

'It is the sentence for a traitor.'

Seymour closed his eyes and sighed wearily. 'He's my brother, John.'

'It's unfortunate... but still.'

'I won't sign it.'

'Edward—'

Seymour slammed his hand down on the desk. 'I will not condemn my own brother. You cannot ask it of me.'

'I'm not asking.'

'For Jesu's sake, have you no mercy?'

'Mercy?' John spat, blood rushing into his cheeks, his black eyes flashing. 'When I was nine years old, I watched my father's head cut off to the sound of the cheering mob, all so King Henry could enhance his popularity with his people. My father was no traitor, yet he was branded one, and my family lived in ignominy for years. I've had to work hard and crawl my way back to favour, and you beg for mercy for your treacherous brother. You waste your breath crying for mercy. Mine's all spent.' He'd been spitting in his anger and wiped his mouth with the back of his hand. 'And isn't this sudden display of brotherly love rather out of place? I'll wager this is all just for show and that truly, all you feel is joy that you're finally going to be rid of him.'

With a roar, Seymour pushed against the desk. It turned on its side, papers and quills tumbling to the floor. John stumbled backwards, shocked, as Seymour landed a punch on his jaw. He dropped like a stone to the floor. Seymour kicked at him, weak, ineffectual kicks that John, when he realised what was happening, easily blocked. He grabbed Seymour's ankle and pulled, making Seymour lose his balance and stumble backwards. John jumped up and grabbed Seymour by the throat, pinning him to the wall. He drew back his arm, fingers curling into a fist. But the fight had gone out of Seymour and he sagged beneath John's grip.

'I'll forgive you for the punch,' John panted, 'because I understand you're upset.' He let go, and Seymour slumped to the floor. John snatched up the warrant. 'Now, will you sign? No? Then I'm going to the king. You can explain to him why you wouldn't put your name to a traitor's death warrant.'

'No. Stop!' Edward grabbed at John's leg. 'I'll sign it, I'll sign it.' He scrabbled around on the floor, found a quill, and jabbed it in a puddle of ink. John handed him the warrant, and Seymour scratched his name on the bottom. 'I am the king's loyal servant,' he whimpered, trying to blow the ink dry.

John snatched the paper from his hands. 'Good for you,' he sneered, and left the room as Seymour sobbed on the floor.

CHAPTER THIRTEEN

John Dudley yawned and wondered at the hour. One or two in the morning, he reasoned, and rolled his head, wincing as bones cracked in his neck. He looked across enviously at William Paget, who was sleeping peacefully, his head resting on his arms.

It was a worrying time for the council. A recent law, the Enclosure Act, had caused outrage. Land that had always been free and open to the people and their animals to graze upon was now fenced in at the whim of landowners who wanted to create deer parks and gardens. With their livelihoods under threat, the people revolted and tore down the hedges and fences, fighting to defend their rights and take back control of the common land. A successful uprising in Cornwall had encouraged others across the south of England to rebel.

John rubbed his knuckles against his weary eyes. Opening them, William Cecil came blearily into focus. 'What news?' John asked with a sigh.

'I'm getting further reports of uprisings in Essex, Hertfordshire, Oxfordshire, Suffolk...' Cecil said. 'The list goes on, my lord.'

'Jesu. How far is this going to spread before the Protector does something?'

'His Grace is in his office, issuing orders.'

John nodded grimly. 'And they'll contradict all the orders we the council have issued. God only knows what's going through that man's mind. First, he's against the Enclosure Act, then he's for it, then he's against it again. Is it any wonder the people think they're not breaking any laws when even the Protector can't decide what's legal and what's not? My own parks have been attacked, Cecil. My pasture land ploughed up and sown with bloody oats.'

'I'm sorry to hear it, my lord.'

'I could bear it better if we had a plan to deal with these rebels. Even his friend Paget,' John gestured at the snoring man, 'has told the Protector he's making poor decisions, but Seymour won't listen.'

'I think the death of his brother has changed my master greatly,' Cecil said sadly.

The chamber doors suddenly burst open and Seymour strode in.

'John,' he declared, 'you must go to Norfolk. A rebellion has broken out there, and one of the damned landowners is leading it. Lord Northampton, who I sent there to maintain law and order, is in my office, quivering like a jelly because they chased him out. You are to leave immediately.'

'I'll talk with Northampton first.' John pushed past Seymour, disappearing into the darkness of the corridor.

'Very well,' Seymour called after him. He looked at Paget, who had awoken with a startled snort when Seymour burst in. 'What the devil are you doing?'

'Nothing,' Paget protested. 'I'm not doing anything.'

'Well, you should be doing something, not just sitting there.' Seymour turned on his heel and stormed out of the room.

Cecil gave the open-mouthed Paget a sympathetic smile and followed his master.

STANFIELD HALL, NORFOLK

Amy Robsart plucked one last flower to complete the daisy chain. Giggling to herself, she arranged it on the head of the boy asleep beside her on the grass. Yawning, she too lay down, making a pillow of her arms. She knew it was getting late and was expected home, but it was very pleasant to lie back and do nothing with the sun warm upon her face.

Ned snorted and woke up. 'I fell asleep,' he said in surprise. 'What are you laughing at?'

'Nothing,' Amy lied.

Suspicion mounting, Ned raised his hand to his head and felt the floral crown. He threw it away with a snort of disgust. 'You let me lay there with that on my head?'

'Oh, don't be cross, Ned, there was nobody to see. Come, lay your head in my lap.'

The offer placated him. He lowered his head to her lap and she ran her fingers through his thin fair hair.

'I shall have to go soon,' she said. 'We have visitors tonight. The earl of Warwick and some of his officers.'

'They're coming because of Kett, I suppose?'

'I suppose so.'

Ned plucked a blade of grass and stuck the end in his mouth. 'Robert Kett and his men tore my father's fences down, you know?'

Amy frowned. 'I heard but I don't understand. Kett's a landowner like your father. Why would he join men who are against the landowners?'

'Father says Kett was never one of us. He's always been a nuisance.'

'Well, I think Robert Kett has a point. After all, what

right do the landowners have to stop the people letting their animals graze where they always have?'

'Amy!' Ned knocked her hand away and sat up. 'You're talking against your own kind when you say such things. Your father and mine.'

'I'm only saying I don't think it's fair.'

'Well, keep your opinions to yourself. If the earl of Warwick heard you—'

'Oh, he won't be paying any attention to me. I'm far too stupid to be of any interest to a man like him.'

'You're not stupid, Amy.'

Amy smiled tenderly at him. 'You're very kind, Ned, but I can't read and I can barely write my own name. I can't compare with London girls, I'm sure.'

'I don't want a London girl.'

'Oh, but you do want me?'

'You know I do, Amy.'

'I know nothing of the sort. It's been such a long time since you kissed me, I thought you no longer cared.'

'I didn't dare. I suppose I should have asked—'

'Why must you ask? Why can't you just kiss me, Ned?'

'Amy,' he said, shocked, 'you sound like a wanton.'

She glared at him. 'Ned, I want you to have a passion for me. So much so that you can't help yourself.'

Ned looked embarrassed. 'You want me to kiss you now?'

'God a'Mercy, yes.'

Ned licked his lips and looked around to make sure no one was watching. He leaned closer to Amy and kissed her, his lips sliding clumsily over hers. She pulled away.

'I must go,' she said, smoothing down her skirts. She looked down at Ned, whose cheeks were reddening, aware his kiss had not been a success. 'Why don't you come to the Hall tonight? You'll be support for me when I make a fool of myself.'

'Yes, all right,' he said, clambering to his feet. 'I'll go home and change.'

Amy watched him as he hurried away, reflecting that he was the boy she supposed she would marry one day. Her heart sank a little at the prospect. Ned was really very sweet, and he cared deeply for her, but he fell so short of what she wanted.

Oh, Amy, she said to herself as she made her way back to her house, *if only you knew what you want.*

'I must go,' Amy said, trying to pull away.

'Not yet,' Robert said, tightening his hold on her.

'It's too soon,' she protested feebly as he pressed kisses to her neck. 'I only met you tonight.'

'But, Amy, I could die tomorrow.'

'Oh, don't say that. I couldn't bear it.'

How was it possible to feel so much for a boy she had only just met? she wondered. Her fears for the evening had been quickly dispelled. The earl of Warwick had been courteous and warm, not at all as she had expected. He had complimented her father on his pretty daughter and praised his house. And then his handsome sons, Ambrose and Robert, had drawn her into conversation, and it had been clever and amusing, so unlike the conversations she had with her family or with Ned.

Ned! How she wished she had not asked him to come. He had arrived late and behaved rudely, taking an instant dislike to Ambrose and Robert, though they had done nothing to deserve it. No, it was just Ned being ... well, Ned. He had stuck his fingers in dishes and sucked them clean. He had told vulgar jokes and been the only one to laugh. Amy wondered how she could ever have thought she could marry him.

She had compared Ned to Robert, and Ned came out

wanting. Ned was fair, lumpy and plain; Robert was dark, slim-limbed and handsome. Ned was dull and slow-witted; Robert was intelligent and quick.

So it was that midnight found them together in a dark corner of a stairwell, with Amy wondering how she dared to make such an assignation, and Robert hardly able to believe his luck.

'It's true. I might die,' Robert said. 'Father will offer pardons, but he doesn't believe Kett will surrender, and we'll have to take Norwich by force.' He slumped against the wall, still holding her hand.

'Are you frightened?' she asked.

'A bit,' he admitted. 'I've never been in battle before.'

'But you know how to fight?'

'Every man knows how to fight. It's what we're brought up to do. I just hope I don't disgrace my father.'

'You won't. I know you won't.'

He smiled then and pulled her towards him. 'Would you miss me if I died?'

'I think I would die myself.'

He kissed her then, hard, and she pressed her body against his. She would have given herself to him if he had asked. But he didn't ask.

'I must get to bed,' he said, breaking their kiss. 'I wish I could stay with you, Amy, but I dare not be tired for tomorrow.'

'And I would not have you so,' she declared. 'Not if it puts you in danger.'

'Shall I see you in the morning? Will you see me off?'

'Oh, I will, I will. And Robert, my sweet Robert, you must come back to me. I couldn't bear it if you went back to London and never thought of me again.'

'I'll come back,' he promised.

. . .

Robert galloped across the fields, glad to be away from the camp and heading for Stanfield Hall. He pulled his horse up abruptly as he neared a large oak and saw Amy sitting beneath it.

She looked up, shading her eyes with her hand. 'Robert,' she cried, jumping up.

Without a word, he dismounted, letting the reins trail on the ground. He embraced her, taking her breath away with his kiss. 'It's over, Amy. The rebels are defeated.'

He left out that most of the rebels were also dead. He didn't want to remember that part, when his father had ordered a gallows built in Norwich's marketplace and had forty-nine men executed. Their legs had kicked in the air as the ropes squeezed the breath from their bodies, and Robert had had to close his eyes and force down the vomit rising in his throat.

Amy's face fell. 'If it's over, you'll be leaving.'

'In an hour or so.'

She stepped away from him, tears falling unchecked. 'But I love you,' she sobbed.

'Amy—'

'No, don't tell me I don't. I know what I feel. I do love you. Won't you say it back? Couldn't you even pretend that you loved me just a little?'

'I don't need to pretend. But I am going back to London.'

'Would you marry me if you could?'

'If I could, yes, of course.'

'You're already betrothed?'

'No.'

'Then why can't—'

'Amy, my father is an earl. Your father is only...,' he searched for a word that would not be too insulting, 'a gentleman. I'm expected to marry someone of my own station.' He couldn't bear the despairing look on her face. 'I can ask my father about marrying you.'

'You will?' Amy asked, her red puffy eyes widening in hope.

'I will,' Robert promised.

CHAPTER FOURTEEN

ELY PLACE

John rubbed at his temples, trying to smooth away the pain. A day spent arguing in the council chamber had left him tired and with a pounding head, so he had returned home, hoping to rest. But there was more work when he arrived home: letters from courtiers pressing their suits, others offering their services in the hope of some reward, and much to his annoyance, letters from the Protector's secretaries with more unnecessary instructions for him.

He reached for the wine his servant had left out for him. As the liquid trickled down his throat, he heard footsteps just outside his door. They didn't pass on, but returned and repeated their measure. He listened for a moment, the noise grating on his fragile nerves.

'Christ's blood,' he roared, wincing as the shout jarred inside his skull, 'whoever that is, either go away or come in.'

The pacing stopped. A moment later, the door opened with a squeal. Robert's head appeared around it. 'It's me, Father.'

'What do you want?'

'It's nothing. It can wait.'

'You've already disturbed me. You may as well come in and tell me what you want.'

Robert stepped inside. 'Well, I'm not sure you will approve, Father, but I've asked Amy Robsart to marry me and I ask your permission.'

John stared at him. 'Who the devil is Amy—? Wait. You don't mean Sir John Robsart's daughter?'

'Yes, Father.'

'You've got her with child?'

'No, Father, I have not,' Robert cried indignantly.

'Then why do you want to throw yourself away on a squire's daughter?' John demanded. 'And anyway, what makes you think you can choose a wife for yourself? Your mother and I will choose who you are to marry, as we did for your brothers and sisters.'

Robert pursed his lips. 'Your answer's No, then?'

John's eyes widened. Must he suffer a thousand petty tyrannies from Edward Seymour at court only to come home and endure insolence from his son? He jumped up from his chair and charged around the desk. His hand whipped across Robert's face.

'You dare talk to me like that again, boy, and I'll have you beaten for an hour. You understand me?'

Robert's eyes were watering from the blow. He turned his face away. 'Yes.'

'Yes, what?'

'Yes, Father.'

John returned to his chair, his hand stinging. 'What has this girl to recommend her other than a pretty face?'

'She is an heiress, Father. She will inherit substantial lands in Norfolk, and I thought that as you have no lands in Norfolk, they might be of some use to you.'

John rubbed his chin as he considered Robert's words.

'Well, you're right. I don't have any influence in that county. And the girl. I suppose you think you're in love with her?'

Robert nodded, his eyes still on the floor.

'As it happens, I don't have any marriage plans for you, and as you say, there would be advantages to the match. Very well, you've persuaded me. I'll write to Sir John in the morning.'

'You mean I can marry Amy?'

'Yes, you can marry the girl,' John said, trying to avoid looking at his son's flaming cheek.

'Thank you. I apologise for my rudeness, Father.'

John gave a tight nod, dismissing him. As the door closed behind Robert, John slammed his hand down on the desk in anger at himself. Never before had he lost his temper so badly with a child of his. It was all this business at court fraying his nerves. Seymour was acting like a man losing his mind. John had returned to court expecting to be greeted with thanks and congratulations for quashing the Kett rebellion. Instead, Seymour hadn't acknowledged his success at all, and had given lands John had promised to a Norwich man who had been useful to him in dealing with the rebels to other men who had done nothing, for no better reason than he could. Seymour had made John look both a liar and a fool.

His only consolation was that Seymour was treating all the privy counsellors with the same distrust and disdain. Even men like William Paget, who had been his staunchest supporters, were complaining about Seymour.

John knew he couldn't go on like this, taking his frustrations out on his family. He would have to do something about Seymour.

. . .

'Really, John,' William Herbert attempted a laugh, 'why all the secrecy?'

John had just ushered him into his study and was now checking the corridor to make sure there was no one lurking. He closed the door and turned to William.

'I'm sorry to involve you in this, William, but I need friends about me now.'

William touched his arm in concern. 'Why, John, whatever's the matter?'

'I've had enough. I can't allow this to go on.'

'Can't allow what? John, talk sense.'

John moved to the window and looked out across the garden. 'The Protector has to be brought down, William. He's gone too far. I put down a rebellion and how does he reward me? With scorn and indifference. And he mocks me. Lands I had promised to one man, he deliberately gave to others. He made me look like a fool and a liar and for nothing but spite.'

'The Protector is acting unreasonably, I agree, John, and not just with you,' William said. 'But he is the king's uncle. His position is secure.'

John shook his head. 'Not as secure as you might think. He's made a lot of enemies at court, not just me, and even the people have turned against him since he sent his brother to the scaffold. Even Paget, who as you know, has been his ally since before the death of King Henry, has been complaining about him and begging him to listen to the council. I promise you, William, the Protector is standing on dangerous ground.'

'Well, you'll have my support, but how can it be done?'

'We'll have to be careful. We can't afford for it to look as if we're just trying to get rid of him to put ourselves in power. And, in truth, that's not what this is about. Seymour will ruin this country if we don't pull him down. I make no bones about it, William. This comes from me and men can either follow me or not. Now, Seymour's taken himself and the king to Hampton Court. He's demanding the council convene there. I shall not go. If he has any sense left in his head, he will realise what that means. Instead, I shall write to the other counsellors, telling them what I intend and if they're with me, to meet here at Ely Place. We'll then send word to the Protector that he no longer has the backing of the council and he should relinquish his post.'

'And if he doesn't?'

'Then we'll have to remove him by force. I don't want to do it like that, but if it's the only way...,' John shrugged.

'And then what?'

'Then the council rules as one, as King Henry originally intended.'

'You seem to have it all planned out, John.'

John gave a mirthless laugh. 'William, it's the only way I work.'

Robert and Ambrose were up in the Minstrel's Gallery, leaning over the balustrade to watch the men trooping into the Great Hall below. Over the past half hour, at least fifty men had come into the hall, there not being room inside for the three hundred and more waiting outside in the courtyard. All the men present had come at John's request because, like him, they had their worries about Edward Seymour.

Seymour's paranoia and belief in his own power had resulted in him forcing the king to leave London and retreat to Hampton Court, telling him only that his life was in danger. To his fellow counsellors, he had been more explicit, telling them John Dudley had threatened the king, and demanding they join him at Hampton Court to defend King Edward. It was nonsense, all the counsellors knew, and not one had obeyed Seymour's order. Instead, they had reported Seymour's words to John, and John had come up with a plan to remove Edward Seymour by force.

Jane came into the gallery, panting a little because the stairs were steep and her stays a little too tight. 'I've been looking for you all over the house,' she said, joining them at the balustrade. She looked down on the packed hall and shook her head. 'I hope your father knows what he's doing.'

'He always knows what he's doing,' Ambrose assured her.

'It's dangerous,' she said, her voice breaking, tears threatening to fall. Ambrose put his arm around her shoulder and was glad when the floorboards creaked and their father joined them.

'There's no call for concern,' John said, shaking his head at his wife. 'We're not marching anywhere. The aldermen agree to muster men to defend London, but not to go to Hampton Court and remove Seymour. We can't march without their support.'

'Then this could all be for nothing,' Jane burst out, 'and Seymour will have you arrested and sent to the Tower.'

John sighed and leant over the balustrade to study the scene below. A dog, brought by one counsellor, barked at one of the household dogs and strained at its leash. Angry shouts and strained laughter resounded around the hall. And then, a young man in Seymour's livery entered the hall, and John's heart banged faster. Had this messenger brought an order for his arrest as Jane feared?

John shouted, 'You!' and the hall quietened. The messenger looked up. 'Come up here.'

'What is this, John?' Jane asked fearfully.

The messenger clattered into the gallery. He held out a letter. John snatched it from the young man's hand, broke open the seal and read it quickly. He laughed out loud. 'The damned fool,' he cried, giving Jane a smacking kiss on the lips and running down the stairs to the hall.

'Listen to me,' John shouted, waving to get the crowd's attention. Silence fell. 'You good men of London, who are mindful of your duty and loyal to our king. Not fifteen minutes ago, you told me you were not prepared to march against the Protector, but only to defend this city should he attack it. But I have just received a letter from him and I feel sure you will change your minds when you hear what he writes.' He paused, making sure he had their complete attention. 'He tells me that if we threaten and intend to kill him, then he will ensure that the king dies first.'

There were loud gasps and exclamations of disbelief from his audience.

'I tell you,' John went on, gratified by the response, 'I and my fellow counsellors never intended the Protector's death. We merely wanted him removed from office. He has claimed I threaten the king. That was and has never been my intention. This letter is proof that it is he who threatens the king. So, now I ask you again. Will you help me remove this pernicious man?'

A loud 'Aye' answered his question, and the men began marching out of the hall.

Up in the Minstrels' Gallery, Jane shook her head, a smile forming on her face. 'Your father,' she said to her sons, 'has the luck of the devil.'

John glanced down at the floor to a chunk of bread that had fallen from the table. 'You haven't eaten.'

Seymour, sitting on a stool by the small window, wrapped in a blanket, turned his back. 'What do you care? Isn't it enough you've imprisoned me? Must you come to gloat?'

John sighed and rubbed his forehead. 'Ned—'

'You will address me as Lord Protector.'

'The council has rescinded your Protectorship.'

'The council can't do that.'

'They can and they have. The council has at last become what King Henry wanted for his son.'

Seymour snorted in derision. 'Does the king know I'm here?'

'He knows you are in custody, yes.'

'Ah,' Seymour turned to face him, 'so he doesn't know I'm here in the Tower. What other lies are you telling him, John?'

'I've told the king no lies. The boy is not a fool. He cannot be ignorant of what you've been doing. You drag him off to Hampton Court—'

'For his safety.'

'For your own. I showed him your letter, Ned. You remember? The one where you promised to kill him if you were in danger.'

Seymour seemed to shrink into himself, pulling the blanket tighter about his shoulders. 'That was written rashly. I wasn't thinking properly. I didn't mean it.'

'That's a feeble defence. You didn't mean it? It's treason to even think of the king's death, let alone threaten to kill him yourself. Do you really think a 'sorry' will excuse you?'

Seymour didn't answer. John wandered around the small room, glancing idly at the graffiti cut into the stone walls by previous prisoners.

'Where's my wife?' Seymour asked quietly.

'At Somerset House.'

'Under guard?'

'We didn't think that was necessary.'

'So, what are you going to do with me? Put my head on the block like you did with my brother?'

'You signed his death warrant,' John reminded him.

Seymour nodded, his chin sinking deeper upon his

chest. 'And I shall be damned for that. I have been damned for it.'

'This has all been of your own making.'

'And a little of yours, confess it, John.'

'You shouldn't have treated me so badly, Ned. You made enemies when you didn't need to.'

Seymour jumped up from the stool and hurtled towards John, thrusting his face at him. John smelt his sour breath and noted the heavy, bloodshot eyes.

'You tell the king I'm here,' Seymour screamed, speckling John's face with spittle. 'I'm his uncle. You can't do this to me.'

John stepped back. The fury in Seymour's eyes was unsettling. He banged on the door to be let out and a guard swung it open. He stepped outside, watching while it was locked and barred. Seymour continued to scream his protests as John walked away.

Robert ran up to his father in the corridor. 'I'm sorry, Father. I couldn't think of a way to stop her.'

'Stop who?' John demanded. He hurried on through to the Presence Chamber and immediately had his answer.

Anne Seymour was on her knees before the king. John stopped dead. He glared at Robert, who had hurried to catch up with him. 'How did she get in here?'

Robert shook his head in answer, mumbling another apology.

Just then, the king caught sight of John. 'Warwick, where is my uncle?'

John stepped up to the dais. 'Under arrest in the Tower, Your Majesty.'

The boy's small, pointed face hardened. 'I was told he was ill. I thought he was being held at Somerset House.'

'He is ill, Your Majesty,' Anne said, her hands shaking,

'because of the threats to his life. The council will kill him if you do not give him your pardon.'

'Godfather.' The king turned to Archbishop Cranmer, who was shifting uneasily from one foot to the other. 'Is this true?'

'We feared for your life if he were to remain at liberty, Your Majesty,' Cranmer said.

'But my uncle has never done me any harm,' Edward cried.

'The lords of the council had good reason to suspect his intentions—'

'No, I will not have it.' The boy stamped his foot. 'I want to see my uncle.'

John silenced a further protestation from Cranmer with a hard, brief stare. 'Of course, Your Majesty, if you wish it. We shall have him brought here so you may see him.'

'At once, my lord,' the king said, stepping down from the dais. John gestured for Robert to follow the boy.

John turned to Anne Seymour and held out his hand. She looked at it scornfully, but then slid hers into it and struggled to her feet. 'I thank you,' she said, and John saw how much it cost her to say those words.

'I serve the king, my lady.'

'As does—,' she sniffed. 'As did my husband.'

'Indeed. Good day, Lady Anne.'

'Why did you agree for the king to see him?' Cranmer hissed in John's ear when she had gone.

John turned to him. 'Would you go against the king's wishes?'

'Not willingly, but the Protector was a threat and had to be removed. I would have thought you were the last person who would want the king and his uncle reconciled.'

'I didn't go through all this for personal gain, Cranmer,' John said heatedly. 'If I had, then I have failed, for Wriothesley has become closer to the king than I.'

'Yes,' Cranmer nodded, his face creasing into even more lines, 'I've been meaning to talk to you about that. Do you know Wriothesley's been corresponding with the Lady Mary?'

John knew, thanks to his spies, but he wasn't about to admit their existence to Cranmer. 'What has he been saying to her?'

'That he hopes and believes that soon she will be allowed to hear Mass again. And he's told the Spanish ambassador the Pope will soon be restored as the head of the Church in England.'

'I would be very sorry if that were true.'

'And what of me?' Cranmer said, clutching his cross. 'If England returns to Rome, all my work will be undone. And my life, very like, forfeit.'

'Cranmer, you must stay calm,' John said. 'Let's just see what happens when the king meets his uncle.'

Cranmer walked away, muttering his unhappiness. John moved to a window seat to consider the changing situation. If the king would not believe his uncle to be guilty of treason, then it would be wise to appear to be a friend to Seymour. It would take a bit of deft manoeuvring on his part and Wriothesley was going to be a problem, John knew, but then, when wasn't Wriothesley a problem? What John needed to do now was acquire friends. All right, he conceded with a wry smile to himself, perhaps friends was the wrong word. Allies then, he needed allies. He began making a mental list of his fellow counsellors, those who were likely to side with Wriothesley and those with him, and was pleased to find that the balance tipped in his favour.

Robert knocked and waited, his ear pressed against the door. He heard the murmurings of his father's voice and then the shouted, 'Come in.'

'Yes, Rob, what is it?' John asked as Robert entered the room. William Paulet stood at his side.

'Could I have a word with you, Father?'

'Of course. William, would you mind leaving us for a few minutes?' It was a command, not a request, and Paulet showed his irritation at having to make way for a boy with a very audible sigh.

'Well?' John asked when he had left. 'What is it?'

'I've just been speaking with the king,' Robert began. 'The meeting you arranged for him with his Uncle Seymour this morning has unsettled him a little, I think.'

'I don't see why it should,' John said with a frown. 'The boy hardly said a word to him.'

'Because he couldn't think of anything to say. He's concerned at how his uncle is being treated at the Tower. He says he looked very much changed.'

'Well, Seymour's thinner, certainly. Worry will do that to a man. But he's not been ill-treated, far from it.'

'I assured him he wasn't, that you wouldn't allow that to happen. But he's no fool. Young he may be, but the king understands what has happened.'

'Is he angry at me?'

'I don't think so. He admits his uncle has behaved foolishly. He even said it would do him good to be shown his place. You know how close the Protector kept him—'

'Seymour threatened to take his life,' John cut in. 'Does he know that?'

'He doesn't believe his uncle would ever harm him.'

John sighed and rubbed his chin. 'Well, what does he want done with him?'

'I think he wants him to be set free.'

'But...,' John sighed loudly. 'I don't believe this. Does he want him back as Protector?'

Robert shook his head. 'He hasn't said so. He understands charges of treason have to be answered, but he doesn't want his uncle to be punished any more than he already has been.'

'He said that?'

'He implied it.'

'Well, then—'

'He sought me out, Father,' Robert said, holding up a hand to halt his father. 'He wanted to speak with me so I would speak to you.'

'He certainly isn't a fool, is he?' John nodded grimly. 'Well, Wriothesley will not like it. But still... I've had your mother befriend Seymour's wife again, much to her displeasure because she thinks her an odious woman, just in case. So, that should serve me well, at least.'

'Can I tell the king anything?'

'You can give him my assurances that Edward Seymour is being treated fairly and I will do my utmost to have him back on the council. But not as its head, Rob,' John pointed a finger at him. 'Make it clear to the king that his uncle no longer works alone. The council of regency, as his father decreed, will act in the king's name.'

Robert departed and Paulet came back in. 'What was that all about?' he asked.

John put his hand on his shoulder. 'William, it seems we're going to have to find a way to work with Seymour again.'

The door burst open and Wriothesley strode in. 'What the devil are you playing at, Dudley?'

John took a sip of wine before answering. 'Playing, Thomas?'

'I've just heard, from William Paulet, mind, not from you, that we're letting Seymour go free.'

'That is correct.'

'Would you care to explain why?'

'The king wishes it.'

'So?'

'I cannot gainsay the king, Thomas. He is prepared to show mercy and we can do nothing but obey.'

'I can see where this is leading,' Wriothesley nodded knowingly. 'Seymour reinstated—'

'No,' John cut him short, 'that will not happen.'

'But if the king—'

'The king understands. Seymour must answer the charges of treason laid against him. Providing he admits to them, he will be released from the Tower and invited back onto the council.'

'Back onto the council,' Wriothesley spluttered. 'After what we had to do to remove him? And besides, I had a plan—'

John's eyes narrowed. 'You had what, Thomas?'

Wriothesley took a deep breath. 'I had hopes that the country would be in better hands than Seymour's.'

'And it will be. Ours. Yours and mine.'

Wriothesley snorted a laugh. 'But we disagree on so many things, Dudley.'

'Only on matters of religion,' John replied smoothly. 'Oh, don't look at me like that, Thomas. I know you cling to the Old Faith. That's no concern of mine. Of course, the king would prefer it if it were not so, but...,' he gestured with his hands. 'Tell me, the hopes you had. Anything in particular?'

Wriothesley stared into John's unblinking black eyes. 'No,' he lied. 'Nothing in particular. I'll go now. Good day, Dudley.'

John watched him leave with an amused smile. *Oh, Thomas,* he thought, *I know exactly what you had hoped for. A return to popery with Mary on the throne. Well, if I have anything to do with it, you're not even going to come close.*

CHAPTER FIFTEEN

1550

'You're the last to arrive, my lord,' Robert informed Wriothesley as he led him up the stairs to John's bedchamber.

'A damned inconvenience having to come here,' Wriothesley muttered. 'What exactly is wrong with your father?'

'A rheum in his head, my lord. He has been very ill.' Robert knocked on his father's door.

The door opened. 'Ah, there you are, Wriothesley,' William Paulet said and gestured him inside.

Wriothesley stepped through and Robert was about to leave when he saw John, propped up in the bed and swamped in blankets, discreetly gesture for him to enter. He did so, closing the door behind him, and moved to a shadowed corner of the crowded room.

John had summoned the council to Ely Place to hold their meeting there. He had been ill for a couple of weeks, but it had become politic to prolong his illness. He wanted to be on home ground when the inevitable happened.

Wriothesley and Paulet had interrogated Edward Seymour in the Tower. Vengeance mixed with envy had led Seymour to admit his treasons, but he had told his accusers that John Dudley had been with him every step of the way. Whether this was true, Wriothesley didn't stop to wonder; he saw an opportunity to get rid of Dudley, his chief opponent on the council. Unfortunately for Wriothesley, he had few friends, and William Paulet was not one of them. Paulet had informed John of everything Seymour and Wriothesley had said. So, John was ready for Wriothesley when he was about to accuse him of treason.

It happened rather sooner than John expected. Arundel had just begun to speak of routine matters when Wriothesley silenced him.

'You must listen to me,' he said. He swelled with importance as all heads turned towards him. 'Edward Seymour has confessed his treasons. Ordinarily, such a confession would mean death, but I'm told the king wishes Seymour to be set free. Now, I have every respect for the king, but he is young and has a kind and generous heart. He does not see the evil in his uncle. And others close to him.'

His eyes met John's and a glimmer of complete understanding passed between them. John knew the moment to act had come.

'My lord,' he cried, throwing back the bedclothes and jumping from the bed, sliding a sword out from between the sheets and pointing it at Wriothesley. 'I believe you wish Seymour dead, though the king would not have it so. I would not have it so. Anyone who threatens the life of Edward Seymour means to have mine as well. You, sir, are a traitor.'

The colour faded from Wriothesley's face. He started towards John but suddenly, Robert appeared before him, his hand pressing firmly upon his chest.

'It's not true,' Wriothesley protested feebly.

'It is true, my lords,' Paulet said, moving to stand beside John. 'My lord Wriothesley planned to remove both

Edward Seymour and John Dudley on charges of treason and establish himself as head of the council.'

The counsellors muttered their astonishment, then loudly voiced their outrage. They appealed to John to act.

'Paulet,' John said, struggling to keep the triumph from his voice, 'Thomas Wriothesley must be placed under arrest. Escort him to Lincoln House and put him under guard. I shall inform the king of what has happened here.' John threw his sword on the bed, his head suddenly swimming, his infirmity of the past few weeks catching up on him. 'Gentlemen,' he said, leaning against the bed for support, 'you must forgive me, but I cannot now continue. We will reconvene tomorrow. Our business can wait until then.'

The counsellors made their bewildered goodbyes, following the dumbstruck Wriothesley and Paulet from the room.

Robert helped John back into bed. 'You should rest, Father.'

'I will today, but I must get up tomorrow and go to the palace. I can't afford to absent myself any longer. I need to write a letter to the king about what's happened here. If I dictate, will you write?'

'Of course, Father. I'll just get some paper and ink.'

'Good boy,' John sighed, sinking into the pillars. 'Oh, and thank you, Rob.'

'What for?'

'For standing between me and Wriothesley. I truly think he would have struck me if you hadn't, and in my poor state, I would have broken like glass.'

'You're welcome, Father,' Robert grinned. 'After all, I need you alive to make sure my marriage takes place.'

'Oh, yes, your marriage. That reminds me. I've had a reply from Sir John. Naturally, he gives his consent and has proposed a dowry, which I have accepted. So, you will get to marry your Amy and live in Norfolk.'

Robert faltered. 'Leave London?'

'I thought that was the whole point. You are to be my man in Norfolk. What's the matter?'

'Nothing, Father, but I will miss being at court.'

'Norfolk's not the other side of the world, Rob. I shall still need you here from time to time.'

'You promise?'

'I promise,' John said with mock solemnity. 'Now, get that ink and paper, will you?'

CHAPTER SIXTEEN

Robert teased open the bed curtains an inch, wincing as a shaft of bright sunlight blasted across his eyes, confirming it was indeed morning. He let the curtains close, pressing his head deeper into the pillow. In the curve of his arm, Amy moaned softly, her warm breath tickling the hairs on his chest.

She stirred and lifted her face to him. 'Good morning, my lord,' she purred.

'Good morning, wife,' he said, enjoying the sound of the new word.

Amy shifted to lean on her elbow. 'Was I good yesterday? I mean, I didn't embarrass you in front of your family, did I?'

'Of course you didn't. Why would you think that?'

'I'm not used to such people, Robert. Just remembering yesterday makes my head whirl. I mean, good heavens, I met the king!'

'It was good of him to attend. I only wish Father could have been there too.'

His father's health worried Robert a great deal. Robert had always thought of John as being very robust, but of late, he had had bouts of illness that confined him to bed for weeks on end. John had been so poorly, he hadn't been able to attend either Robert's or his brother Jack's wedding.

'I don't think your mother was very impressed with me,' Amy said.

Robert assured Amy his mother had just been anxious that the day went well but the truth was Jane was disappointed with Robert's choice of wife. She had made her disappointment obvious by criticising the clothes Amy brought with her from Norfolk, exclaiming they were not good enough to be seen by the servants, let alone the king. And so Amy had gone to the altar in one of Mary's dresses, seamstresses working through the night to make the alterations necessary for Amy's plumper figure. Amy had accepted all this meekly, holding back the tears as Jane spoke about her to Mary as if she wasn't in the room.

'I will be glad to return to Norfolk,' she said. 'Father is making Syderstone Hall ready for us. It's such a lovely house, Robert. I wish we could leave London today.'

'We can't,' Robert said firmly, resisting the pleading in her voice. 'I must conclude my duties at court and take leave of the king before we go to Norfolk.'

Amy sighed and laid her head once more upon his chest, and Robert was relieved she was letting the matter drop. He felt the smallest twinge of resentment against her, for it was because of her he was having to leave London and his family. He knew he would miss them and almost wished he hadn't married. But maybe Norfolk wouldn't be so bad, he told himself, as he turned over in the bed and hugged Amy to his chest.

Robert quickly came to love Norfolk, and he found he did not miss London as much as he had feared, for there was much to do as lord of estates and tenancies. Almost every day, he would rise early and ride out on his beautiful chestnut mare, Salome, a wedding present from his parents.

This morning had been no different, and Robert walked Salome back into the stable yard feeling his blood pounding through his body, the way he always felt when he had been alone with his horse and galloping across the country. Nothing bothered Robert when he was riding, and it was the only time he felt truly free.

He slid his hand along Salome's hot, damp neck, feeling the throb of her heart. He pressed his face in the hollow behind her jaw and gave her a kiss. 'A wonderful ride, my sweet,' he murmured, and she snorted in pleasure. He handed her reins to the stable boy with an instruction to take good care of her and made his way into the house.

Robert entered through the kitchen, greeting the servants cheerfully and winking at two young maids whose smiles dimpled their cheeks. As he entered his study, his steward rose from his desk.

'Good morning, Farrow,' Robert greeted him. 'What business have we today?'

Farrow consulted his papers. 'Two complaints from tenants about the state of their roofs. A woman asking for your help in a matter of arbitration. And a letter from your brother.' He held out a paper.

'It's about time Ambrose wrote, the lazy dog,' Robert said, taking the letter. 'I'll read his letter first and then you can show the tenants in. And tell my wife to get out of bed if she's still in it.'

Farrow left, leaving Robert alone. Robert dropped into his chair and broke open the seal on Ambrose's letter.

Rob,

Sorry for not having written to you sooner, but as you read on, you'll understand how busy I've been. I don't know if you will have heard, living in that backwater you call home, but there has been a plot at court to murder our father. You will not believe it after all Father's kindness towards him, but it is all the work of Edward Seymour.

Now, before you rush off to come here, I assure you Father is well and in no danger. The affair is all over. Edward Seymour is once again imprisoned in the Tower, and I rather fancy the king will not be so forgiving this time. It is almost certain Seymour was raising the people of London to attack and remove the council so that he could rule once again as Protector.

The king misses you, by the way. He relies on Father a great deal and trusts him completely, and you will be pleased to hear that Father will soon be given the dukedom of Northumberland. We Dudleys do rise!

Father needs men around him he can trust, so I'm sure he'll be sending for you soon.

Until then, I remain your loving brother, Ambrose.

P.S. Mary is going to marry your old friend Henry Sidney.

Robert screwed up the letter, wishing it was Seymour's heart. How dare that man cause his father so much trouble?

The door opened, and Amy shuffled in wearing only her nightgown. She eased herself onto his lap, curling her arms around his neck.

'Why did you make me rise so early?' she said in a soft, whiny voice, her face tilted to his so that he tasted the sour tang of her breath.

'It's not early, Amy,' he said sharply. 'It must be at least nine o'clock.'

'That is early. Won't you kiss me?'

He pushed her off his lap. 'Get dressed.'

'Why are you angry with me? What have I done?'

'I've had a letter from Ambrose. My father's life has been threatened. If I'd been in London instead of idling here with you…'

Amy clutched at his arm. 'You're not leaving?'

'I must. My family needs me.'

'Then I'll come to London with you.'

'It's better I go alone. You'll just get in my way.' She sniffed, and he knew she was going to cry. 'Don't weep. You knew I would have to leave at some time.'

'But not so soon, Robert,' she pleaded.

'I'm going. Now leave me. I have much to do before I go.'

GREENWICH PALACE

The court had changed. People now spoke in whispers and looked carefully about them as if wary of being overheard, and when they looked at Robert, he saw respect in their eyes. He was now, he realised with pride, the duke of Northumberland's son.

He hurried to his father's rooms and threw open the

door, too impatient to knock. He caught his breath and stared. Was this his father sitting at the desk? This thin, grey-skinned man with tired, purple-ringed eyes?

'My word,' John said with a little laugh, 'I must indeed look ill for you to stare so.'

Robert rushed to his father's side and knelt, taking his hand. 'What is it that plagues you, Father?'

'I'm a little tired and there is a pain in my stomach that tortures me from time to time, but you mustn't worry. It will pass.' He shook off Robert's hand and nodded at the stool on the other side of the desk. 'Sit.'

Robert obeyed. 'Ambrose wrote and told me all the news.'

John nodded. 'Seymour will be executed on the twenty-second.'

'You seem sad at the prospect. After all he's done to you, why weep for Seymour?'

'He was once my friend, Rob,' John said with a shake of his head. 'And I take no pleasure in bringing a man to his death.'

'It reminds you of Grandfather?'

John didn't answer, but instead rifled through the papers on his desk. 'It's just as well you've come. I was going to send for you. I've arranged for you to take up the post of Master of the Buckhounds, so you'll need to move back to London.' He passed a folded parchment with a heavy red seal dangling from a ribbon to Robert. 'That's your commission. You can sleep with Ambrose for tonight and I'll get my secretary to find you some rooms of your own tomorrow.'

'Thank you, Father. I suppose I had better see the king.'

'He'll be pleased to see you. He's had quite a rough time lately.'

'Ambrose wrote he was ill.'

'He was, but he seems to be over the worst. This business with Seymour hasn't helped, though. Cheer him up, Rob, take his mind off things. You're good at that.'

'I'll do my best,' Robert promised, heading for the door.

'And after you've seen the king, come back here and we'll have a family supper,' John called.

'I don't want to keep you all waiting for me, Father. There's bound to be a corridor full of people wanting to see the king and I'll have to wait my turn.'

John laughed and shook his head. 'You won't have to wait. Just tell the guards who you are and you'll be let straight through. You're a Dudley, Rob. No door is closed to you now.'

The king was sitting on a cushion on the floor in his bedchamber, his back against the wall. He looked up as Robert entered, and Robert saw his eyes were swollen and red and snot dangled from his nose.

'Hello, Rob,' Edward said, attempting a smile.

'You are unattended, Your Majesty,' Robert said, surprised.

'I didn't want anyone to see me like this.'

Robert made a move back towards the door. 'I should go, then.'

'No, don't,' Edward said. 'I'd like to talk with you. It's been so long.'

Robert crossed the room and sat down beside Edward. 'Will you tell me what's wrong?'

Edward wiped his arm across his eyes. 'Don't tell your father you found me like this.'

'I won't,' Robert said, knowing he would break his promise that very evening. 'Why are you crying?'

'Because of Uncle Edward. I'm killing him just like I

124

did Uncle Thomas.' Edward cried again and Robert put his arm around him. 'I killed my mother, too. What next? Shall I kill my sisters too?' He searched in his doublet for a handkerchief, failed to find one, so Robert gave him his.

'You mustn't think like this. You have done nothing wrong.'

'I try to be a good king,' Edward said, 'but I am worried I will not have the chance. I've been ill, Rob, very ill, and it made me think. What if I were to die?'

'You will not die, Your Majesty. Do not fear that.'

'You misunderstand me, Rob. I'm not afraid of dying. I'm afraid of who would succeed me.'

'I suppose your sister Mary would.'

'That's exactly what frightens me. I've worked so hard to bring this country to accept the New Religion. Mary would undo it all and return England to Rome.'

'Perhaps,' Robert said, the thought never having occurred to him. 'But what can be done? Your father was very clear about the line of succession. After you comes Mary and then Elizabeth.'

'I don't suppose my father imagined I would die without issue,' Edward said. 'He cannot have truly meant for Elizabeth to ascend the throne. He knew she was illegitimate.'

Robert frowned. 'If not Mary or Elizabeth, then who does that leave?'

Edward made a face. 'My cousin, Lady Frances Brandon. But there again, she has only daughters and is too old to have any more children. There just aren't enough males in our family.'

'So, unless you marry and have a son, the crown must surely go to a woman?'

'I don't think I'm going to live long enough to marry,' Edward said sadly. 'Your father suggested I name Lady

Frances's eldest daughter my successor. You remember Jane?'

'Oh, yes, I remember Jane. Small, thin, pointed chin and freckles across her nose.'

'That's her. I like Jane. She's clever, and she's a Protestant, and if my successor must be a woman, then I would rather it was her.'

'Sounds like she would make a good wife for you.'

Edward coloured. 'Uncle Thomas suggested that once, but I feel Jane is too close in blood to me. Better she marry someone who can give her sons. That's why your father has suggested your brother as a husband.'

'What?' Robert burst out. 'You can't mean Guildford? Guildford marry Jane? Do you mean to say my idiot younger brother could be king of England one day?'

'Only if I die,' Edward said, handing Robert back his now soggy handkerchief.

Robert took it, not noticing the wetness. 'For England's sake, to save her from King Guildford, I sincerely hope you live forever, Your Majesty.'

CHAPTER SEVENTEEN

1553

Robert hurried through Durham House, past the servants in the Great Hall laying the tables for the wedding feast and up the stairs to Guildford's bedchamber, taking them two at a time. He gave a smart rat-tat-tat on the door and entered.

His youngest brother lay splayed out on his bed, his long legs hanging over the sides. He was half-dressed in silver hose and pumps, his torso bare, one arm thrown across his eyes.

'Guildford, you lazy dog! Father will whip your backside if you're late.'

'There's plenty of time,' Guildford murmured sleepily.

'No, there isn't. The church bell has already struck twelve and you're getting married at one.'

Guildford propped himself up on his elbows, his dark blonde hair falling over his forehead. 'Why the devil do I have to marry her?'

'Because Henry's too young.' Robert snatched a shirt from the back of a chair and threw it into Guildford's lap. 'I don't know why you're complaining. Can't you see what Father's doing for you?'

'He's marrying me to a sour-faced girl.'

'Jane Grey is actually quite pretty. And has it occurred to you, Gil, that she may not be overjoyed at the prospect of being married to you either?'

Guildford pulled on his shirt. 'Why? What's wrong with me?' Robert raised an eyebrow. Guildford stuck out his tongue and finished dressing. 'There,' he said, holding his arms out and turning around. 'How do I look?'

'Beautiful,' Robert mocked. 'Now, come on.'

They clattered down the stairs back into the hall, Guildford pulling at his collar as though it were strangling him. As they entered from one end, John and Jane's father, Henry Grey, the duke of Suffolk, entered from the other.

'Ah, there he is,' John said cheerily to Henry Grey, but to Robert, the cheer felt forced. 'This is Guildford, Henry.'

Henry Grey looked Guildford up and down. 'He doesn't look a bit like you, John. I thought all the Dudley boys were dark. He's got fair hair. Are you sure he's one of yours?'

'He has his mother's colouring. Are you ready, Guildford?'

'Yes, Father,' Guildford answered, struggling to keep the sulkiness from his voice.

'My daughter's waiting,' Henry said brusquely, edging back towards the door.

'Yes, let's to the chapel.' John gestured for the duke to lead, looking behind him to make sure Robert and Guildford followed. 'A pity the king is too ill to attend, but he sends his best wishes for the day.'

'You see?' Robert said in Guildford's ear. 'Your marriage has the blessing of the king.'

Guildford grimaced. 'The only thing that makes this bearable is knowing that if Edward dies, Jane inherits and I become king.'

Robert grabbed his arm and pulled him roughly around to face him. 'For Christ's sake, Gil, hold your tongue. Never talk about the king dying. If anyone heard you—'

'To hell with you. I'll stand for Mother and Father telling me what I can and can't do, but I'll be damned if I have to take it from you.'

'Gil, I'm only—'

'I know what it is. You're jealous, aren't you? There's a chance I might be king one day and you're wishing it could be you.'

'That's ridiculous,' Robert said.

'It's not, and you know it. If you hadn't been so keen on your stupid country girl, you would be marrying Jane. Now, let go of me.' Guildford tugged his arm free and hurried after their father and the duke.

Robert had not dared admit it even to himself, but he was jealous. Why had he set his heart on having Amy? He had spent but a day with her before promising to marry her, throwing himself away on a girl who could neither read nor write and was an embarrassment to him and his family. What a fool he had been!

Robert knocked quietly on the door of the king's privy chamber. He heard footsteps on the other side and peered into the subdued light of the interior as it opened.

'Father?' he whispered.

John waved him inside and the stench hit Robert immediately. Vomit, excrement and herbs, and something else he couldn't place, all mixing together to create a metallic tang that hit the back of his throat. He looked towards the bed. The curtains were drawn.

Robert turned to his father. John looked old in the candlelight. 'How is the king?'

'He's not at all well,' John said grimly. 'I don't think he has long.'

'Is he in any pain?'

'Yes, a great deal. The medicine the doctors give him,' John gestured towards two men sitting before the fire examining a bowl of the king's urine, 'make him feel worse than the illness. I've half a mind to tell them to stop, to let him die, but I dare not. The poor boy can't even escape into sleep. He is tormented by what he will leave behind.'

'The succession weighs heavily on his mind, I know.'

A sudden cry arose from outside the window and John heaved a sigh. 'I wish they would go away.'

Robert moved to the window. Peering through the glass, he saw a large crowd below, all staring up at the window. 'What are they doing there?'

'Hoping to see the king,' John said. 'There's a rumour going around London that Edward is dead and the people want proof he isn't. Rob, I need you to show him to them. Come.'

Robert joined his father at the bedside and peered over his shoulder as he carefully drew back a hanging. His breath caught in his throat as he looked upon the king. The hair on Edward's head was thin and patchy, the skull was covered with scabs. His fingernails had fallen out, leaving the hands as blood-blistered claws that clutched spasmodically at the sheets. His legs were swollen, but it was his skin that was the most shocking sight of all. Edward was turning blue.

'Your Majesty.' John bent low over the boy so he could hear. 'Please forgive me for this, but we must show you to the people.'

Edward's eyelids flickered open. 'Do they think I'm dead, John?'

John smiled sadly. 'They're concerned about you. You don't have to do anything. Robert will carry you.'

Robert nodded understanding as John turned towards him and stepped aside. He slid his arms beneath Edward's body and lifted him from the bed, shocked by how little effort was required. Edward was nothing more than a bag of bones.

'Gently, gently,' John said, opening the window.

As the gentle summer air wafted in, contrasting with the foetid odour of the room, Robert understood what the smell was that he hadn't been able to place. The king's very flesh was rotting.

Edward groaned with each step Robert took. Reaching the window, Robert leaned forward slightly, angling the boy so his head was just poking out of the window. The crowd saw him and cheered.

'Can you wave to them, Your Majesty?' John asked.

Edward tried to raise his arm, his face grimacing with pain. 'I can't,' he gasped, his head falling back against Robert's shoulder.

'It doesn't matter,' John said. 'It's enough. Bring him back, Rob.'

Robert returned Edward to the bed. John replaced the bedclothes, and with a tenderness that surprised Robert, stroked the king's cheek and bid him sleep. As he drew the hanging back, Robert saw tears in his father's eyes.

They both left the bedchamber quietly. Once in the antechamber, John wiped his eyes and became once more the man Robert knew.

John shook his head. 'Do you know, Rob, it makes me wonder what God is about to let such a good servant as the king suffer so.'

'I expect God has his reasons, Father.'

'Then I wish I knew what they were. Still, enough of that. It's obvious the king does not have much time left. We must proceed with his Device for the Succession that makes Jane Grey his successor. Tomorrow, I must convince the council to ratify it and that will be no easy task, I tell you.'

'What if they will not?'

'Oh, they will,' John assured him vehemently. 'Even if I have to shout and threaten, they will do what that boy wants. I refuse to let him die in fear of what he leaves behind.'

John re-read the signatures on the Device for the Succession. It had been hard work to get all the signatures, but it was done and would become law. Jane Grey would succeed to the throne when Edward died.

He looked up as William Cecil, Seymour's former secretary, now his, lit a candle on his desk, for though it was only just past eight o'clock, the sky had darkened and a thunderstorm was threatening. 'It's signed, Cecil.'

Cecil blew out the spill. 'So I understand, my lord.'

John leaned back in his chair and studied his secretary. 'I get the impression you don't approve.'

'It's not my place—'

'What exactly do you object to?'

Cecil hesitated and glanced down at the parchment. 'If I may speak plainly, my lord. I fear the people will not like a change in the succession.'

'It is their king's decree.'

'The people may not see it that way.'

'What you mean is that they'll think it's all my doing, but it's not. The king came up with the idea.'

'As you say, Your Grace.' Cecil moved away.

'But I'm being unrealistic, aren't I?' John murmured to himself. 'How can I expect the people to believe me when my own damn secretary doesn't?'

The door burst open, and Robert hurtled into the room. 'Father,' he panted, 'the king is dead.'

It took a long moment for Robert's news to sink in. Then John got to his feet. 'We have no time to lose. Rob, you and Jack must escort the Lady Mary to London. I want you to make sure she comes straight here from Hunsdon. No detours, no delays.'

'What about Elizabeth?' Robert asked.

'Elizabeth says she's ill and cannot leave Hatfield. But I'll have her here, one way or the other. Don't dally, Rob. Take men from the Tower and be on your way.'

Robert ran out of the room. John looked across to Cecil, who was standing by the desk, awaiting instructions. It was impossible to tell what he was thinking.

'Now then, Cecil,' John said briskly. 'Whether you like it or not, the king is dead and we must issue a proclamation naming Jane Grey queen of England.'

HUNSDON PALACE

The man kept his hood up, despite Mary's insistence that she wanted to see with whom she was speaking. His message was brief and to the point.

'For your own safety, do not go to London. John Dudley will have you in the Tower.'

'What of my sister?' she cried.

'She too has been warned of the duke's intentions. She keeps to her house.'

'At least tell me who sent you,' Mary called after him as he mounted his horse.

But he pulled his hood even further over his face and would only say, 'A friend.'

The chambers of Hunsdon echoed with their emptiness. Jack Dudley checked all the rooms, the heels of his riding boots making clipping noises on the flagstones. Back in the

Great Hall, something glinting on the floor caught his eye. He bent and picked up a gold coin almost hidden by the rushes. 'She left in a hurry.'

'Perhaps she's on her way to London,' Robert suggested.

Jack shook his head. 'There's only one road to London from here. We would have passed her. No, she's probably gone to Kenninghall. She could expect to find allies there.'

'Allies? Against us?'

'Someone has obviously warned her we were coming,' Jack said impatiently. 'Plenty of people are unhappy with what Father has planned. Any of them could have sent word to Mary to flee.'

Robert kicked at the rushes. 'What do we do now, then?'

Jack thought for a moment, then headed for the door. 'I'll go back to London. Let Father know what's happened. You ride on to Kenninghall. See if you can catch up with her.'

'And if I do catch her?'

'Not if, Rob,' Jack said, putting his hand on Robert's shoulder. 'You must find her, else we will all be in danger.'

Robert rode fast when Jack left him, but as swift as he was, Mary had been faster. He didn't find her at Kenninghall. He rode on, growing desperate as he was told time and again at the houses where he made enquiries that he had missed her by only a few hours.

He didn't know what to do. He could keep on searching for Mary, but he suspected it would be pointless. Wherever she was, she had men joining her by the hour. Her followers were increasing, and Robert, with his few men, was no match for them. Should he return to London? Where would he be of the most use to his father?

He set up camp at King's Lynn and sent his most trusted servant, Taylor, to discover what news he could. Robert was sitting in the entrance to his tent, doing the only thing he could think of to do, polishing his sword, when Taylor returned. He set his sword aside and rushed over to meet him. Taylor's face was bruised and bloodied, his clothes torn and dusty.

'What happened to you?' he demanded.

Taylor gulped for air. 'Followers of the Lady Mary attacked me. They saw my badge of Warwick and pulled me from my horse. Then they tore my badge from me and called me a wretch for serving such a vile traitor.'

'A traitor?' Robert echoed. 'They called my father a traitor.'

'The Lady Mary has been proclaimed queen, my lord.'

'That's not possible.'

'It is true, my lord,' Taylor said. 'Even your father, the duke, has proclaimed her queen.'

'No, you're wrong. You have to be wrong. Jane is queen.'

'Jane Grey is imprisoned in the Tower, my lord, along with your father and brothers.'

Robert's blood ran cold. It couldn't be true, could it? Mary proclaimed queen and all the Dudleys in the Tower? He studied Taylor's face and saw truth in his eyes.

'Perhaps we should flee, my lord,' Taylor said. 'There's nothing you can do for your family, but you can save yourself.'

'We will stay.'

'But they will come for us.'

'They will come for me.'

Taylor shook his head. 'You're wrong, my lord. We will all be taken. They will punish us.'

'You will not be taken, Taylor. You have my word.'

Taylor grabbed Robert's arm. 'What good is your word now?'

Robert pushed him roughly away, then balled his fist and, summoning up all his anger and sense of failure, punched Taylor on the jaw, felling him. 'Leave if you want, or stay. But do not dare to show your face to me again.'

He glowered at the men who had clustered around to watch the altercation between master and servant, and retreated to his tent to await his arrest.

CHAPTER EIGHTEEN

THE TOWER

'They're bringing Rob in now,' Ambrose said from the window.

Jack joined him and looked down at his brother walking between two guards. 'He looks grim.'

'You know Rob. He's going to blame himself for all this.'

'So he should,' said a sulky voice from behind them. They turned to their brother, Guildford, lying on a truckle bed. 'Don't look at me like that. All Rob had to do was capture a silly woman and he couldn't even manage that.'

'It wasn't his fault, Gil,' Jack said. 'Mary moved too fast for us. We had no idea how much support she had.'

'And if you're going to blame anyone, blame your wife,' Ambrose said, kicking Guildford's foot hanging over the side of the bed. 'If she hadn't been so stupid as to insist Father leave the court to lead the men against Mary, he would have been able to keep control of the council. They turned on him as soon as he left. And to think they're calling Father a traitor. The bloody hypocrites.'

Jack looked around the small chamber. 'We shall have to make room for Rob. Maybe we can—.' He broke off as he heard a bang and pressed his nose to the window. The guards were leaving. 'What are they playing at? They've left Rob downstairs.' He turned to Ambrose. 'Why would they leave him on his own?'

Robert was wondering the same thing. He would have given anything to see a friendly face. It was cold there in the stone chamber, despite the warmth of the late summer day, for little light penetrated through the narrow slit windows. He sat down on the bed. It creaked and spread beneath his weight. He pulled his legs up to his chest and hugged them tight.

He could hardly believe this had happened. Even when he had been arrested and taken before Mary, forced to his knees to do her obeisance, it hadn't seemed possible he was her prisoner. Entering the Tower under guard had made it all too real.

Fear was making him shiver. Fear for himself, fear for his family. He thought of his mother, and it hurt him to think how worried she would be. Then he thought of Amy, sitting at home in Syderstone Hall, wondering what had become of him. He cried without even knowing he did so and curled himself into a ball on the bed. Exhaustion over-whelmed him, and he fell into a fitful sleep.

Robert was left on his own for two days. On the third, his guard came in without his breakfast and told Robert to get up from his bed.

'Why? Where are you taking me?' Robert asked, his fingers trembling as he hurried to pull on his boots.

'The Tower's filling up,' the guard said, unlocking the

inner door. 'We're having to put prisoners together to make room. So, you're going in with your brothers.'

Robert grabbed his cloak, bundling it under his arm. He didn't move fast enough for the guard, who grabbed his arm and shoved him through the doorway.

'Don't you dare push me, you dog!' Robert growled.

His rage amused the guard. 'Haven't you worked it out yet?' he said, looking Robert up and down with contempt. 'You're nothing. You're nobody. Soon, you'll be out on Tower Hill on the scaffold, pissing yourself because your head is about to be cut off, after they've ripped your guts out first, mind. I might be a dog to you, but I'm a dog who will be alive this time next year, which is more than you'll be. Now, are you going to walk up those stairs there or do I have to drag you up?'

The door closed behind him. Robert blinked at the sudden brightness of the upper chamber. His brothers were sitting around a small table in the centre of the room, playing a game of cards.

'Rob?' Jack jumped up and rushed at him, arms outstretched.

Robert melted into his brother's arms, burrowing his face in his neck and breathing in his warm, comforting smell. Then Jack let go and stepped aside so Ambrose could embrace their brother.

'It's good to see you, Rob,' Ambrose said. 'How are you? Have they mistreated you?'

'I'm well enough.' Robert pushed aside his examining hands. 'I'm so sorry.'

'Enough of that,' Jack said sharply.

'But if I had found Mary—' Robert protested.

'It wouldn't have made any difference, Rob. The council turned on Father.'

139

'Have you seen him?'

'He's in the Garden Tower with Henry.' Ambrose said.

'But Henry is so young. They can't believe he was involved in any of this, can they? He was home with Mother, wasn't he?'

'He was, but our young brother is a Dudley and therefore cannot be left at liberty to cause more trouble.'

Robert groaned. 'What's going to happen to us?'

'There will be a trial, I expect,' Jack said, 'at which we'll be found guilty of treason. After that...' He threw up his hands. He didn't need to finish the sentence. They all knew what happened to traitors.

They all turned as the door opened. Robert's truckle bed from the downstairs chamber flew through the air and clattered in a heap on the floor.

'Don't expect anything else,' the guard grunted, pulling the door shut and locking it.

Ambrose went to the bed and began setting it straight. 'Gil, shove along so we can get this in.'

Robert watched as his brothers rearranged their prison furniture. His eyes stung with tears. 'For us to come to this.'

'It is to be expected, Rob,' Ambrose said.

'How can you say so? We are Dudleys, Ambrose.'

'We are traitors, Rob. Don't you understand what we've done?'

'What have we done?' Robert cried. 'Tell me, brother. What have we done but tried to save England from a Catholic queen?'

'Rob's right, you know,' Guildford said. 'After all, it was King Edward who wanted to change the succession—'

'Edward had no right to do that, Gil,' Jack said.

'No right?' Robert cried in exasperation. 'What does it mean to be king if one cannot dictate the law of the land?'

'This is not a land of tyrants, Rob,' Jack shouted back,

'where a sovereign can act without the consent of the people.'

'He had consent, Jack. Parliament consented.'

'Only after Father bullied them.'

'I can't believe you're speaking so, Jack. If this is what you've always thought, why didn't you say so to Father?'

'I did my duty by Father, as I would always do, whether I believed him right or not.'

'Well, I know he was right, and I did my duty out of more than loyalty.'

Guildford snorted. 'You can't claim to have done your duty, Rob.'

Robert turned on him. 'What did you say?'

'I said you didn't do your duty. If you had caught that bitch, Mary, we wouldn't be here.'

'You think I am to blame.' He turned to Ambrose and Jack. 'Do you think so too? Have you been lying to me?'

'No, we haven't,' Ambrose said with a sigh. 'And neither does Gil. He's just talking nonsense, like always.'

'I'm not. I'm right and we all know it.'

'Shut your mouth, Gil,' Jack yelled, stepping up to his young brother and glaring at him. 'Just shut up.'

'And I'll tell you something else. If Rob had done his duty, I wouldn't allow you to speak to me like that. If Father had succeeded, you would all have to bow your knee to me.'

'Bow our knees to you?' Jack sneered, looking Guildford up and down with contempt. 'I don't think so. Not after Jane refused to crown you.'

'She refused you a crown?' Robert scoffed. 'Did even your wife realise what a blockhead you are?'

'And I suppose you think you would make a better king?' Guildford shot back.

'You're bloody right, I would,' Robert yelled into his face.

Jack pushed the brothers apart and held them at arm's length. 'That's enough. We mustn't be like this. Do you think it would please Father to see us at each other's throats?'

'Maybe he should have considered what his actions would lead to,' Guildford said.

'Father isn't to blame,' Robert insisted.

'How can you say that? No one who matters agrees with you. They're probably already building his scaffold.'

Robert turned to Jack. 'They wouldn't do that, would they?'

Jack shook his head sorrowfully. 'It is likely, Rob.'

'No,' he said, the blood draining from his face. 'They won't do that to Father, Jack. They won't.'

CHAPTER NINETEEN

John Dudley pulled his cloak up to his chin and dug his fingers into his side in a futile attempt to press away the pain. The pain there was almost constant now. Or perhaps he was imagining it? Had failure made it seem more real?

He swore as the imaginary knife twisted, and turned it into a curse against his daughter-in-law. It had been Jane sending him out of London that had been his undoing. If he had been allowed to stay as he had tried to tell her he should, his fellow counsellors wouldn't have been able to stab him in the back. He knew he was growing angry, knew too it would do him no good, so he willed his anger away. After all, it was ridiculous. Dudley the queenmaker! He had been a fool to think he could have done it.

John looked up as his cell door was unlocked and Stephen Gardiner walked in. Gardiner's countenance still bore the pallor that five years' imprisonment in the Tower during King Edward's reign had given him.

'Is my wife safe, Stephen?' John asked. 'And where has Henry been taken?'

'Your wife is safe. The queen bears her no malice. Your

youngest son has joined his brothers in the Beauchamp Tower.'

'How are they?'

Gardiner sighed. 'I neither know nor care, Dudley. I came only to tell you your trial is set for three days hence. You will be found guilty, you and your sons.'

'And what will follow?'

The look Gardiner gave him was steely. 'Death, of course.'

'For me, yes, I understand that, but not my sons, please. They don't deserve to be executed. They were only doing what I told them to do.'

'They are old enough to know it was treason, Dudley. They must pay the price.'

'They're my sons. There must be something I can do for them. Let me write to the queen. I will beg her to show mercy.'

Gardiner's eyebrow rose. 'The duke of Northumberland beg?'

'To save my sons, yes, I will beg.'

Gardiner considered him for a moment. 'There is something you could do that might make the queen feel merciful towards you. Admit your religion is false. Admit the error you have made in following the Lutheran heresy and return to the True Faith. Admit this and your sons may be saved.'

John stared at him. 'But that's not what I believe.'

'You won't do it?'

'It's no small thing you're asking of me.'

'Then I see no point in my remaining.' Gardiner turned towards the door.

John grabbed his arm. 'Wait. Will it really save my sons?'

'The queen is not vengeful, Dudley. Your life is forfeit,

but a public recantation of your faith will save your sons. You have my word.'

'Then I'll do it, if I have your word. I'll say I've been wrong all these years and that the Catholic faith is the true faith. I only hope God will forgive me.'

Gardiner's lips twitched as he tried not to smile. 'You'll be able to ask him soon enough.'

This was the way his father had died. John had been there that day, so many years ago, on Tower Hill as a small boy, crushed between the bodies of the spectators. The sound of the cheers as his father's head was hacked off had stayed with him to haunt his dreams. Now, the cheers were for him, an eager mob shouting for his head to be hacked off. He was so tired, he could almost be glad his life was soon to be over.

John moved to the block, shuffling through the sand and straw laid down to soak up his blood. He felt someone step up behind him, and a white cloth was thrown over his eyes, making him flinch. A knot was hurriedly tied and John felt hands on his back, guiding him to the block. His trembling legs gave way, and he fell onto his knees, gasping at the jolt of pain that shot up through his spine. He leaned forward, feeling for the curve in the wood. As he lowered himself, the blindfold slipped and fell down around his neck. It made him shudder to look again upon the baying crowd with his head so near the red-stained stump of wood. He sniffed to hold back his tears, but it didn't work. *God damn you*, he chided himself, as they flowed so obviously down his hollow cheeks. His fingers fumbled at the knot, untying and repositioning it, this time tying it so tightly it dug into his skull. He thrust his neck into the hollow and shouted, 'Jesus, into your care, deliver me.'

John spread his arms wide, the signal for the executioner to strike. He felt the cold metal of the blade against the back of his neck as the executioner marked out his target, a terrifying few seconds as he imagined the blade arcing into the air, then an exquisite shock of pain and the world went black.

Jack, leaning against the fireplace, closed his eyes. He had just seen the cart carrying his father's body returning from Tower Hill.

'It's done,' he said.

Henry rushed to him, pressing his face against Jack's chest.

Guildford, his face white, swallowed. 'Is Father—'

'Yes, Gil,' Ambrose cut him off sharply, adding more kindly, 'yes.'

He turned to look at Robert. Robert lay on his side on the bed, his back to the room. He was shaking. 'Oh, Rob,' Ambrose whispered, and moved to the bed. He reached out a hand and stroked the thick black hair.

Robert flinched beneath his touch. Jerking upright, he knocked Ambrose's hand away. 'I'll never forgive them,' he said, his black eyes fierce behind his tears. 'Not as long as I live.' His face crumpled. 'What am I going to do without him, Am?'

Ambrose looked across at Jack, hoping he had an answer, but Jack lowered his eyes. 'I don't know, Rob,' Ambrose said sadly.

'For Christ's sake, what's the matter with you?' Robert grabbed at him. 'Why aren't you angry?'

'I am angry,' Ambrose retorted, stung by the accusation. 'Do you think you're the only one who loved him?'

'I wish they'd killed me, too.'

'Don't say that,' Jack scolded, giving Henry's head a savage caress. 'And don't believe what Father said in the chapel about recanting his faith. It was a lie, said to save us from the same fate. It hurt him to say what he did, but he did it for us. That's the kind of father he is. Was.'

'They didn't have to kill him,' Robert said, punching the mattress. 'They could have just kept him a prisoner. Why'd they have to kill him?' His sobs began afresh.

Ambrose pulled him close and held him tight. 'Because that's what the Catholics wanted,' he said bitterly. 'A human sacrifice to their religion, so they can say, "Look, even the duke of Northumberland admitted he was wrong and we are right." They're heartless bastards, Rob. Every one of them.'

Jack nodded his agreement. 'The sooner that bitch, Mary, is dead and Elizabeth sits on the throne, the better for all of us.'

CHAPTER TWENTY

Simon Renard, the Imperial ambassador, looked down at the woman sitting in the chair and felt sorry for his master, the king of Spain. This was the woman King Philip was going to marry, and an older, uglier, less appealing woman than Mary Tudor Renard could not imagine.

'No, I cannot do it.' Mary slapped her hand down on the pommel of her chair. 'They're innocents.'

Stephen Gardiner moved away from the window to stand before his queen. 'Jane Grey and her husband were never that, Your Majesty. This recent rebellion of Wyatt's has shown how insecure your hold on power is.'

'I am loved,' Mary declared indignantly. 'The people supported me against Dudley, and Thomas Wyatt claims to have only been protesting against my marriage to King Philip, not my right to be queen.'

Gardiner shrugged. 'What Wyatt claims and what he would have done once he had achieved power are two different things.'

Mary wrung her hands desperately. 'I still don't see why Wyatt's treachery affects my cousin Jane and her husband.'

'Her father, the duke of Suffolk, was free to join the rebellion,' Renard pointed out, reminding Mary of her former ill-judged mercy in not imprisoning Suffolk, too. 'And had Wyatt succeeded, the duke would have put his daughter on the throne once more. While that girl lives, she is a constant danger to your security. And while she lives and has a husband, she is the perfect candidate to be queen.'

'I agree with Senôr Renard, Your Majesty,' Gardiner said. 'The Grey girl is a threat to your throne and your life. You have shown great mercy in allowing her to live this long.'

'She is my cousin,' Mary protested.

Gardiner gave Renard a look that urged him to speak. Renard nodded and said, 'Your Majesty, King Philip will not feel secure in a country whose citizens are allowed to rise up against their sovereign without fear of punishment. He may not agree to your marriage.'

'But he must.' Mary stumbled towards him in agitation. 'We are betrothed.'

'Alas,' Renard shrugged, 'these arrangements are easily undone.'

'No, Philip must come here. My heart is given to him. He must, he must.'

'Then you must sacrifice your noble feelings towards your cousin, Your Majesty,' Renard said with as sympathetic an expression as his face could muster. 'You have no choice. Jane Grey must die.'

'Help me,' Guildford screamed, grabbing at the cloak Jack wore to keep out the cold.

Jack wrenched it from his hands. 'There's nothing we can do, Gil.'

'But you can't let them kill me. I did nothing. Why do I have to die?'

Ambrose stepped away from the door where he had been listening. 'They're coming.'

The door opened. Sir John Brydges, the Lieutenant of the Tower, stood in the doorway, two halberdiers behind him. 'It's time,' he said solemnly, staring at Guildford.

'You can't do this, Sir John,' Ambrose said, moving to stand in front of Guildford. 'He's only a boy.'

Brydges looked away. 'Stand aside, sir, if you please. I have a warrant signed by the queen.'

Ambrose and Jack looked at each other, knowing there was nothing they could do to stop this. Jack grabbed Guildford and pulled him into an embrace. 'Be brave, Gil. I love you.'

Ambrose put his arms around Guildford when Jack reluctantly let go, and his words were ones of love, too. Henry pressed his face against Guildford's, their tears mingling. He was too young to hold back his tears. 'Sorry,' he slobbered and released his brother.

Robert reached for Guildford and wiped his wet cheeks with his thumbs. Curving his hand around the back of Guildford's neck, he pulled his brother to him and held him fast.

'I love you,' he said through gritted teeth.

'It's not fair,' Guildford sobbed.

'I know.'

They had no more time. Brydges tugged Guildford out of Robert's embrace and hurried him through into the passage beyond. The guard swung the door shut, pointing his halberd at Ambrose and Jack as if fearing they would hurry after him, and locked the door.

The brothers heard Guildford's cries as he was taken down the stone stairs. They hurried to the window, waiting for him to appear. As he emerged into the sunlight, he looked up at the window and gave them a weak smile, the last they would ever see.

CHAPTER TWENTY-ONE

Mary had married and was happy for perhaps the first time in her life. The Dudleys were no longer a threat to her throne or her contentment and when it became clear the queen had no other plans for the brothers but to let them rot in the Tower, Sir John Brydges invited the Dudley brothers to dine with him. The week before, he'd invited Jack and Henry. Tonight, was the turn of Ambrose and Robert.

Brydges gestured to his servant to pour more wine for his guests. Robert and Ambrose added water to their cups when Brydges wasn't looking as Jack had told them to, knowing it wouldn't be wise to have muddled brains or loose tongues before a servant of the queen.

'I am heartily sorry for your present condition, my lords,' Brydges mumbled, setting down his cup. 'I don't care to see the sons of the duke of Northumberland in such a place as this.'

'We don't much care for it ourselves,' Robert replied sourly.

'But we thank you for allowing us to dine with you, Sir

John,' Ambrose said, giving Robert a warning kick beneath the table.

'You are very welcome, my dear young man,' Brydges said, patting his hand affectionately. 'Though, I fear I may not have the pleasure of your company once the Lady Elizabeth is brought here.'

Ambrose and Robert glanced at one another in surprise. 'Elizabeth is coming here?' Robert asked.

'As a guest?' Ambrose added.

Brydges shook his head. 'As a prisoner, like you and your brothers. It seems she was involved in the Wyatt Rebellion, receiving letters from that young man telling her what he had planned. But if you want my opinion,' he leaned forward conspiratorially, 'I don't believe she received any letters, or if she did, that she replied to them. If you ask me, she shouldn't be sent here at all.'

'Then why is she?'

'The queen is grown very suspicious of her sister, from all I hear.'

'It will be good to see Elizabeth again,' Robert said.

'Ah, there now, you hope in vain, Master Robert,' Brydges wagged a finger at him. 'I have orders she is to be close confined. No visitors.'

Robert winked at him. 'We'll see.'

'No, no, no. On this, I must stand firm,' Brydges insisted. 'It could mean my head if I do not.' He glanced at the window. 'Oh my word, it's late.'

'Yes,' Ambrose said, draining his cup. 'You had best be locking us up for the night.'

Sir John bid them goodnight and instructed the guards waiting outside the door to take the brothers back to their cell. They reached the open air and their nostrils were filled with the scents of flowers from Brydges's garden. Robert could almost believe himself back in Norfolk.

'I don't believe Elizabeth would be so stupid as to join a rebellion,' Ambrose said.

'Nor do I.' Robert leant closer so the guards would not hear him. 'But I wouldn't put it past her to know about what Wyatt intended and to sit back and watch to see how it turned out.'

'You make her sound so duplicitous. Surely, she would warn the council if she knew her sister was in danger?'

'Not if it wasn't in her interest, she wouldn't. I wonder if we will see her.'

'Brydges said not, and I don't think you should nag him about it. It wouldn't be fair when he's been so kind.'

'But I have to see her, Am,' Robert said earnestly. 'I have to have something to look forward to. Tell me, is it cruel of me to be pleased she's coming?'

'Twice in as many weeks,' Robert murmured as the Tower guards escorted him and Ambrose into Brydges's apartments. 'Sir John must be lonely.'

'Don't complain,' Ambrose said. 'The dinner here is better than in our chamber.'

'I'm not complaining, but Henry and Jack were. It was their turn to dine with him. Why did he ask us?'

'Perhaps Sir John prefers our company.' Ambrose stared at the table. 'Look. The table is set for four. Maybe Henry or Jack was supposed to come with us.'

Robert shook his head. 'The guards were very specific. Just you and me.'

'Then who is the fourth place for?' Ambrose wondered.

'It's for me.'

They whirled around at the voice.

'Bess!' Robert cried.

Smiling, Elizabeth held out her hands to him. 'Why, Robin, how you stare at me. Do you think I'm a ghost?'

'Of course not,' he laughed, though she was paler and thinner than when he had seen her last. He took her hands and kissed them. 'I'm surprised, that's all.'

Elizabeth turned to Ambrose. 'How are you, Ambrose?'

Ambrose bowed. 'Very well, my lady. Sir John,' he called as Brydges walked in, 'what is this? You said to meet with this lady would be impossible.'

Brydges brushed past Elizabeth, frowning. 'The Lady Elizabeth can be very persuasive.'

'What he means,' Elizabeth said, 'is that I hounded him until he agreed to let me see you. Are you glad I did, Robin?'

'Glad beyond words,' he said, and meant it.

'You?' she mocked. 'Well, beyond words you may be, but I doubt if you are beyond dinner. I know you of old.'

Robert led her to the table, guiding her to Brydges's accustomed seat. Brydges considered protesting but did not want to seem churlish and sat down next to Ambrose.

'You seem quite cheerful, my lady,' Ambrose observed. 'Considering.'

'Considering?' Elizabeth raised an eyebrow.

'Considering why you're in here,' Ambrose said, uncomfortable beneath her glare. 'You've been accused of conspiring with Wyatt, Sir John tells us.'

A flicker of annoyance crossed Elizabeth's face. 'It's a complete fabrication. I never conspired with that man, and my sister cannot prove I did.'

'How can you be imprisoned without proof or even a trial?' Ambrose asked. 'I thought there were laws against such injustices.'

'A queen can do what she wants,' Elizabeth said coldly, 'especially when she listens to the advice of her council.'

'Are you so unpopular with Mary's council?' Robert asked.

'To them, I am a heretic and a bastard,' she said. 'They prefer having me out of the way. They even had me brought here in secret so the people wouldn't make any protest.'

'My lady,' Brydges said. He looked very uncomfortable at the way the conversation had turned. 'I feel I must stop you speaking so of the queen and council. If they were to hear I allowed you to say such things—'

Elizabeth laid her long fingers upon his arm. 'Forgive me, Sir John. I do not wish to make trouble for you, especially as you have been so kind as to reunite me with old friends.' She turned to Robert. 'Come, Robin, we will change the subject to make Sir John content. We will eat and talk of happier times.'

And talk they did. Ambrose, who had not seen his brother so happy for such a long time, drew Brydges into conversation and encouraged him to engage in a drinking game, downing cup after cup until their heads drooped and they slept, snoring a little.

'It seems they have no head for wine,' Elizabeth joked, rubbing her arms. 'I feel a little cold, Robin. Let's sit by the fire.'

Robert tossed two cushions onto the floor beside the hearth. He held her hand as she lowered herself to the floor.

'Of course, I should hate you,' she said.

Robert plumped down next to her. 'Why should you?'

'For what your father did. For using Jane. For all of it.'

'What did you ever care for Jane?' he scoffed.

'She was my cousin,' Elizabeth said sternly. 'And I did care for her, in my way. She didn't deserve what happened to her.'

'Nor did Guildford,' Robert returned. 'Nor did my father, for that matter.'

'Really, Robin, after all that has passed, can you still be blind to his faults?'

'What do you know of his faults? You didn't know my father as I did.'

'I know he meant to take Mary's life, and he would have taken mine.'

'That's not true.'

'Why then did he send for us to come to London?'

'Edward was dying. My father thought you would want to be with him.'

'So you say, but I received word Edward was already dead. Your version of the story doesn't cover the facts.'

'Who sent word to you?'

'I don't know. I received an anonymous letter.'

'But who do you think it was?' he pressed. 'You won't tell me. Well, that's all right. I can guess who betrayed my father and put ideas into your head to falsely accuse him. William Cecil. I've never trusted him. I'm right, aren't I?'

Elizabeth reached for his hand. 'Robin, think. With Jane on the throne and your father expecting Guildford to be made king, what need would he have for Mary and me?'

'He wouldn't have hurt you, Bess. He was doing what Edward wanted. Mary forced his hand. I tell you, the man who sent the letters ruined everything. He put my father's head on the block as surely as Mary did. I'll never forgive him.'

'I am sorry you lost your father, Rob,' she said.

Robert smiled sadly. 'When he died, I said to Ambrose I wished they had taken my head too. I still miss him so very much, Bess.'

Elizabeth held his hand to her breast. 'You must have loved him very much. I wish I had loved my father as much as you loved yours. But I hardly knew him.'

'I thought you did love him.'

157

'I loved his magnificence, I think, not him. Kat, you remember Kat? She said he must have been a hard man to love, but I think she was thinking of my mother when she said it.'

'Do you remember her?'

'I have one memory of her. A woman with black hair and black eyes, crying as she held me. I suppose that was just before she was arrested. Maybe I am to suffer the same fate as she.'

'Well, my father followed his. Maybe I will follow mine.'

'How dreary this conversation has become,' she said. 'Let's talk of something happier.'

'Tell me what to talk about, Bess. Soon, the sleeping Sir John will awake and we will be locked in our cells once again. Tomorrow will pass much as today has. What have we to look forward to?'

'It's selfish of me, I know, but I am glad to have you here for company. It makes me feel less alone.' She quickly kissed his cheek. 'Are you as frightened as I am, Robin?'

He returned her kiss. Her lips were cold. 'Just as frightened, Bess.'

'Some letters from your ladies.' Brydges handed them out.

'It's from Mother,' Jack said, as Henry stood to look over his shoulder.

Brydges made to leave but turned back to Robert. 'Oh, I thought you would like to know that the Lady Elizabeth has gone.'

Robert looked up from Amy's letter. 'Gone?'

'They took away her last night. Gone to Woodstock, I'm told. Sir Henry Bedingfield has charge of her now. I can't say I'm sorry to see her go. One month of that young lady was enough to try the patience of a saint. No, you must not keep me, Master Robert. I have much to do today.' Bridges pulled the door shut and locked it.

'Why didn't she warn me she was going?' Robert said, kicking at a stool. 'To just go off.'

'She hasn't just gone off,' Ambrose said. 'You heard Sir John. She was taken. She's still a prisoner.'

'Stinking bitch,' Robert cursed, screwing up his letter and throwing it into the fireplace.

'Elizabeth?' Ambrose asked in surprise.

Robert shook his head. 'Mary.'

'Well, I imagine Elizabeth is glad to be out of the Tower.'

'Oh, you imagine, do you?' Robert mocked. 'What of me? What about us?'

'She probably didn't give us another thought, Rob.'

'You think not?'

'Well, would you, if you hated this place as much as she did?'

'I do hate this place and with more reason. We've lost more than she has, Am.'

'Yes, I know,' Ambrose agreed. 'Yet do not wish her back again, Rob. That would be unkind.'

'Well, I do,' Robert said, falling onto his bed. 'No, I don't. Oh God, Am, I fear I shall go mad in this place.'

'We may see freedom yet, Rob,' Jack said, holding their mother's letter in front of his face. 'Read how Mother works for our release.'

'Yes, begging the queen.'

'The queen will take pity on her.'

'Pity!' Robert repeated, disgusted. 'Our mother going begging to a half-Spanish mule. My stomach turns at the thought of it.'

'Mother has found more friends among the Spanish at court than the English,' Jack snapped. 'So, stop your moaning and read Amy's letter you have so thoughtlessly thrown away.'

Fever infected the Tower. Jack succumbed and Jane Dudley petitioned the queen ever more vigorously to take pity on her sick son. The queen, grown once again merciful, granted him his release and Jack was carried out of the Tower on a litter, delirious and drenched in sweat, unaware he was leaving the dreaded fortress. Mary awaited her brother's arrival at her house, Penshurst, with a mixture of joy and dread. Doctors were summoned, but their medicine could do nothing. Three days later, Jack died.

Jane Dudley, worn out with cares, died less than three months later. The very day of her death brought release for the three brothers left in the Tower. Queen Mary pardoned them. The brothers were free.

The news came too hard on the heels of misfortune to cheer them greatly, though they hurried from their prison, not once looking back. They made their way to Penshurst, where all the remaining family gathered. Reunions were tinged with sadness. Their mother's will was read, and Robert heard with indignation how she had not wanted a grand funeral, preferring to be laid to rest privately and quietly.

Robert would not allow it. He made all the funeral arrangements, borrowing money to pay the coffin-maker and tradesmen. His mother would not be buried quietly, ignominiously. Her funeral would be a lavish affair, as befitted the duchess of Northumberland, widow of a once great general of England.

CHAPTER TWENTY-TWO

Amy Dudley lay in bed, looking at the man lying asleep beside her. Sunlight fell across his face, making his skin look almost golden. How handsome he was, and like this, asleep in their bed, Robert was entirely her own. It made her stomach lurch when she thought of how close she had come to losing him; first, when his father had been executed, then Guildford, and then when Jack had become ill. But Robert was strong and had survived, and she thanked God daily for it.

He had changed, of course. He was thinner, older, and there was a new wariness in his eyes. The joy had gone out of him, too. She must try to make him feel it again.

Smiling to herself, she slid her hand through the opening of his nightshirt, the hairs on his chest springy against her fingers. He moaned softly and turned his head towards her. His eyes flickered open. She smiled down at him. He closed his eyes and turned his head away. She cuddled up to him, her hand delving deeper inside his nightshirt.

'Amy,' he chided, pushing her hand away.

'Don't you love me?' she asked playfully.

161

'I'm tired,' he said.

'What shall we do today?' she asked after a few moments when he failed to respond to her caresses.

With a groan, he opened his eyes. 'I should go over the estate and see what needs to be done. You should see about the household staff. See if there are any servants we can do without. Perhaps there are some tasks you can take over, Amy.'

'You want me to work?'

Robert sighed. 'We haven't any money, Amy, as well you know. If it wasn't for Ambrose giving us this house, we wouldn't even have anywhere to live.'

'Oh yes, do remind me we're living on your brother's charity.'

'Why the devil do you say that?' Robert snapped, sitting up. 'It's not charity, it's a financial arrangement. Ambrose has given us the house in exchange for paying off our mother's debts.'

'And making me work like a drudge.'

'If the idea of work pains you so much, you can always go back to your father.'

'You want to be rid of me, don't you?' Amy turned on him, her eyes filling with tears. 'Why don't you just say it?'

'Oh, for Christ's sake, Amy,' Robert said, throwing back the bedclothes. 'Don't start.'

'Where are you going?'

'Away from you,' he returned through gritted teeth, slamming the door behind him.

Amy buried her face in the pillow and cried.

'So, how are you?' Elizabeth bit down on an almond biscuit, crumbs tumbling down her dress.

Robert watched her brush them away. 'Well enough.'

'That didn't sound convincing, Robin. I was sorry to hear about Jack and your mother.'

'Thank you.'

She leant forward and placed her hand beneath his chin, forcing him to look at her. 'What's wrong?'

Robert sighed, taking hold of her hand. 'I'm finding it difficult, being free.'

'Surely you wouldn't rather be back in the Tower?'

'No, but the only worry I had in the Tower was staying alive. Now,' he shrugged. 'I've been released, but there's nothing left for me. We have no estates. They've all been taken by your sister. I have no money, it's all gone to pay off debts. Ambrose had to give me a house to live in and the only horses I have are the ones that work the land. If I want to go riding, I have to borrow a neighbour's horse.'

'Poor Rob. I hadn't realised things were as bad as that.'

'Well, they are. But never mind. They'll get better, I'm sure.' He smiled at her.

'How's your wife?' Elizabeth asked.

The smile fell from his face. 'She's fine. It's me,' he went on as Elizabeth looked at him doubtfully. 'I've changed, and she's stayed the same.'

'You don't love her anymore?'

'Not as I once did, but that's not her fault. I'm not the man she married. How could I be, after what I've been through?'

'Perhaps when you have children—'

'There won't be any children,' he cut in angrily, throwing her hand away. 'We've been married for five years and not once has she been with child. She must be barren.'

'Then I'm sorry for you, Rob,' Elizabeth said sincerely. 'I think you would like to be a father.'

'Anyway,' he waved his hand in the air, signalling he

wanted to change the subject, 'you're pleased to be back at Hatfield?'

'Immeasurably.' Elizabeth rolled her eyes. 'I wouldn't wish Sir Henry Bedingfield on anyone. My sister couldn't have chosen a better gaoler.'

'Do you hear any news from the court?'

'I have my spies.'

'Indeed!' He made a face, impressed. 'And who would they be?'

'I'm not telling you,' she slapped playfully at him. She became serious. 'Philip wants to war against the French.'

'A war? He'll be needing men, then?'

'Oh, look at you,' Elizabeth snorted in disgust. 'Why do men get so excited at the idea of war? And you would fight for the king of Spain?'

'I would fight for the Devil. I need to do something, Bess. I need money.'

'You could get yourself killed!'

'And what loss would that be?'

Elizabeth glared at him. 'Your wife would miss you. Your family would miss you. I would miss you.'

'Would you?'

'Yes, God help me, I would.'

'Who should I write to? Oh, come on, Bess, tell me. Who should I write to, to offer my services?'

Elizabeth shrugged. 'To my sister's secretary, I suppose. But how are you going to equip yourself for war? That takes money, Robin, or hadn't you thought of that?'

'I'll have to borrow more, or sell some of the land around Hales Owen. I don't suppose you could...?'

'Me?' Elizabeth laughed. 'Next in line to the throne I may be, Robin, but I have no money of my own that isn't already spent twice over. My household costs a fortune to maintain. I should ask *you* for a loan.'

'If I could, I would, you know that.'

'I know.' She leaned over and touched his knee. 'Money, I may not have, but I do have horses. Shall we go for a ride?'

Robert took her hand and kissed it. 'I was hoping you'd say that.'

'And now you want to go to France?' Ambrose threw up his hands in exasperation. 'After what happened in London?'

Robert wanted to forget London. He had gone there, dragging Ambrose and Henry with him, needing to smell the stink of the city in his nostrils, desperate to feel part of some- thing, if only for a short while. He had arranged to meet two brothers he had always thought of as friends. They turned out to be anything but. They had looked down their noses at him, reviled him for being a traitor and mocked his father. A fight followed, Ambrose having to pull Robert away. They had returned to their lodging house to find a stranger waiting for them. He answered none of their questions, merely informed them it would be better, safer, for them to leave London immediately. They had left the next morning.

'Forget London,' Robert retorted.

'I thought you had learnt your lesson when we were warned to stay out of court affairs.' Ambrose shook his head wearily. 'We're not welcome.'

Amy poured Robert another cup of wine. 'Ambrose is right. Can't you be content with me here?'

Robert looked away with a deep sigh. 'No, I can't. Oh, for heaven's sake, Amy, be quiet,' he snapped as she whimpered. He leant across the table, his hands held out to Ambrose. 'Come with me, Am. Henry and I are going to France whether you do or not, but I would so much like you to be with us.'

'You haven't dragged Henry into this?'

'I didn't have to drag him. He wants to go.'

'And what will going to war achieve? Tell me that.'

'Maybe we'll make our fortune. King Philip needs men, and if we serve him well, who knows what he may grant us?'

'*If* we come back,' Ambrose pointed out. 'We can't afford to equip any men, Rob, so we'd have to serve under someone.'

'I've already spoken with the earl of Pembroke. We can serve under him. Oh, say you'll come, Am.'

'Of course I'll come,' Ambrose said. 'God knows what would become of you both if I let you go on your own.'

Robert laughed and clapped his hands. 'Oh, you won't regret it, Am, I promise. We will do so well, King Philip won't be able to ignore us.'

The field stank.

Battered bodies spilt their lifeblood into the mud of St Quentin. Robert held himself up by hanging over the side of a horse-cart and thanked God he was still alive. A moment's rest was all he allowed himself. Pushing away from the cart, he stumbled over outstretched limbs, sinking ankle deep in the mud with each step. The mud had got everywhere, inside his boots, through rips in his shirts. His handsome face was grimed with it, merging with the blood of those he had fought.

Over the crackle and snap of fire, the moans of the dying and the shouts of the living, one voice rang out, hard and urgent, calling his name. He tried to find its origin, but black smoke blew into his face, blinding him. He stumbled forward, knuckling out tiny pieces of ash and grit from his eyes. Strong hands grabbed him and spun him around.

He blinked. 'Ambrose?' he croaked, his throat sore

from the roar of battle cries. Ambrose was struggling for breath, his fingers digging painfully into Robert's flesh.

'Henry,' Ambrose gasped, his tears marking channels down his mud-streaked cheeks. 'Cannon shot. He's dead.'

Robert stared at him, his mouth hanging open. 'No,' he cried. 'No.'

'I've seen him. Lying by his horse, half his body gone.'

'You left him?'

'I wanted to find you.' Ambrose pulled Robert close. 'There was nothing I could do for him.'

Robert pushed away. 'Where is he?' he shouted, trying to hurry through the gripping mud. 'Where?'

Ambrose lurched after him. 'There's nothing you can do,' he protested, grabbing Robert by the arm and pulling him back, almost collapsing on top of him. 'He's dead.'

He repeated the two awful words until he felt Robert accept the truth of them and stopped struggling. The two brothers, half-lay, half-crouched in the mud, spent, struck down with grief, while around them England lost the war.

Queen Mary's eyes, set deep in her sallow, jowly face, squinted down at him. She sniffed pointedly at Robert's riding clothes, caked in mud and manure and stinking of sweat.

'You bring news from my husband?' she growled.

'I have, Your Majesty. Despatches from France.'

Mary stretched out her hand. 'Give them to me.'

Robert untied the leather roll and pulled out the documents. Mary held them close to her face as she read.

'I see you have lost your brother, Dudley.'

'Yes, Your Majesty.'

She offered no condolences. 'My husband is pleased with you. He professes you have been most valiant in France.'

'The king is generous to say so.'

'Indeed, he is.' Mary frowned, her mouth twisting as she looked down at him. 'More than you realise. My husband requests that your family be restored in blood.'

Robert waited, not daring to breathe. He heard her rings tapping against the pommel of the chair.

She sniffed once more, then said, 'Rise, Lord Robert.'

He took hold of the hem of her skirt and kissed it, taking a moment to breathe in the dusty smell of the cloth and slow the blood pounding in his hears. He rose and bowed his head.

'I cannot adequately express my gratitude, Your Majesty.'

'Hear me, Lord Robert,' Mary said sternly. 'Though I do as my husband wishes, I do not forget that you are the son of the traitor Northumberland, whose actions caused me to take the life of that poor girl, Jane Grey. An innocent, who would never have thought of the crown had it not been thrust upon her by your father. I will not have you at my court.'

Robert kept his head down. 'I ask nothing further of Your Majesty. Your bounty has already been most generous. My only desire now is to return to the country.'

'A sensible desire, Lord Robert. You may go.'

He backed away from her, hearing the whispers of the courtiers as they discussed his new fortune. In a daze, he found himself back in the stable yard, laying a shaking hand against the brick wall. The Dudleys were back in the game. But what a price they had had to pay!

He walked towards the stalls. His horse was still resting, so he fell down in the straw and closed his eyes. It didn't bother him that the queen didn't want him at court. He had no desire to serve Mary. No, he would go back home and wait for the next queen to come along.

CHAPTER TWENTY-THREE

1558

Elizabeth waited beneath the oak tree.

Cecil had sent her word that Mary was dying and to expect to be named queen before the day was out. It troubled her she felt no sense of grief or loss for her sister. If the situation had been reversed, if it was she who lay dying, Mary would weep for her.

She saw them coming, smoothing her skirts and holding herself erect, determined to look like a queen.

Sir Nicholas Throckmorton climbed down from his horse and fished inside his velvet purse for the ring that he had taken from Mary's stiff, icy finger, the ring that would symbolise the transference of sovereignty from the dead queen to the new one. He hurried towards her. He noticed her trembling lips, the eagerness in her eyes and knew he need waste no words of condolence. He fell to his knees and delivered his news that the queen was dead. He handed her the ring.

'This is the Lord's doing,' Elizabeth said, trying hard not to smile. 'It is marvellous in our eyes.'

She sank to her knees before him, clapped her hands together and silently mouthed a prayer. Did she pray for her dead sister? Throckmorton doubted it.

'Come, my lord,' she said, holding out her hand for him to help her to her feet. 'Sir William Cecil is with you, I hope?'

'He follows not far behind, Your Majesty.' He heard her breath catch at the new title.

'Good. I shall need him. Escort me back to the house, my lord. There are plenty of letters to write.'

Amy looked up from her sewing as Robert stamped into the chamber and fell into a chair. His expression was thunderous.

'Robert, what's the matter?'

'That damn carthorse threw me.'

'You're hurt?'

'No,' he said, shrugging off her searching hands. 'What's that?' He pointed at a crumpled paper peeping out from the top of her bodice.

She pulled it out and tried to smooth out the creases. 'It just came for you.'

He snatched it from her and broke the seal. 'Oh, Amy,' he breathed, his face breaking into a grin, 'the best news. Mary has died. Elizabeth is queen.'

'Oh, really?' Amy said, unimpressed. Robert disappeared up the stairs, and she hurried after him. 'What are you doing?' she asked breathlessly, falling onto their bed.

'Elizabeth has sent for me.' He flung off his riding coat and washed hurriedly, slapping water under his armpits and down his back.

'Elizabeth wants you, so you go?'

'Yes, that's right.'

'And what about me?'

'What about you?'

'Can I come with you?'

'No,' he said, pulling on a clean shirt.

'Why not?'

'I can ride quicker on my own.'

'I suppose you think I'll be in the way?'

'Amy, please understand. This is what I've been waiting for.'

Amy looked away, determined to hold back her tears. 'When will you be back?' she asked quietly.

'Come here.' Robert held out his arms and Amy rushed to him. 'I'll return as soon as I can.'

'Promise?' she looked up at him with her large brown eyes.

'I promise.'

Robert had been made to wait, like all the others, in the Presence Chamber, and he was growing bored. The room was filling up. Courtiers jostled for space, and he'd been elbowed aside to make room more than once. He was relieved when a page called out his name and instructed him to follow.

The page showed him into a much smaller room. Elizabeth was standing by the window, watching the new arrivals. She was dressed in a simple gown of black and white, her red hair brushed straight, falling like a curtain down her back. Robert took a step towards her.

'Good morning, Lord Robert.'

Robert turned. William Cecil stood behind a desk, its surface littered with papers. 'Cecil. What are you doing here?'

'I am made Her Majesty's Secretary, Lord Robert.'

'Indeed,' Robert said. He turned pointedly away,

171

striding towards Elizabeth and sinking to one knee. 'Your Majesty.'

Elizabeth held out her hand. 'Robin,' she purred as he pressed his lips to it. 'How good it is to see you again! We have both had changes of fortune, haven't we?'

'Indeed, we have.'

'Oh, get up. I can't have my Master of Horse on his knees.'

Robert rose. 'Master of Horse?'

'Of course. Who else is more suited to the position?'

'No one,' he agreed.

'But I warn you, this won't be a sinecure. You'll probably have more work than you realise.'

'I'll be glad of it. I've had years of nothing to do.'

'Your first duty,' Cecil said, 'will be to arrange the transportation of Her Majesty and her household to London. May I ask if your wife accompanied you?'

'No. She stayed in the country.'

'Good. We haven't much room to accommodate too many spouses. Of course, once we are at court, arrangements could be made for her. Perhaps as one of the Ladies of the Bedchamber?'

'No,' both Robert and Elizabeth said.

Elizabeth turned away, her face reddening.

'My wife does not care for the town,' Robert explained. 'She would much rather stay in the country.'

Cecil raised his eyebrows, looking between Robert and Elizabeth. 'I see.'

'But I know my sister, Mary, would be pleased to serve you, Bes—,' Robert corrected himself, 'Your Majesty.'

'Mary! Of course,' Elizabeth said delightedly. 'Send to Lady Sidney, Cecil. She can be one of my Ladies.'

Cecil made a note, gesturing towards the paperwork on his desk. Elizabeth nodded.

'You must go now, Robin. I have so many other people to see.' She held out her hand once more for him to kiss.

Robert took her hand, his fingers warming hers. 'I hope to see you later, Your Majesty.'

'Yes,' she answered, neither a promise nor a denial.

THE TOWER

Robert pushed open the heavy oak door to the chapel. It creaked on its hinges. He stepped inside, his footsteps echoing around the vaulted chamber. Passing the rows of wooden pews, he came to the altar. Flat stones served as grave markers for the executed, their names carved into the stone: Anne Boleyn, Catherine Howard, Edward Seymour, Jane Grey. Robert knelt and ran his fingers along the grooves of the last two names: John Dudley, Guildford Dudley.

'Robin?'

He started. 'Your Majesty. I didn't hear you come in.'

'Stay still,' Elizabeth said, walking swiftly towards him.

She looked down at the gravestones, then across to him. 'You've been crying.'

'Have I?' He wiped his hand across his cheeks and was surprised to find them wet. 'So I have. You're unattended, madam.'

'My Ladies are just outside. I saw you come in. Do you mind my being here?'

'Why should I mind?'

'I thought you might want to be alone.'

He gestured towards his face. 'Look what being alone does to me.'

She knelt down next to him and stroked his cheek. 'Poor Robin.' She nodded towards the stones. 'I wonder if they can see us now.'

He sniffed. 'They can.'

'You sound very sure.'

'I am sure.'

'My mother would be pleased, I think.' She smiled sadly. 'Would it please your father to see me on the throne?'

Robert stiffened. 'He would have served you, Bess, as he would any king or queen. I know what everyone thinks of my father. God knows they do not try to hide their opinions from me. But it was your brother who thought of changing the succession to Jane and Father was doing his duty by him. I don't deny there were certain advantages to our family in the change, but Father never would have thought of it himself. And when it came to it, he was reluctant to carry it out at all.'

'But you understand that people have a difficult time believing that, Robin?'

'Because they didn't know him, as I knew him. And Edward was right. Look what a state Mary brought this country to.'

'I know. When I think of those poor souls she sent to the flames in the name of her religion. Archbishop Cranmer—.' She shook her head. 'But I will change it, Rob, I promise you. And you will help me, won't you?'

'I give my life to you. It's yours to do with as you please.'

'And if I please to have you near me, always?'

'Then that is what I will do.'

'Your wife may not like that.'

'My wife can go to the Devil.'

She laughed, pleased. 'Oh, come Rob, let us leave here. We've paid our respects to the dead. Besides, Cecil will send a search party to find me if I'm away much longer.' Robert made a face. 'Oh, I know what you think of him.'

'With reason,' he said, helping her to her feet.

'With nothing more than suspicion. But he is as dear to

me as you and you will have to find a way of working with him.'

'Oh, I can work with the man, as long as you don't expect me to like him.'

'No, I won't expect that.' She squeezed his hand. 'And I must ask of you a favour. I want you to meet with John Dee and ask him to divine the best day for my coronation. The day must be propitious. I can't send Cecil on such an errand. He would disapprove.'

'Leave it to me,' Robert said.

CHAPTER TWENTY-FOUR

WHITEHALL PALACE

The black crows were moulting and their fallen feathers were crunched underfoot as their owners half-skipped, half-danced to the edge of the stage. Their scarlet red robes flounced higher and crucifixes bounced against their chests to the sound of laughter.

Elizabeth, her chin upon her hand, glanced sideways at her secretary. 'What's wrong, Cecil? Does it not amuse you?'

Cecil smiled politely. 'Yes, Your Majesty.'

'Now, don't pay me lip service. What is it you object to?'

Cecil cleared his throat. 'I applaud the anti-Catholic sentiment behind this entertainment, madam, but I question the wisdom in performing it, especially in front of the Imperial ambassador.'

They both looked towards King Philip's envoy, who looked anything but amused.

'Lord Robert devised it,' Elizabeth said carelessly.

'Ah,' Cecil nodded, as if that explained everything.

Elizabeth laughed. 'Oh, Cecil, we shall have to forgive him for his daring. I like a man to be daring.'

'Daring, indeed, madam! But when daring becomes foolish or even reckless...'

The smile dropped from Elizabeth's face. 'I won't allow him to be reckless or foolish. I am his mistress, not he my master.'

Cecil looked her straight in the eye. 'I am very glad to hear it, madam.'

Elizabeth sank back in her chair, frowning as she looked about her. 'Where the devil is he, Cecil? I can't see him.'

At that moment, Thomas Howard, Duke of Norfolk, walked past and Elizabeth clicked her fingers at him.

Norfolk halted, a flicker of annoyance crossing his face. 'Yes, Your Majesty?'

'Norfolk, kindly find my Master of the Horse. Remind him his place is by me.'

Norfolk's jaw clenched. 'Yes, Your Majesty,' he growled.

Cecil lowered his eyes as Norfolk passed on, embarrassed for the duke, but Elizabeth seemed oblivious to the insult she had just given. He would have to find a gentle way of reminding her of the duke's nobility.

Robert was standing at his desk when Norfolk strode into his room. 'Your Grace?' he asked, making a bow, wondering what on earth the duke could want with him.

Norfolk moved to the desk. 'What is this?' he asked, gesturing at the paperwork.

'I'm working on the route for the coronation.'

'Proving difficult?'

'No,' Robert said defensively, 'but there is such a lot to do and I want it to be perfect.'

'Perfect?' Norfolk laughed. 'I hear the queen had a necromancer decide the date for the coronation.'

'John Dee is no necromancer, Your Grace. He is a scholar.'

'A scholar.' Norfolk looked disgusted. 'I tell you, it won't happen at all if my cousin can't find someone to crown her.'

Robert knew that many of the bishops, Catholics left over from her sister's reign, had refused outright to perform a coronation of a woman they believed to be doubly cursed, first as a bastard and second as a heretic. 'She'll find a bishop to do it.'

'She has less than two weeks. All this,' Norfolk gestured at the paperwork, 'may be for nothing.'

'She will find someone.'

Norfolk sniffed, bored. 'I hope you've put me in my rightful place in the procession.'

'Yes.'

'The first in line?'

'Yes.'

'Good. And make sure my horse has been purged by nine in the morning. I won't have it shitting all the way to the abbey.'

Robert sighed in annoyance. 'I do know what I'm doing.'

'Yes, I suppose I can trust you with the horses, at least. Though why my cousin gave you such a prominent position eludes me. She may have forgotten your recent history, but I haven't. Once a traitor, always a traitor, in my opinion. She wants you, by the way.'

'What for?'

'I'm damned if I know. Perhaps her Fool has let her down, and she needs someone to make her laugh.' He slouched out of the room, laughing at his own joke.

Had he been ten years younger, Robert would have

struck the duke to the floor, despite his nobility, and to hell with the consequences. But if his sojourn in the Tower had taught him anything, it was his place in the world. He was newly risen, and he would do nothing to jeopardise that. He shrugged on his doublet and closed the door behind him.

Mary Sidney lifted the pearl-encrusted headband from Elizabeth's head, sensing her mistress's relief at its removal.

'Are you unwell, Your Majesty?'

Elizabeth rubbed at her temples, squeezing her eyes shut. 'Oh, Mary, my head feels like it is splitting in two. You wouldn't believe how heavy the crown and the ceremonial robes were.'

'And it's been such a long day,' Kat Ashley said, warming a nightgown before the fire. 'You must be tired, my sweet.'

'I am, Kat. Hurry with my— why, Robin!' she cried as Robert entered the bedchamber, Cecil close behind.

'I come to bid you goodnight, Your Majesty,' Robert said with a smile, 'while Cecil comes with yet more paperwork for you.'

'The business of government is never at an end, Lord Robert,' Cecil replied tersely. 'Your Majesty, I have documents which require your signature.'

Elizabeth barely looked at him; her eyes were fixed on Robert. 'I think John Dee must be losing his powers, or else you passed on the wrong information, Lord Robert, for I tell you, today has not been at all propitious.'

Robert frowned. 'Pardon me, madam, but I had thought the day went very well.'

'Maybe it did for you, but you have not had to endure what I have this day. The oil Bishop Oglethorpe anointed me with was rancid. I've had it plastered all over my body

179

and I have a terrible headache. It has been a very long day, Robin.'

'I'm sorry to hear you are not well, madam.'

Elizabeth grunted and sat down at her dressing table, signalling for Mary to brush her hair.

'Even more reason for you to get some rest,' Robert continued. 'Cecil, the paperwork can wait.'

Cecil bristled. 'It is for the queen to dismiss me, my lord. I go at none other's say so.'

Robert rolled his eyes. 'Here,' he said, snatching up the nightgown and holding it out.

Elizabeth's lips twisted into a reluctant smirk. 'You really are too impertinent, Robin. Do you think I will undress before you?'

'I can but hope.'

She laughed out loud, her humour restored. 'Give it back to Kat, you monster, and be gone. Both of you go. I am exhausted and the government of my country must wait until tomorrow, Cecil.'

Cecil hid his annoyance poorly, bidding Elizabeth goodnight with an audible sigh. Once in the corridor, he turned to Robert. 'I must confess your sense of humour escapes me, Lord Robert.'

Robert frowned at him. 'What are you talking about?'

'To talk with a queen about her state of undress or make insinuations of a, shall we say, familiar nature, is most improper.'

'Oh, nonsense,' Robert started off down the corridor, his long legs taking such lengthy strides that Cecil had to hurry to keep up. 'I was only joking.'

'Yes, I understand. But you must see how I could be mistaken in thinking you were in earnest?'

Robert came to a sudden stop. 'I don't care what you think. Elizabeth knew I didn't mean it.'

'You two are of a similar age, of course,' Cecil said.

'You understand the queen better than I. But I would advise you to be careful, my lord.'

'For God's sake, careful of what?'

'Lord Robert, you are a married man whose wife is, you'll forgive me, conveniently in the country. And the queen is an unmarried young woman who cannot afford gossip to ruin any future marriage prospects.'

'I would do nothing to endanger the queen's reputation.'

Cecil looked into his dark eyes. 'I trust you will not, my lord. Goodnight.'

CHAPTER TWENTY-FIVE

SYDERSTONE HALL

'ROBERT!' Amy screamed with joy and rushed towards him.

I mustn't be impatient with her, Robert reminded himself as he slid down his horse's flank. *She hasn't seen me for months. It's only natural she's excited.*

Amy threw herself against him, nearly knocking him over. 'Oh, why have you stayed away so long, Robert?'

He gently pushed her away. 'I have duties at court now, Amy. I'm not free to come and go as I please.'

She stared up into his face. 'Are you tired? Are you working too hard?'

'Nothing of the sort. I'm very well. Now, tell me, how does my little wife fare?'

They walked into the house. Robert strode to the fire to warm his cold hands. She clung to his arm.

'To tell the truth, my love, I am not very well. I have a pain here.' She pointed to her left breast. 'And there is a lump.'

He frowned. 'Have you seen a physician?'

'No.'

'Why ever not?'

'I hoped it would go away, and then, when it didn't, I grew frightened and now, I don't want to think about it.'

'Amy, you can't just ignore—'

'Oh, please don't be angry with me. Now that you're home, I'm sure I will feel better.'

Robert hesitated. *Best to tell her now*, he decided. 'I'm not home to stay.'

'What?' she said sharply.

'I have to leave no later than Saturday.'

'But that's only three days away.'

'I am Master of the Horse, Amy.'

'Well, then, I shall return to London with you.'

Robert shook his head. 'I can't take you with me. The queen doesn't care for wives at court.'

'But your sister's at court. Is she not a wife?'

'Mary's a Lady of the Bedchamber. That's an entirely different thing. Even Cecil's wife has to stay at home.'

'But—'

'And I'll wager she doesn't complain to her husband for it, but accepts that it must be so.'

'Well, isn't Mistress Cecil a marvel, then!' Amy retorted scornfully.

'Amy!'

'I think you don't want me at court. That's what I think,' Amy said, her face screwing up in anger. 'You don't want me there so you are free to whore with your women.'

'My women?' Robert laughed. 'I don't have any women. Good God, Amy, you're enough for any man.'

'Well, I see I must vex you very much, husband. Why you even bother to come home, I can't imagine.' She sat down and stared out of the window.

'I will send for the doctor to examine you,' Robert said quietly. 'Illness mustn't be ignored, Amy.'

'If you want,' she sniffed. 'Maybe you're hoping he'll tell you I haven't long to live. Then you'll be happy.'

He stepped up behind her and placed a kiss on her flushed neck. 'You mustn't say such things, Amy. You know that isn't true.' She remained silent. 'Could you arrange for dinner for me? It's been a long, cold ride from London.'

'Dinner will be brought shortly,' she replied curtly. 'You had best change your clothes. You stink of horses.'

Only as he walked away from her, did she trust herself to look at him. She hadn't meant to be so shrewish with him. She had wanted him to be pleased to be home. He would leave the sooner now, she knew it, eager to be away from her and her complaints. Oh, why had she not held her tongue? She could have worked upon him when they were in bed. He wouldn't have refused her anything then. The thought of their lovemaking reminded her of her earlier accusation. She didn't believe him when he said there were no other women. She had seen, too often, the wives of their neighbours making eyes at him, and she had been proud that they should covet her husband. But then he had been at home, where he could not have disguised any infidelity. But at court he was free to do as he pleased, and she didn't doubt that he did.

A servant brought in a platter of beef and set it on the table. 'Oh, forgive me, my lady, I was told the master had returned. Shall I take this away?'

'Your master is but changing his clothes, Richard. He will be down for his dinner directly. And he wants the doctor sent for.'

'Is he unwell, my lady?'

'The doctor's for me,' she said almost wearily. 'I don't think I'm very well.'

Elizabeth was so much easier to work with without Lord Robert Dudley around to distract her. It pleased Cecil to have her all to himself. He passed her another document and watched as she made her elaborate signature.

'Next?' she asked as she passed it back.

'Your Master of the Horse has written, madam. He requests a further three days leave of absence from court. It seems his wife is unwell and wishes him to remain until she feels better.'

'What's the matter with his wife?' There was no trace of concern in her voice.

'He did not say in his letter, madam, but I have told him he may take the three days. I trust I was right to do so?'

'Yes, perfectly right.' Elizabeth seemed annoyed. 'His duty to his wife must come before his duty to me. What's next?'

Cecil passed a paper across the table. 'This is a list of names suggested by your council as possible suitors for your hand, madam.'

Elizabeth read. 'Sir William Pickering, the earl of Arundel, the earl of Arran, King Eric of Sweden and ... King Philip of Spain.' She looked up at Cecil. 'He is my brother-in-law!'

'Dispensations for consanguinity can be obtained, madam,' Cecil replied, refusing to apologise for the inclusion of Philip's name.

She grunted doubtfully. 'Sir William Pickering, I already know. He is much older than me, Cecil.'

'But a very sensible man, Your Majesty.'

'These others. Will any of them come to England so I may see them?'

Cecil tried hard not to appear shocked by her question.

What was Elizabeth thinking? That her suitors would parade before her so that she could look them over to see if one took her fancy? Some of these men were princes, for heaven's sake. 'I don't believe that would be possible, madam. We could request likenesses if you wish to see their faces.'

'I have no intention of marrying a man I have not set eyes upon, Cecil. I do not want to start a marriage with that kind of disappointment.'

'There are other virtues besides a handsome face, madam. The nobility of princes—.' He broke off as he noticed Elizabeth scowl. 'I shall request likenesses.' He began shuffling once more through his documents.

'Enough,' Elizabeth said, slapping her hand on the desk. 'No more work. I'm getting a headache. I've been inside for too long.'

Cecil stifled a protest. 'Shall I send for your Ladies, madam?'

'Yes, I will go riding.' She rose and moved to the window. 'I don't need Robert,' he heard her mutter. 'I do not need him.'

Robert leaned over the pommel of his saddle and stroked Mirabelle's neck. 'I hope you've been looking after my horses, Samuel.'

'I have, my lord,' Samuel replied proudly. 'But they've missed you, that I will say.'

'I'm told the queen is out riding.'

'Yes, my lord.'

'Which way did she ride out?'

'Towards the lake, my lord.'

'Who was with her?'

'Some of her Ladies and Sir William Pickering.'

'Pickering?' Robert frowned. 'He hates horses.'

'The queen commanded it, my lord,' Samuel grinned. 'He didn't look too happy about going.'

Robert nudged Mirabelle's sides and rode off towards the lake. Ten minutes later, he saw the queen's party by a clump of trees and he cantered up to them.

Elizabeth was wearing a green riding habit which showed off her red hair. He was thinking how handsome she looked until that thought was shunted from his head by the stare Elizabeth turned on him.

'Your Majesty,' he greeted her with an uncertain smile.

'Why, Lord Robert! How good of you to return to court.'

'My duty lies here, madam,' he answered.

Elizabeth brought her horse alongside his. 'I assume your wife is better now, as she has allowed you to leave her side?'

'She is more settled in her mind than she was.'

'Well, that is something. Perhaps now your duties as my Master of the Horse can be attended to.'

'I trust you have not been neglected in my absence?'

'Not at all. Sir William Pickering has kept me most happily entertained.'

Sir William Pickering, keeping his seat with some difficulty, managed a proud smile.

'I'm glad,' Robert said, even as Elizabeth moved away. He had been wrong to stay away, he realised. Elizabeth thought he wasn't dedicated to his position. Maybe she was even considering giving the Horse to someone else. Damn Amy and her insistence he stay longer!

'Rob?'

He jerked in surprise as someone touched his arm. 'Oh, Mary, it's you.'

'I startled you.'

'I was thinking. Mary, has the queen said anything about me while I've been away?'

Mary brushed a strand of hair away from her cheek. 'In private, she has spoken of you often. Too often, to my mind.'

Robert looked sharply at her. 'What do you mean by that?'

Mary hesitated. 'I think you should be careful, Rob.'

'Of Elizabeth? Is she displeased with me, Mary?'

'Oh, how can you be so blind? She cares for you, Rob.'

'Of course she cares for me—'

'More than a queen should care for a subject. More than a friend.'

Robert stared at her. 'You don't mean—'

'Yes, I do mean. She's in love with you, Rob. That's why she's so annoyed.'

'She's in love with me, so that's why she's angry with me?' Robert asked, thoroughly confused.

Mary groaned in exasperation. 'You've been spending time with your wife instead of with her. She's jealous. So, what was wrong with Amy?'

'Apart from the usual complaints, you mean? She has a lump in her breast. I sent for the physician.'

'And?'

'He said it could be a tumour.'

'She's in pain?'

'A little, yes.'

'Poor Amy. You should have brought her back with you.'

'I can't do that, Mary. Elizabeth won't have wives at court unless they're in service to her.'

'But if she knew how ill Amy is—'

'Oh, talk sense. If, as you seem to think, Elizabeth loves me, she won't want my wife here, spying on us.'

'Spying on you?' Mary repeated incredulously. 'Robert, your behaviour with the queen can be nothing other than honourable or her reputation will be ruined. She cannot marry you, so she must not love you. What do you think? That you can lie with her?'

'For Jesu's sake, keep your voice down,' he hissed at her. 'Spying was the wrong word. I didn't mean it.'

'I think you meant exactly that. My God, Rob, sometimes you disgust me. You don't care about Amy at all.' She snapped her whip against her horse's rump and sped away after the queen.

Robert stared after Elizabeth. Was Mary right? Could Elizabeth be in love with him? He searched his memory. That night in the Tower, when they had sat before Brydges's fire and shared their fears; the times since her accession when they had laughed together, gone riding together, danced. Her flushed cheeks as he held her during a dance, the holding of his hand just that moment longer than necessary as he helped her mount her horse. Other little intimacies too numerous to even catalogue. Good God, how could he have been so blind? Had he been so caught up in his new work, so eager to make a success of it, that he hadn't noticed the signs?

Elizabeth, the queen, was in love with him!

CHAPTER TWENTY-SIX

Cecil clasped his hands behind his back and fixed his impatience behind an expression of polite attention. 'You wanted to see me, Your Grace.'

Norfolk was polishing a dagger, his full mouth pursing as he stroked the cloth along the blade. 'Yes, I did.' He set the dagger down and looked up, his brow creased in a frown. 'Tell me, Cecil, how long are you going to allow this to go on?'

Cecil stifled a breath of irritation. 'Forgive me, Your Grace, but allow what to go on?'

'The damned Gypsy.'

'Ah,' Cecil nodded, understanding. 'I believe you mean Lord Robert Dudley.' He had heard the nickname going around the court. He suspected Norfolk had coined the term as a slur on Dudley's dark skin and also for the reputation of gypsies as pickers-up of anything they could get their hands on.

'Yes, I do mean Lord Robert Dudley. Did you see that display tonight?'

'The dancing, Your Grace?' Cecil was prevaricating, but he knew exactly what Norfolk was getting at. the queen and Dudley had danced together practically all evening, their bodies moving closer with each measure.

'Dancing? Is that what you call it? They may as well have rutted right there on the floor.'

'Really, Your Grace,' Cecil admonished, his cheeks reddening.

Norfolk stood, his hands on his hips. 'Well, you may not care what everyone is saying, but I don't want this court made the laughing stock of Europe. He's her bloody stable boy, for Christ's sake.'

'Master of the Horse, Your Grace,' Cecil corrected with a wry smile.

'He's a Dudley,' Norfolk said, his voice growing louder with annoyance. 'When is she going to understand the kind of man he is?'

'And what kind would that be?'

'A traitor. He comes from tainted stock.'

'In truth, Your Grace, I am inclined to agree with you. The queen does, in my opinion, act with little discretion in her relationship with Lord Robert. But,' Cecil shrugged helplessly, 'I am at a loss to see what I can do about it.'

'Well, can't he be got rid of? Some way or the other?'

Norfolk had always been a brute. Cecil smiled politely. 'An assassination, Your Grace? He's hardly worth such an endeavour, surely?'

'I'd stick a dagger in him myself if I thought he was worth the trouble.'

Or worth the risk to your neck, Cecil thought. 'Perhaps the queen will grow tired of him, Your Grace. He has but a handsome exterior to recommend him.'

'I agree, the man has no nobility, but what does that matter to this queen? She likes handsome men, doesn't she, Cecil? You remember Thomas Seymour?'

Cecil held up a warning hand. 'Your Grace, the

queen's involvement with him was never proven. She was but a child at the time.'

Norfolk leered unpleasantly. 'Oh, come now, Cecil, we both knew old Thomas. He couldn't walk past a woman without trying to get beneath her skirts.'

'Perhaps so, but I think it would be wise not to mention the late Lord Admiral, to the queen, or anyone else for that matter. He is a part of her history I believe she would not care to be reminded of.'

Norfolk pouted and fell back into his chair. He snatched up the dagger once more. 'Well, then, let's hope she doesn't allow the Gypsy the same freedom as poor dead Thomas or it might be more than a maidenhead that is lost.'

Cecil had avoided looking again at the letter. There it lay, on the furthest corner of his desk, occasionally getting covered by other paper during the day, but always a sliver of white showed through to remind him it was there.

But now he had no excuse. The work of the day was completed, his clerks had been sent away and the letter just had to be dealt with. He rubbed his chin, enjoying the rasping sensation as his fingers crushed his short beard. With a resigned sigh, he picked up the letter and re-read the words that had so disturbed him earlier.

The queen's behaviour with Lord Robert Dudley has become the scandal of the French court. There is talk of Her Majesty visiting Lord Robert in his bedchamber, and he visiting her while she undresses, and other such that I shrink to commit to paper. I myself cannot

believe these rumours to be true, but the injury
they do to Her Majesty's reputation is
undeniable.

Good sir, you have the queen's trust. Cannot
you persuade her to amend her favour towards
Lord Robert, whose reputation here in France
and the rest of Europe is near as black as his
heart?

Your servant
Nicholas Throckmorton

Nicholas was a good man, unwilling to believe the
gossip, but he wasn't at court. The gossip was true. Was
this what he had waited for? The girl, whose friendship
and trust he had cultivated over many years, who had
sought his advice, who had said that she knew him to be
honourable and true! Was this the reason she had wanted
the crown, so she could be free to sport with a married
man of dubious reputation? Was this to be his reward?
When he had struggled to find among her mutinous
bishops one man who was prepared to crown her, and
what persuading he had had to do to get Bishop
Oglethorpe to agree! When he was even now negotiating
with the crowned heads of Europe to find suitable
contenders for her hand. Would there be any takers for a
queen who was behaving like any common bawd from the
Southwark stews?

Cecil refolded the letter, his fingernail rhythmically
tapping the broken red seal. Norfolk was right. Something
would have to be done about the Gypsy.

.   .   .

'She's like a hobgoblin sitting there.' Robert glanced over his shoulder and smiled at Kat Ashley, ensconced on a seat in the far corner of the box garden.

Elizabeth slapped his hand playfully. 'Don't be cruel. Kat's there for my protection.'

'You need protecting from me?'

'Yes, from you. She thinks you have designs on my honour.' She laughed, but stopped when she realised Robert wasn't laughing too. 'What is it?'

He shrugged sulkily. 'Dishonour seems to follow me around.'

'How very melodramatic you sound.'

'You think I don't know what's being said about me? The Gypsy?' The look he gave Elizabeth dared her to deny she had heard the nickname.

'It's only name-calling, Rob.'

'It hurts, Bess. Especially when what's being said involves you. Oh, don't pretend you haven't heard the gossip. Why else the hobgoblin?'

'Gossip. That's all it is. You and I know the truth.'

'No, we don't. I don't know if you care for me.'

'Oh, Robin, how can you not know?' She reached out and stroked his cheek. 'Of course I care for you.'

'Yes, but how much?' he asked earnestly, grasping her hand and holding it to his chest.

She hesitated before answering. 'Rob, you are married.'

Robert let out a breath of exasperation. 'Oh, it's always "Rob, you're married". I damn well know I'm married.'

'Why can't you be content with what we have?'

'We have nothing. I'm your Gypsy, the pampered pet you like to have following you around. I command no respect.'

'You're my Master of Horse.'

'Your stable boy, as Norfolk puts it.' He lowered his

voice. 'Bess, Amy is ill. She has a cancer in her breast. The physician says it's unlikely she will get better.'

'Rob—'

'No, let me finish. I sound callous, I know, as if I don't care for her. I do care for her, Bess.'

'Care?' she scoffed. 'She's your wife. You're supposed to love her.'

'I can't say love, Bess, not anymore. All that time apart when I was imprisoned, all that I lost then. It's difficult to explain. Amy couldn't understand what I had suffered. She wanted to pretend nothing had happened. She wouldn't let me talk about my family – I suppose she thought it might upset me. But it upset me more not being allowed to remember them, as if they meant nothing. If I even mentioned Father or my brothers, she would change the subject and start talking about other things, her clothes or her bloody embroidery. I hated her when she did that.'

'So, you're just waiting for her to die and then... what? You think you and I can marry?'

'Couldn't we?'

'I... no... I don't know,' Elizabeth shook her head. 'You mustn't ask me.'

'Well, maybe I should just go back to Norfolk. Back home to Amy.'

'You can't leave. I won't let you.'

'There's nothing for me to stay for, is there?' he shouted, not caring who heard.

'Rob!' she shushed, shaking her head at Kat, who was rising from her seat in alarm. 'What do you want from me?'

'I want what Thomas Seymour got!'

Elizabeth stared at him, stunned. 'You believe that about me?'

He snapped off a leaf from the hedge and crushed it between his fingers. 'Everyone believes it.'

'It's not true. I never lay with him. I was but fourteen years old.'

'It's said you had a child by him.'

'I am still a maid.' She went to him and touched his arm. 'You do believe me, Rob?'

'You promise?'

'I swear it.'

He pulled her to him and kissed her forehead. 'Then I believe you.'

'I can't lie with you, Rob,' she said. 'If I were to have a child—'

'It wouldn't matter if we were married.'

'I can't marry you. I'm a queen. I must marry someone of noble birth.'

'Oh, I see. I'm not high enough for you.'

'No, forgive me, but you're not.'

'My father was a duke, Bess.'

'And he lost that title, Rob.'

'Then give me another one,' he suggested with a laugh.

She smoothed down her skirts. 'Not just yet. I show you too much favour as it is.'

Robert didn't press the matter. 'So, who are your prospective bridegrooms?' he asked carelessly.

'Much the same as they were,' Elizabeth said. 'Although, I think I have finally persuaded Cecil that I will not be considering Philip of Spain.'

'Where is Cecil? I haven't seen him for days.'

'In Scotland. The French regent, Mary de Guise, has agreed to negotiate with us.'

'Oh, yes?' Robert said with little interest, studying Elizabeth's face. 'Will it always be like this, Bess? You pushing me away?'

She brushed back a curl of hair from his forehead. 'No more questions.'

CHAPTER TWENTY-SEVEN

No wonder the Romans never bothered with Scotland, Cecil thought as he shuffled wearily into his rooms. How could any civilised woman (and though she was a Catholic, he would concede that Mary de Guise was civilised) live and rule in such a place? The country was inhospitable and the people filthy savages.

And yet, he had reason to be proud of his time in Scotland, for had he not just negotiated a masterpiece of a treaty? The Auld Alliance, that centuries old agreement between France and Scotland to unite against a common enemy, was now broken thanks to Cecil, and the French ordered to withdraw their troops from Scotland.

He wanted to see the queen to inform her of his success. He looked up as the door opened and his page returned with a jug of hot water. 'Set it down over there. Tell me boy, where is the queen tonight?'

'She takes supper in her chambers, Master Cecil,' the boy replied.

'Why in her chambers? Is she not well?'

The boy smirked. 'Oh, she's well enough. But she has

company there. Lord Robert Dudley dines with her most nights.'

'Take that insolent grin from your face, boy,' Cecil said sharply. 'Find me a clean shirt in that trunk and be quick about it.'

'Cecil,' Elizabeth hallooed from the dinner table. 'Come in.'

'Your Majesty,' he bowed. 'Lord Robert.'

Robert grinned up at him, but did not rise from his seat beside Elizabeth. 'Cecil. How was Scotland?'

'Cold,' he answered tersely, 'but productive, I am pleased to say, Your Majesty.'

'Indeed?' Elizabeth raised an eyebrow. 'How so?'

Cecil swallowed uneasily. She sounded doubtful. Worse, she sounded scornful. 'The Auld Alliance is no more. A new treaty, the Treaty of Edinburgh, now takes its place.'

'It hasn't been signed though, has it?' Elizabeth said sharply, scrutinising a plate of sugared almonds Robert waved beneath her nose. She selected one and looked up at Cecil enquiringly.

'Not yet, but it will be,' Cecil replied stiffly, realising with dismay she had already heard his news. *From whom*? he wondered.

'This is the treaty that removes any claim Mary Stuart has to my throne?'

'Yes, madam.'

'Do you honestly think that woman will renounce her claim?'

'I do, yes.'

Elizabeth's eyes narrowed. 'I never took you for a fool, Cecil.'

Cecil could have sworn Robert sniggered. 'Even if

Mary Stuart doesn't sign, madam, and I am confident she will, there are other terms in the treaty that benefit your realm greatly. French troops are preparing to withdraw from Scotland even now. The Royal Arms of England have been removed from the royal flag of France. Mary Stuart can no longer lay claim to your throne.'

'That won't stop her. Still, I suppose you have done well enough, Cecil. What, Robin?' She bent towards Robert as he whispered in her ear. 'What of Calais? Do I get Calais back?'

Cecil glared at Robert. 'No, madam. Calais belongs, irretrievably, to the French.'

'And you dare to stand there and call it a victory?'

Cecil was taken aback. 'I claim no victory, madam, but I have toiled for your sake and I have, I believe at least, achieved a great deal.'

'Toiled?'

'Yes, madam,' he interrupted her almost savagely. 'And had your head not been turned, you would now agree with me.'

'My head turned?' Elizabeth screeched. 'How dare you speak so to me?'

'Madam, if you will give me leave to speak with you alone.'

'No, I will not.'

'Then you break that promise you made me on the day of your accession, Your Majesty, when you said if I ever needed a private audience, you would grant it.'

'I will not hear you alone so you can malign my friends,' she stammered uneasily.

Cecil straightened. 'I have delivered my news, Your Majesty, and long for my bed. If you would be so good as to peruse this paper,' he said, holding out a list to her. 'It is an account of my personal expenses contracted during my business in Scotland.'

Elizabeth glanced at it. 'Do you think to dip your hand in the privy purse to pay your petty expenses?'

He felt the burn of humiliation upon his cheeks. 'I was in Scotland on official business, madam.'

She tossed the paper aside. 'Get the playing cards, Robin.'

'Of course, madam. Let me show Cecil out first.' Robert rose and took Cecil's arm.

Cecil shook him off. 'I know my way, sir,' he growled.

Robert smiled. 'Of course you do. I thought perhaps you needed help.'

'I need none from you.'

'You may find that you do soon enough,' he said, keeping his voice low. 'There may come a time, Cecil, when you will need all the help I am prepared to give you.'

'When, and if, that day ever comes, I will not stay around to ask for it.' Cecil looked pointedly over Robert's shoulder. 'Goodnight, Your Majesty.'

Elizabeth gave a tight nod. 'Goodnight, Cecil. We will speak again in the morning when you're rested.'

'What an insolent fellow he is,' Robert said when Cecil had gone. He pulled open a drawer in a chest by the wall and retrieved a pack of cards.

'No more insolent than you,' she snapped. 'Why did you make me speak so to him?'

'I? What did I do?'

'You made me speak harshly when I had no cause.'

'Oh, his pride's just a little wounded, that's all,' Robert said, shuffling the cards. 'He'll be fine in the morning.'

'I did make him a promise.'

'So? He's only your secretary.'

'He's a good man.' Elizabeth snatched up the cards

200

and threw them at him. She rose and crossed to the window to stare out into the darkness.

'Bess?' Robert asked quietly. 'Forgive me.'

His voice was soft, and her ears loved the sound of it. She turned and her anger melted as she looked upon him, his face half in shadow, the candlelight glinting in his eyes. It made her stomach flutter just to look at him. 'I do. I fear I'll forgive you anything.'

He moved to her and took her hand in his. 'What sweet words, Bess,' he whispered, leaning in close, his breath hot upon her cheek.

'Sweet words,' she whispered back. 'Sweet Robin.'

He heard the door close behind him. They were probably laughing at him now, her and Dudley. He could just picture them. Even the warders on either side of the door were exchanging glances. That one, the one with the crooked mouth, was smirking. Cecil glared at him.

'Look to your business,' he snapped and stormed off down the corridor.

'Master Cecil,' a heavily accented voice called out.

Cecil halted and turned. The Spanish ambassador, Bishop de Quadra, was hurrying after him. 'Bishop?'

'Master Cecil.' de Quadra peered into Cecil's face, noting his flushed skin. 'Are you unwell?'

'Not unwell, bishop. Angry and disappointed.'

'Why so?'

Cecil took a deep breath. He was not used to sharing confidences, but why the hell not? 'I'll tell you why. I return from Scotland, having been away on the queen's business, spending so much of my own money that I shall be in debt for years, only to find that the queen scorns all my efforts and bids me go so she can dally with Lord Robert Dudley.'

'Ah, Lord Robert,' de Quadra nodded, understanding

completely. 'It is unfortunate the queen should have so ill regarded a man as Lord Robert so close to her. It does her reputation no good, no good at all. And he a married man.'

'Disgraceful, I agree. Though he may be a widower soon enough. Apparently, his wife has a malady in one of her breasts and is thought likely to die.'

'Indeed?' de Quadra raised both eyebrows in interest.

'And,' Cecil hurried on, 'I have heard that his wife believes there are attempts to poison her.'

'By whom?'

'Who can say?' Cecil shrugged.

'The poor lady.'

'Of course, these are just rumours,' Cecil said. 'There may be nothing in them.'

'And yet, they must spring from somewhere.'

'Time will tell. But, sir, as you know the queen and are a friend to her, I beg you, say nothing of this. I fear for her reputation.'

'You need beg nothing of me, Master Cecil,' de Quadra assured him, his brain already working on the wording of his next letter to his master, the king of Spain. 'If you will excuse me.'

Cecil willed his heart to slow as he watched de Quadra hurry away. He knew his words would be written down and repeated and was glad of it. Perhaps hearing the rumours of poison would shock Elizabeth into ridding herself of Dudley. Better still, if Amy Dudley died, with all these rumours bruited abroad, Dudley himself would come under suspicion and then the queen could not afford to have him near her. Oh yes, that would wipe the grin off his handsome face. Cecil allowed himself a little smile as he walked back to his rooms.

CHAPTER TWENTY-EIGHT

Amy had heard them talking, whispering among themselves, thinking they couldn't be heard. Their filthy gossip had meant her mind had not had a moment of rest. She hadn't slept properly for months. She would wake in the middle of the night, stretch out a bare leg and feel only the cold mattress beside her and, for a sleep-befuddled moment, would wonder where her husband was. Then she would remember and there would be a drag at her heart.

It had been three months since she had last seen Robert. He had returned to Syderstone, full of concern for her, but had seemed distracted, as if he was merely doing his duty, and his mind, and perhaps his heart, was elsewhere. He had moved her to Cumnor Place to lodge with his friends. For her comfort, he had told her, and for his, of course, so he would know she was being looked after. She agreed without argument, even though the Odingsells bored and irritated her with their kindnesses. Every time she took a sip of wine or a mouthful of food, she wondered if the gossip was true and Robert was poisoning her. She found she didn't care. She felt half dead anyway.

This morning, the pain had been terrible, waking her

from a troubled sleep and bringing tears to her eyes. She had pushed herself upright, gasping and wincing, clutching her left breast as if touch alone could stop the pain.

Her maid, Pinto, had taken up residence on a truckle bed in her mistress's chamber for the last month, concerned at Amy's diminishing weight and pale, gaunt appearance. She had awoken early, as the first shafts of dawn's light penetrated the chamber, but had lain still, listening to the breathing of her mistress. At the first rustle of bedclothes, she had sprung up and rushed to the bedside.

Nothing could be done, of course, save giving Amy her medicine that would numb the pain. It would soon wear off, leaving her tired and irritable. As the pain faded and her eyes grew heavy, Amy complained about the noise from below. The servants were being too noisy; did they not know she was ill?

'Isn't there a fair today?' Amy had mumbled. Pinto had answered in the affirmative. 'Well, send them out to it. I want some peace.'

'They won't enjoy going on a Sunday,' Pinto had said. 'Only the common folk go then.'

'I don't care. I want them gone.'

'What about Mistress Odingsell? I can't make her go.'

'She can do as she pleases. The servants will go. And you, too.'

'Me?'

Despite Pinto's protestations, Amy had been adamant. So, Pinto went to the fair and made her complaints to the other servants, finding them more receptive than her mistress.

As the hours passed, Amy found she did not enjoy her solitude as much as she had expected. And the pain was returning. She fumbled through the medicine chest, cursing herself for not getting Pinto to make up her medicine before leaving. Well, she had seen Pinto make it often enough, she would do it herself. It tasted good, even if the consistency was rather thicker than usual. It didn't matter. If she had put too much in, it would last the longer.

Mistress Odingsell knocked on her door around noon and asked if Amy wanted to dine with her in her chamber. Not overly fond of the old woman, but restless and wanting company, Amy agreed. She soon regretted it. Mistress Odingsell chattered and ate, chattered and ate until Amy grew sick of her fat, snapping mouth. She rose, saying she needed some fresh air and would walk in the garden. The old woman volunteered to accompany her if she would but wait until she had finished her dinner. Amy assured her she would be fine on her own, especially as she knew her friend would want to take a nap after eating. She shuffled from the room before Mistress Odingsell could protest further.

She headed for the stairs. Her foot caught in her long skirt as she stepped onto the third tread. She kicked the heavy fabric away, annoyed at how fuddled her head seemed. Her need for fresh air had not been a fabrication. She needed it to blow the cobwebs away. She stepped down on another tread. Again, her foot caught. She stumbled forward, coming down heavily on the next step, the impact juddering up through her spine. She cried out in pain.

And then she was falling... falling...

WHITEHALL PALACE

Tamworth stood at the foot of his master's bed and looked down at the sleeping man. 'My lord,' he exclaimed. 'My lord, you must wake up.'

Robert turned his face into the pillow and mumbled for Tamworth to go away. But Tamworth persisted and eventually Robert opened sleep-encrusted eyes. 'What is it?'

'My lord, a man is here from Cumnor. He brings sad news.'

Robert was wide awake in an instant. He sat bolt upright and threw back the sheets. 'Is it my wife?'

'I'm afraid so, my lord.'

'Has she...?' he swallowed. 'Is she...?'

'Yes, my lord.'

Robert swung his legs to the floor and rose, crossing to the window and pressing his forehead against the glass. He closed his eyes. 'Was it peaceful?' he asked hopefully.

Tamworth hesitated. 'My lord, I think you should see the man who has come.'

Robert turned to him, wondering at his evasiveness. 'What is it?'

'The messenger can explain better.' Tamworth hurried to the outer chamber and returned with a short, red-faced man, dusty from the road. 'This is the man. Bowes.'

'You brought the news of my wife,' Robert said, pulling on a dressing-gown.

'Yes, my lord,' Bowes said. 'Lady Dudley was found yesterday evening.'

'Found?' Robert thought it was an odd way to describe it.

'Yes, my lord. Lady Dudley was found at the bottom of the stairs with her neck broken.'

'What?' Robert gasped, taking a few shaky steps forward. 'But I thought her illness—'

'No, my lord,' Bowes shook his head. 'It was the fall that killed her.'

'But how did she come to fall?'

'No one can say. No one saw it happen. Only Mistress Odingsell was in the house and she was in her chamber.'

'But where were the servants?'

'Lady Dudley had sent them to the fair at Abingdon.'

'But my wife hated to be left on her own.'

'It's true, my lord. She even sent her maid away.'

Robert sat down on the bed. 'I don't understand it.' He put his head in his hands.

'My lord,' Tamworth said, 'I think perhaps you should dress now. You should see the queen and tell her of this yourself before she hears of it from other quarters.'

Robert looked up and Tamworth saw he had been crying. 'Yes, of course. Get out my black doublet and hose, Tam.'

'Yes, my lord.'

Elizabeth had not yet risen. Robert was told by a grim-faced Kat Ashley that it was unreasonable to ask to see the queen at such an early hour.

'I must see her,' he said.

Kat looked at him. This wasn't the brash Robert Dudley she was used to. She noticed the tear tracks down his cheeks, the sniff of his nose. 'Is it important?'

Robert nodded.

'Wait here,' she said. She went back into the bedchamber and shook Elizabeth's shoulder gently. 'Your Majesty, Lord Robert needs to see you urgently.'

'Is something wrong?' Elizabeth asked, sitting up.

'I think so. He's been crying.'

Elizabeth hurried out of bed and Kat helped her on with her dressing-gown. 'Let him come in,' Elizabeth said. 'Rob.' She went to him as he walked in and took hold of his hands. They were cold. 'What's happened?'

'Amy's dead.'

A pause. 'Oh my God,' Elizabeth breathed. 'When?'

'Yesterday.'

'You'll be leaving, then.'

Robert's eyes widened. 'Yes, I'll be leaving,' he said incredulously.

'Why are you looking at me like that?' Elizabeth retorted.

'Not "Sorry" or "How are you?" Just, "You'll be leaving, then".' He turned and headed for the door.

'You want me to say I'm sorry?' Elizabeth called after him. 'Are *you* sorry?'

'How dare you ask me that?' he cried. 'She was my wife. I didn't want her dead. And certainly not from falling down some damned stairs.'

'She fell? But I thought her cancer—'

Robert shook his head.

Elizabeth fell silent, her mind busy. This news changed things. Perhaps she should have made an effort to be sympathetic, but her heart had been thumping so hard at the realisation that Robert was now free. He would want to marry her now and she would have no excuses left. But a death from a prolonged illness was one thing; Amy dying from a fall quite another. She had heard the rumours and knew people would be wondering whether Robert Dudley's poor, long-suffering wife had fallen down the stairs or if she she been pushed.

'There will have to be an inquest,' she said.

Robert shrugged. 'I suppose so.'

'You can't stay at court.'

'I'll be leaving for Cumnor as soon as I am packed.'

'No, I mean…,' Elizabeth sighed. 'I mean, you won't be able to come back until the inquest is over and…'

'And what?' he asked.

'Rob, for heaven's sake. There have been rumours about you and I circulating around this court for a year. Rumours that Amy was being poisoned to get rid of her. And now, your wife dies, very conveniently, by falling down stairs.'

Robert looked at her, aghast. 'You think I killed her?'

'No,' Elizabeth shook her head emphatically. 'I don't. But don't you think others will if it suits them?'

'It's monstrous.'

Elizabeth pointed to the door. 'You should go now.'

'You can't wait for me to be gone, can you?'

'I can't risk being accused of complicity in this,' she said. 'Until it's proved Amy's death was an accident, Rob, you must stay away from me.'

CHAPTER TWENTY-NINE

Slouched in a chair by the window, his feet propped up on a stool, Robert turned the pages of a book idly. His shirt, stained with sweat, fell open to his navel and stubble showed dark upon his cheeks.

Robert tossed the book aside. It was no good trying to read. His mind kept wandering. He stood and stretched, groaning as he felt bones crack in his shoulders. Pushing the window open further, he leant out on the sill, breathing in the scent of the lavender bush below. Looking towards the gateway, he was surprised to see a mule and pony trotting along the gravel path.

He hastily tied his shirt and snatched up his doublet from the back of the chair. Thrusting his arms through the sleeves, he hurried outside, shooing away the servant who was heading for his guests. The gravel crunched beneath his feet. Masking his surprise at the identity of the rider, he took hold of the mule's bridle.

'Cecil, I wasn't expecting you.'

Cecil climbed down from his mount with relief. 'I trust my coming is not an unwelcome surprise.'

'Not at all,' Robert replied with sincerity. 'You will stay and dine with me, I hope?'

Cecil noted the quiet desperation in his eyes and was pleased. 'I thank you, yes. Can my page be attended to?'

'Of course. Boy, go around to the stables and ask for Gregson. Cecil, please come in.' Robert led Cecil back into the house. 'Forgive the mess,' he said, as he hurried to tidy up.

'That is a great deal of correspondence,' Cecil nodded at a pile of letters stacked precariously on a small table.

'Yes. Letters of condolence.'

'Of course.'

'Can I get you something to drink?'

'Thank you.' Cecil took a seat. 'You must wonder why I'm here.'

'You have a message from the queen?' Robert asked hopefully, handing him a cup of beer.

Cecil inclined his head sympathetically. 'I'm afraid not. I come on my own account to see how you are.'

Robert slumped in his chair, disappointed. 'I am as you see me. In truth, I am not surprised the queen sends no message. We parted badly.'

Cecil had heard of their last encounter. 'I'm sure there is no ill feeling on the queen's part, my lord. Indeed, she is most distressed by this situation. Is there any news from Cumnor?'

'My steward, Anthony Blount, has spoken with all the servants in the house, including my wife's maid, Pinto. It seems Pinto made a comment which I find disturbing, to say the least.'

'Which was?'

'That she had often heard Amy pray to God for a release from her pain.'

'You think, then, that your wife may have taken her own life?'

Robert shook his head vehemently. 'Not for a moment. Amy was a good Christian and would not throw away the life that God gave her. Besides, if you wanted to kill yourself, would you trust Death to take you by throwing yourself down a flight of stairs? No, I can't believe it. I do believe she simply fell.'

'A tragedy, my lord.'

'In more ways than one,' Robert murmured. 'I must thank you for coming to see me, Cecil. I had not expected such kindness, I confess.'

Cecil was almost moved. 'Think nothing of it, my lord. After all, we are both servants of the queen.'

Mary Sidney exchanged a glance with her husband. He nodded his head in encouragement, and they both looked back at Robert.

'How are you really, Rob?' Mary asked.

Robert, who had been pushing his food around his plate, looked up at her with tired eyes. 'Fine,' he said.

'You don't look fine. You look tired. And worried.'

'Of course, I look worried,' he laughed sourly. 'The entire world thinks I'm a murderer.'

'Oh, please don't say that.'

'My dear sister, even Elizabeth has her doubts of my innocence.'

'I'm sure she doesn't,' Mary said, stabbing a piece of meat with her knife.

'She sent me away, didn't she?'

'She explained why she had to do that.'

'Oh yes, Elizabeth is very careful of her honour. It doesn't matter that I may have needed her support. These calumnies against me would not have dared to have been spoken if she had kept me with her.'

'Can we not go over this again?' Henry pleaded. 'Once the coroner has declared Amy's death an accident, you can go back to court. The queen specifically instructed Mary to send her word of how you are. So, you see, she hasn't deserted you.'

Just then, the door opened and Anthony Blount strode in with a huge smile upon his face.

Robert jumped up from his seat. 'What news?' he demanded.

'Accidental Death, my lord,' Blount said.

'Oh, God be praised,' Robert gasped as Mary threw herself against him. He clutched her tight and buried his face in her neck. Beneath her arms, his body shook with sobs.

Embarrassed, Henry led Blount outside. Mary pushed Robert back into his chair and she knelt at his feet.

'Rob,' she said, taking hold of his hands. 'It's over now.'

'I know,' he nodded. 'I don't know why I'm crying.'

'It's grief and relief, you idiot. Now, Rob, look at me. It's over. Say it.'

'It's over.' He took her face between her hands and kissed her. 'Oh, Mary, what a time it's been.'

'I know. It can't have been easy.'

He pulled out a handkerchief from his doublet and wiped his eyes. 'Will Elizabeth send for me now, do you think?'

'Of course she will. There's no reason for her not to, is there? Maybe Cecil will come and get you.'

Robert snorted. 'Cecil! I'll wager this verdict will not please him.'

'He came to see you last week. You told me how kind you thought it was of him.'

'My brain wasn't working then, Mary. I was so lonely and distressed, I would have welcomed the Devil. He came to gloat. Elizabeth had got rid of me and he was back at her side. He's no friend to me.'

'Oh Rob, you see enemies where there are none.'

'Mary, how is it possible to have spent your entire life at court and still think well of people?'

'I do not know, Rob,' she said, her voice heavy with sarcasm. 'I cannot think where I get my good nature from.'

He laughed and pulled her towards him, embracing her so tightly she protested she couldn't breathe. Henry and Blount returned, and the hours passed happily in their company. At eight o'clock that evening, a messenger arrived. He had a letter for Robert from the queen, informing him his presence was required at court.

GREENWICH PALACE

Elizabeth thundered ahead of him, her horse kicking up great clods of earth. She headed for a clump of trees that provided cover from spying eyes and waited for him.

Robert slid down from his saddle and stood by Mirabelle. Elizabeth stood by her horse and they stared at each other for a long moment. Then Elizabeth's face crumpled, and through her tears headed towards him, her arms wanting, needing to hold him. He let her press against him before he relented and cradled her in his arms.

'Oh, Robin, you can't imagine what I have had to endure while you were gone.'

'I think I can imagine it, Bess. I wasn't exactly enjoying myself exiled at Kew, you know.'

'I was all alone.'

'You had Cecil.'

She pulled away from him. 'What is Cecil to me? A

trusted counsellor, someone I can depend on. Not a... not a...,' she faltered.

'A what? A lover?' he suggested. 'Well, no more am I.'

'No, not in the physical sense,' she admitted as she wiped her cheeks. 'But what we have is so much more. True love, Robin. True and enduring.'

'True love is all very well, Bess, but I need more.'

Elizabeth made a gesture of despair. 'Why must you have more? I don't need it.'

'Because men are different.'

'Why can't you understand? If I were to have a child—'

'All the country would rejoice at that if we were married, Bess.'

'How can we marry with things as they are?' Elizabeth had quite recovered herself and her eyes were blotchy but dry. 'It may have escaped your notice, Robin, but you are hated the country over. I would be despised as well if I were to marry you. They may even turn against me.'

'Never. The people love you.'

'I wish I could be as sure as you. Perhaps in a few years' time, the situation will be different.'

Robert turned to Mirabelle and stroked her neck. 'Will it ever be different? You will always be queen and I will always be the traitor who isn't fit to kiss your feet.'

Elizabeth didn't disagree. 'The others will catch up soon. Help me mount my horse.'

Robert cupped his hands for her to put her foot in and heaved her up into the saddle.

'Don't be angry with me,' she begged.

'What good would it do me to be angry?' he said, climbing back onto Mirabelle and nudged her sides, goading her to a gallop, leaving Elizabeth to follow.

CHAPTER THIRTY

1561

'It's not right, you know,' Mary said, shaking her head. 'Ambrose is the elder. He should be ennobled before you.'

Robert grinned at her. 'It's not my fault. It's the queen's decision.'

'I haven't heard any protest from you.'

'Mary,' Ambrose scolded, slipping an arm around her waist. 'Don't fret so. My time will come. Quiet now, she's coming.'

Elizabeth strode into the room, her brow heavily creased and her mouth so pursed that her thin lips had turned almost white. She headed straight for the desk where the ennoblement documents were laid out, ready for her signature.

Robert wondered at her expression, but now was not the time to ask questions. He sank to his knees before the table and looked up at her.

Elizabeth seemed to study his face for a long moment, and Robert couldn't guess what she was thinking. She picked up the topmost document and squinted at it. 'Robert Dudley, to be raised to the peerage and given the title of...,' She stopped, tapping her finger rhythmically upon the wood.

Robert glanced at Mary and frowned. Mary gave the slightest shake of her head, as confused as he.

'No,' Elizabeth said, picking up a paperknife and stabbing the centre of the document. She drew the knife down, tearing the paper in two.

Robert scrambled to his feet, barely registering the rising murmur of the watching courtiers' whispers. 'What... why?'

'I have my reasons,' Elizabeth replied coolly, quickly signing the other documents laid out for her.

Robert was speechless. Why was she humiliating him like this? As she rose from the desk, he grabbed hold of her arm.

Elizabeth shrugged him off angrily. 'You want reasons? Very well, here they are. Your family has been traitors to the crown through three generations. You have been suspected of murder throughout my kingdom and Europe. Your arrogance and ambition threaten my throne—'

'I would never...,' he began, but broke off. 'Why are you doing this?'

'I'm your queen, Lord Robert. Take care you never forget that.'

There was a sternness in her eyes Robert had not seen before. He released her and Elizabeth left the chamber, Cecil trotting at her heels.

Then Robert heard the laughter, the scoffs, the jeering, and God's Death, how they hurt! But he was damned if he would lose control for them all to see. He raised his chin a little higher and strode back to his room.

But once inside, Robert's control deserted him. He yanked off his cloak, throwing it on the floor. He rammed his fist against the bedpost, swallowing down the sickening pain it brought.

There came an almost tentative knock on the door. For a moment, he actually thought it might be Elizabeth come to explain herself, maybe even to apologise.

The door opened and Mary poked her head around. 'Rob?'

'Leave me alone, Mary,' he said, disappointed.

'No, I won't,' she said, entering and closing the door. 'Oh, Rob, that was so cruel.'

'I'm well enough.'

'Don't pretend with me. I know how much that hurt you.'

'How dare she!' he exploded. 'How dare she humiliate me like that?'

'Perhaps someone advised her to do it?' Mary suggested.

'Don't make excuses for her, Mary. Elizabeth doesn't need anyone to tell her to be cruel. It comes naturally to her.'

'Well, don't think on it. Let her think you don't care.'

'Turn my back on her if she comes calling, you mean? My, what an innocent you are! She's the queen, Mary. Like it or not, I have to take her insults, her taunts, and what's more, thank her for them.'

'No, Rob, you mustn't accept this insult. Let Elizabeth know she can't treat you so.'

'Our family's future rests entirely upon the queen's good graces, Mary. To relinquish her favour would be to relinquish all my hopes.'

'Well, maybe that is true,' Mary agreed ruefully. 'But I don't have to like it. What are you looking for?'

Robert was rummaging through a trunk. 'My riding boots. I have to get out of the palace. Why don't you come with me?'

'I expect the queen will notice my absence. I should get back.'

'She won't want a Dudley around her.'

'I'm a Sidney, Robert,' she replied, teasingly.

'You were a Dudley first, sister. Never forget that. Oh, come riding with me, Mary. Don't make me get down on my knees and beg.'

'Very well, Rob,' she agreed with an indulgent smile, 'but you must defend me if the queen demands to know where I've been.'

'I may very well need defending myself. Come on, let's leave before we're noticed.'

At that moment came a loud, peremptory knock on the door. Robert sighed and called out, 'Come in.'

A page entered. 'The queen demands your presence, my lord.'

'You see, Mary,' Robert cried. 'The queen demands and I must obey. Come, sister. Let's find out what Her Majesty wants of me now.'

Elizabeth turned as Robert and Mary entered the Presence Chamber, a sly smile playing on her lips. 'Robin,' she purred, holding her hands out to him.

He went to her. 'Your Majesty,' he greeted her coldly.

'Now, Robin,' she said, adopting a mock scolding tone, 'your face is as sour as vinegar.'

'With reason, madam.'

'Oh, nonsense. Are you so easily overthrown?' she asked, laying her long fingers upon his cheek. The gesture was curiously sensual and intimate. Robert could hear no laughing now.

Henry Sidney, sensing an advantage, spoke up. 'So great a man is fit for a greater place. Do you not agree, Your Majesty?'

'Indeed, Sir Henry?' Elizabeth said. 'And what greater place would you suggest?'

Henry gave a broad smile and shrugged as if the answer were obvious. 'At your side, Your Majesty. What other would suit?'

'You mean, none other would satisfy him.' Elizabeth gave a sideways glance at Robert. 'No, I will not marry a subject, for then men would come to ask for my husband's favour and not mine.'

'Your sister had no such fears with her husband, Your Majesty,' Henry pointed out.

'And remember how that turned out,' Elizabeth snapped. She turned to Robert. 'I will have here but one mistress and no master. Remember that, my lord.'

Robert nodded, his courtier's nod which hid the disappointment he felt. For he was beginning to believe Elizabeth meant every word she said.

CHAPTER THIRTY-ONE

1562

Cecil waited until the other counsellors had filed out and the door had closed. Then he looked at Elizabeth and licked his dry lips thoughtfully.

'What is it?' Elizabeth asked, her eyes narrowing with curiosity.

'I wanted to speak to you in private about Mary Stuart.'

Elizabeth grunted. Her cousin was the last thing she wanted to talk about.

'Have you had any thoughts about who she should marry?' Cecil continued.

'Marry?' Elizabeth said. 'Cecil, she's only just been widowed. Her husband is hardly cold in his grave.'

'Nevertheless, madam, if Mary Stuart isn't considering her next husband, then her Guise uncles will be. I have received intelligence from Sir Nicholas Throckmorton. You are aware of the animosity between Mary Stuart and the queen Mother, Catherine de Medici. It is believed that Catherine will not allow Mary to stay in France. If that should be the case and she doesn't marry soon, Scotland will be the only place Mary Stuart can go.'

'Well, it is her country, Cecil. Why should it concern me if she is there?'

'Madam, she is a Catholic.'

'But Scotland is Protestant. Her half-brother, James, takes our money to keep it so.'

'Indeed, but he is a bastard and ineligible to rule. Of course, he will hope that Mary will merely be the figure-head of Scotland with himself in actual charge, but, I hear, she is strong-willed and may choose to be a queen in more than name. That would be a pity. If James were to lose his position of power, it could cause trouble for us.'

'She *is* a queen, Cecil. She has a right to rule.'

Cecil's face twitched. 'Indeed, she does. But not all monarchs have the ability to rule. If I may say so, madam, Mary Stuart is not Elizabeth Tudor.'

Elizabeth's eyes softened. 'Have you turned flatterer, Cecil?' she asked with a smile.

'It is not flattery to speak the truth, madam. Remember, Mary Stuart has a personal allegiance to France and a religious allegiance to Spain. And if she were to choose a husband not inclined towards friendship with England—'

'Yes, yes, I understand.' Elizabeth waved her hand at him impatiently. 'You want me to suggest a husband to her? Why would she pay attention to anything I say? She has already shown herself careless of my feelings. Does she not lay claim to my throne?'

'She does indeed maintain that position, madam, but has not the power or support to enforce it. But she may also have need of your goodwill. To get to Scotland, she will need to pass through English waters. You could with-hold permission for her to do so, forcing her to take a different, perhaps more dangerous, passage.'

'Good idea,' Elizabeth said, impressed. 'If she intends to return to Scotland, I will withhold permission. She can go the long way around.'

'And a husband, madam?' Cecil prompted.

'You have someone in mind, Cecil?'

Cecil coughed nervously. 'I was thinking of Lord Robert Dudley.'

Elizabeth stared at him. She couldn't speak. She was stunned. Had Cecil just suggested Robin marry Mary Stuart?

'Consider the advantages of such a match,' Cecil continued quietly. 'Lord Robert is a great friend to you and therefore to England. He is a Protestant. He is ambitious and such a match would raise him very high indeed. The only issue would be if...,' he paused and took a deep breath, 'if you could not bear to lose him.'

Elizabeth's mouth tightened. She smacked her hand down on the table angrily and rose, striding across to the window. Cecil got to his feet, tasting sweat on his upper lip, and waited. He could see the tension in her shoulders as she leant on the windowsill and stared out into the gardens.

She slowly turned to him. 'Robin would never agree.'

'If you ordered it, madam, how could he refuse?'

'There must be other possibilities. Is she not supposed to be beautiful?' Elizabeth sneered. 'There must be plenty of princes across Europe eager to wed her.'

'None that would be so advantageous to England, madam. And is Lord Robert not a handsome man?'

'The most handsome.' Elizabeth could not help but smile. 'Does Mary like handsome men, Cecil?'

'What woman doesn't?'

Elizabeth shot him a sharp look. 'I shall have to think about this, Cecil. Say nothing to anyone for the moment.'

'Of course not, madam. You will consider it then?'

'I've said I will, haven't I? But I will not be hurried into anything. Mary can marry no one until her mourning is over. There is plenty of time to consider husbands for my dear cousin.'

Cecil gathered up his papers and left the council chamber, leaving Elizabeth alone.

It was an outrageous suggestion. How could she let that woman get her hands on Robin? She pictured Robert in Mary's bed, Mary enjoying him as she, Elizabeth, had never dared to do. Oh God, it hurt to imagine such things. But then, she admitted, there was security in the idea, for England and for her personally.

Oh Cecil, you clever man. In one stroke, you could secure Scotland as an ally for England, tame a dangerous Catholic queen, and rid yourself of a nuisance rival.

Elizabeth had to admire Cecil for his ingenuity.

HAMPTON COURT PALACE

'Oh, have pity on me, Rob, and sit down.'

Elizabeth rubbed her eyes as there came another stab of pain. God's Death, how they ached tonight! And Robert would keep fidgeting.

'But Elizabeth,' he continued, heedless of her discomfort, 'they are Protestants. The Huguenots are being persecuted in France for their religion, a religion this country shares. If we do not answer the appeal of the Huguenots—'

'I don't care about the Huguenots. Let the French go hang themselves. Why are men always so eager to go to war?'

'We can't ignore them, Bess. If the Catholics were to gain the upper hand—'

'So, what then?'

'Then the balance of power in Europe would be heavily in favour of the Papists. And England could face a joint French and Spanish alliance.'

Robert was trying to frighten her into action, she knew, but Elizabeth was too tired to think.

'And if we aid them,' Robert continued, 'they have promised to cede to us the port of Newhaven. Think of it, Bess, a port in France once again. We haven't had one since Calais was lost.'

'I know, and how did we lose that?' Elizabeth said testily. 'By my sister, Mary, embroiling us in a foreign war, urged on her by men.'

'That was an ill-advised expedition. The gains this time would far outweigh the risks. And once we have Newhaven—'

'If we win.'

'Yes, if we win,' Robert conceded. 'And then we may even be able to reclaim Calais.'

'Cecil would prefer to act as intermediary between the Huguenots and Guises. Bring them to a reconciliation.'

'I imagine Cecil would. He is nothing if not cautious. But it would be wrong, Bess. Ask your council.'

'Oh, is there any need?' Elizabeth asked, raising her eyebrows. 'I thought you had already been canvassing their opinions.'

Robert smiled, half-embarrassed at being caught out. 'Well, I wanted to ensure my argument had support.'

'You don't have enough support, Rob. I'm not deciding anything yet.'

He took her hand, meaning to try to persuade her with sweet words and kisses. Closer than he had been all evening, he saw now that she looked quite ill. Her cheeks and forehead were flushed and blotchy, her eyes bloodshot and sweat shined on her top lip.

'Bess, are you ill?'

'I'm tired. I want to go to bed and you keep me talking.'

'Well, then, let's get you to bed.' He took hold of her arms and pulled her up from the chair. Even as he held her, Robert felt her strength fall away. She slumped against him, and he struggled to hold her upright.

'Guard!' he yelled over his shoulder. Two Yeoman Warders rushed in, their halberds lowered and pointing at Robert. 'The queen has fainted. Help me get her to the bed.'

One guard dropped his halberd on the floor and took hold of Elizabeth's legs. Between them, they managed to lay her on the bed.

Her Ladies were coming in from the antechamber, clustering around her prone body. Robert ordered one of them to fetch the queen's doctor before Kat Ashley shooed him out of the room.

Robert ran a hand over his face. 'For God's sake, how long does it take to find out what's wrong with her?'

'Doctor Burcot is a fine physician,' Cecil said, distractedly tapping a quill against upon the council table.

'He had better be.'

'There is an outbreak of smallpox in London. I understand two boys from the kitchens succumbed only yesterday.'

'Smallpox? Please God, not that.'

'I know. The disfigurement can be terrible. If the patient survives at all, that is.'

They glanced at each other, both considering the possibility of Elizabeth's death and the awful consequences when Mary came into the room.

'What news?' Robert demanded, jumping up from his chair.

'Doctor Burcot says it's smallpox,' Mary said. 'The queen woke shortly after you left, and when the doctor told her she had smallpox, she grew so angry, she shouted at him to get out. The earl of Sussex had to drag him back.'

'I must see her.' Robert headed for the door.

Mary grabbed his arm. 'She's asleep again. And besides, you don't want to catch it.'

'I won't catch it. I don't catch anything. And I don't care if she's asleep. I just want to be with her.'

Mary nodded wearily, seeing it would be pointless to argue further. 'Come with me then,' she said and led Robert to the bedchamber.

Elizabeth lay in her bed, eyes closed, mouth hanging open, hair clinging to her sweat dampened forehead and neck.

Mary pulled a chair to the side of the bed and pointed Robert to it. He sat, finding Elizabeth's hand between the folds of the red flannel blanket she was wrapped in and pressed her clammy fingers around his.

'I'm here, Bess,' he whispered. 'I'm here.'

Elizabeth slipped in and out of consciousness for days. Robert stayed by her side. When eventually he was persuaded to retire to his room to sleep, Elizabeth, perversely, awoke. She thought she was dying. She had the council brought into her bedchamber and once they were all assembled, declared that Robert Dudley be made Protector of the Realm in the event of her death. No one wanted to argue with a dying queen, so they all murmured their agreement while giving each other uneasy looks. Dudley as Protector! Preposterous.

But then, Elizabeth rallied, and there was no need to contemplate a Protectorship. Robert felt strange; his emotions were at odds. He felt great happiness that Elizabeth was recovering and yet disappointment that he would not be Protector, however remote that possibility had been.

Mary Sidney had no reason to rejoice, however. Elizabeth, by some miracle (or witchcraft, some murmured) had escaped the horrific disfigurement that smallpox could inflict, but Mary caught the disease. She too survived, but her face, which had once been so very pretty, was now painful to look upon, so altered and ugly had it become. She could not bear the embarrassed glances of people who didn't know where to look, nor their expressions of sympathy, and retired to her house at Penshurst.

CHAPTER THIRTY-TWO

Cecil rubbed his nose, leaving a smudge of ink upon its tip. 'Lord Robert has once again petitioned the council to send men to Newhaven, Your Majesty.'

Elizabeth took up the paper upon which Robert had detailed the advantages and disadvantages of a campaign against the French in support of the Protestant Huguenots and which he had presented to the council earlier that morning. Despite herself, she smiled at his assiduousness. 'He is proving a most energetic counsellor.'

'Indeed,' Cecil agreed regretfully.

Since Elizabeth had made Robert a member of the Privy Council, Cecil had not had a moment's peace. Robert and Norfolk, who had been made a counsellor at the same time, were either too high in rank or too close to the queen to be ignored, and neither believed in holding their tongue.

'Shall I tell him the answer is once again no?'

Elizabeth smiled ruefully at him. 'I believe this time I must say yes, Cecil.'

'Your Majesty?' Cecil asked, not quite believing he had heard correctly.

'I know you are of my mind that wars are costly businesses, but Lord Robert has been most persuasive.' She pointed to Robert's list. 'And thorough. Two ports in France would benefit England greatly and, in truth, I am inclined to help our Protestant cousins. And Robert is not the only one pressing me to act. My good Sir Nicholas Throckmorton in France urges me to it almost daily.'

'Yes, I'm aware he has written. Well, madam, if you are indeed resolved to act, then I shall begin with the preparations. But I do have one question. Who is to head the expedition? I know Lord Robert believes he should lead it as the Huguenots have been appealing to him directly.'

Elizabeth nodded. 'Yes, well, Robert is going to have to be disappointed. I will not be sending him.'

'He will be very disappointed, madam,' Cecil said, trying not to smile.

'His brother can go instead. Now that I have ennobled Ambrose, it is proper that he should. And that way, the Dudley name will be represented.'

Cecil made a note. 'Ambrose Dudley, the earl of Warwick, to head the army.'

'Is that all?' Elizabeth asked with a sigh. 'Lord Robert is waiting for me to ride.'

'Yes, that is all for the moment, madam. I shall let Lord Robert know of your decision.'

'No, I shall tell him myself,' Elizabeth said, getting to her feet and waving him to sit still. 'He will be petulant and argumentative, no doubt, and I, like a mother, must soothe and comfort him. That's not a role for you, Cecil.'

Cecil smiled gratefully.

'Rob, stop.'

Elizabeth reined in her horse and waited for him to come back to her.

'Tired already?' he asked, looking at her horse, not her.

'No, but I don't want you sulking all day. Walk on,' she nudged her horse's sides. 'I know you're disappointed, but I really can't let you go. Ambrose will do well, I'm sure.'

'Of course he will.'

'Good. So, take that look off your face.'

Robert knew he was being childish, and he made an effort to improve his temper. 'Sorry,' he mumbled.

'Well, I hope this will make you feel better. You remember Kenilworth?'

'Yes. It's a castle up in Warwickshire. It belonged to my father for a short while.'

'Well, now it's yours.' She gave him a sideways glance and was gratified to see a growing look of astonishment cross his face. 'You heard me. I'm giving you Kenilworth.'

'Oh, Bess!'

'It will need a lot of work. I hear it's almost a ruin.'

'I don't care. I'll rebuild it.'

'It might be cheaper and easier to build new, you know. That's what Cecil's doing with his house.'

'No, not for me. I like to keep the history of a place.'

Elizabeth laughed. 'It's always history with you, Rob. Everything you do, every action you take, you're not thinking of now, what it means at this moment. You're thinking far ahead, years even. You're thinking of the legacy you'll leave behind. And I want you to have plenty of time to build that legacy. Which is why you're not going to France. You understand me?'

He met her eye. 'Yes, Bess, I understand.'

CHAPTER THIRTY-THREE

1563

Robert jumped down from his horse and beheld Kenilworth. *His* Kenilworth. Elizabeth had not understated the matter when she said it was ruinous; some of the older structures had crumbled away and several chambers had lost their ceilings and were open to the air. But it was still impressive.

'Good day, my lord.' A large man with a shaggy beard waved a trowel at Robert from the bottom of a deep trench, touching his muddy fingers to his cap in deference.

'Turner. A fine day, is it not?'

'Aye, you picked the right day to come visiting, my lord. The sun hasn't shone this bright for many a day.'

'Has it slowed down the work?' Robert asked, wandering along the path. Turner climbed out of his ditch and hurried to catch his master up.

'A bit. But we have done quite a lot already.'

'Yes, it seems to be progressing well,' Robert agreed, trying to stop his nose from wrinkling at the smell coming off of Turner. 'How soon before it will be habitable, do you think?'

'Oh,' Turner shook his head, 'you've got quite a wait

for that, my lord. There's a fair amount of work to be done before you can think of settling.'

Robert gave him an apologetic smile. 'You'll have to forgive my impatience, Turner. My enthusiasm sometimes doesn't reconcile with common sense. The queen will visit here when it's done, you know.'

'Well, in time, my lord, it will be fit for such a great lady. Have no fear.'

Robert moved away, up the causeway, which he was having turned into a tiltyard. Already the earth had been turned, the ramparts built, the weeds plucked out, and the foundations of the viewing galleries at each end marked out with pegs. And there, to the right, would be the new stable block he had designed to house all the beautiful horses he was planning to buy, strong, graceful creatures from Ireland he knew Elizabeth wouldn't be able to resist.

'Robert!'

A female voice broke into his musings. He turned, one hand shielding his eyes from the sun to see a woman climbing down from a coach. She wore a dull grey dress, and a veil covered her head and shoulders.

'Mary!' He waved back. He ran up to her and kissed her through the veil. 'Why didn't you tell me you were coming? I might have missed you.'

'I came to see the castle, not you.'

'Oh, so you're not pleased to see me,' he teased.

'Of course I am,' she said, taking his arm. 'I'm glad you're here.'

'Well, what do you think?' he asked as they walked back along the causeway.

'I think it's going to take a lot of work. And money. Do you have enough?'

'I'll find it,' Robert shrugged. 'I can always find money.'

'I'm not sure the queen was being generous giving you

this. Couldn't she have found one that wasn't falling down?'

'It seems Elizabeth knows me better than you, sweet sister. I couldn't have hoped for anything better than Kenilworth. There isn't anything better. Anyway, enough about me. How are you?'

'As well as I can be.'

'I wish you would come back to court. I miss you, and so does the queen. I'm sure you exiling yourself at Penshurst makes her feel even more guilty.'

'So she should,' Mary retorted feelingly. 'Is it fair that I should bear all the scars of her disease and she emerges unscathed? Could she not have suffered just a little, too?'

'Don't be cruel, Mary.'

'Cruel?' she cried, throwing away his arm. 'Is it not cruel that my husband looks on me with disgust and not desire? And I can't blame him.'

'You are still his wife, Mary,' Robert said, grabbing her shoulders and bringing her to face him. 'He married you for yourself, not your face.' His fingers pulled gently at the veil. He meant to tear it from her head, to show her she had nothing to fear from showing her cruel affliction to the world, but her pitiful, half-smothered scream halted him. Instead, he put his arms around her waist and pulled her to him. 'I won't do it, I promise.' He felt her relax, and he released her. His eyes caught a movement back at the coach and his face broke into a grin. 'Is that who I think it is?'

Mary followed his gaze. 'It is. He jumped from the coach before I could stop him. I imagine he's been running around the castle, getting in everyone's way.'

'PHILIP!' Robert waved furiously.

The boy halted and looked around, startled, to find out who called his name. 'UNCLE ROB!' he yelled. He ran towards them and flung himself into his uncle's outstretched arms.

'Well, now I see who the favourite is in our family,' Mary laughed, as Robert propped his nephew on his hip.

'It's been ages since I've seen you, Uncle,' the boy scolded.

'I quite agree. It's a great fault in your mother not to bring you to see me more often, Phil. You can't be nagging her enough.'

'Mother told me this was a castle.'

'It *is* a castle,' Robert replied indignantly.

'But it's all broken.'

'At the moment, Phil. But you see all the men hereabouts? They're going to make this a dream castle and there will be no place like it in the whole of England. Shall it not look grand, Phil?' He tweaked the boy's nose and set him on his feet.

'The queen will visit, of course?' Mary asked.

'Of course, and she shall enjoy her stay. By Christ, she shall, Mary. But enough of her.'

Robert patted Philip on the shoulder, gave him a complicit wink and sprinted away, his spindly legged nephew running after him.

CHAPTER THIRTY-FOUR

Despite Robert's assurances, the French campaign to help the Huguenot Protestants was not a success. Ambrose tried, but the Huguenots inexplicably turned on their English allies to join with their Catholic enemies. It seemed Englishmen setting foot on French soil was enough to unite the two factions and turn them both against the English.

Ambrose asked for more men, more weapons and money to fight the French forces, but Elizabeth would not send them. And then disease swept through Ambrose's army, weakening it still further. All Ambrose could do was to seek a dignified surrender. He asked for permission from Elizabeth and she gave it, cursing Robert and Nicholas Throckmorton for persuading her to send men in the first place.

So Ambrose stood on the city walls of Newhaven, bargaining with the French below for terms of surrender. And a French musketeer, either bored or careless, shot him with a musket in the thigh. The surrender was made, and Ambrose and his army returned to England.

. . .

Robert rushed into the best bedroom in Master White's house, his face smeared with the dirt of the road. 'Ambrose. Dear Jesus, you look terrible.'

Ambrose tried to sit up, but he was too weak and sank back against the pillows. 'I can, at least, rely on you not to mince your words, Rob.'

Robert pressed his lips to his brother's fevered forehead and sat down on the edge of the bed. 'Have you seen a doctor?'

'Yes, he left not half an hour ago, and Master White is looking after me very well. How is it you've come here?'

'Thomas Wood wrote to me, said you were ill. Is it just the fever or is it your leg as well?'

Robert pulled back the bedclothes, wincing when he saw the bandage on Ambrose's thigh, his bright red blood staining the cloth.

'The fever is better than it was. My leg is very painful.'

'Trust you to get in the way of a musket ball.'

'I know. You should not get so close to me, Rob,' Ambrose said, giving him a gentle shove away. 'It would not do for you to catch my fever.'

'Oh, I never catch anything.' Robert waved away his concern and threw off his riding cloak.

'Still, you shouldn't have come.'

'Well, what could I do? I get a letter telling me my brother is gravely ill and it's a miracle he's still alive. As if I could stay at court once I knew that. Well, now that I have seen you and you are not likely to die just yet, I think I should let you sleep. I will ask Master White to put me up here until you are better and can come back to court with me. No, no argument. Sleep, Am.'

He stroked his fingers over his brother's already closing eyes.

. . .

'My lord.'

Master White stood at the foot of the stairs as Robert descended, his hand outstretched, holding a letter. 'This has just arrived for you. I believe it is from the queen,' he said reverentially.

'Thank you, Master White,' Robert said. 'It seems my brother will need to stay here for a while. May I too trespass upon your good nature and beg a bed for myself until he can move?'

'Certainly, my lord,' White said, his mind already calculating the extra expense he would incur for their provisioning. 'It would be an honour. I can arrange the chamber next to the earl for you if that would serve.'

'It would serve admirably, I thank you. And don't worry about the cost.' Robert untied the purse at his waist and passed it to him. 'That should be enough for a few days, at least.'

'Oh, my lord, it's not necessary,' White protested gratefully, clutching the money bag to his chest. 'Really.'

'Not another word,' Robert silenced him. 'Now, Master White, could I have somewhere private to read my letter?'

'Of course. Take my room, my lord. There is a comfortable chair and a jug of excellent wine you might wish to partake of.'

'I will gladly. I could also do with some food. It was a long ride here.' Robert smiled his charming smile and Master White scuttled off to order dinner for his guest.

Robert fell into the fireside chair and opened Elizabeth's letter. It was full of complaints. How dare Robert leave the court without permission? Ambrose had a fever, didn't he? Robert could catch it, become ill and then where would Elizabeth be? And what about her horses? Only at the close of the letter did Elizabeth think to ask how Ambrose fared.

Robert screwed up the letter and threw it in the fire.

CHAPTER THIRTY-FIVE

1564

Cecil leaned over Elizabeth's shoulder and murmured in her ear. 'Madam, the question of Mary Stuart's marriage has risen once again.'

Elizabeth glared up at him. 'Why so?'

'It seems she is now actively looking for a husband.'

Elizabeth glanced across the room to where Robert was talking with Henry Sidney. She knew Cecil still thought Robert was the best candidate for Mary's hand.

'Sit,' Elizabeth instructed. 'Lord Robert would have to be ennobled before Mary would even consider him.'

'You had planned to do that anyway, madam,' Cecil said, taking a seat. 'Indeed, it is time he was.'

'Are you so eager to be rid of him you would advance him so, Cecil?' she asked sharply.

'No, madam, but as you ennobled his brother, it is not unreasonable you would do so for one so close to your heart.'

'He is close to me, Cecil, but not so close that I am blind to all else. I see the advantages such a marriage would bring.' She paused. 'Write to Mary Stuart and propose Lord Robert.'

Cecil caught his breath. *A decision*, he thought. *A miracle.* 'I shall do so at once, madam,' he said and left before she changed her mind.

Elizabeth sighed and raising her hand, caught Robert's eye and crooked her finger at him. She watched him excuse himself from Henry's company and make his way towards her.

'You wanted me, Your Majesty?' he asked.

'Come and sit by me, Robin,' she said, indicating the chair vacated by Cecil. 'I need to talk to you.'

'This sounds serious,' he said, settling himself down.

She took hold of his hand beneath the table and held it in her lap. 'I've told Cecil to write to Mary Stuart. He is going to propose you as a husband for her.'

The colour drained from Robert's face. 'What?' he gasped.

'Now, don't be angry. I have my reasons.'

'The devil you do,' he declared. Elizabeth shushed him to lower his voice. 'What have I done to deserve this?'

'It's an honour, my sweet. You would be married to a queen.' She added sharply, 'I thought that was what you wanted.'

He glared at her. 'You're the only queen I want to marry. I don't want to be packed off to Scotland. You may as well kill me now.'

'Scotland isn't that bad.'

'You'd know that, would you? You, who have travelled so very extensively?'

Elizabeth's mouth pursed. 'I'll forgive you your temper. I admit, it took me a while to get used to the idea. God's Teeth, Robin, I no more want to lose you to Mary Stuart than you want to go. But for my security and for England's, I need her to have a husband whom I can trust.'

'What makes you think she'll even have me? I have no

rank. And worse, everyone knows I am your lover, don't they? Do you think she'll want your cast-off?'

'There's no need to be vulgar, Robin. And as for your rank, well, that can be easily remedied. I had planned to do it anyway,' she said, idly fingering a pearl on her dress.

'Do what?' he asked sulkily.

'Raise you to an earldom. I had thought Leicester would suit.'

Even that news could not lift Robert's spirits. 'Thank you,' he muttered. 'Did you say Cecil was writing to Scotland about me?'

'Yes.'

Robert shook his head understandingly. 'I see. He's outmanoeuvred me at last, hasn't he?'

'It *was* Cecil's idea,' Elizabeth admitted, adding slyly, 'I didn't think of it, wouldn't have thought of it, if it hadn't been for him.'

Robert stared out across the room, watching the dancers as they passed before him. 'Well, maybe it won't be as bad as I imagine. Mary Stuart is very beautiful, by all accounts, and comely. She'll keep my bed warm, if nothing else.'

Elizabeth threw his hand away and said, 'You can go now.'

Robert rose and gave a slight, very slight, bow. 'I hasten to do your bidding, Your Majesty, in this as in everything. Good night.'

Elizabeth watched him leave with tears in her eyes.

Cecil stifled a sigh. He had thought the queen beyond this kind of display. But there she was, placing the heavy ermine-trimmed robes around Robert Dudley's shoulders and running her fingers along his neck to play with the short stubs of his dark brown hair. And there was Norfolk. He had seen the familiarity too and was fuming. Unlike Cecil, Norfolk could never keep his temper in check.

So, Robert Dudley was now earl of Leicester and suitable for marriage with the Scottish queen. But Cecil had found out that Robert had written to Mary Stuart and told her he wasn't interested in becoming her husband. Cecil had wondered whether he should tell Elizabeth about it, but he wasn't sure the news wouldn't please her. She would, no doubt, interpret it as a reluctance to leave her. And now, seeing her act so familiarly, he wondered if she had ever really intended to let Robert go.

Women! Cecil thought in despair.

'What do you think of my new creation, Sir James?' Elizabeth asked.

Sir James Melville, the Scottish ambassador, looked over to where Robert chatted with Cecil and smiled. 'The earl of Leicester well becomes his new position, Your Majesty.'

'He does,' Elizabeth agreed. 'Will your queen like him, do you think?'

'How could she not?'

'She would be foolish indeed if she did not,' Elizabeth remarked. 'I must give you a present to give to my dear cousin, Mary.'

Melville followed her around the bed. He watched as she lifted the lid of a silver casket. Taking a piece of cloth, she unwrapped it and handed him a miniature of herself.

'A remarkable likeness,' he said. 'My queen will treasure it always.'

'I would like to have a picture of her in return.'

'I shall see to it. And who else is in there?' he said, peering into the box.

Elizabeth showed him the other miniatures in her box. 'This is my late stepmother, Queen Katherine. This, my father. This, my sister. And this...,' she hesitated.

Melville took the picture from her hands. 'Ah, Lord Robert. Forgive me, I mean the earl of Leicester. Perhaps I should take this to my queen. She has not got a likeness of the earl.'

Elizabeth snatched the miniature from his hand, placed it back in the box, and slammed down the lid. 'When my cousin has the earl of Leicester, I will have need of his portrait.'

Robert was playing with his new badge with its emblem of the bear and ragged staff.

'Can't you leave it alone?' Elizabeth teased.

'Give me something else to play with.'

She ignored the wink he gave her. 'You'll be playing tennis tomorrow. I've arranged for you and Norfolk to entertain the court with a match.'

'Can Norfolk even play?'

'He's actually very good.' Elizabeth leant forward and snatched the last almond biscuit from the plate as Robert reached for it. 'I hope you'll make it interesting.'

His eyes narrowed. 'What do you mean by interesting?'

'That's up to you.'

Robert frowned at her. 'I believe you want me to fight with him.'

'Don't be ridiculous. Why would I want my nobles fighting?'

'Because he's an idiot?' Robert suggested.

Elizabeth laughed. 'Robin, how dare you say such a thing about the noblest peer in the land?'

'Everyone thinks it.'

'Well, I will just say it would please me greatly if you

were to win tomorrow. Norfolk doesn't care for me, which doesn't trouble me greatly, for I neither need nor desire his affection, but I do want his respect. So, I would quite like to see Norfolk suffer a public defeat at your hands. That would hurt his pride a very great deal, I think.'

'Bess,' Robert said admiringly, 'you are a wicked woman.'

So much for putting Norfolk in his place, Robert thought, as the ball bounced past him and Norfolk scored another point. It looked as if he was going to lose the match and it would be he who would look like a fool. He raised his arm to serve, and sent the ball spinning across the net, heading directly for Norfolk. It punched into Norfolk's stomach, causing the duke to double over in pain.

'My apologies, Norfolk,' Robert called out, pleased to hear sniggers from the viewing gallery. 'Perhaps if you were quicker on your feet.'

That remark earned him a ripple of laughter from the spectators. Robert served again. Norfolk returned it with a vengeance, but Robert side-stepped it neatly. He lobbed the ball high. It hit the angled wall and bounced off. Norfolk was too slow and missed it. Another point to Robert and he cheered up. Norfolk's anger only increased and his frustration hampered his game. He lost point after point and Robert won the match easily.

'Congratulations, my lord,' Elizabeth called to Robert, 'and commiserations to you, Your Grace.' She unclasped a jewelled brooch from her bodice and threw it to Robert as a prize. He caught it and kissed it. 'God's Death, but you are both sweating like pigs.'

Robert grinned, leant over the railing and took her handkerchief from her lap. He wiped his forehead.

Norfolk's red face turned purple at his impudence. 'You knave,' he roared, quieting all the voices around. 'How dare you take such a liberty?'

Robert stared at him, open-mouthed. He could not believe Norfolk was serious, but the duke was trembling all over with rage. Robert shook his head, laughing.

Norfolk lunged at Robert and grabbed his shirt. 'You bastard,' he hissed, spittle dabbling Robert's chin. 'I'll teach you.'

'Enough.' Elizabeth's voice rang out loud. 'How dare you presume so much, Norfolk?'

Norfolk lowered his arm. 'I was thinking of your honour, Your Majesty.'

'Indeed? Is my honour so fragile that it cannot stand some honest fellow's handling?'

'Honest fellow?' Norfolk scoffed, his bluster returning. 'Hardly a label I would credit a Dudley with.'

'Kiss my feet, you miserable dog,' Robert snarled and the two men squared up again, but Elizabeth had had enough.

'Will you brawl in my presence? Two of my nobles making such a spectacle of themselves! You, my lord,' she pointed at Norfolk, 'learn to contain your spleen or I will have you sent from court. And you, Lord Leicester, show due courtesy in future. Ladies, away.'

Mary followed her brother back to his rooms. He had persuaded her to attend court for a few weeks, but had not persuaded her to remove her veil.

'Honestly, Rob, you should be careful.'

He threw open the door to his bedchamber and strode inside. 'Careful?' he scoffed. 'I have nothing to worry about.'

'Not from the queen. I mean, you should be careful of the duke. The Howards are a crafty lot, they always have been. Are you going to change your clothes?'

'In a minute,' he said, pouring himself a large cup of beer. He gulped it down, wiping his sleeve across his mouth. 'By Christ, I needed that.'

'Thirsty work?'

Both he and Mary turned. Elizabeth was in the doorway, smiling.

'Damned thirsty,' he replied. 'Are you coming in or are you planning to linger there?'

She stepped inside, one of her Ladies, Lettice Devereux, close at her heels. 'Lettice, you may go. Lady Sidney is here to attend me.'

Lettice glanced at Robert as she dropped a curtsey, gave him a quick flutter of her eyelashes and retreated, closing the door as she left. Elizabeth sat down on the bed.

'Mary was just saying I should be careful of the Howards.' Robert poured water from a jug into a large bowl. 'She doesn't like the duke.'

'Few people do,' Elizabeth said. 'He's not an easy man to like.'

'He's a pompous ass,' Robert said, leaning against the cabinet.

Elizabeth looked him over, her gaze taking in his long legs, his chest where a thin long triangle of skin and dark curly hair peeped through his open shirt. She looked away as heat flooded up her neck.

Robert caught his sister's eye and jerked his head at the door. Mary understood and frowned, but his eyes were insistent.

'Madam,' she said huffily, 'would you give me leave to fetch something from my room?'

'Of course, Mary,' Elizabeth answered quickly, a quiver in her voice.

Mary exited. Robert turned back to the bowl of water and pulled his shirt over his head. With his back to her, Elizabeth could look at him all she pleased; the smoothness of his skin, the curves of it as it stretched over bone and muscle. She watched as he splashed water on his face, over the back of his neck and chest. Water trickled down his spine. He turned, grabbed a linen cloth and slowly, deliberately, rubbed his chest dry. Elizabeth met his eye, and a tremor ran through her.

Robert moved to the door and locked it, turning the key slowly, giving her a chance to protest. But Elizabeth said nothing.

She stood up to meet him, tilting her head back, ready for his kiss. His lips pushed against her, his tongue lapping at her teeth to open. She gave in and he thrust his tongue deep into her mouth. Her hands ran over his naked back, grabbing and scratching at the wonderful feel of his skin. Robert pushed her back onto the bed and made a grab at her skirts.

Her heart was pounding as she felt his hand on her thigh. Panic gripped at her stomach and she couldn't breathe. Wrenching her mouth from his, she pushed him away and scrambled to the other side of the bed.

'Unlock the door,' she cried. 'UNLOCK IT.'

Robert hurried to the door and turned the key. 'Bess,' he asked quietly, 'what have I done?'

'It's not your fault.'

'I wouldn't hurt you.'

'I know. I just... I can't, Robin, I can't.'

She rose on shaky legs from the bed and smoothed down her skirts. She pressed her fingers to her lips, tentatively, as if they were bruised. 'You should get dressed. And then... then we will play a game of cards. I'll wait for you. In there.' She strode into the adjacent chamber, closing the door behind her.

'You took your time,' he heard her say, and he realised Mary had returned. He pulled on a clean shirt and doublet. Taking a deep breath and fixing a smile upon his face, he joined the women.

CHAPTER THIRTY-SIX

Elizabeth was experimenting, trying to see if she could bear to live without Robert by her side. Thomas Heneage was handsome and very attentive. She liked him and his company made a change. Yes, perhaps Heneage would do. For a while, at least.

Heneage suggested a walk. Elizabeth agreed, taking his arm as he led her out into the gardens. She caught Robert's eye as they passed his card table, but she wasn't able to read his expression.

'Your turn, Rob,' Henry Sidney prompted. 'Is something wrong?'

Robert selected a card and laid it down. 'No.'

Henry cast a look at the retreating queen and her companion. Her ladies trailed a discreet distance behind. 'Has the queen upset you?'

'Why would she have upset me?'

'Well, she seems to spend a great deal of time with Thomas Heneage.'

'She can spend time with whomever she likes,' Robert said carelessly, winning the game and taking his money. A ripple of laughter filtered through the window from the group outside. 'Heneage has taken her fancy, that's all. You know how she is, Hal. She's like a butterfly, flitting from one flower to the next. She gets bored and moves on to another.'

'The queen's bored with you? I can't believe that.'

Robert shrugged.

'I'm surprised you're taking it so calmly. It can't mean good for you if you're no longer in favour.'

'What harm can it do me? I have my earldom. I have my estates and, if the plan holds, I'll soon have a royal wife as well.'

Henry's mouth dropped open. 'You mean you *are* going to marry—'

'Not Elizabeth. Mary Stuart. Maybe. Thomas Heneage is obviously my replacement.'

'The queen would send you to Scotland?'

'That's why I was given my earldom, to make me more suitable for a queen.'

'You want to marry Mary Stuart?'

Robert leant back in his chair and blew out a puff of air. It was hot and he could feel his shirt sticking to his skin. 'The idea is growing on me. Especially now I see how Elizabeth treats me. She toys with me, Hal, and I am getting mightily tired of it.'

'So, seek a diversion. There must be plenty of willing women at court.'

'Oh, they're willing enough, but if Elizabeth found out, you know how possessive she is. Then again, now she has Heneage, she may not be watching me too closely.'

'Well, then. Let's pick one for you.'

'Henry,' Robert scolded, almost embarrassed as Henry twisted in his seat to peruse the company.

'I know,' he said. 'Lettice Devereux. Now, she, Rob, is a beauty.'

'A beauty with a husband.'

'Who is in Ireland, I believe, and none too sorry that he is there, I should say. What do you think of her?'

Robert glanced over Henry's shoulder, out of the window to where Lettice stood, looking bored and glancing longingly back to the chamber. He had noticed Lettice often, for her auburn hair, thicker and more lustrous than her cousin the queen, made her stand out. She had perfect and soft, creamy skin, a comely figure and inviting eyes that often looked his way. They were doing so now. He met them with his own and inclined his head towards her. Lettice returned a surprised, radiant smile.

Robert said, 'I think she will do very well.'

Robert hadn't planned to approach Lettice in the corridor, but he had been on his way to the stables to inspect the horses when he bumped into her.

'Good morning, Lady Essex.' Robert made a deep bow, which she returned with a low curtsey, the fingers of her right hand playing with the low neck of her bodice. He noticed the round swell of her breasts beneath the green silk and felt the first stirring of lust. He sighed dramatically. 'What a very lucky man your husband is, Lady Essex.'

'To be serving in Ireland?'

'To be married to you.'

She gave a little laugh, smooth and low. 'Much good it does him, being so far away.'

'Do you mind so very much?'

'I find I can bear it well.'

'You're not lonely, then?' Robert moved closer.

She lowered her eyes. 'I sometimes yearn for company.'

'But you have the constant company of the queen's Ladies.'

Lettice shook her head. 'The company of women can

become very tedious. I find the company of men more agreeable.'

She looked at him, and he knew they need not play the game any longer. They both wanted the same thing.

'Dine with me, Lettice,' he said, lowering his voice.

'When?'

'Tonight.'

'I'd love to.'

'Lady Essex!' Elizabeth's strident voice made them both jump. 'What do you do here?' She strode up to them and glared.

'Nothing, Your Majesty,' Lettice said, her voice trembling.

'And you, my lord?'

'I was on my way to the stables,' Robert said, damned if he was going to show fear of Elizabeth.

'Indeed. Are my horses to be found in the corridors of my palace?'

Robert looked away, irritated by her sarcasm.

'The earl of Leicester was kind enough to enquire of my health, Your Majesty,' Lettice said.

'Your health is no concern of his,' Elizabeth snorted derisively. 'And from the look of you two, I doubt very much that was his concern. Or is enquiring of your health a euphemism for intending to cuckold your husband, madam?'

Lettice let out a gasp of shock and surprise, her cheeks flushing red as the other Ladies giggled.

'That remark is not worthy of you, Your Majesty,' Robert growled feelingly.

'Get out of my sight,' Elizabeth hissed, the tendons in her neck sticking out. 'Before my temper gets the better of me. By Christ, if my father were alive, he would have had your head for what you just said to me.'

'That being the case, perhaps you wish me to leave the court,' Robert suggested, his chin rising defiantly.

'Oh, no, sir. You have duties, do you not? And besides, it suits me to have you here. For when people see you trotting around court like the dog you are, they know I am here. And damn you, sir, you will be brought to heel.'

Elizabeth adjusted her bonnet and made her way across the lawn. She stood back a little as Robert drew the bow and watched as the arrow thudded into the edge of the butt. She clapped the poor shot to make her presence known.

Robert glanced over his shoulder. At first, the spectator appeared to be a dairymaid, and he thought it impertinent of her to stop and watch him, let alone applaud. But then he looked a little harder beneath the flapping cloth cap.

'Elizabeth?'

She folded the fabric back. 'Yes, it's me.'

'What the devil are you doing dressed like that?'

'It was the only way I could escape the prying eyes of my Ladies. Kat got the dress for me.' She held out the loose skirts and twirled round. 'Do you like it?'

He lied and said yes. In truth, the dowdy garb did little to flatter her thin, boyish body. Elizabeth needed the sparkle of jewels and fine fabrics to make her beautiful.

'Why did you need to escape?' he asked.

'I wanted to see you alone.'

'Oh, yes?'

'I wanted to say sorry.'

'Well, that can't be easy for you.'

Elizabeth held her tongue. 'Your aim's off,' she said, pointing to the butt.

'You called me a dog.'

'I know, I'm sorry. But you did provoke me.'

'By talking to Lettice Devereux?'

'She's a wanton.'

'She's your cousin. And did she deserve to be banished from court?'

'I don't want to talk about Lettice,' Elizabeth sighed. 'Robin, say you forgive me.'

'Get rid of Heneage and I'll forgive you.'

'I will,' she said gratefully.

'Very well, then,' he shrugged. 'After all, you can have him back when I'm in Scotland.'

'Yes, I suppose I can,' Elizabeth said quietly, handing him another arrow.

'I hear Lord Darnley wants to go to Scotland to look over his estates,' Robert said. 'Maybe he and I could travel up together. I'd be glad of the company.'

'Darnley's not going to Scotland.'

'Why not?'

'Darnley has a claim to my throne and Mary Stuart knows it.' Her voice grew hard. 'If she laid her greedy eyes on him, she would probably marry him to strengthen her own claim and annoy me. Mind you, I could wish her joy of him. Do you know, his mother thinks he's an angel? She has no idea of what he gets up to when he's out of her sight.'

'He's a great frequenter of the Southwark stews, I hear.'

'So Cecil tells me. His mother spoils and indulges him and he thinks himself the loveliest creature alive.'

'Well, if you won't let him go, I'll have to go on my own, then.'

Elizabeth was silent for a long moment. Then she asked, 'Dine with me?'

'If you want me to.'

'I'll expect you.'

She walked away. She was hoping he would say something, call her back, apologise for sulking, but Elizabeth made it back to the palace without Robert saying a word.

Elizabeth couldn't sleep. What Robert had said about taking Heneage back when he was in Scotland troubled her. As if Thomas Heneage could take his place! She had thought that perhaps he could, once. But the past week when she and Robert hadn't been talking had been unbearable. She couldn't live the rest of her life like that. No, Robert must not, could not go. She couldn't let Mary Stuart have him.

But what to do about Mary? Resolved on the matter of Robert, her mind cleared. She knew Darnley's parents had ideas of marrying him to Mary Stuart, hence the sudden plan to inspect his Scottish estates. Did they think she was a fool? How she loathed Darnley; there was something about him that made her skin crawl. To think that he had Tudor blood!

No doubt Mary would think he was wonderful. Elizabeth felt almost sure of that. It was strange. Although they had never met, Elizabeth felt she understood her cousin, despite their differences. The thought of Mary being wedded to that poor excuse for a man! What a jolly dance Darnley would lead her. She pulled the covers up to her chin and closed her eyes.

Seconds later, they snapped open. *Yes*, she thought with pleasure, *what a jolly dance*! Maybe Darnley should be allowed to go to Scotland after all.

They were listening to the boy singing. Robert reached for another grape and popped it into his mouth. With juice squirting over his tongue, he asked, 'So, when am I going to Scotland?'

255

Elizabeth slid him a sideways glance. 'You're not going. You know you're not going. Don't pretend to be ignorant.'

Robert smiled smugly. 'So, Mary Stuart has definitely married Lord Darnley.'

'Well and truly wed,' Elizabeth confirmed, biting down on a walnut. 'The stupid woman.'

'You really don't like her, do you?'

Elizabeth curled her lip. 'She rules with her heart, not her head. A woman like that is not fit to be a queen. And she wants my throne.'

'Might she not get it, with Darnley as her husband?'

'It's a risk, I know,' she acknowledged. 'But Cecil has heard Darnley is already causing Mary problems and my hope is he will cause her more. She has had the sense not to make him king, and he resents that. I suppose you take his part on that issue?'

Robert ignored her remark. 'Has Cecil heard anything about the little Italian, the Pope's spy – oh, sorry, the queen's musician?'

Elizabeth laughed at his wit. 'He seems to be befriending Darnley.'

'Befriending? I know Darnley is game for anything, but is Rizzio a catamite?'

Elizabeth shrugged. 'He's a filthy little Italian. Who can say what he gets up to?'

'They're very cunning, Italians.'

'They're not the only ones,' Elizabeth said pointedly. 'I thought you might tell me what you've been up to, Robin. With Norfolk, your newfound friend.'

Robert shifted uneasily. 'I don't know what you're talking about.'

'Oh, yes you do, you little toad. I know you and him and others on my council are trying to get rid of Cecil. Don't deny it,' she held up a hand to halt his protestations. 'I know all about it.'

'Bess, I can explain—'

'I hope for your sake you can.'

'Norfolk approached me. He said it was because of Cecil's contriving that we had not married, that it was Cecil's idea to marry me to Mary Stuart and—'

'And you believed him?'

Robert gestured helplessly. 'He sounded plausible. Cecil has done me many an ill turn over the years. I know that to be true, if nothing else. And I was angry with you at the time, all that business with Heneage and Lettice. I suppose I wasn't thinking properly. You can understand that?'

'I suppose I can. But what an idiot you must be to think I would ever give up Cecil. He is worth ten of you, all of you, and let me tell you, any mistakes he makes, I will forgive, as I would forgive them in you.'

'You mean—,' he reached for her hand and she didn't draw it away. 'You mean I'm not to be punished?'

'Oh, you're quite safe. It's Norfolk I blame. Oh, why am I plagued by such cousins?'

'Why don't you send him away? Back to the north, where he belongs?'

'Because he could cause more trouble for me there than here. No, I want him under my eye.'

'I'm sorry, Bess, truly. Tell me, does Cecil know about what we were planning?'

Elizabeth threw his hand away with a snort of contempt. 'Of course he does. Who do you think told me?'

CHAPTER THIRTY-SEVEN

1566

'Rob, Rob,' Elizabeth shook him roughly. 'Oh God, please wake up.'

Robert opened his eyes. 'Bess?'

She was leaning over him, strands of hair escaping from her nightcap and hanging down to tickle his face. The moonlight darkened the hollows of her face. 'I need you.'

'What time is it? What's the matter?'

She propped herself on the edge of his bed. 'I didn't know it would happen like this. I swear to God, I didn't.'

'Bess,' he took hold of her arm, 'tell me what's happened.'

'David Rizzio has been murdered. Cecil just told me.'

'But we knew that was going to happen. We saw a copy of the murder bond the Scottish lords signed.'

'I know, I know, but they killed him in front of her.'

'They did what?' Robert was aghast.

Elizabeth shifted on the bed to face him. 'They were having supper, Rizzio and Mary. The lords burst in on them and told Rizzio he was about to die. Rizzio clung on to her skirts and begged Mary to help him, but they dragged him into the next room and stabbed him, again and again.'

'My God!'

'Mary must have heard his screams. They held her back. Those brutes took hold of their sovereign queen and used force against her.'

'Was her husband there?'

'Oh, he was there, the miserable wretch. He watched as Rizzio was killed and did nothing to protect her, not even when Ruthven held a pistol to her swollen belly and threatened to shoot. His wife and unborn child threatened and Darnley did nothing.'

'Is Mary hurt?'

She buried her face in her hands. 'I don't know. Bothwell helped her to get away. He had horses, and they rode to ... somewhere.… I can't remember.'

'She's seven months gone with child,' Robert said in astonishment. 'To take to horse at such a time—'

'Could kill her and the child,' Elizabeth finished. 'Think how desperate she must have been.'

'So, she has Bothwell with her?'

Elizabeth gave a short, hard laugh. 'And Darnley.'

'Darnley?'

'She had to take him with her. She convinced him the lords meant to kill him next, so he would help her escape. By Christ, if I had been her and had a dagger, I would have stabbed him for his treachery.'

'So, it seems Mary is safe for the moment, Bess. What upsets you so?'

She drew in a deep, shuddering breath. 'Is it my fault? Is it, Rob? I sent Darnley to her. I wanted him to cause trouble. Did I make this happen?'

'Bess, that's ridiculous. How could you have foreseen

this? Darnley, of his own accord, made himself a friend to the Scottish lords. He may not have wielded a dagger himself, but he signed their bond to murder the little Italian. All your council knew of it and decided not to act. This is not your fault and I don't want to hear any more such nonsense that it is. You hear me?'

He wrapped his arms around her, and she leant against his chest. 'Oh, none other can comfort me as you can,' she said. 'I thank God for you, Rob.'

'I'll always be here for you. But Bess – not that I mind, you understand – but I think it will do your reputation no good if you stay much longer in my chamber at this time of night.'

She laughed and gave a small nod. 'I'm sorry for waking you, Rob.'

'Don't be sorry. Come,' he gestured for her to move and he threw back the bedclothes, tugging his nightshirt down to cover his legs. 'I'll take you back to bed.'

He put his arm around Elizabeth's waist and led her back to the bedchamber, past the two Ladies who had been searching the corridors, wondering where their mistress had got to in the middle of the night.

'How is she?' Cecil asked anxiously as Robert emerged from the queen's chamber.

'Better, I think,' he sighed.

Cecil rubbed his forehead. 'I had no idea the news would distress her so, else I would not have told her in such a way.'

Elizabeth had been dancing in the Great Hall when Cecil had delivered the news that Mary Stuart had given birth to a son.

'Don't blame yourself. Elizabeth seemed merry enough.'

'Do you know what she meant by "I am of barren stock"?'

'It's obvious, isn't it? The Tudors were never good breeders, Cecil. Mary Stuart now has a son and heir and Elizabeth does not.'

'Maybe now she will look to remedy that,' Cecil said hopefully. 'With a suitable nobleman,' he added.

'Of course,' Robert replied sarcastically. 'Come, there's no point loitering outside her door. She will be abed soon enough. Do you care for a drink before turning in, Cecil?'

Cecil would not ordinarily be inclined to spend time with Robert, but he wanted news of his concern for Elizabeth to get back to her, and he followed Robert to his chamber. They settled before the fire, each with a cup of Rhenish wine in their hands.

'It's a wonder Mary didn't lose the baby, really,' Robert mused. 'That long ride after Rizzio's murder. I suppose it is healthy?'

'The report from Sir Nicholas says the child is quite robust and, more importantly, Darnley has acknowledged it as his, which should put down the rumours about Rizzio being the father.'

'So, the boy is confirmed legitimate.'

'Indeed.' Cecil nibbled at his bottom lip. 'The queen will be all right, won't she?'

'Cecil, Elizabeth will be fine. She has these sudden moods, you know, ever since Rizzio's murder.'

'Yes, I've noticed.'

'Talking of which, what has happened to the Scottish lords who killed him?'

'They've been imprisoned, all except Mary's half-brother, James Moray. He's on his way here because he is not safe from his sister in Scotland.'

'Is Mary Stuart safe on her throne?'

'It appears she is.'

Robert rubbed his chin. 'I can't quite work out whether that's a good or bad turn of events for us.'

'Well, it means Scotland has a stable government once again, but it also means a Catholic rules it with affiliations to both France and Spain. Oh, if only Moray had been born on the right side of the blanket and he was king of Scotland.'

'What a lot of problems that would solve,' Robert agreed.

The Rhenish was making Cecil languid; he slouched in his chair. 'What is it, Leicester, that the queen has against Mary Stuart? Do you know?'

'Other than the political reasons, you mean? In my honest opinion, Cecil, vanity and jealousy. Mary Stuart is reputed to be a great beauty, a great charmer of men. She is a rival to Elizabeth and Elizabeth has never liked competition.'

'Was she like that as a child?'

'She certainly liked to have her own way,' Robert laughed, 'but then, what royal child doesn't? I remember Edward could be almost uncontrollable at times, demanding this and that. Barnaby Fitzpatrick would often have to take a beating for Edward's behaviour. Elizabeth was a little different. She knew what liberties she could take and never went beyond them, but she always had to win, that I do remember.'

'And, of course, you let her.'

'Not always,' Robert replied with a grin. 'Well, she was a girl and, royal or not, I had my pride, too.'

'I've met Mary Stuart, and she was very charming and quite lovely. She might be different now, of course, after what she's been through. She had a softer appearance than Elizabeth, I think. More womanly.'

'Elizabeth will be interested in your opinion,' Robert said, hiding his smile behind his cup.

Cecil sat bolt upright in the chair, holding his hand out to Robert. 'Oh, no, I didn't mean—'

'Cecil, I'm teasing,' Robert said, his eyes twinkling. 'She'd box my ears if I said that to her.' His face became serious. 'Is Darnley back in the conjugal bed?'

'I wonder,' Cecil shrugged. 'Is Mary Stuart a forgiving woman? I don't think so. Her great love for him seemed to die almost as soon as they had married. She had little time for him before the Rizzio murder and she stuck with him out of necessity. It is rumoured Darnley has the pox.'

'That doesn't surprise me. I hear he was as great a frequenter of the Scottish brothels as he was of the English ones.'

'He certainly took no pains to conceal his visits.' Cecil looked down at his empty cup. 'There is another rumour bruited abroad. That of a relationship between Mary Stuart and the earl of Bothwell.'

Robert's mouth fell open. 'Is it true?'

'It's a rumour. I can get it neither confirmed nor denied.'

'But if it is true?'

'Then the future may be very bleak indeed for Darnley.'

'You don't mean—'

'The Scottish are very fond of murdering people, Leicester, and they don't care if they're seen to be doing it.'

'You think Darnley's life could be in danger? But even if Darnley was out of the way, Mary would surely not marry Bothwell. He's a Protestant and only an earl.'

'You are only an earl,' Cecil pointed out, 'and yet you were considered suitable as a husband for her.'

'Don't remind me,' Robert muttered. 'But what then? I mean, if she were to marry Bothwell?'

'Who can say?' Cecil said. 'I think we're looking a little too far in the future to speak with any accuracy. Now,' he put down his empty cup and rose. 'I must get to my bed. You will, no doubt, see the queen before I do tomorrow. You will convey to her my concern for her wellbeing?'

'Of course I will, Cecil. Get you to bed.'

'Thank you. Goodnight, Leicester.'

'I think you must be a Master of the Dark Arts, Cecil,' Robert whispered in his ear, making him jump.

Cecil looked at him, shocked. 'What do you mean?'

'Well, don't you remember, you predicted this – why, it must have been nearly two years ago now. You predicted Darnley would be in danger, and before long, Darnley is dead. Mary Stuart promptly marries Bothwell, who probably killed him, with or without her knowledge or instigation.'

'I merely prognosticated a chain of events based on experience, Leicester. I do not appreciate accusations of necromancy being hurled in my direction.'

'It was only a joke, Cecil,' Robert protested with a laugh. 'But you got it right, didn't you? If only you hadn't stopped there and foretold the rest.'

'I could not have predicted what followed,' Cecil assured him.

The Scottish lords had risen up against Mary and Bothwell and defeated them. They had imprisoned Mary at Lochleven Castle and Bothwell fled to Denmark. But then, Mary Stuart escaped and made her way to England, foolishly thinking her English cousin would be sympathetic to her plight and help restore her to her throne.

'What a convenient memory that woman must have,' Robert mused. 'To have forgotten all the insults and trouble she has given Elizabeth over the years, and to think Elizabeth would too.'

Cecil grunted. 'Must you hover about my shoulder like a bad angel?'

'Prickly today, aren't we?'

'This situation makes things very difficult.'

'Why?'

'What are we to do with Mary Stuart?' Cecil gestured hopelessly. 'The Scottish don't want her back, which suits us very well. Catherine de Medici won't have her in France. Spain may offer her a place to live in view of her Catholicism, but the truth is they don't want her, either.'

'We'll have to keep her,' Robert shrugged.

'I suppose we will, but at a very great expense. And it's a dangerous situation to find ourselves in, Leicester. With Mary in England, it is a perfect opportunity for the English Catholics to try to put her on the throne. You know how they feel about our queen. I promise you, Elizabeth's life will not be safe as long as Mary is here.'

'Have you told the queen this?'

'Yes, I have,' Cecil said, stiffening.

'And?'

'And she told me that if I was thinking of having Mary Stuart done away with, she would get one of her guards to run me through with their halberd.'

Robert burst out laughing. 'So that's why you're so touchy. And were you?'

'Was I what?'

'Thinking of having Mary Stuart killed?'

'No, my lord, I was not.'

'Well, I don't care what's done with her, as long as I'm not expected to marry her again.'

'She's still married to Bothwell.'

'I'm glad to hear it. So, the queen's in an ill temper, is she? Well, I've suddenly remembered I've got some work to do. If she asks, tell her I can't be found, will you, Cecil? There's a good fellow.'

Robert patted his shoulder and sauntered away. Elizabeth looked up and crooked her finger at Cecil.

Cecil took a deep breath and headed towards her.

CHAPTER THIRTY-EIGHT

1571

Robert stroked the smooth white thigh laying over his own. It caused the owner to moan and turn over, presenting him with a full, rounded buttock. He smirked, raising his hand to give it a playful slap, but changed his mind. *Let her sleep*, he thought.

He yawned as there came a knock at the door. 'Wait,' he called, easing his legs to the floor. He retrieved his shirt from the floor and pulled it over his head where it barely covered his nakedness. 'Come in,' he said, pulling the bed hangings together.

Peters pretended not to notice the dress thrown over the chest at the foot of the bed. 'My lord, the duke of Norfolk is in the antechamber. He wishes to speak with you.'

Robert groaned. 'What the devil does he want?'

'He didn't say, my lord. I told him you were not to be disturbed, but he insisted.'

'Very well.' Robert pulled on his hose and slipped his feet into shoes. 'But he shall have to take me as I am.' He followed Peters into the adjoining chamber, closing the door behind him. 'You wanted to see me, Your Grace?'

Norfolk looked Robert up and down, his lip curling at his disarray. 'Did I get you from your bed?'

'Just a brief nap. The queen didn't need me.'

'A nap? Really?' Norfolk raised a sceptical eyebrow. He sighed impatiently and glanced around the room, anywhere but at Robert and his naked legs. 'There is a rumour bruited about the court that I should marry Mary Stuart.'

'Yes, I've heard that rumour. But isn't she still married to Bothwell?'

'The Pope has already agreed the marriage was forced upon her. An annulment could be easily arranged.'

'You sound as if you want to marry her.'

'If it would serve Her Majesty, I am prepared to marry the Stuart woman.'

'Well, I would wish you luck. Her husbands are not the most fortunate of men.'

Norfolk waved that concern aside. 'I am, of course, eminently suitable to marry with someone of her rank. I am the highest peer in England. I have royal blood in my veins—'

'And you are a Catholic,' Robert interrupted, bored with the pedigree, 'which should make you even more agreeable to Mary Stuart.'

Norfolk's eyes narrowed. 'I am of the New Religion, Leicester—'

'No, you conform to it, Norfolk. You hide your true allegiance poorly.'

'I don't care what you think you know about me—'

'Oh, come now, you must care a little.'

Norfolk stepped up to Robert. 'Let me make one thing clear between us. We care not a jot for one another, and if it wouldn't mean my head on a block, I would gladly kill you where you stand. But the queen has a misguided attachment to you and I admit you have your uses. That is the only reason I am standing here now.'

'What do you want from me?' Robert asked.

'Nothing but your support for this marriage.'

'You want me to join forces with you again, after the fiasco of your Cecil intrigue?'

'We were foolish to think that the queen would turn against Cecil,' Norfolk admitted. 'But she will see the sense in this.'

'Well, *I* don't see the sense in it.'

'For God's sake, Leicester, if I were her husband, I would tame Mary Stuart. There would be no need for the queen to fear her. With England's help, Mary Stuart could be reinstated on her throne—'

'And you would get a crown.'

'Which is no more than you desire here in England.'

Robert considered. 'Do you think you could stomach Scotland, Norfolk? It's a savage country.'

'So is the north of England, Leicester. I manage that well enough.'

'Well, in that case, you have my support.'

'I wonder...,' Norfolk began and paused, embarrassed. 'I wonder if you would speak with the queen about it.'

'You want *me* to ask her?'

'I thought it might be better coming from you.' Robert smiled, which annoyed Norfolk. 'Very well.'

'Good.' Norfolk shuffled his feet, unsure what to say or do next. Gratitude was called for, he knew, but he couldn't bring himself to thank Robert. 'I'll be going then.'

'You're welcome,' Robert called out as he left, causing Norfolk to nearly walk into the doorframe.

Elizabeth had declared it was too hot to move about and had instructed all the windows to be thrown open. Cushions had been strewn upon the floor and she and Robert lay there like bees drunk with pollen, too stupefied to move.

'Is that Norfolk hovering?' Elizabeth jerked her chin towards the opposite end of the corridor.

Robert glanced behind him. 'I'm rather afraid it is, Bess.'

Elizabeth groaned. 'Oh, what can he want? Go and find out, Rob, but don't bring him back with you. I don't think I can bear him today.'

Robert got to his feet and sauntered over to Norfolk. 'Can I help you, Your Grace?'

'Have you spoken to her yet?' Norfolk demanded.

'No, not yet.'

'Why the devil not?'

'I've been waiting for the right moment to approach her.'

'So, what's wrong with now?'

'All right, I'll talk to her now. But don't wait here. I'll let you know later.'

'I'll come to your rooms after six. Don't keep me waiting.' Norfolk strode off.

'Well, what did he want?' Elizabeth asked as he plumped back down on the cushion.

'He asked me a few weeks ago to speak with you on a delicate matter. Regarding Mary Stuart.'

Elizabeth looked away. 'Oh, yes?'

'He wants—'

'Since when have you and Norfolk been such good friends?'

'We're not,' Robert assured her.

'Then why are you doing his begging for him?'

'I'm not begging. Besides, you don't know what I'm going to say yet.'

'I do know what you're going to say,' Elizabeth replied energetically. 'You must all think I'm stupid.'

Robert was startled. 'What am I going to say, Bess?'

'Norfolk wants to marry Mary Stuart. He wants you to find out if I'm agreeable to the idea.'

Robert stared at her, open-mouthed. 'I think you must be a witch, Bess.'

'Cecil keeps me fully informed,' Elizabeth said. 'Unlike some.'

'You think I should have told you this before?'

'Well, don't you?'

'It's only a question of marriage, Bess.'

'It's not just marriage,' she cried, her voice rising. 'God, what a fool you are! He's plotting rebellion, Robert. Do you hear me? Rebellion. Marriage to Mary Stuart is only the first stage.'

'Bess, I didn't realise,' he protested.

'There seems to be much you don't realise.'

He swallowed and licked his dry lips. 'I'll tell him no then, shall I?'

'You'll tell him nothing, for the present.'

'Why not?'

'He expects me to say no, so he's making contingency plans. He's written to Mary, offering himself, and she's accepted him. They're not prepared to wait for my permission. What they are preparing for is to act. As uncrowned king of the North, he thinks he can raise an army to rise against me.'

'Bess, for God's sake, you must have him arrested.'

'Not yet.' She shook her head and reached for her fan.

'But if he's plotting against you—'

'We will wait. That's what I want, and Cecil agrees with me. We wait.'

'I don't understand. Wait for what?'

'For Norfolk to incriminate himself. Which he will do, before long.'

'How can you be so sure?'

'Why, Robin,' she looked up at him, wide-eyed, 'it's a gift we witches have.'

'What is Elizabeth playing at?' Robert shoved Ambrose's letter across the table to Cecil. 'My brother tells me it is common knowledge the Northern earls are planning a rebellion, so why aren't they under arrest?'

'We want time to gather evidence against them.' 'Surely there is evidence enough!' Robert scoffed. 'We want more,' Cecil replied simply.

'What about Norfolk then?'

'Ah,' Cecil raised an eyebrow, 'there I have some news that will please you. The queen has ordered his arrest.'

'But Norfolk has left the court,' Robert said, sitting up in agitation. 'I saw him leaving.'

'Don't concern yourself. He is being pursued and will be brought back to the Tower.'

'Thank God for that. Let's just make sure he stays there, where he can't cause us any more trouble.'

But Elizabeth released Norfolk. He behaved himself for a while, but he soon grew restless and began writing to the Scottish queen again. They picked up where they had left off, with talk of marriage and usurpation. Cecil knew about it from the start, of course. There wasn't a noble's house in England that did not house his spies. So, Norfolk was arrested and went back to the Tower. The Northern earls he had been plotting with heard of his arrest and decided to go ahead without him. Their rebellion failed, and they were punished.

Norfolk, meanwhile, begged the queen to show him mercy. Elizabeth may have been prepared to forgive Norfolk, but there were men on her council who would not.

Cecil winced as he shifted his swaddled foot on the stool. He looked across the bed. 'I didn't hear what the doctor said.'

Robert kept his eyes on Elizabeth, asleep in the bed. 'She's suffering from pains in the chest. He couldn't find any cause.'

'I wonder...,' Cecil scratched his temple. 'I wonder if it could be because of the duke.'

Robert frowned at him. 'Norfolk?'

'Well, this latest treachery of his has struck at her hard, Leicester. She is ever inclined to be merciful, you know. She had expected the duke to have learnt his lesson when she allowed him to leave the Tower. For him to betray her once again...,' Cecil shook his head.

'Why doesn't she just sign his death warrant and be done with him?'

'The queen has not ordered an execution before, Leicester.'

Robert leant forward and gently took hold of Elizabeth's cold hand. 'Let Norfolk be the first, I say. If anxiety is the cause of this sickness, then she should execute him without further delay.'

'Have you spoken to her of the duke?'

'I've tried. She signed the warrant once and then tore it up.'

'Well,' Cecil sighed, 'he is her kin.'

'But she's not fond of him, so her hesitation can't be because of familial affection. It can't be a question of whether he's guilty. He's admitted his treason.'

'And the Commons want his death. They petition me almost weekly to press the queen to it.'

Elizabeth suddenly jerked, her feet kicking out beneath the blankets, and she cried out, her face screwing up as if in pain.

'Bess,' Robert said softly, reaching out to stroke her cheek. 'It's all right, I'm here.' She seemed soothed and turned on her side, drawing her legs up, becoming small like a child.

'I'm sure Norfolk plagues her dreams,' Cecil said, almost angrily. 'I wish she would act.'

'We'll have to work on her when she's better, Cecil.' Robert rubbed at his eyes. 'You know, you don't have to stay up, Cecil. I'll sit with her.'

'I'm quite comfortable, really.'

'But your gout must be painful.'

'It's better than it was. And I wouldn't be able to sleep if I went back to my rooms. I'm quite content sitting here.'

'Did you get any sleep, Bess?' Robert asked, watching Elizabeth as she picked at a loose thread on a cushion she clutched to her chest.

She gave him a derisive look. 'How could I sleep?'

'Will you take some breakfast?' Robert asked, gesturing towards a table where bread and meats were laid out.

'I can't eat,' she cried, incredulous. 'The duke of Norfolk, the highest peer in the land, my cousin, Robin, is even now walking out to his death on Tower Hill. At my command! I signed my name to his death warrant. His blood will be on my hands.'

'How many more times?' Robert slammed down his cup of beer. 'All your council, the Commons, urged you to this. For your own safety, Bess.'

'I know, I know.' She sat down next to him. 'I wonder what he will say on the scaffold. Will he speak against me?'

'You'll get a report.'

'I'm not sure I want to know.'

'Then I won't let you see the report, Bess. Now, please, eat. You'll make yourself ill again.'

'Is there still time to stop it?'

'No,' he replied curtly, and placed a plate of meat before her. She nibbled at a slice of beef until the Tower cannon fired and announced the death of the duke.

As their thunder died away, Elizabeth began to shake.

Robert hastily moved to her side and drew her to him.

'It's over,' he whispered into her hair. 'There will be no nightmares, I forbid it. And you will be safe, Bess. We will make you safe.'

CHAPTER THIRTY-NINE

1572

Lady Douglass Sheffield sat stiffly upright as she heard Robert's voice in the hall. She pinched her cheeks, fearing they might be too pale just as the door opened and Robert walked in.

'Douglass,' he cried, holding his arms out. 'Why didn't you let me know you were coming tonight?'

'Sit down, Robert.' She patted the chair beside her. 'I have something to tell you.' Douglass took a few deep breaths and said, 'I'm with child, Robert.'

'You're...,' he gasped, his eyes widening. 'Good God.'

'It is quite natural, I assure you,' Douglass replied. 'The wonder is it hasn't happened sooner. And I need to know what your intentions are.'

'My intentions?'

Douglass's eyes filled with tears. 'Oh, Robert, are you going to make me beg?'

'Douglass,' he said, dropping to his knees and taking her hands, 'don't cry.'

'We must marry.' She slid her hands away and delved inside her bodice for a handkerchief.

Robert clambered back into the seat. 'Douglass, let's not be hasty—'

'I won't be known as the mother of your bastard, Robert.'

'Please understand, I have to be careful. You know how the queen is.'

'I don't care about the queen. She can't stop us from marrying.'

'No, but she can make it damned unpleasant for us. All I have, I owe to her generosity. She could withdraw everything just like that.' He clicked his fingers to indicate the swiftness of Elizabeth's disapproval.

She grasped at his hands. 'Don't let me be your whore, Robert. I'll beg you, if that's what you want. Please, please, let us marry.'

Robert took his own handkerchief and wiped her eyes. 'Just give me a little time, Douglass. I have to go to Kenilworth in a few days to see how the building work is coming along. I'll be back in about a month and we'll sort it out then. Everything will be fine, I promise.'

'I rode over to Kenilworth last week,' Ambrose said, pulling his fur cloak tighter about his shoulders. 'I couldn't believe the change in it.'

Robert stared into the fire. 'I'm going to see it tomorrow. It should be impressive, the amount of money it's costing me.'

'That sounds like regret.'

'No, not at all.' Robert ended the sentence with a sigh. Ambrose narrowed his eyes. 'What's on your mind, Rob?'

Robert looked up. 'It's Douglass,' he said sulkily.

'The delectable Douglass?' Ambrose raised a surprised eyebrow. 'Whatever can she have done?'

'She's with child.'

'But Rob, that's wonderful. Why aren't you pleased?'

'How can I be pleased?'

'You've always wanted children.'

'It's difficult, Am.'

'Oh, you mean the queen?' Ambrose nodded. 'Well, I admit it will be a trifle awkward for you, but surely she'll understand?'

'Oh, you think so? She'll be understanding? Finding out I've had a mistress for almost four years and that she is going to bear my child? Can you really believe Elizabeth won't mind?'

'I'm sure she'll be angry at first. But what does her anger matter when you have the prospect of an heir before you? And Douglass will make a fine wife.'

Robert grimaced.

'You don't still have hopes of marrying Elizabeth, do you? Oh, Rob, surely not?'

'She still might agree,' Robert said with a shrug.

'Rob, if Elizabeth was going to marry you, she would have done so years ago. You must marry Douglass.'

'Must I?'

'Of course you must. You don't want your child to be a bastard, do you? After all, who else do you have to leave all your worldly goods to?'

'I can leave what I have to anyone I choose, bastard or no. And bastards can be legitimised. Anyway, when Douglass and I began our relationship, I told her then she couldn't expect me to marry her. I kept nothing from her.'

Ambrose shook his head. 'I think you're a fool,' he said, his annoyance showing. 'You're free to wed whom you please. You have the prospect of an heir before you, yet you still hold out for a woman who has no intention, and to my mind, has never had any intention of marrying you.'

'And you don't, or won't, understand,' Robert retorted angrily. 'Everything I have, I owe to Elizabeth. What she has so freely given, she can take away. And then where would I be?'

'I do know that. What then of Douglass?'

'I don't want to hurt her, Am.' Robert rubbed his forehead. 'I have thought of a way out. What if I were to seem to marry her?'

'What do you mean seem?'

'I mean go through a ceremony but have no witness to it. That way, Douglass will be content believing herself married, but I can deny the marriage if Elizabeth ever agrees to marry me.'

'Rob!' Ambrose cried in horror.

'You think it despicable.'

'You know it is.'

'But I don't see I have any other option, Am. After all, I'm not saying I will disavow her. Just that I can if I need to.'

CHAPTER FORTY

1573

Robert shook the rain from his cloak and handed it to his servant. 'Wine and cakes,' he ordered.

'At once, my lord,' the servant replied. 'Sir Henry and Lady Sidney have arrived. They are in their chamber.'

'Very well.' Robert, tired, climbed the stairs slowly. He knocked on the door and opened it. 'Hello, you two.'

Henry, stretched out full length on the bed, waved to him and lazily sat up. Mary, her ravaged face uncovered in the safety of her chamber, turned to him from the window and held out her arms. 'How dare you not be here when we arrive,' she scolded as they embraced.

'Forgive me, I've been in Esher.'

'And what were you doing in Esher?' Henry asked jauntily.

Robert hesitated, looking from one to the other. 'Has Ambrose not told you?' Both shook their heads. 'I've married Douglass. Sort of. Well, she's going to have a child.'

He accepted their cries of joy and congratulation tetchily.

'How is she?' Mary asked.

'She's well enough. I've sent her up to Warwick. She's going to stay with Ambrose until Kenilworth is ready and the baby is born.'

'But why have we heard nothing of this?' Henry asked. 'The court should be buzzing with this news.'

'The court knows nothing of this and that's the way I intend to keep it. The queen must never find out.'

'But if you're married, she'll have to know. And what do you mean, sort of?'

Robert sighed impatiently. 'It's complicated, Mary. Oh, look, write to Ambrose, he'll explain. I'm sick of talking about it.'

'Forgive us for being pleased for you,' Mary replied haughtily, more than a little put out.

'Oh, don't be like that.' He put his arm around her waist. 'Are you going to court while you're in London?'

'Yes,' Henry said, 'we must pay our respects to the queen.'

'Well, then, for God's sake, don't mention any of this to Elizabeth. She mustn't know.'

'Don't worry,' Mary assured him, 'we won't.'

Robert hurried along the corridor. Clutched in his hand, a letter from Douglass he dared not read until he was back in his own room and alone. Courtiers importuned him as he went, hurrying alongside him even as he brushed them off. At last, he closed the door to his bedchamber behind him, moved to the window for the light, and opened the letter.

Douglass's news was brief and to the point. She had given birth to a son and was calling him Robert. A cry of joy, relief, disbelief burst from him and he realised with happy astonishment his cheeks were wet. A son. He had a son. He was a father at last.

He wiped the tears away and read on. Both the child

and Douglass were healthy and wishing he were with them. Robert thought it was the most perfect letter he had ever received. He pulled out the chair to his desk and hurriedly wrote a reply, sending them both his very great love. Then he shook sand over the wet ink, folded and addressed it, sealed it, and left it for his secretary to send.

Then he gave his face one last wipe, clearing any trace of happiness from it, and began the walk back to Elizabeth.

CHAPTER FORTY-ONE

1575

Henry Sidney helped his wife down from the carriage. 'He must have half the county here.'

Mary shielded her eyes against the sun. 'Robert does nothing by halves, you know. Well, Phil, it's been a while since you were here. What do you think of Kenilworth Castle?'

Philip Sidney climbed out after his mother, a tall, serious-looking young man. 'Uncle has certainly improved it.'

'Let's find him, shall we?' Henry led the way, past the people running to and fro, their ears ringing with the shout and clamour of voices. 'There he is. ROBERT!'

Robert turned around, a harassed expression on his face. He walked towards them, even as he continued to bark orders over his shoulder. 'Hello, Henry.' He kissed Mary through her veil. 'Phil.'

'Uncle.' Philip stepped forward and embraced him.

Robert held him tight for a moment. 'Oh, just what I needed.'

'Are things as bad as that?' Henry asked.

Robert nodded grimly. 'I've organised this sort of thing before, but never on this scale. And this has to be good. An extravaganza! Well,' he turned back to the castle and spread his arms wide, 'it's finished. What do you think?'

'It's wonderful, Rob,' Mary said. 'Fit for a queen, Uncle.'

Robert turned to him, grinning. 'You remember me saying that, Phil?'

'I remember everything you tell me, Uncle.'

'I'm very glad to hear it.' Robert turned as a worker called out to him. 'I'm sorry, I've still got so much to do. You know where your rooms are, don't you? Make yourselves comfortable and we'll meet for supper.'

'Is there anything I can help you with, Uncle?' Philip asked as Robert made to go.

'Actually, yes, Phil, I could do with some help. I have some players waiting for me. They should be in the hall. Could you go and see them, make sure they know what they're doing and run them through the play?'

'Of course, Uncle.'

They made off in different directions, making promises to meet later.

'You know, Mary,' Henry said ruefully as they began walking towards the castle, 'I sometimes wonder whose son Philip thinks he is.'

'What do you mean?'

'Well, his father's only a knight. His uncle's an earl.'

'Oh, Henry, you're not jealous?'

Henry looked away. 'Do you blame me? Rob's been given all this,' he gestured towards the castle, 'he has the queen's favour, he has power and prestige. What do I have?'

Mary grabbed his arm, halting him. 'Now you listen to me. You have your knighthood and you're Lord Deputy of Ireland. And more importantly, you have me, you have your children. Rob may have power and prestige, but he's not allowed to publicly own a wife. He's not free to acknowledge his own son. He has to take the taunts and insults of Elizabeth when she's in a temper, for it's not all billing and cooing in their relationship, I can tell you. So, I don't want to hear any more about how you're not good enough. Do you hear me, Henry Sidney?'

'I think the whole damned castle heard you,' he said with an embarrassed smile. 'And you're right. I have everything I could want. But I'm right too, you know.'

'About what?'

'You don't need this thing,' he gestured at her veil. 'Take it off. Please.'

'Don't make me, Hal,' she said, and he heard the tremor in her voice. 'I can't bear people to see me. They look at me for a moment and then they're too embarrassed to look any longer, so they look away. I'd rather they didn't see me at all. So, please don't make me take it off.'

Henry sighed. 'Very well, I won't. Come on, let's get to our bedchamber and have a lie down.'

'It's the middle of the afternoon, Hal,' she said, her voice curling with her smile.

'And we have nothing to do until supper,' he said, taking her hand.

Their horses trotted side by side as he brought her to the bridge of Kenilworth, just as the blue sky was darkening. The castle rose out of the water, the reflections of a thousand torches glinting and rippling on the surface, the pennants on the battlements swelling with every breeze.

'It's beautiful, Robin,' Elizabeth congratulated him. She smiled down upon the people crowding around her, eager to see a glimpse of their monarch. 'I want your people to see how high in my favour I hold you.'

'They're a good people,' Robert said, 'and loyal.'

'I'm very glad to hear it. I've learnt my lesson with the

duke of Norfolk. I don't intend to foster traitors in my country again.'

'No traitors here, madam. You have my word.'

'And I trust your word, Robin,' she said, reaching over to place her gloved hand on his. 'Hallo! What's this?'

They brought their horses to a stop and Elizabeth peered over the side of the bridge. Fifteen feet below, a raft covered with green grass and flowers floated. Standing upon it, her naked feet crushing the flowers, was a young woman, clad in white silk, her golden hair, far too beautiful to be her own, streaming over her shoulders. Two children, cupid-like, with tendrils of green ivy wrapped around their legs and arms, knelt behind her, offering up bunches of wild flowers.

'I am the Lady of the Lake,' the woman said. 'Keeper of this sacred pool since the days of the great and glorious Arthur, king of all the Britons. Never until now has England had such majesty. Never until now have I been able to entrust the keeping of this lake to anyone but our most gracious queen.'

The Warwickshire accent was unmistakable and spoilt the mythic quality of the speech, but her words pleased Elizabeth and she smiled down at the woman. 'I thank you for your generous gift, but we had thought the lake had belonged to us already.'

Robert's jaw tightened. Couldn't Elizabeth accept a compliment gracefully, just for once?

'Very nice, Robin,' Elizabeth murmured.

A cannon discharged its shot. Robert touched Elizabeth's arm and pointed to a large ornate clock high on the tower he had named Caesar's. The hand moved slightly and then stopped. 'While you are here, Bess, no time will pass.'

'Old Father Time stands still. A happy thought.' She

looked around her, at the fairyland Robert had created for her. 'If only.'

Days passed, all of them spent in pure enjoyment. Fireworks, dancing, hunting, masques, food, food and more food. Robert had prepared well and there were only words of praise for his accomplishments and murmurings of jealous admiration from the courtiers as the entertainments played themselves out.

One warm night, Elizabeth and Robert stood on the bridge by Mortimer's Tower, looking down at the dark, moonlit water where a mermaid glided through the water. Beside her, a dolphin, expertly crafted, floated and atop him sat a masked Arion. When they were directly below Elizabeth, the mermaid thrashed her tail and Arion kicked his heels until the water foamed and tumbled. Up swam Triton, his long hair entangled with seaweed. He held a hand aloft.

'You winds, return unto your caves and silent there remain. You waters wild, suppress your waves and keep you calm and plain,' Triton shouted into the night, determined to play his part well.

But Arion whipped his mask from his face and looked up at Elizabeth. 'I heed him not, my queen. Triton commands not me, for I'm not Arion but only honest Harry Goldingham.'

Robert scowled. The idiot had spoilt the entire scene. Was this what he had paid for?

But Elizabeth was amused. 'Well, honest Harry Goldingham, I would rather have you than Arion and I've enjoyed this more than all the other entertainments put together. Here.' She threw him a gold coin. 'A sovereign from your sovereign.'

Honest Harry waved it above his head in triumph as a sulky Triton dragged away him.

Elizabeth moved off, laughing with her ladies.

'Is something wrong, Lord Robert?' Lettice Devereux's smooth, low voice curled into his ears.

'Not really,' he said. 'I was just thinking of how easily a fool can spoil my plans.'

'It wasn't spoilt. The queen laughed.'

'Laughter wasn't the response I was after. I suppose it doesn't matter. So, Lettice! Are you enjoying yourself?'

'Well, you certainly put on a good show, my lord. But I cannot help feeling that there is more sport to be had indoors of a night.' She edged nearer so their sleeves touched.

Robert checked over his shoulder to make sure Elizabeth was not in earshot. 'How is your husband, Lady Essex?'

The green eyes looked slyly at him. 'He is well, and in Ireland, which is the best place for him.'

'You,' he said with an admiring grin, 'are a saucy wench.'

'As you would have discovered had you not abandoned me all those years ago.'

'Ah, yes, so I did. Tell me, were you very upset?'

'Devastated,' she mocked, laying an elegant hand upon her breast. 'To be wooed by the most handsome man at court and then forsaken as soon as the queen clicked her fingers. And I can't believe the queen ever offered you more than I could. She has not the experience. At least, that is what she claims, our dear virgin queen.'

Robert said nothing.

'I believe you still wish to wed her,' Lettice said sharply, irritated by his silence.

'Only a fool would not want to.'

'But would you be marrying her for her crown or her

body? Will you not answer me, my lord?' She moved closer, her mouth at Robert's ear. 'You will find my bed warmer than the queen's, and free to visit whenever you wished.'

'And if I wished to visit tonight?' he asked quietly, turning at last to look at her.

Her lips curled as her heart beat faster. 'Then you would find my door unlocked, and I, alone in my chamber, waiting for you.'

'Leicester!' Elizabeth's voice, hard and angry, cut into their conversation.

Robert turned to her immediately. 'Yes, Your Majesty?'

'You're neglecting your duties as host, my lord.'

Robert moved to her. 'Forgive me. I had thought you were attended.'

'So I was, but not by you.' Elizabeth's fierce eyes flashed at Lettice. 'You and I, sir, shall walk alone.'

She took his arm, and they walked on through to the gardens, flaring torches on long poles casting shadows across the path.

'You have been most direct these past few days,' Elizabeth said as the scents of flowers filled their nostrils. 'Day after day, I am told I should marry. In masques, in poems, by people who jump out at me from behind trees. And who am I told I should marry? None but you.'

'It's my greatest desire and no strange news to you, Bess.'

'No, indeed. But I'm afraid all your efforts have been in vain. For I do not mean to marry. Not you, not anyone.'

Robert came to a halt. 'I see.'

'I am sorry, Robin,' she said. 'When I think of the expense you've gone to—'

'Be sure, Bess,' he turned to her, his face grim. 'Be very sure. I'm going to ask you one last time. Marry me.'

He was in earnest, she realised. 'I am your queen. You are oath sworn to serve and love me.'

'I will always love you, Bess,' he said, bending his head to kiss her.

She pushed him away, angry. 'I can't marry you, Rob. I can't.'

'Why not?' he demanded.

'I have reasons you could not possibly understand. Now, you have your answer. Hate me if you wish.'

'I can't hate you, Bess, nor will I ever. You're my queen and my friend. But lover no more.' He sighed and looked back at the company. 'Shall we walk back? It's getting late.'

He pushed down the handle and opened the door. A solitary candle burned beside the bed. Lettice lay beneath the sheets, her hair fanned out over the pillow. Bare shoulders above the bed sheet, undulating over her breasts and hips. Robert stepped inside and turned the key in the lock.

She giggled as he pulled the sheet away from her body. 'I was beginning to think you wouldn't come.'

He whipped the sheet away and drank in the sight of her. 'How could I resist such an invitation?'

Her toes prodded his codpiece. Robert grasped her ankle and pulled her further down the bed, spreading her legs and placing himself between them.

'Oh,' she moaned, curving her body towards him, 'thank the Lord for a proper man.'

CHAPTER FORTY-TWO

'Your Majesty, the entertainments for today—'

'Are cancelled,' Elizabeth finished sharply.

His feeling of happiness faded quickly. *God's Death*, he thought, *here we go again*. 'Why, Your Majesty?'

'Get out!' she barked at her attendants. They retreated hurriedly, kicking against one another's feet in their haste. Robert watched them go and prepared himself for another quarrel. 'Where were you last night?'

'Why, Your Majesty?' Robert repeated.

'Answer me. Where were you?'

'I did not retire to my bed until late last night, Bess. At what time exactly do you mean?'

'Two o'clock this morning.'

'I do not rightly remember. Perhaps in my study.'

'Liar,' she hissed. Her hand thudded against the pommel of her chair and he watched her knuckles turn white as she gripped it. 'You were in some harlot's bed.'

He sighed heavily and ran his fingers through his hair. He was tiring of this game. 'If you knew where I was, Bess, why ask me?'

Elizabeth jerked from her chair and slapped his cheek.

Robert staggered back. The inside of his cheek had caught against his teeth and he tasted his own blood.

'Madam, you deny me your bed. Would you deny me comfort elsewhere?'

'Why do you need comfort, Robin? I do without. Why can't you?'

'It's not natural for a man to do without. To keep me from other women's beds, you will need to send me to the Tower, madam, for I swear I was not made to live the life of a monk.'

The light of anger faded from Elizabeth's eyes. She fell against the chair, missed, and tumbled to the floor. She fell on her face and sobbed into her arms. Robert was too angry to go to her.

'You will torment me to my death, Robin. I cannot bear the thought of you with other women.'

'Then don't think of it, Bess,' he said, none too gently.

'Who was she?'

'Does it matter? Besides, the less you know, Bess, the less it will torment you. How did you know I was not in my chamber last night?'

'I went to you. I wanted to talk to you. You weren't there. You were sweating in some bitch's bed. It hurt, Robin. I have cried all night long.'

'I'm sorry that you were upset, Bess. I didn't mean for you to find out.'

Elizabeth sat up and wiped her eyes with her fingers. Robert took a lace handkerchief from his sleeve and handed it to her.

'You're right, Robin. I don't want to know.' She pushed herself back into her chair, sniffing. 'As for the entertainments today, I'm sorry, but I'm not in the mood. Perhaps tomorrow. I have a headache. Leave me.'

Robert nodded and bowed out of the room. 'See to your mistress,' he instructed her ladies, who clustered outside the door. 'Wait a moment,' he said, grabbing Lettice's arm.

'Gladly, my lord,' she said. 'Are you in disgrace again?'

'In disgrace and yet forgiven. She knows I wasn't in my chamber last night.'

'Does she know whose you were in?' Lettice asked hurriedly.

'No, Lettice. Fear not, I didn't inform against you. It's better she knows nothing.'

'She shall not hear it from me,' Lettice promised. 'It's not to be the end though, is it, Robert?'

Robert pulled her to him and nuzzled her neck. 'I enjoyed you too much to forsake you again, sweetheart. I shall come—'

'Tonight?' she clutched at him. 'Come tonight.'

'Tonight,' he promised.

'Lettice,' Elizabeth's imperious voice called from the chamber. 'Cousin, is that you?'

Lettice shot a quick glance at Robert, then hurried to her mistress. 'Yes, Your Majesty,' he heard as he pressed his ear to the door.

'We will leave here in the next day or two,' Elizabeth said. 'I would like to stay at Chartley, cousin. You may leave at once to see to the arrangements.'

'Oh, but Your Majesty,' Lettice protested. 'Kenilworth is far more comfortable than my home can ever be.'

'If you don't want me there, cousin, just say so.' The tone of Elizabeth's voice made Robert wince.

Lettice continued. 'No, Your Majesty, I just want you to be comfortable. I will leave at once to make all ready for you.' She backed out of the room and watched the door close upon her. 'She's sending me away. Do you think she knows?'

Robert shook his head. 'No, she would have said. She

just wants to get away from here. Damn her. All the money I've spent!'

'I won't be able to see you tonight,' Lettice pouted, poking her finger inside his shirt and stroking his chest.

'No,' Robert agreed ruefully, 'but there'll be other nights.'

'Will you be coming to Chartley?'

'It depends. Elizabeth may not want me with her.'

Elizabeth did want Robert. At Chartley, she thought she would find some peace, but not solitude. One thing Elizabeth never wanted to be was alone.

'I came on ahead,' Robert explained to Lettice when he arrived at Chartley, 'to make sure everything was ready for her.'

'She's coming already?' Lettice asked despairingly. 'I thought she wouldn't be here until tomorrow, at least. Just look at the place.'

'It's fine,' Robert said, looking around. 'Just have your servants throw fresh rushes down and all will be well.'

'Rushes? Oh, yes, rushes. I will tell them.'

'Not yet.' Robert put his arms around her waist and pulled her to him. 'You haven't said hello properly.'

'Robert,' she protested weakly, as his kisses trailed down her neck, 'my children might walk in.'

He hurriedly released her. 'I forgot your children. Your husband is a most fortunate man. He has you and four children to carry on his name.'

'I really believe you mean that,' Lettice said in surprise.

'Of course, I mean it. What else did God put us on this earth for if not to have children?'

'Walter would agree with you,' Lettice said, settling herself onto a couch. 'Honour and family are all he thinks about.'

Robert smiled down at her. 'And you have other things on your mind?'

'Several other things. Oh, there are the children.'

Four youngsters tumbled into the room and stopped dead at the sight of Robert. 'Who are you?' the tallest demanded.

'Robert Devereux,' Lettice scolded, 'that is no way to address the earl of Leicester.'

The young boy stared up at Robert. 'The earl of Leicester?'

Robert nodded. 'That's my title. My name is Robert too.'

'What do you say?' Lettice said to the boy.

'I am most honoured to meet you, my lord,' the boy answered dutifully.

'Now, my darlings,' Lettice said, 'the queen is coming to visit. She will be here shortly and I want you all to be on your best behaviour. Is that understood?' The children nodded. 'Very well. Now, all of you, go and play some-where. I don't want you back in the house before six o'clock. There is a lot of work to be done and I don't want you underfoot. Now, go on. Go and play.'

'You were very strict with them, Lettice,' Robert said after they had gone. 'And what work have you to do? I told you all you have to do is lay down fresh rushes…'

Lettice twined her fingers into his and pulled him towards the stairs. 'Sometimes, Robert, I believe you are the stupidest man in England.'

CHAPTER FORTY-THREE

1577

Douglass shifted her son on her hip as she strode along the alley. The child was getting heavy and she would gladly have put him down, but he couldn't walk as fast as she and she was determined not to be slowed down. She ignored the stares of those who passed her by; a small child was an uncommon sight at court. There were a few glimmers of recognition, but Douglass wasn't prepared to be waylaid by friendly greetings. She kept her eyes on the path before her and her feet moving fast. She was going to find Robert.

But she had no idea where Robert would be. The court was so large, it seemed ridiculous to try to find him, but Douglass suspected that where the queen was, Robert would be too.

But then two ladies passed by and one said, 'That must be Lord Leicester's bastard' to the other, and Douglass's courage left her. She hurried on, now hearing whispers all around her.

'Boy,' she stopped a young page. 'Where are the earl of Leicester's rooms?'

The page directed her and she set her son on his feet and, holding his hand, they walked slowly to Robert's apartments. She half-feared seeing a guard on the door, but there was none. She knocked, and the door opened.

'Is your master here?' she asked of the servant who answered.

'No, my lady, he's in the council chamber.'

'I'll wait,' she declared, stepping through the doorway. 'Perhaps you could take a note to him?'

Douglass's note told Robert she was waiting in his chambers to see him. She was prepared to wait however long it took, but Robert appeared within fifteen minutes.

'Douglass, what the devil are you doing here?' he erupted upon entering the room. Then he saw his son playing with his pack of cards on the floor by the bed and he picked up the little boy and held him close. 'Hello, Robbie,' he kissed the pink cheek. 'How does my little man?'

'He does well enough,' Douglass said. 'Which is more than can be said for his mother.'

'What's the matter?' Robert asked with a sigh.

'The matter is I haven't seen you for months.'

'I've been busy.'

'You're always busy.'

'I see you as often as I can, Douglass.'

Little Robbie laid his head against his father's shoulder and closed his eyes. Robert pressed his cheek to the top of the little head, feeling his warmth. It was worth risking the queen finding out just to have his son in his arms like this. He wouldn't admit it to Douglass, but she was right; it had been too long since he was with them.

'As I came here, a woman called our son Lord Leicester's bastard. You see what people think? They think I'm your whore, not your wife. Why can't you admit we're married, after all this time?'

'It's not the right time—'

'Oh, it's never the right time. It won't ever be the right

297

time.' She fell onto a wooden bench and cried. Her tears had worked on Robert before, but not this time.

'Stop crying,' he said sharply. 'That won't do any good.' He hitched himself up onto the bed. 'You should go home before anyone else sees you.'

'Home to Kenilworth, I suppose?'

'Leicester House. I'll come there tonight. You can stay for a week. But then you must go home, Douglass.'

'Why? Afraid I'll be in your way?' She turned to him, her tears drying.

Robert looked at her. 'What's got into you?'

'I'll tell you, shall I? Lettice Devereux.'

Robert started, jerking the slumbering boy awake, who began to cry. 'There, there,' he said soothingly. He looked back at Douglass. 'I don't know what you're talking about.'

'Don't pretend with me. I know she's your mistress.

There's no point lying.'

'Very well,' he said, laying Robbie on the bed, 'so you know.'

'Is that all you can say? Don't you care that you're hurting me?'

'Of course I care,' he snarled. 'But I can't change what's done.'

'You can stop seeing her.' She saw the look on Robert's face. 'But you won't, will you? After all, you've killed her husband so you can see her more often.'

'What the devil are you saying? Killed Walter Devereux? Of course I didn't.'

'It's what's being said. Didn't you know?'

'I don't know where these rumours start, but they're a pack of lies. He died of the flux. What good would it do me to have him killed?'

'So you can marry her. But, of course, you'd have to have me killed, too, to do that.'

Robert bit his tongue, not ready to disillusion her about

their so-called marriage. 'Go to Leicester House, Douglass. I'll come there as soon as I can.'

He strode past her and left the room. Douglass curled up on the bed, curving herself around her now sleeping son, and held him close. She'd lost Robert, she realised.

Perhaps, she thought, *I never really had him.*

CHAPTER FORTY-FOUR

1578

'Oh, Christ's blood, is this nonsense to be resurrected?' Robert flung the letter he had been reading across the table to Francis Walsingham, the new secretary of the council, whose thin lips curled up in distaste.

'It appears so, my lord.'

'I had thought it all dead and buried.'

'The queen and Cecil believe it expedient to pursue the matter.'

'It amazes me that anyone can still believe the queen will ever marry. This charade has been played out so many times before.' Robert sat down heavily and pointed at an empty chair. 'Is Cecil attending the council today?'

'I fear not. He has sent word he is unwell again.'

'Hmmm. Ah Hatton, there you are.'

Christopher Hatton, the tall, elegant chancellor entered the chamber, munching on a crust of bread. 'Good morning, Leicester, Walsingham. What business today?'

'Have you heard about this?' Robert demanded, pointing at the offensive letter.

'About what?' Walsingham passed the paper to him.

'Oh, Alençon. Yes, unfortunately, the queen has mentioned it to me.'

'No more than a mention?'

'No, not really. She wondered if he is really as ugly as everyone claims, that is all.'

'I wish I knew her thoughts on the subject,' Robert smacked the table irritably.

'She has not confided in you, then?'

Robert shook his head.

'Negotiations would be easier to carry out if we knew the queen's mind,' Walsingham said. 'Does she wish to marry or no?'

'Walsingham, I tell you, this is a charade, like all the others,' Robert insisted.

'I hope it is, my lord,' Walsingham said sincerely. 'It would be a black day for England were a French Catholic sitting on the throne beside the queen.'

Robert and Hatton exchanged a glance. Walsingham had been in Paris when the massacre that became known as St Bartholomew's Eve sent shockwaves of horror throughout Europe. French Catholics, whipped into a frenzy of religious hatred, pulled Protestant women and children from their homes and hacked them to death in the streets, while the corpses of the men were thrown into the Seine, their blood turning the river red. Walsingham had taken refuge, along with Philip Sidney, in the English embassy, but even from behind its walls he had still heard the screams. Any wonder then that he had no liking for Catholics, especially those that were French?

'This will be just for policy, Francis,' Robert said.

Walsingham nodded a curt appreciation.

'Perhaps it would be better to ask the queen,' Hatton suggested.

Robert laughed. 'You mean ask her outright if she means to marry the ugly dwarf?'

'Well, perhaps not couching it in such terms, but yes.'

'You may be right. Anyone know where she is?'

'I left her in the gardens,' Hatton said.

The other council members trooped in as Robert left, and he gave them all a cursory greeting. The sunlight hurt his eyes as he entered the gardens. They were full of courtiers, the day too lovely to spend indoors. Several people plucked at his sleeve, requesting an audience with him at some convenient time. He told them all the same thing; that they should contact his secretary to arrange the meeting. It never annoyed him, these calls upon his person. Indeed, he feared the day when people did not ask him for help, to intercede for them. He cherished his closeness to the queen. In council, the other members looked to Robert to speak for them when they did not have the courage to persuade the queen and sometimes feel the sharp edge of her tongue on their behalf.

He turned corner after corner before he came upon Elizabeth. She sat on a wooden stool, three of her Ladies on the ground, each with a book in their hand.

'Your Majesty,' Robert bowed.

Elizabeth looked up and frowned. 'Yes, Robin?'

'The duke of Alençon.'

'What of him?' she muttered, keeping her eyes upon her book.

'You are considering marriage with the duke?'

'I am.'

'Seriously?'

Elizabeth looked up at him slyly. 'Maybe.'

'There is no need for such a marriage, Your Majesty.'

'No? Cecil seems to think so.'

'Cecil is wrong.'

'And I agree with him.'

'For God's sake, why?'

Elizabeth closed her book and looked up at him. 'You

have been saying for months England should get involved in the Netherlands and protect those poor people from the Spaniards. My marriage with a prince of France would do that.'

'I proposed sending men and money to the Netherlands. I never countenanced you sacrificing yourself.'

'All I sacrifice is my virginity, and that is mine to do with as I please.'

'To which there are dangerous consequences, madam,' Robert said carefully.

All three of the women at his feet glanced nervously up at him.

Elizabeth bit her lip angrily. 'Enough of this, Robin. This is for discussion in the council chamber.'

'There was a time when I had your ear, madam.'

'And there was a time when I had your love,' she retorted, standing suddenly, her book falling to the ground.

'Your Majesty?'

'I said enough, and I meant it, Robin. Now leave me.'

'Not until you explain,' Robert insisted.

'How dare you!' Elizabeth sneered. 'Must the queen answer to her horse master? You will learn your place, my lord.'

'Have I not learnt my place well enough, madam?' Robert burst out angrily. 'Have I not been the recipient of your scorn more times than I can remember, endured your displeasure without complaint, denied myself—'

'Denied yourself?' Elizabeth repeated incredulously. 'I have never known you to deny yourself. Where do you think you are going?' she demanded of her Ladies, who had tried to slip unobtrusively away. They about-turned abruptly and resumed their places. 'Denial would mean no fornication with Douglass Sheffield. Or my own damn cousin, Lettice.'

Robert was stunned. She knew about Douglass and Lettice! 'Madam,' he protested.

'Make no excuses.' She waved him silent. 'I know what men are.'

'Why then condemn me for it?'

'Because you try to stop any chance of happiness that may come my way while you enjoy yourself shamelessly.'

'You told me once, madam, that you would have no master. Has that changed?'

She raised her eyebrow contemptuously. 'I said that to you. I may not say it to a prince.'

'I am nothing to you, then?'

She hesitated a mere moment. 'You are nothing to me. As I am to you.'

LEICESTER HOUSE

Robert went home, unable to remain at court after the quarrel. He went straight through to his private parlour and was surprised, and extremely pleased, to see Lettice there, sitting before the fire with a glass of wine in one hand and a plate of sweetmeats in the other.

'Lettice, why didn't you tell me you were coming here today? I only came home by chance.'

'Well, I would have sent for you,' she said, tugging at his arm to sit down next to her.

'Why? Is something wrong?'

'Not wrong exactly,' she shook her head, 'it's just that I have something to tell you. I'm pregnant again, Rob.' She laughed as Robert embraced and kissed her. 'You're pleased, then?'

'Of course I'm pleased. It's wonderful news.'

'Is it?' she frowned. 'I wonder. After last time. I lost that baby. Who is to say this time will be different?'

'It'll be fine this time.'

'You say that, but we are still in the same position we were before. I still have the same worry.'

'What worry?'

'That I may end up in the Tower. Or worse.'

'You won't.'

'If the queen finds out…'

'There is no need to worry anymore, my love. Elizabeth already knows about us.'

Lettice stared at him. 'She knows? How do you know she knows?'

'She told me.'

'Oh my God, Robert,' she cried, grasping his hand. 'And she doesn't care.'

'Doesn't care? She does care, if I know my cousin.'

'Well, you're not in the Tower, are you? Nor am I, so she can't, can she?'

Lettice looked down at her hands, two fingers playing with her rings. 'Would she care if we were husband and wife?'

Robert rubbed his forehead thoughtfully. 'When is the child due?'

'October.'

'Let me think about it.'

'We haven't time. We have only a few months. Oh, Robert,' Lettice pushed him away and moved to the fireplace. 'What are you still hoping for?'

'I don't know,' he admitted.

'Or is it Douglass? Do you want to pretend to be married to her still?'

'Douglass hasn't anything to do with us.'

'So, deny your marriage to her, Robert, and marry me. Answer me this. Do you ever believe the queen will marry you? Yes or No.'

Robert was silent for a long moment. 'No,' he admitted finally.

'Then why should you not marry when and whom you please? I am to have your child. I shall pray for a boy and you shall have your heir.'

'I already have a son, Lettice.'

'Douglass's bastard.' Lettice said sharply. 'That's hardly the same thing.'

Robert looked at her. He loved her; he wanted to be married, and he wanted a son. Her son. 'Very well, Lettice. We'll get married.'

'When?' she asked breathlessly.

'Soon.'

'And married with witnesses, Rob. I do not want you disavowing our marriage when you grow tired of me.'

'Oh, Lettice,' he said, drawing her into his arms, 'as if I could ever grow tired of you.'

Robert waited in the gardens. He paced up and down, ignoring the stone bench which would have given him some bodily ease. He had been easy and cool with Lettice, talking of ridding himself of Douglass, but now it came to it, he felt uneasy. *No, not uneasy*, he scolded himself, *ungallant, unkind, cruel.* He turned at the crunch of gravel. Douglass was walking towards him, her arms outstretched.

He brushed her aside. 'Don't, Douglass. That's not why I'm here. Won't you sit down?'

'What's wrong?' she asked, and he heard the fear in her voice.

He turned aside. 'Lettice is pregnant,' he said, and heard her gasp. 'And she wants me to marry her.'

Douglass grabbed his shoulder and spun him around. 'I spit on your whore, do you hear me? I spit on her.'

'Douglass—'

'Let her have her bastard. Give it your name, if you want, but she won't have *you*. You belong to me.'

306

'I don't, Douglass,' he said angrily. 'We were never married, not properly. I am free to marry whom I please, and it pleases me to marry Lettice.'

Douglass stared at him, her mouth open. 'You're lying,' she breathed. 'Of course we're married. We went through a ceremony.'

'Not a legal one. I did it because you insisted on being married. You left me no option, Douglass. I had to act as I did.'

'You deceived me!'

'I did, and it was wrong of me.'

Her tears fell. 'Then you never loved me. It was all a lie.'

'Not all of it,' he sighed.

'But we have a son, Robert.'

'And he will be provided for.'

'He's a bastard,' she cried, sinking onto the bench. 'All these years, he's been a bastard, and I never knew it. How could you do this to your own son?'

Oh, how her words hurt! His chest tightened and tears pricked at the back of his eyes, but he willed himself to be resolute. 'I shall give you seven hundred pounds a year, Douglass, for your welfare and our son's. It should be enough. I will even help you find a husband, if you wish it. I couldn't bear the thought of you being lonely. Would you like me to do that, Douglass?'

Douglass rose from the bench and stared at him, her cheeks blotchy and her eyes puffy and red. 'I don't want you doing anything for me. I want you to rot, Robert Dudley. You and your whore.'

CHAPTER FORTY-FIVE

Robert decided he would marry Lettice at his new house in Wanstead, close enough to London to get there and back to the court within a few hours, yet distant enough to be away from prying eyes. He took his friend, Lord North, with him to act as a witness. Lettice had insisted on witnesses. When he and North arrived at Wanstead House, they found the rest of the wedding party already there.

'Robert,' Lettice hallooed from her chair beside the hearth. She gestured at the man sitting opposite her. 'Father was worried you would not come.'

Sir Francis Knollys frowned at his daughter. 'Not at all. Leicester, good morning.'

'Sir Francis,' Robert nodded, taking his hand. 'You know, seeing as we are about to be related, you should call me Robert.'

Knollys snorted, whether in agreement or not, Robert could not tell and decided not to pursue it. 'My love.' He moved towards Lettice, taking her hand in his and laying his lips to her fingers. 'How are you?'

'Fat and hungry,' Lettice smiled up at him. 'Lord North, how pleasant to see you again.'

North bowed, his eyes noting the swell of Lettice's stomach beneath her loose red gown. 'It's a very great pleasure to be invited, my lady.' He turned to greet Ambrose. 'A secret wedding. This is the most excitement I've had all year.'

Ambrose and Robert laughed. Sir Francis frowned. Lettice asked when dinner would be served and they all drank a toast to the wedding that would take place later that day.

'Husband,' Lettice smiled and held out her arms to him. He stretched full length on the bed and wrapped his arms around her, pressing his lips to hers. The deed was done and there was no going back. He was well and truly, lawfully married. He pulled away from her.

'Rob, what's the matter?'

'Nothing.'

He kicked off his shoes and untied his doublet and shirt. Lettice watched him with pleasure. A nightshirt hung over the back of a chair next to the bed and he began pulling it over his head.

'Robert, why ever are you putting that on?'

'It is best we don't make love,' he explained. 'I don't want to endanger the child.'

'But it's our wedding night. Walter never let my being with child stop him, and it did no harm.'

'Nevertheless, Lettice. Not tonight. I have very weary brains for lovemaking.'

He climbed into the bed. She leaned into him, her slender fingers poking through an opening in his night-shirt, and pulled gently at the greying hairs on his chest. 'It's not your brains I require, husband. You're not paying any attention, are you? Are you thinking of her?'

Robert did not need to ask who she meant; 'her' was always Elizabeth.

'Yes, Lettice, and before you shout at me, I must think of her. Everyone who knows of us keeps asking me the same thing: does she know? And they are all worried about what will happen if she finds out. I must tell her of our marriage before someone else does.'

'That dried up old hag,' Lettice growled, pulling the bedcovers over her breasts. 'I trust this is not the effect she will always have upon you, making you unwilling in bed.' And with that, she turned on her side, yanking the covers over her shoulder and ending the conversation.

At length, her even breathing told Robert that she slept, and he felt guilty enough to curl up behind her, laying his arm over her waist, and clasping her hand in his, his chin on her shoulder. He felt supremely content, more so than he could ever remember feeling in his life before. He had a wife he loved who was already carrying his child, and his influence and power at court stretched far and deep. But at the back of his mind, there was the knowledge that he owed almost all of that he prized most dear to Elizabeth, and he could lose it all so very easily.

WHITEHALL PALACE

'Ah, Leicester, you're returned,' Cecil said as his page helped him into his chair.

'How's the gout?' Robert asked, noting the bandage on Cecil's foot.

'Better than it was, which is all I can hope for.'

'Leicester,' Hatton hallooed him cheerfully as he entered the chamber and clapped him on the shoulder. 'It's good to see you back. And you have some news, I hear.'

'Oh, God's Death,' Robert slapped his gloves upon the table. 'How do you know about it?'

Hatton laughed. 'Leicester, the entire court knows about it.'

'The queen, too?'

'Everyone except the queen. There isn't anyone brave enough to tell her.'

'Tell her what?' Cecil demanded.

'You don't know?' Hatton looked at him in surprise.

'I have been ill in my bed, Hatton,' Cecil said irritably. 'I have had very little news from the court and no gossip.'

'Don't you fret, Cecil. I have no doubt you shall find out soon enough,' Robert assured him grimly.

Cecil, annoyed, began slapping his documents about him on the table. 'Is Walsingham attending today?' he muttered.

'I saw him earlier. He said he would join us as soon as he is able,' Robert said. 'Now, tell me, has anything been decided about this damned Alençon affair?'

'Yes, you've missed quite a lot,' Hatton said. 'The little frog is sending his chief darling as he calls him, to woo on his behalf. A fellow named Simier.'

'And what do we know of him?'

'Only that he's a rogue. Murdered his brother when he caught him in bed with his wife.'

'Indeed? And what did he do to his wife?'

'No one seems to know.'

'Well, we can only hope his bad character will disgust the queen,' Robert said.

Cecil looked up from his paperwork. 'You are still opposed to this marriage, Leicester?'

'I am, Cecil, and will remain so. Such a marriage is not fit for the country, nor the queen.'

'The queen does not agree.'

'Only because she listens to your advice. I wish I could persuade you of the danger such a marriage would mean.'

'But the negotiations are just for policy, aren't they,

Cecil?' Hatton asked. 'The queen does not really mean to marry this Frenchman, does she?'

'That, Hatton, only the queen knows. But until she informs us otherwise, we must proceed with the negotiations as if the marriage was a decided affair.'

'When is this Simier arriving?' Robert asked.

'At the end of the week, if the Channel permits,' Hatton said.

Robert sighed and shook his head. 'Well then. We can do nothing until he arrives and declares their terms. So, what other business for us today?'

CHAPTER FORTY-SIX

'Rob, what's the matter?' Lettice asked him as they lay in bed.

'I've been thinking. Hatton told me that the entire court knows about our marriage. Elizabeth is bound to find out eventually and I think it would be better if it came from me.'

'Are you sure?' Lettice asked, propping herself on her elbow and staring down at him.

'You said it yourself, I am allowed to marry. And the duke of Alençon's envoy arrives tomorrow and I want to get this out of the way before all this French marriage nonsense starts. Leave for Wanstead in the morning, Lettice. I will get Elizabeth to come here, away from the court.'

'Well, if you're sure,' Lettice said, settling back down. 'I just hope I will have a husband to come back to.'

Robert stared out of the window and looked down onto the river. It had been over two hours since he had sent the note to Elizabeth asking her to come to him. Surely Elizabeth would not ignore him? Surely, she would come?

His breath fogged a patch of window glass. He wiped it away with his sleeve and as the pane cleared, Elizabeth's barge came into view. One of his servants was waiting at the barge steps, his arm outstretched to help her from the barge, but Elizabeth hurried past, gathering up her skirts above her knees. She half-walked, half-ran up the path to the house.

Robert waited.

The door swung open, banging against the wall behind.

'Why aren't you in bed?' Elizabeth demanded. 'Are you ill?'

Robert stepped around her and closed the door. 'No, Bess, I'm not. I just needed to get you here quickly.'

'Then you've worried me for nothing.'

'Forgive me. It was the best stratagem I could devise.'

'And it has worked well in the past,' she frowned, taking a seat by the fire.

'For us both, Bess.'

'Well, what is it you want to say to me? If it is more about the duke of Alençon, save it for the council chamber.'

'No, Bess. It is not of your marriage I wish to speak of, but mine own.'

Elizabeth stared at him. 'Yours? You wish to marry?'

'I have married,' he said quietly.

'If this is some joke, Robin…'

'No joke, Bess. I have married Lettice.'

She turned her head towards him, her expression almost incredulous. 'You married that whore?'

'Elizabeth, please, do not speak of her like that.'

'That whore?' she repeated. 'For God's sake, why?'

'She is carrying my child.'

'A child,' Elizabeth whispered.

'Yes. I have always wanted children and this, well, this could be my last chance for an heir.'

'You already have a son with Douglass Sheffield.'

'I wasn't married to Douglass.'

'There was a ceremony.'

'But it wasn't valid. I paid a man to marry us but he wasn't a clergyman. I wasn't sure I wanted to be married then. I was still hoping for you,' he smiled wanly, reaching for her hand, but she pulled it away.

'Why did you have to marry Lettice?' she wailed.

'God's Death, Bess, shall I tell you why? You told me there was no chance of our ever marrying and I believed you. Neither Ambrose nor I had a legitimate heir to carry on our Dudley name, and I am not about to let everything we have worked for and spilt our family's blood for vanish into the dust when we are gone. I want a son, and I married Lettice because I love her. And you know why? Because she is so like you. Except that she allowed me into her bed and you did not.'

'Is that it? Is that your reason? Is it me you think of when you two are rutting?'

'I told you once, I could not live like a monk. And why exactly are you angry? Because I am married, or because I am married to Lettice?'

'I don't know why I'm angry,' she cried, burying her face in her hands. 'I understand, Rob, I do, about you wanting a son. It's just that, that... I thought you loved *me*.'

'I do. I always have. That hasn't changed. But a man can only take so many refusals.'

'Robin, if we had bedded, would you have married her then?'

'I don't know, Bess. Why?'

'We will bed, if you disavow her,' Elizabeth said, looking up at him desperately. 'You can come into my bed as often as you like, if you do, and promise never to see her again.'

Robert was stunned. After all these years, after all those refusals, she was now submitting to him? For a moment, the thought of taking her to bed, of having her in his arms and burying himself in her, shut out all thought of wives and heirs. But the moment passed. He shook his head.

'I can't disavow her, Bess. The marriage was legal, and we had many witnesses.'

She covered her mouth with her hand, stifling a sob. She felt her stomach lurch, sick and yet strangely relieved he had refused. 'I am alone,' she whimpered.

He knelt before her. 'No, you're not. I'm still here. I still love you.'

'How can you? When you say you love her?'

'I can't explain it, but I know I do love you still. And I hope you can forgive me.'

She looked at him, his handsome face so earnest. How she had dreamt of that face, dreamt about kissing it. How she had admired his body, felt her own heat just thinking of him. Now, she would not be able to do that, because in her thoughts, he would be with Lettice, not her.

'I don't know,' she said. 'I can't believe you can love two women at the same time. At the moment, Rob, I hate you.'

'No, Bess, please—'

'I hate you,' she repeated, trying to make herself believe it. 'I hate you. I want to hate you.' She grabbed his head and kissed him fiercely. She pushed him back onto the floor and climbed on top of him. Her sharp teeth dug into his lips and he tasted blood. He pushed her away.

With a wrenching cry, Elizabeth stumbled to the window, pressing her burning forehead against the glass.

316

Robert lay where she had left him on the floor, catching his breath, his lips reddened with blood. He closed his eyes and waited.

Her head, her eyes, her throat, all were strained and aching. She focused her eyes on the boats on the river and waited for her heart to stop pounding. She could not look behind her, could not bring herself to look back at him. What must he think of her? Desperate, pathetic? To want him even when he no longer wanted her. She flinched when he spoke.

'What will you do?'

'I don't know,' she answered meekly. 'Will you send me to the Tower?'

Running her hand across her face, she said, 'I don't know.' She rose unsteadily from the window seat.

'Stay.'

'No.' She glanced at him, saw his bruised and bloodied lips, and looked away, cringing with shame. She strode to the door. 'You will not return to court. At least, not until I give you leave.'

She clambered onto the barge, knocking past the hands extended in aid, and fell into the cushioned seat. For a long moment, she stared into space, an image of Robert declaring love for another woman imprinted on her lenses. She called out to the boatmen to row and yanked at the hangings to shut herself in. The future lay before her, barren and bleak. Robert would leave her, more and more often, and she would be alone. Then Alençon walked into her mind, the prospective bridegroom she had thought to play with, make use of and then discard when his useful-ness was spent. In him was a chance to not be alone.

Oh God, she prayed silently, *make me love him. I will need him now and I want to be married. And I so want to not be afraid of love any longer.*

CHAPTER FORTY-SEVEN

1579

1579

Elizabeth eyed Jean de Simier surreptitiously as the players enacted their scene. He was concentrating hard, the bawdy humour of the English stage a mystery to him. Hatton had told her of Simier's history, of his savage revenge and the murder of his unfaithful wife and his brother, and found she did not care. Hatton had hoped such a history would dissuade her from receiving Simier. Poor Hatton. He never understood her.

Simier must have felt her eyes upon him, for he turned his head and his bold, dark eyes glinted at her. She smiled, a tight, one-sided smile, not giving too much. He was, after all, the servant of a foreigner, not one of her own.

But she liked him. Typically French, dark, all of him dark, lips that were too plump, too red to be attractive on a man, but his intelligence showed in his face. Elizabeth liked clever men. She enjoyed the conversations she could have with them, especially when they were peppered with phrases of love.

And God's Death, but Simier knew how to make love with words!

They were alone now, taking supper in her private apartments. 'The earl of Leicester—' he began.

She didn't want to ruin the evening with thoughts of Robert. 'What of him?' she answered shortly.

'He has a reputation.'

'For what?'

Simier waggled his head. 'For his admiration of Your Majesty.'

'Admiration?' she snorted. 'Is that what it is called now?'

He pouted. 'Perhaps admiration is not quite the word I meant. Forgive me. English does not come easily to me.'

She patted his hand. 'You speak it very well. But I know what you have heard and I can tell you it is not true.'

'Then there is no love between you. I see it is just duty that binds the earl to you and nothing more.'

Elizabeth bit her lip. 'It is I who has misunderstood you, Simier. I thought you meant malicious gossip about our relationship.'

'My master will be greatly relieved. He was not looking forward to the prospect of sharing you with another.'

'My Monkey,' she said, addressing him with the nickname she had bestowed upon him, 'your master will have to share me with my entire kingdom.'

'Subjects he will love, as you do yourself, but rivals...' He laughed and shook his head.

'But Robin…,' Elizabeth said hastily, 'the earl of Leicester is no rival, no danger to your master. Tell him that. The earl cannot have me.'

Simier nodded understandingly. 'I understand. And that being so, I trust you will not allow the earl to influence you against my master, who is a goodly prince and one who loves you dear.'

'I am not so easily swayed. You have reason to believe the earl will speak against your master?'

'Your Majesty, I confess to no great talent with your language, though you flatter me I speak well. But I do know people.'

'And you always suspect the worst of them?'

'I fear it is in my nature to do so,' he grimaced playfully. 'But I feel it to be no bad thing. That way, I am never disappointed.'

Elizabeth threw back her head and laughed, then remembered that he might see the gaps between her teeth and quickly covered her mouth with her hand. 'The earl will be back at court within a few days,' she said sourly. 'But I tell you, I know my own mind, Simier.'

'I am glad to hear it, Your Majesty. It would grieve me to have to comfort a disappointed master. He is hard to bear when he is melancholy.'

'Is it a humour he is prone to?'

'No, Your Majesty, no. Do not mistake me. He is of a most pleasant turn, amiable. But he has thought of nothing but you these many months and it would take much to remove you from his mind. Ah, such beautiful hands,' he said, taking her long fingers and pressing her knuckles to his womanly lips. It was an impertinent gesture for a servant to make, and he knew it. He saw her eyes narrow and knew she was wondering whether or not to rebuke him. 'Such hands should not belong to a mortal.'

'They do not, sir. I am God's deputy on this earth. I am above you.'

'But madam, we all have feet of clay. And I am thankful for it. If you were not mortal, a woman not of flesh and bone, your divine magnificence would blind us poor fools. As it is, we can look upon your beauty and wish ourselves princes.'

CHAPTER FORTY-EIGHT

Leicester,' Hatton waved. 'How was Buxton?'

Robert hesitated. 'Oh, pleasant enough. The queen told you …?'

'She said you had gone there for your health. I trust the waters helped?'

There was no hint of duplicity in his question. Robert's greatest fear, that the queen had forsaken him and would waste no time in informing everyone, had not come true. She had told no one.

'A little. But I fear this pain in my stomach will be with me for the rest of my days, Hatton.'

'No remedy, then,' Hatton said sympathetically. 'Will you dine?'

Robert nodded and gestured for Hatton to lead the way. As they walked through the corridors of the palace courtiers pressed their backs to the wall to clear the way for the great earl of Leicester, and a look of relief passed over Robert's face. Nothing had changed.

'Have you met him yet?' Hatton asked, as they entered his small chamber where food was already laid out on a table.

'Who?'

'Have you not been listening to me? Simier, the duke's envoy.'

'Oh, no, not yet, I've only just arrived,' Robert said, sitting and wrenching the leg off a chicken. 'Walsingham wrote to me about him but didn't commit too much to paper. Tell me, what is he like?'

Hatton made a face. 'Exactly like I thought he would be. But the queen, God's Wounds, Leicester, the queen thinks the world of him. She pets him, gives him presents. She's even given him a nickname. Her Monkey, she calls him.'

'Monkey?'

'Simier, simian,' Hatton explained. 'She has him to dine almost every night in her private chamber. I wish you had been here to distract her.'

'I don't think my presence would have done so.'

'Why? Has something happened between you and the queen?'

'Why do you ask that?'

'Well, you left hurriedly, without a word, and the queen has hardly mentioned you.'

'I am returned!'

'Ah, yes, but you have not seen the queen yet, and here you are, dining with me. Usually the queen is the first person you see and you would dine with her. This doesn't speak of high favour to me, Leicester. You will forgive me if I am prying?'

'You're right, Hatton,' Robert admitted. 'I'm not in favour at the moment, though I trust I will not remain so.'

'That is a thousand pities. May I know why?'

'You may, if I can trust you to keep it to yourself.'

'You can trust me.'

'Well, you know I've married. The queen now knows it, too.'

323

Hatton whistled. 'And I thought you would end up in the Tower when she found out.'

'I thought it possible myself.'

'What made you confess it?'

'She would have found out sometime. Better it came from me.'

'And so you're in disgrace. What did she do when you told her?'

'Suffice to say, she wasn't pleased,' Robert said dismissively. 'Now, I have told you enough, Hatton, and you will repeat it to no one.'

'None shall hear it from me,' Hatton promised solemnly. 'Has your wife returned with you? When do I get to meet the new countess of Leicester?'

'You don't. At least, not at court. Walsingham sent word that my presence was required but that I was to come alone. Decoded, that means Lettice is forbidden to ever join me.'

'That will be hard for her to bear, I should think.'

'Extremely. Lettice is not used to being forbidden anything.'

'But perhaps it will make these marriage negotiations easier,' Hatton mused. 'If personal feelings between yourself and the queen are at an end—'

'We still care for one another, Hatton,' Robert said sternly. 'Don't think otherwise.'

'I stand corrected, Leicester. I merely meant you cannot be accused of selfishness regarding this marriage.'

'No, my reasons against this marriage will be purely political.'

'On the other hand,' Hatton said, 'it could make things difficult for us.'

'How so?'

'Well, it might make the queen… eager.'

'I don't understand you, Hatton.'

'You haven't seen how she is with this Simier. I truly think he can make her forget herself.'

'With him? A mere servant?'

'He is greatly in her favour. He has fair put me in the shade.'

'No, I can't believe it, Hatton,' Robert said. 'You're wrong.'

'I hope I am, Leicester. But if she feels she has lost you, one whom she considered as her very own, well, I fear you may have made her desperate.'

'Desperate enough to make a bad marriage?'

Hatton shrugged. 'See for yourself. The queen is probably with him now.'

'I think I will. Excuse me, Hatton.'

Elizabeth's laugh cut off abruptly as Robert entered. He studied her face, looking for a clue of how he should be with her, but she merely stared back at him.

He bowed. 'Your Majesty.'

'You're returned, Robin,' she said coldly.

'As you instructed, madam.' Robert glanced at her companion. 'Good evening, sir.'

Jean de Simier half rose and made a slight bow.

Impertinent fellow, Robert thought, *am I not due more respect than that?* He looked at Elizabeth, but she had a sly smile on her face. *I see*, Robert thought, *that's how she's playing it.*

'I merely came to make the acquaintance of the duke's envoy and to let you know I had returned, madam. But as you have no obvious need of my company, I shall leave you to–'

'You will stay,' Elizabeth said sharply. 'I will decide if I have need of you or not, Robin.'

Robert smiled, wallowing in the dismay exhibited on Simier's face. 'Of course, madam. Whatever you wish.'

325

. . .

Elizabeth kept him for an hour, but then he said he should really check on his horses and he left for the stables. Robert tickled the nose of his favourite mare and she nuzzled his hand affectionately. He had missed the stables, missed the smell of them, of straw, horse sweat and warm manure. He talked and joked with the stable hands, gave medical instructions when he noticed sores on Arundel's bay, and watched the progress of the newest addition.

'So, what do you think?'

Robert jumped. 'Damn it, Hatton. How long have you been there?'

Hatton leaned against the stable door. 'Just got here,' he said, turning his foot to look at the sole. He muttered something and scraped his boot against the ground.

'What do I think of what?' Robert asked.

'The Monkey.'

'Oh, him. I think,' Robert paused, searching for the correct demeaning word, 'he's a typical Frenchman.'

'Ah, judgement enough.'

'He's dining with me tomorrow.'

'And are you going to warn him off or welcome him in?'

'Neither. I want to see what he's all about, that's all.'

'Huh, I could tell you that,' Hatton said sourly. 'He's the perfect courtier. Says all the right things, makes all the right gestures, never puts a foot wrong.'

'We'll see.'

'Shall I dine with you, too?'

'No, I don't think so. I may get him to talk more if we're alone.'

'I would not place a wager on that. Anyway, I can see you want to be alone. I shall leave you to your horses.'

. . .

'That was a fine dinner, my lord,' Simier said, dabbing a napkin against his mouth. 'You dine as well as the queen.'

'Better,' Robert said, signalling to a servant to refill the wine cups. 'The queen never has much of an appetite, and we have to finish when she does, so often we at court go hungry.'

'Well then, moderation does indeed have some virtue. The queen is most slender.'

'She is virtuous in many ways.'

'Really?' Simier smirked.

'What do you mean by that, sir?' Robert asked, his face darkening.

'I have known virtuous women, my lord, and I have known whores. The queen falls somewhere in between.'

'How dare you!' Robert was astonished at Simier's language. 'I shall tell the queen of how you abuse her.'

'And I will tell her you lie, my lord. I am not one for pretences,' Simier said, picking through the debris on his plate. 'I know it is you who is most vocal against my master marrying the queen. It is you who persuades your members in Parliament to protest against a French Catholic marrying the queen. Why should I pretend with you?'

'I won't deny that I don't want this marriage and I have done all I can to prevent it and will continue to do so, Simier.'

'I expect nothing less from the earl of Leicester.'

'As I am earl of Leicester, how is it you dare to speak so of the queen, to speak so disrespectfully of her?'

'I speak knowing that you are not what you once were,' he shrugged. 'In truth, I so wanted to meet with the great earl of Leicester, the queen's notorious bedfellow. And what do I find? That you no more have access to the queen's bed than I do. Perhaps even less.'

Robert was bursting with rage, but he was determined not to let Simier see.

'There is something I would like from you,' Simier continued. 'Your support for this marriage.'

Robert barked an incredulous laugh. 'After all you've said? You believe I have no influence with the queen.'

'Ah, but you still have influence in the country. And I admit, there may be some remnant of affection for you in the queen's heart.'

'Why should I change my policy for you? What do I get?'

'The queen does not find out about your marriage with Lettice Devereux.'

Robert drew his napkin to his face, hiding a smile behind the cloth. So that was why the Monkey was being so indiscreet with his words. He thought he had the upper hand.

'I see,' he said, pretending to consider. 'You must let me think on it, Simier.'

'Of course, my lord,' Simier said, popping a grape into his mouth. 'Now, I thank you for my dinner, but I promised the queen I would attend her this evening. Bon nuit.'

CHAPTER FORTY-NINE

'Leicester, if this is your doing...'

A purple-faced Sussex thrust himself at Robert as he entered the council chamber, his spittle spraying Robert's doublet.

'Is what my doing?'

'Simier was shot at on the queen's barge.'

'My lord Sussex,' Hatton interposed, 'there is no proof that Simier was a target.'

Sussex ignored him. 'The man responsible is one of your people, Leicester.'

'And you think I had something to do with it? Oh, this cannot be believed. Cecil,' Robert appealed, shoving Sussex out of his way, 'I know nothing of this.'

'Simier has himself accused you,' Cecil said.

'And the queen?'

'The queen does not seem overly concerned about the Monkey, Leicester,' Hatton said. 'Here, sit down.'

'No, I must speak with her.'

'She is with Simier as we speak, Leicester. I advise you to wait,' Cecil said. 'My lord Sussex, will you not take a seat?'

'Was anyone hurt?' Robert asked Hatton.

'A boatman was shot through the arm. The queen behaved magnificently, Leicester. She tied a bandage for the man herself.'

'She is most brave,' Robert said, running his fingers through his hair distractedly. 'But why accuse me?'

'The man was wearing your livery,' Sussex spat.

'I'm not responsible for the actions of everyone in my service, Sussex.'

'Simier is no fool. He knows it is you who most often speaks against him. It would please you greatly to have him out of the way.'

'Yes, and I know I can rely on you to think the worst of me, Sussex. You are ready to believe I am the devil himself.'

'I know a rogue when I see one, Leicester.'

'And I a coward when *I* see one, Sussex. Meet me in the gardens and we shall settle this like men.'

They put their hands on their swords. Hatton and Walsingham stepped between them.

'What is all this?' Elizabeth stood in the open doorway, her hands on her hips, her face red with rage. 'Fighting in my Privy council? Did I hear you challenge the earl of Sussex to a duel, my lord Leicester? You know I have forbidden duelling and do not think you will not be punished for attempting one. Sussex, sit down before you hurt yourself, and you, sir,' she turned back to Robert, 'you explain yourself.'

'Your Majesty,' he began, 'I had nothing to do with this attempt on the duke's envoy, if indeed one has been made.'

'What reason had you to draw your sword on Sussex here?'

'He accused me.'

Elizabeth glared at Sussex. 'Is this true, my lord?'

330

'The man was wearing Leicester's livery,' he exclaimed.

'An accident, Sussex,' Elizabeth said coldly, 'as I have told Monsieur Simier, who accepts the explanation. If he can, then so can you.'

'But what of the man, madam?' Sussex blustered. 'What was he doing on the river with a loaded weapon near you? Can the earl answer that?'

'Can you, Robin?'

'Of course I can't,' Robert replied angrily. 'I can't know the whereabouts of every man who wears my colours.'

'Sounds reasonable to me, Sussex,' Elizabeth said.

'Madam, I cannot believe the French will let this lie,' he persisted. 'The man must be punished.'

'If I punish a man who may very well be guiltless, how would my people react? They would be outraged, Sussex.'

'I understand your reluctance, madam. But what do you think the duke of Alençon will think of such mercy?'

'Oh, let the duke thinks what he likes,' Robert said. 'Who in God's name cares what a Frenchman thinks?'

'*I* care, Robin,' Elizabeth turned on him furiously. 'And keep a civil tongue in your head about the duke. I have invited him here and I command you to be respectful.'

'If you wish it, madam, then I will be no other when he comes.' Robert bent his head in obedience.

'Then settle, you dogs,' Elizabeth sneered. 'Walsingham, keep these schoolboys under control or I shall dismiss you all.'

The music had been playing for over four hours, and everyone, save the queen and her partner, wished it would stop. Cecil's head sagged upon his chest. Hatton waved away offers of dance partners wearily, Walsingham read paperwork surreptitiously and Robert drank cup after cup of wine.

Robert belched loudly and wiped his mouth with the back of his hand. Pushing away from the table, he staggered over to the corner of the room where Walsingham sat with his secretary, William Davison, the two of them oblivious to the entertainment around them.

Walsingham looked up angrily as the table jolted against his leg. 'Take ca—, oh, Leicester. Davison, quick, get the earl a chair.'

'Have mine, my lord,' Davison said, guiding Robert to his seat.

'What a farce this is,' Robert said, shaking his head. 'Are you well, my lord?' Walsingham asked carelessly, running his eye down a list of names Davison handed him.

'I am sick, Francis.'

'I am sorry to hear that, my lord.'

'Oh, for Christ's sake, leave that accursed paperwork and talk to me.'

With reluctance, Walsingham put down the document. 'What do you want to talk about, my lord?'

'Anything. That is if we can hear ourselves over this damned noise.'

'Indeed,' Walsingham nodded. 'The music has played overlong to my mind.'

'So has this scene.' Robert waved his arm at the dancers. 'This makes me sick.'

'The dance?'

'The dancers. Francis, do not play the fool with me. The queen. When did she sign the duke's passport so he could come here?'

Walsingham grimaced apologetically. 'When you were away, my lord.'

'Damn it, could you not have dissuaded her?'

'I made no attempt to, my lord. I know my limits regarding Her Majesty.'

'Oh, look at them,' Robert scowled, as the duke of Alençon leapt into the air. 'How ridiculous they look! He barely comes up to her shoulder.'

'Her Majesty seems pleased with him. See, they kiss.'

'How can she bear it? I thank God the people cannot see this.'

'But how long can his visit be kept a secret?' Walsingham wondered as Robert reached over and refilled his cup.

'When's he leaving?' Robert asked.

'He is here for about a fortnight.'

'Hell, we have to endure him that long?' Robert cried loudly. 'It will cost me a fortune.'

'The queen will expect you to entertain him?'

'Do I not always entertain her guests, though it near ruin me?'

'You do, my lord,' Walsingham agreed, setting aright the jug Robert's elbow had just knocked over. 'Though you usually take pleasure in it.'

'Not this time. You are very quiet on the matter, Francis. What do you think of the duke being here?'

'I think it is a step towards disaster for England, my lord. I would be grateful if you could allay my fears that the queen means to marry.'

Robert sighed and shook his head. 'I can't. I hope she doesn't mean to marry, but I can't promise you she will not. Is there no more wine?'

'That was the last of it,' Walsingham said. 'We have a council meeting early tomorrow, my lord. Perhaps it's as well the wine is gone.'

'Are you saying I am in my cups?'

'No, my lord. I am merely trying to spare you an unpleasant morning.'

333

'A broken head will only add to the unpleasantness,' Robert said. 'I understand you want me clear-headed, not brain sodden. Tell me, Francis, are you so used to people lying to you that you do not know how to speak clearly yourself.'

'There is a distinction, my lord,' Walsingham said haughtily, 'between civility and dishonesty. I flatter myself I am exercising the former when we speak.'

'Oh, all right, all right. I am a little drunk, I confess. What is to be discussed at the council meeting tomorrow?'

'The queen desires our opinion on whether to wed or not.'

'She has had our opinions,' Robert cried exasperatedly. 'How many more times must she hear them before she will make up her own mind?'

'The indecision wearies me,' Walsingham agreed, his eyes looking longingly at his papers. 'Ah, at last the music stops.'

They looked towards the dancers, the queen and her stunted partner. They exchanged a few words in French before the duke took Elizabeth's hand and kissed her fingers, cradling her hand in his own as though it were a precious thing. A few more teasing words, a dozen meaningful glances, and the evening's entertainment was at last at an end. The queen rustled from the chamber, followed by her weary Ladies. Courtiers took their leave of each other gratefully and the crowd thinned.

'Well, now we can go to our beds,' Robert said, getting to his feet unsteadily. 'Our cold, lonely beds.'

'I sleep better alone,' Walsingham said.

'Do you? I prefer company.'

'It's a pity that the queen will not relent and allow your wife to come to court.'

'It's a pity for me. Lettice complains continually. Perhaps when the child is born, she will not miss it so.'

334

'Her confinement must be near.'

'Next month. Well, till the morning, Francis.'

'Till the morning,' Walsingham said. 'Sleep well, my lord.'

CHAPTER FIFTY

Robert groaned as Sussex slammed his hand on the table. Could the man never make a quiet argument?

'The queen desires the marriage—,' Sussex was saying.

'She has told you this?' Hatton asked in surprise.

'She has not actually said so. But her actions all point towards such a desire.'

'I do not think it wise to assume the queen's desires, my lord,' Cecil said.

'Well, it is safe to assume our own, I suppose,' Sussex retorted. 'And I, for one, wish her to marry the duke.'

'As do I,' Cecil nodded.

'I do not,' Hatton said fiercely.

'Nor I,' said Robert quietly, rubbing at his temple. 'Walsingham?'

Walsingham laid down his pen. 'I am against such a marriage.'

There was silence for a moment while the clerk's quill scratched and bowling balls clicked in the gardens outside.

'And if the queen informs us she wishes to marry?' Cecil asked.

'Then we will support her, of course,' Hatton said. 'But

it is not just us. Parliament will have to decide and they will not give their approval. I know they will not.'

'That, fortunately, is not our concern, Hatton,' Robert said with a smile. 'Let us tell the queen that her council is divided, but we will support her in whatever decision she chooses to make.'

'And who is to deliver this report?' Cecil wondered. 'It's not what the queen wants to hear and she will rail at whomever tells her so.'

'I shall tell her,' Walsingham said, getting to his feet. 'It's my duty as Secretary, and I am not likely to lose favour with Her Majesty for the news as some might.'

'She's in her chamber, Francis,' Robert said. 'We will wait here for you.'

Walsingham nodded and left.

'There goes a brave man,' Hatton said seriously. 'I would not wish myself in his shoes.'

'Nor I,' Robert agreed. 'I fear the queen will not take this well.'

Robert's prediction was correct. Not ten minutes had passed before the council door flew open and Elizabeth stormed into the room.

'Is that all you can say to me?' she demanded as they got to their feet. 'You will support me whatever I decide? That is not the advice I need to hear, gentlemen.'

'If you would just say whether or not you wished to marry, madam, then we could advise you,' Hatton said.

Elizabeth glared at him. 'How can I decide to marry if you will not advise me on it?'

'What Hatton means, madam,' Robert interjected, bored by her prevarication, 'is do you love the duke and wish to be his wife? It's a simple question.'

'Do you dare to mock me?' she growled. 'You mock me, sir?'

'Indeed, madam, I do not.'

'Do I love him?' she cried incredulously. 'Love him? What does it matter if I do or not? I, sir, do not have the luxury of marrying whom I love. Policy governs my decision.'

'Then I shall counsel you on policy,' Robert said. 'It would not be good for England if you were to marry the duke, madam.'

'In what way would it not be good, Leicester? Is an heir for England not a good thing? Is it not a good thing that the line of Tudor not die with me?'

'Then your reason for marrying would be the getting of an heir?'

'To have a child of mine own. Is it so unnatural?' she pleaded. 'You have wives, you have children, and yet you would deny me the comfort of family.'

Robert moved to her side and took her hand. She met his gaze with softened eyes. 'Madam, the time for that is past.'

Her eyes lost all their softness. She pushed him away. 'You rogue,' she rasped and rushed from the room, pushing past Walsingham, who hovered in the doorway. Her sobs echoed along the corridor.

Walsingham stepped inside and closed the doors. 'I am glad it was you who said that,' he said wryly.

'Leicester, what possessed you?' Sussex asked. 'You as good as called her old.'

'What if I did? It's time some of us faced the truth. How old is the duke? Seventeen, eighteen? And the queen nearing six and forty. I tell you, Sussex, bed her with the duke and we will lose her.'

'That is by no means certain.'

'It would be dangerous for her to bear a child now,' Robert persisted. 'Or does your ignorance prevent you from even realising that fact?'

'It seems to me that she wants to marry, despite her talk of policy,' Hatton said gloomily, falling into his chair.

'There is no other business today, gentlemen,' Walsingham announced, gathering up his papers.

'Do you really think she wants to marry?' Robert asked as he sat down next to Hatton, watching the others file out.

'I fear so, Leicester. I have heard from her Ladies such things that... well, I shudder to believe them.'

'What have you heard?'

'That Simier had... Well, before the duke arrived, the queen permitted him great freedom with her person. And she visits the duke in his bedchamber before he has risen. She stays and dallies with him. Alone.'

'I cannot believe it. She would not... No, I will not believe it.'

'I told you, Leicester, your marriage may have made her desperate.'

'I should see her. Ask her to forgive me for what I said.'

'If she will see you,' Hatton said doubtfully, looking towards the door as there came a knock upon it.

'I must try. Come in,' Robert called.

A page entered. 'A message from the queen, my lord. Her Majesty decrees her counsellors are no longer required and will retire to their private homes.'

Robert and Hatton looked at one another in total surprise.

Lettice was in bed when Robert arrived at Leicester House. He told the servants they could retire and went up to her, opening the door quietly and peering round. Lettice lay back in the bed, the sheets stretched over her bulbous belly. He tiptoed in and began undressing.

'I'm awake, Rob,' she said. 'I didn't wake you, did I?'

'No, I was waiting for you.' She propped herself up on

one elbow, her red hair falling over her shoulders. 'Well, what news?'

'No change.'

'You mean she still has not made up her mind?'

'No, and blames the council for it.' He sat down on the end of the bed. 'Are you well? Your face is flushed.'

'No,' she said, pressing her fingertips to her forehead, 'I haven't felt well all day.'

'You should have sent word. I would have returned.'

'There was nothing you could do. I always feel like this when I am near my time. Don't fret so, Rob. Childbirth is something I am used to.'

He smiled and kissed her cheek. 'Well, you shall have me for company for the next few days, my love, whether you want me or not.'

'Why? Are you not needed at court?'

'Seems not. None of us are. Cecil, Walsingham, Hatton, myself, all of us are banished from the court because the queen is annoyed with us.'

'Oh, she is being ridiculous. Get into bed and rub my back,' she ordered. 'How is she supposed to govern without you all?'

'She's frightened, Lettice.'

'Of what?'

'Of marriage. Of the wedding night, I think.'

'Someone should tell her to ignore the panic and enjoy the pleasure.'

'She's not like you, Lettice.'

'What do you mean by that?'

'The act of love is something to be feared for Elizabeth. Believe me, I know.'

Lettice turned to him, her interest aroused. 'And how do you know? Is our revered virgin queen no virgin?'

'Of the queen's virginity, I can say only this. I, nor no man before me, ever took her maidenhead.'

'But you doubt her now? Why?'

'Hatton told me that Simier has been allowed certain liberties. Ones that I thought a mere servant, and a Frenchman at that, would never be allowed.'

'You don't mean to say—'

'But they are only rumours,' he insisted. 'And I prefer not to believe them. Elizabeth would not forget herself with such a man.'

'You hope?'

'I hope. But you're tired, Lettice. Put out the light.'

Someone was shaking him, but he didn't want to wake up. He was warm and happy. It was a bright, breezy summer day, and he was playing. Winning, of course, until Guildford started crying and his mother said he was to let his brother win. Robert should have been cross, but he hadn't seen Gil for such a long time and Robert was happy to do anything to make him happy. A hand on his shoulder made him jump. He turned and there was his father, smiling at him. But then his father started talking. He looked as if he was shouting, but Robert could barely hear him.

'Rob. Rob. ROBERT!'

He reluctantly pulled his eyelids apart. 'Wh… what?'

'The child,' Lettice panted, gripping his arm.

'It's coming?' Robert asked, suddenly wide awake.

Lettice groaned in answer. Within minutes, Robert had roused the household, lamps had been lit, doctor and midwife sent for and now all there was to do was wait.

Before the sun rose, Robert was holding his son.

CHAPTER FIFTY-ONE

Elizabeth and her counsellors waited in the council chamber. Elizabeth spoke quietly and tiredly, patting Cecil's hand and shaking her head. He was ill again and should have been in bed, but Elizabeth had summoned him and he was a dutiful servant.

The chamber door opened and Alençon rushed in, Simier and the French ambassador, Fenelon, following more sedately behind. Alençon grabbed Elizabeth's hand which, to Robert's eye, she reluctantly offered and he pressed his thick misshapen lips to it.

'My lady,' he exclaimed in French, 'how cruel of you to keep me waiting for a glimpse of your face.'

Elizabeth smiled thinly and withdrew her hand. 'I would not willingly be cruel,' she answered in English, 'but my face is the better for seeing yours.'

Alençon began talking again in French. Elizabeth waved a reproving finger.

'My lord, English, if you please.' She indicated the council members, though she knew they all understood the French language. Alençon looked contrite, bowed his head and took a seat alongside his countrymen.

'Let us to business,' Elizabeth said, looking pointedly at Walsingham, who seemed to be taking his time at starting the meeting.

Walsingham, who had been expecting the flattery and love play to go on a while longer, looked up in surprise and opened his mouth to speak.

'When are we to marry?' Alençon interrupted.

Elizabeth flicked a glance at him. 'Patience, my lord.'

'I am not a patient man.'

Elizabeth's lips tightened.

Robert saw his opportunity. 'My lord,' he said, leaning forward and placing his elbows on the table, steepling his fingers beneath his chin, 'there are further terms to be discussed before a date can be settled on.'

'I am not aware of further terms, Leicester,' Cecil said, frowning.

'No, I believe you were ill when it was discussed in council,' Robert lied smoothly.

'When what was discussed?'

'A concession on the duke's part.'

'A concession?' Alençon queried, looking between Robert and Simier.

Simier's eyes narrowed as Robert continued.

'Indeed, for the many that England has already ceded.'

'Concessions have been made on both sides, my lord,' Fenelon pointed out in his best diplomatic voice.

'I agree, sir. But England has borne the brunt of the negotiations, and if you'll forgive me, we come off the worst for it. But let there be no lack of harmony between us. Our proposal is that since the late Queen Mary was so unfortunate as to lose Calais, we have had no port in France where we can trade and come and go in as we please. So, we propose that Calais be restored to English sovereignty.'

Robert sank back in his chair, enjoying the long

moment of stunned silence as his words sunk in. Then the room seemed to explode with noise. The duke rose to his feet, and exclaimed in ridiculously fast French the outrage he felt at the earl's words, while Fenelon appealed to Elizabeth to explain. Sussex harangued Robert for not having discussed this new tactic, while Simier sat, still and silent, his eyes locked in an understanding with Robert, whose own eyes dared him to act.

'Your Majesty,' Simier said in a low voice and, astonishingly, the room quietened. 'The earl has made a most audacious proposal, and despite what he says, I do not think it a proposal discussed or agreed upon in council. The earl himself puts this forward to shatter any chance of making my master's happiness or your own.'

'That is a bold assertion, sir,' Robert declared. 'The queen's happiness is more important to me than anything, second only to that of England, as the queen would agree. If I thought she could find happiness in marriage to a prince of France, I would not oppose you.'

'So, you do oppose me?' Alençon demanded.

'I find you a most personable and charming man, my lord, a credit to France and an ornament to our court. But I would be no good counsellor if I did not advise the queen what is best for her country as well as for her.'

'You deny that marriage would be good for Her Majesty?' Simier countered.

'Marriage between princes is a political contract. As I have said, the welfare of the country is the queen's and my first concern.'

Simier slammed his hand on the table. 'You profess such concern for queen and country.'

'I am devoted to both, sir, and you will address me as 'my lord'.'

'Indeed, my lord,' Simier sneered. 'And how does your wife feel about being third in your consideration?'

'My wife is none of your concern.'

'But she may be of concern to Her Majesty, who has no knowledge of her, as you have seen it fit to keep her existence a secret.'

A silence fell upon the group. All eyes were upon Elizabeth. 'You will all leave,' she said finally. 'The earl will remain.'

The company rose, the duke reaching out to take her hand, but Elizabeth kept it resolutely by her side. Simier plucked at his sleeve and the duke followed him out of the chamber.

'Bess,' Robert murmured.

'Must I be made a laughing stock, Robin?'

'You should have told them you already knew about Lettice. Why didn't you?'

'And admit to them all that you didn't care for me?' She gave a hollow laugh. 'Well, they've known all along, I suppose.'

'You know that's not true,' he said, taking her hand. 'God strike me dead the day I stop loving you.'

She squeezed his hand. 'How can I face them?'

'You're the queen. You can face anyone.' He reached up and smeared her tears across her cheeks. She nestled against his hand and smiled weakly.

'The pretence has turned sour now,' she said.

'What pretence?'

'I don't want to marry the duke.'

'I'm so glad to hear you say that, Bess.'

'Even though you have the pleasure of being wed yourself?'

'I assure you, Bess, there are times when being a married man is anything but a pleasure.'

She stroked his face. 'You are a terrible liar, Rob.' She sniffed. 'They'll expect me to send you to the Tower.'

'Send me, then. If it will help you face them.'

'I could never send you to that place, not again.' She smoothed her skirts and took a deep breath. 'You had best call Cecil in.'

Cecil entered, surprised to find Robert still in one piece.

'Oh, don't look so wary, Cecil,' Elizabeth said. 'I haven't murdered Leicester, nor do I intend to.'

'You see, Cecil,' Robert got to his feet, 'Simier thinks he has surprised the queen. He has not. Her Majesty has known for some time that I am married.'

'Indeed,' Cecil raised an eyebrow. 'I was not aware.'

'I'm afraid I have an unpleasant job for you, Cecil,' Elizabeth said. 'You must tell the duke there will be no marriage between us.'

'But—,' Cecil started.

She cut him off with a wave of her hand. 'I am resolute. There is to be no marriage. I have no doubt he will have to be bought off, but I rely upon you to do it as cheaply as possible. Now, I dismiss you both. I am not to be disturbed for the rest of the day.'

The brush pulled gently at the queen's thinning hair. She was melancholy tonight and unusually silent. No gay chatter, no laughter broke the quiet tension of the room. Her ladies looked at one another from beneath lowered lids and each trod carefully lest their footfalls rouse their mistress.

Someone knocked on the door. Elizabeth pointed to her wig with its tight red coils and jewels. With it fixed in place, she signalled for the door to be opened.

'Has he gone?' she asked as soon as Robert entered.

He nodded. 'I left the duke of Alençon on a sandbank, madam.'

'Stranded?' she gasped. 'Oh, Rob, you didn't?'

'I did,' he assured her, taking a seat and helping

himself to wine. 'And from what I hear, the Monkey is in high disgrace. One of my men overheard an almighty quarrel between him and the duke.'

'Really?'

'Yes. My man doesn't understand French too well, but he got the gist of it. Alençon seemed to think that Simier had let him down, that he shouldn't have said what he did and that he ruined everything.'

'Leave us,' Elizabeth waved away her Ladies. They scurried from the room. 'The duke was right. Were it not for Simier... I suppose I should be grateful to him.'

'A pox on gratitude. You owe him nothing.'

'I am glad they're gone. And do not flatter yourself it was done for you.'

'What?'

'That I ended it. I always said I never meant to marry. I was keeping my promise.'

'Hatton believed you wanted to marry the duke,' Robert said.

'Oh, and you did not?'

He shrugged. 'I knew better.'

'You presume to know me better, do you? Well, I tell you, little man, you know me not at all. What do you know of my heart?'

'Forgive me. I meant no... I merely meant—'

'Yes, merely. You would do well to remember your place, my lord.' She moved away to the fireplace, kicking at a log sticking out from the hearth with a slippered toe.

Robert searched his mind for something to say, wanting to ease the sudden tension between them.

'I have news, madam,' he ventured. Elizabeth turned her head slightly, still frowning. 'I have a son.'

'A boy,' she said dully. 'He is well?'

'Yes, bonny and lusty.'

'His name?'

347

'Robert.'

'You already have a son called Robert.'

'Yes, but this one is legitimate. The other was base born.'

'Oh,' she rolled her eyes, 'I remember your sister telling me about you.'

'What did Mary tell you?'

'Your obsession with the family name. How it must be continued.'

'I see nothing wrong with that,' Robert said defensively. 'My father thought the same.'

'As did mine,' Elizabeth agreed, 'but it is I who bears the scars for it. I wonder if he can see me now. Sovereign of such a country, with subjects a queen can be proud of. He would never have believed a woman could rule alone.'

'If ever a woman could, that woman would be the daughter of Henry the Eighth.'

'And of Anne Boleyn,' Elizabeth said quietly, looking down at her hands. 'I killed my mother, you know. Had I been a son, she would have been safe. It's strange, but when I was a child, I thought my father was a god. He seemed one to me. People worshipped him, obeyed him, and he had the power of life and death over them. And he exercised that power all too often.' She leant over to a side table and pulled a mirror towards her. She stared into it.

'No one ever told me when my mother died, but I knew something was happening. All the servants, they all tiptoed around me, and everyone, everyone was whispering and casting furtive glances at me. My dear Kat, God bless her, told me as sweetly as she could. She said that my mother was in a better place but that I would not see her again, and I must not ask for her or say anything to anyone. I was but child of three, but I understood she was dead. I asked Kat why my mother was gone. As far as I knew, she had not been ill and I could not comprehend any other reason. I remember Kat hesitated. I suppose she was wondering what she could tell me. And then Kat told me my mother had offended the king, and she had been punished. She would not tell me more. Only later, when Katherine Howard died, did she give me the full story, of what my mother had done. I believed her, believed that my mother was such a wanton, that she would fornicate with her own brother. If I didn't believe it, then my father was a murderer and my father couldn't be that. But the same thing happened to Katherine, and I started to doubt.'

'After Katherine,' Robert said slowly, 'that was when you told me you would never marry.'

'Now you understand why I said it. I still cannot think ill of my father. Odd, isn't it? I know he had my mother murdered. And those crimes she was accused of would never have been brought against her if I had been the son my father craved. No one would dare to attack the mother of the heir to the throne. But the only child she had was a girl and I couldn't protect her.'

'You blame yourself? But Bess, it wasn't your fault. How could it be?' He reached out and squeezed her shoulder.

'You may not touch me,' she said, shrugging off his hand. 'I am pleased you have a son.'

'I could bring him to you, if you wish,' he offered.

'In time. Perhaps. When he is older.'

'My wife could bring him any time.'

Elizabeth's eyes narrowed. 'Robert, this is the last time I will tell you. As far as I am concerned, your wife does not exist.'

CHAPTER FIFTY-TWO

1584

Robert opened one bleary eye. 'What is it?' he mumbled into the pillow.

The head poking through the bed hangings smiled roguishly. 'The queen wants to ride, my lord,' Johnson, his manservant, said. 'You had best rise.'

'Now?' Robert said incredulously.

'I am afraid so, my lord.'

Robert threw the bedclothes off and sat up. 'Get me my slippers. And take that grin off your face, you knave. How the devil does she do it?'

'Do what, my lord?'

'Stay up most of the night and still get up with the lark. Oh, who is that?'

Johnson opened the door. 'Sir Christopher,' he announced, holding the door open wider for the chancellor to enter.

'Leicester,' Hatton said loudly, 'are you still not dressed?'

'Should I be at this ungodly early hour?' Robert grumbled, moving behind the screen that enclosed his close-stool and emptying his bladder. 'What do you want, Hatton?'

'The queen sent me to hurry you along. It's a good job I came.'

Robert grunted, shrugging off his nightshirt and grimacing at the sight of his rotund belly. 'Quick, give me my clothes.' He was almost dressed when there came another knock at the door. 'If that is someone else sent to hurry me...'

'Who are you?' Johnson demanded of the tall, ginger-haired lad standing in the doorway.

'Tom.'

'Tom who?'

But Robert recognised the voice. 'Tom, what are you doing here? Is something wrong?'

'The countess sent me to fetch you, my lord. She begs you to return to her with all haste. Your son—'

Robert grabbed Tom's shoulders and swung him round to face him. 'Not dead?'

Tom blinked and swallowed uneasily. 'Not when I left. But he was very sick then, my lord.'

Johnson touched Robert gently on the arm and he flinched as if he had been struck. 'My lord, shall I pack?'

'No,' Robert's voice came out cracked. 'No time. We must leave at once.'

'Just your boots then, my lord,' Johnson said, leading him by the elbow towards a chair. Robert obeyed meekly, feeble hands, his own, tugging at the boots to pull them on. Johnson threw a riding cloak over his shoulder and tied it deftly under Robert's left armpit.

'Hatton,' Robert said, looking up at him blankly, 'will you tell the queen—'

'Yes, yes,' Hatton waved him silent, 'don't worry, I shall tell her. You get to your son, my friend. I pray to God that all will be well.'

.   .   .

351

Robert rode like the devil, Johnson and Tom struggling to keep up. When they reached Wanstead and the house was in sight, Robert closed his eyes. *Please God*, he prayed, *please do not let my son die.*

Robert flung open the front door and charged into the hall. 'Where is your mistress?' he demanded of a huddle of girls at the bottom of the stairs.

'In the nursery, my lord,' one answered timidly, pointing upstairs. They scurried out of his way as he sped past them. He paused on the top stair to catch his breath; he had caught sight of the nursery door, a weak light melting through the gap at the bottom. He continued on, his hand shaking as he reached for the handle.

Lettice sat beside the small bed that contained their son, the faint glow of the candles throwing into perfect relief the bear and ragged staff emblem carved on the wooden frame. She turned as Robert entered, her face oddly crumpled. Her hand flew to her mouth as their eyes met, muffling fresh sobs. She looked back at the bed, not wanting to waste a moment when she could look at her son. Robert's throat tightened as he approached his wife and child. Clutching at Lettice's shoulder for support, he felt her hand, cold and bony, grasp at his fingers.

The Noble Imp, their nickname for their little boy, so lovingly bestowed when he had run into their bedroom not three months before wearing the tiny suit of armour Robert had had made for him as a surprise, lay pale and unmoving, save for the slight rise and fall of his chest beneath the covers. His breathing was too shallow and his mouth, so sweetly cherubic, lay open, his lips pale and cracked. Someone, one of the doctors perhaps, stepped from the shadowy corners of the room and provided Robert with a chair. He sat down next to Lettice, held her hand, and with the other, took hold of his son's. He bent and kissed the small fingers.

Robert prayed every prayer he knew, promised anything. Lettice prayed beside him, all the servants in the house prayed, Hatton and Walsingham prayed, everyone at court friendly to Robert prayed.

But God was not listening.

At least he wasn't listening to them. A jealous woman who had been told of the news thought a wicked thought. It was brief, and she regretted it at once, but it had existed and it could not now be undone. If the boy died, she had thought, Robert would have no reason to stay with Lettice. As her father had once said, when a monarch prayed, God listened.

CHAPTER FIFTY-THREE

'Rob?' Mary stepped into the room. She saw her brother sitting by the fire, one hand against the side of his head, his dog, Boy, lying on the rug, his chin upon Robert's feet. She laid her hand on his arm. Robert looked up, startled.

'Mary,' he said croakily, and made to rise.

She stayed him with her hand and moved to the place vacated by Boy, who was pushing his wet nose into her hand. She knelt down and grasped Robert's hands, looking up earnestly into his face.

He smiled weakly, stroking her lumpy cheek. 'You're not wearing your veil.'

'How are you?'

'I'm not sure, to be honest.'

'How's Lettice?'

'She cried herself to sleep.'

'Shouldn't you be resting?'

'I'm not tired. I'm...,' he shrugged, 'I'm not anything.'

'I can't imagine how you must be feeling.' Mary looked up into his face and saw tears streaming down his cheeks. 'Oh, Rob.' She pulled him down to her, putting her arms about him, resting his head against her breast.

'Mary, I am cursed.'

'Cursed? What do you mean?'

'Everything I love dies.'

'Oh, Rob, that's ridiculous. You have Lettice. You have me and Ambrose. Now, sit back up in your chair.'

'Oh, my head hurts.' He smiled meekly. 'So, tell me, what do I do now?'

'Go back to work?' she suggested.

'What there is of it.'

'What do you mean?'

'Mary, I'm not what I once was. My influence is on the wane, the queen doesn't care for me as she used to, my work abroad is being undone by my colleagues on the council, and now, all hope of the Dudley name living on for centuries is gone.'

'You may have more children.'

He shook his head. 'Lettice is past bearing now. There won't be any more children. Ironic, isn't it? I have a healthy son, whom I have made a bastard, and Lettice had four healthy children by Walter Devereux to carry on his name. And yet, together, we couldn't make even one strong enough to carry on mine.'

'You will go back to court?'

'There is nothing there for me.'

'Robert,' Mary said sharply, 'you will be missed.'

'By whom, exactly?'

'The queen will miss you. Despite what you say. She wrote to me.'

'She sent a very sympathetic message. To *me*. Not to Lettice.'

Mary shook her head in disgust. 'She should have sent something to your wife.'

'No, not her. Even a mother's grief wouldn't soften that hard heart.'

'You sound so bitter against her.'

'I am. I have had to endure her scorn and public humiliation time without number. I tell you, if I don't go back to court, I shall not miss that.'

'But what else would you do? You tried your hand once at being a country gentleman and that nearly drove you mad.'

'I was younger then. And lustier. I did not have this belly when I was twenty.'

She rubbed at his stomach. 'Does it still pain you?'

'Now and again. It's nothing I can't endure. If I can endure losing my son....' He began to cry again.

Mary pulled a chair alongside her brother and once more laid his head against her breast.

WHITEHALL PALACE

'Has Leicester returned yet?' Hatton asked, stopping Walsingham in the corridor.

'He's arriving this afternoon. I've just had a letter from him.'

'How does he sound?'

'Melancholy,' Walsingham said. 'And who can blame him?'

'Indeed.'

'And I curse the papists who put this together,' Walsingham held up a green book. 'A libel,' he explained. 'Against Leicester. A vile and malicious slander. Coming on the heels of the death of his son, I dread having to show it to him.'

'Must you, then?'

Walsingham sighed. 'I fear I must. It should be repudiated publicly. It will, no doubt, have a wide distribution by Catholic agents.'

'Can I read it?' Hatton asked eagerly.

Walsingham stiffened. He often found Sir Christopher

Hatton's appetite for gossip distasteful. 'I have only this copy on me at present.'

'Oh, well, I shall read it in council, I'm sure.'

'Yes, well, if you will excuse me, Sir Christopher.'

'Of course. I shall see you soon.'

Walsingham continued on his way. He liked Hatton, who had not a vicious bone in his body, but Walsingham did not want the contents of the book spread before Robert had read it himself. He whiled away a few constructive hours with his secretaries, who had intercepted at least half a dozen letters sent to the Spanish ambassador and were busily decoding their contents. The room grew dark and Walsingham reasoned that by now Robert would have arrived at court. He picked up the book and made for Robert's apartments.

'Am I disturbing you, my lord?'

Robert, dressed head to toe in black mourning, managed a smile in greeting. 'Not at all, Walsingham. Come in.'

'I thank you. Are you well? And your wife?'

'Well enough. Thank you for your letter, Francis. It was most kind.'

Walsingham nodded awkwardly. 'I should really have waited until you are settled.' He waved at the trunks being unpacked.

'Oh, no, not at all. This won't take long. It's just some mourning clothes. But you need me for something?' he asked, almost hopefully.

'Yes. This.' Walsingham proffered the book.

'What is it?' Robert asked, taking it and opening it to the flyleaf. '*The Copy of a Letter written by a Master of Art of Cambridge to his friend in London, concerning some talk passed of late between two worshipful and grave men about the present state, and some proceeding of the earl of Leicester and his friends in England.*'

'A rather cumbersome title. I must warn you, my lord, it is not complimentary.'

'And it's about me?'

'Indeed.'

'I fill up an entire book?' Robert cried incredulously.

'The writer had a lot to say about you. I can give you the main points, if you wish, though I find them embarrassing to repeat.'

'Never mind the embarrassment,' Robert said, flicking through the pages as they both took a seat. 'Leave that till later,' he said to a servant, who was unpacking. 'Go, get your dinner.'

'The main points are,' Walsingham began when they were alone, 'that you have arranged the murder of the following: your first wife, your present wife's former husband, the husband of Douglass Sheffield, the Cardinal de Chatillon, Lady Lennox, Sir Nicholas Throckmorton and the attempted murder of Jean de Simier. Shall I continue?' he asked as he noticed Robert's shocked expression. Robert nodded, open-mouthed. 'That none of Her Majesty's gentlewomen are safe from your lust, that you are the sole reason why the queen has never married—'

'Enough,' Robert snapped, his face as red as Walsingham's. 'I cannot believe it.'

'My lord, the people who write this filth do not know you.'

'Safe from my lust? I am probably one of the chastest men at court.'

'As I said, my lord, scurrilous filth.'

'It must be suppressed. How many copies do you think are in the country?'

Walsingham shook his head. 'It's difficult to say.'

'You are having the usual entry points watched?'

'Of course. But some copies are bound to get through. I can't stop them all.'

'Why am I so hated, Francis?'

Walsingham hesitated. 'It's not just you, my lord. All of us come under attack from time to time. Why, I had to suppress a similar pamphlet about Cecil only last month.'

'Was it as bad as this?'

'No,' Walsingham admitted. 'This is the worse I have seen.'

'Does the queen know of this?'

'I have not yet informed her of it, but she will need to know if we are to issue a proclamation.'

'Let me read it first.'

Walsingham nodded. He looked at Robert for a moment. 'Have you seen the queen yet?'

Robert snapped the book shut and met Walsingham's eye. 'No.'

'Oh. Do you not think you should?'

'I suppose so. Has she asked after me?'

'Only to ask if I had heard from you.'

Robert nodded, as if that was the answer he had expected. 'Will you dine with me?'

'I would like to, my lord, but I expect the queen will want you to dine with her.' He got to his feet. 'Shall I see you in council tomorrow?'

Robert sighed. 'Yes, Francis. Tomorrow.'

Walsingham left, and Robert began to read.

'How long have you been back at court?' Elizabeth demanded as Robert was shown into her chamber.

'A few hours.'

'Hours?' she stamped her foot petulantly. 'How dare you not present yourself sooner? I have to send someone for you—'

'Forgive me, madam,' Robert stopped her before she

could really get started. He was in no mood for a display of her temper.

She glared at him, then noted the sombre blackness of his clothes and suppressed her irritation. 'What have you been doing?'

'Reading. Walsingham gave me a book.'

'Something special about it?'

'He thinks we need to suppress it. And I agree with him. If I may sit down?'

'What is it?' she said, also taking a seat.

'A libel about me.'

'Another?' Elizabeth rolled her eyes. 'Suppress it, like all the others.'

'It is rather more virulent than the others. I am used to being disliked, but this goes past all bounds.'

Elizabeth's eyes narrowed. 'Does it say anything about me?'

'Only by association. It's me who comes in for the filth.'

'Well, let us eat. I shall see Walsingham about it later. Now, tell me how you are.'

'Well enough.'

'I am sorry.'

'I believe you,' he said, fidgeting with his doublet. 'But would it have hurt you to say as much to my wife?'

'I wrote,' she said testily.

'You wrote to me, and while I am grateful for the letter, it hurt me that even a mother's grief had not softened your heart towards Lettice.'

'She has my sympathy, Robin. That's enough.'

He nodded and cut a wing off a chicken. 'I see it will have to be.'

Elizabeth watched him eat. He still had an appetite. That was good. And the wine was disappearing fast enough. His belly was getting big, and she remembered Mary writing that it pained him sometimes. She wished he would talk to her, really talk, and not just pass barbed comments. She wanted him to talk of his son, tell her how he felt. But no doubt he kept that for his wife. Oh yes, Lettice had all the confidences, all his words. Well, Lettice would have to grieve alone. Robert was back at court. And he was staying.

CHAPTER FIFTY-FOUR

'Who is this fellow?' Robert gestured at the tall, handsome man with the country accent who was talking with the queen.

'Walter Raleigh,' Hatton said.

'I know his name,' Robert said irritably. 'I mean, *who* is he? What is his background?'

'A Devon man, a respectable though poor family. I believe there is some family connection to Her Majesty's late mistress, Katherine Ashley. Perhaps that is why he is favoured by the queen.'

'He's in favour because he's handsome and has a pleasing wit,' Robert said bitterly. 'It was ever so with her. Francis,' he reached out and touched Walsingham's arm as he passed. 'Have you got that information I asked for?'

'On the Netherlands? Yes.'

'Excellent,' Robert said. 'Hatton, please excuse me. Well, Francis, what can you tell me?'

Walsingham moved closer and lowered his voice. 'We should expect an embassy from the States, offering a crown.'

'They are willing to cede their sovereignty to us?' Robert asked in surprise.

'It seems so.'

'Will the queen accept?'

Walsingham raised his eyebrows. 'She will not turn down a crown, surely?'

'She would,' Robert said, 'if it meant war with Spain. You know how she dislikes the very idea.'

'But it's a war we should be fighting,' Walsingham said passionately.

'You and I and a hundred other people in this court know that, but every time I broach the subject, she refuses to listen.'

'The queen was ever wont to heed your words, my lord.'

'I know it,' Robert said grimly, 'but now, she has other things to occupy her.' He cocked his head in Raleigh's direction.

'He has found great favour with the queen,' Walsingham agreed.

Robert's lips curled in distaste. 'Well, I'm not staying here to watch her fawn over him. I'm going home to Leicester House in the morning.'

'Then I shall bid you good day, my lord.'

'And you, Francis. Send me any further news you have.'

LEICESTER HOUSE

'Rob, what *is* the matter?'

He had been staring at his book for the last half hour, never once turning the page. 'Hmm? Oh, nothing, my sweet.'

'Very well,' Lettice said huffily, 'don't tell me.'

'It's Raleigh,' he said grumpily.

'Bess has taken a fancy to him, has she?' Lettice

laughed. 'Well, I cannot say I am surprised. He is very handsome.'

'And when have you seen him to know that?' Robert demanded.

'I have passed him on the river, husband. Do not raise your voice to me because you are in a temper.'

'And is his pretty face reason enough to turn a blind eye to the plight of the Netherlanders?'

'If I remember rightly, your pretty face distracted her from policy in your time.'

'That's not true,' he said emphatically. 'She never neglected government. But this Raleigh.'

'Is he really that dangerous?'

'Dangerous? No, I don't think he is—'

'I meant,' Lettice interrupted impatiently, 'dangerous to our interests.'

'Possibly.'

'Then check him.'

'How?'

'By providing her with another distraction. One of your own choosing, who will serve your interests and not his. Give her my son.'

'Give her Essex?'

'Why not? He's as handsome as Raleigh, and as charming, I have no doubt. And it is your duty to advance him.'

'I know that,' he said irritably. 'Then why object?'

'I don't object to taking him to court. I am just doubtful of his reception. Lettice. He *is* your son.'

Lettice glared at him. 'He is also his father's son, and she always claimed a fondness for Walter. Take him to her and see, but don't palm me off with feeble excuses, Robert. If she rejects him, then at least you will have tried. But if she does, she is a greater fool than I think her already.'

'Your Majesty, may I introduce my stepson, the earl of Essex to you.'

Elizabeth squinted down at the young man and looked him over critically. She had known the she-wolf's cub would turn up at court one day and she had resolved not to favour him. But when she had made that decision, she had not expected him to be so handsome.

'Young Robert Devereux,' she said. 'Come nearer, my lord. Why, how like your father you are. Dear Walter.'

Robert rolled his eyes, causing Hatton to smile. She had never called Walter Devereux 'dear' when he had been alive. From the corner of his eye, he saw Raleigh stiffen as the queen smiled on the new boy.

'You are most welcome to court, my lord,' Elizabeth said, evidently having made up her mind to be friendly.

The young man beamed, turned, and grinned again at his stepfather. Robert nodded and smiled, surprised at how easy it had been.

'What did the queen speak about with you?' Robert questioned when his stepson returned to his chambers after spending the afternoon with the queen.

'Oh, many things,' came the answer, as the young Robert helped himself to some wine from the jug and propped his tall body in the window seat. 'I must confess, I had thought I would not care for her, after what Mother has told me.'

'You shouldn't heed everything your mother says about the queen. She has cause to resent her. You do not. Now, I want you to listen, my boy. I've brought you to court because it is my duty to do so, but I'm not going to allow you to waste your time here. I shall be honest with you. I need you.'

'*You* need *me*, sir?' Essex shook his head. 'I can't believe that.'

'Believe it. The queen does not like to be reminded of the passage of time. Entertain her, take her mind off such things. She likes young people about her. I remind her of growing old.'

'She doesn't seem old to me.'

Robert eyed him curiously. 'It's good you think so. It should make your flattery to her all the more convincing. Anyway, your role here is to take some of the attention away from that Raleigh fellow. You understand?'

Essex nodded. 'Completely.' 'Good. I'm relying on you, my boy.'

CHAPTER FIFTY-FIVE

1585

'His Highness, William of Orange, has been shot dead in the Prinsenhof. By a Catholic.' Robert calmly folded the letter he had been reading from and resumed his seat at the council table.

'Shot dead?' Sussex repeated incredulously.

Robert nodded.

'The Catholics.' Walsingham shook his head as if he expected nothing less.

'This changes things,' Robert said, blinking away tears. He was genuinely upset at the death of the sovereign of the Netherlands. He had met the duke, and they had formed an immediate friendship, maintained by family ties. Robert's nephew, Philip Sidney, had been acting as an unofficial ambassador for the queen and a conduit of information and contact-making for Robert.

'I don't see how,' Cecil said.

'Of course it changes things,' Robert said. 'A Catholic has assassinated a Protestant leader, a long-standing ally of England, whose country is being overrun by Spaniards.'

Cecil waved his hand in an understanding gesture. 'Yes,

yes, but we don't want to start a crusade over the death of one man.'

'I'm not speaking of a crusade,' Robert said impatiently. 'Too long have we sat back and watched, done nothing, while the king of Spain's forces conquer that which we should defend.'

'The Netherlands are not England's problem,' Cecil said.

'Then they should be. What are we without them?' Robert demanded, looking appealingly at his colleagues. 'Without them, who do we trade with? The Spanish have all the other trade routes and ports under their dominion.'

'That is not strictly true.' Cecil pulled out a letter from his sheaf of papers. 'Drake has sailed right through Spain's supposed rights of way and is coming back with a shipload of treasure. He anticipates there will be profit in the thousands for the queen and those who invested in his venture,' he finished, looking pointedly at Robert.

'I, too, have had a letter from Drake, Cecil. He has managed to get through this time, I grant you, but King Philip's ambassador, Mendoza, is already insisting on punishment and restitution. Drake shall not do so well again. Besides, this is more than a mere financial argument.'

'I disagree,' Cecil snapped his folder shut, indicating he had said all he intended.

Robert raised his chin higher. 'Then I shall take this to the queen.'

'I advise you not to trouble the queen with this, Leicester.'

'I shall do as I think best, Cecil.'

'As you wish, my lord, but I doubt you will hear what you want.'

. . .

It was some hours before Robert was granted an audience with the queen and it soon became obvious that Cecil had got to her first.

Elizabeth was at her desk reading when Robert entered. He glanced at the book over her shoulder. 'Ah, Spenser. He's one of my secretaries, you know. Good fellow. He gets on very well with my nephew, Philip.'

'That impudent pup,' Elizabeth snorted. 'I have not forgiven him for that letter he wrote to me years ago, telling me I should not consider marriage with the duke of Alençon.'

'Which he wrote for me.'

'Well, of course he wrote it for you. I am no fool, I know that,' she scolded. 'I will not have him back at court, so save your breath.'

'No, madam, that is not what I would say. In fact, he serves me better where he is.'

Elizabeth raised an eyebrow. 'And where is that?'

'At present, in the Netherlands. I received a letter from him today. Would you read it, please?' He held out the letter to Elizabeth.

She turned her head away. 'I already know what it says and your opinion of what we ought to do about it.'

'I see,' Robert nodded, and refolded the letter slowly.

Her eyes narrowed. 'What do you see, Robin?'

'Cecil has prejudiced you against me.'

'Oh, don't be so melodramatic.' She looked up at him and grinned. 'Cecil tells me that Drake is returning laden with bounty.'

'Yes, your pirate is on his way.'

'My merchant adventurer, Robin,' Elizabeth smirked.

Robert settled into a chair. 'Bess, as you know, I have many friends in the Netherlands. With the Spanish running amuck, they're appealing to me to help them.'

'So Cecil told me. What form do they envisage this help taking?'

'They ask for an army. With me at its head.'

Elizabeth studied him for a moment. 'And how long has that idea been brewing, my cunning Rob?'

He smiled. 'For quite a while, I admit.'

'Then I will consider it,' Elizabeth said. 'For quite a while, I think.'

Robert smiled at the two men sitting opposite, the deputation that Philip Sidney had promised were coming from the Netherlands. One of them spoke so little English he had barely said a word since he had arrived, while the other had been so flattered by Robert's greeting that it had made him appear a little self-important.

He smiled back at Robert. 'Our terms are these. Your sovereign provides aid to our poor country in arms and money. And in return, when the war is over and we have won, she will reign over our people.'

Cecil leant forward, peering at a piece of paper in his wrinkled hands. 'Just so I understand, sir. In exchange for men and money, the sovereignty of the States General will pass to Elizabeth, our queen?'

'That is correct.'

'That is quite an offer,' Robert said.

'We are in great need,' the envoy said earnestly.

'So it would appear,' Cecil said, his reluctance evident.

'We were led to believe,' the envoy said hastily, 'that our offer would be accepted.'

'And who led you to believe such a thing?' Cecil asked. The Dutchman glanced at Robert. Cecil caught the look. 'I am afraid the earl of Leicester is not placed to provide you with assurances of any kind regarding Her Majesty.'

Robert felt the heat flood his cheeks. How dare Cecil humiliate him like this!

'Cecil,' he snapped, 'you mistake the situation. Her Majesty is quite aware of my involvement in the affairs of the States General. Understand, I speak for the queen, and the Dutch need only confirmation from her regarding appeals.'

'Really, my lord?' Cecil raised a sceptical eyebrow. 'I spoke with the queen this morning and she made no mention of such a bestowment of power.'

'You cannot blame me, Cecil, if Her Majesty does not keep you informed.' Robert laughed, sharing the joke with the Dutch envoy.

Cecil and Robert stared at one another for a long moment, then Cecil rolled up his papers and addressed the Netherlanders. 'This offer, gentlemen, will have to be discussed with the queen before any decision can be made. I and my colleagues thank you for coming to see us. You will be shown the way out.' He gestured to a secretary. Cecil squinted at Walsingham. 'What is that you are writing?'

'A note to Her Majesty,' he said, still scribbling. 'Requesting her presence.'

'Surely this can wait?' Cecil said huffily.

'If you will forgive me, my lord,' Walsingham replied, 'I am secretary of the council and that is a decision for me to make.'

'I am here, gentlemen,' Elizabeth announced, flouncing into the room. 'What did the Netherlanders have to say?'

'As I mentioned to you last week,' Robert began, 'they offer you sovereignty of the Netherlands in return for aiding them against the Spanish invaders.'

'And as I told you last week, I will not accept.'

Cecil snorted quietly. Robert ignored him. 'I understood that you would consider their terms before making a final decision, madam.'

Elizabeth saw Cecil gloating and had no wish to embarrass Robert. 'Yes, I did, I remember now. Well, what are their terms?'

'Francis, that paper.' Walsingham handed it over. 'These are their terms.'

Elizabeth took the sheet he handed her and glanced down the page. Her frown confirmed Robert's fears.

'No, I will not have it,' she said, tossing it aside. 'Madam—'

'I have done as you asked, Robin, I have read their terms and I am still not convinced. If I were to accept a crown from the Dutch, it would mean an open declaration of war on Spain, which may be what you want, Rob, but it's not what I want.'

'It's not a case of my personal wishes, madam,' Robert insisted. 'Francis, what do you say?'

'Aiding the Netherlanders is in all of our interests,' Walsingham said. 'If we do not become involved, the Spanish will take full control of the Netherlands and our wool trade will suffer, probably to the point where it will collapse altogether.'

'Oh, you exaggerate, Sir Francis,' Elizabeth said dismissively.

'No, he does not,' Robert said. 'Our trade will suffer, and if that is not reason enough, then it is our duty to aid the Netherlanders against the Catholic menace.'

'When Philip of Spain has done with the Dutch, he will turn his attention to England,' Walsingham said.

'Oh, his Enterprise of England?' Elizabeth said sceptically. 'He's been talking about that for years and nothing has ever come of it.'

'If the Netherlands were to fall, madam,' Walsingham continued, 'it would make the Enterprise far more likely.'

'I will not accept a crown,' Elizabeth said firmly. 'England is quite enough for me.'

'Then what of aid, madam?' Robert asked impatiently. 'I have agreed to aid them with men and money.'

'With whom at their head?' Walsingham asked.

Elizabeth glanced at Robert. 'Whom do you suggest, Sir Francis?'

Walsingham gestured towards Robert. 'The earl is well known as sympathetic to the Netherlanders cause, madam. He is a known advocate of Protestantism and is one of the foremost peers of the realm.'

'And they know how close he is to me, so I am likely to favour him in any cause that concerns them,' Elizabeth finished.

'That was not what I was going to say,' Walsingham said tersely.

'That is what they are thinking though, isn't it, Rob?'

'I trust they are not, madam.'

'I hope not for their sake. You will not go. Someone else. Sir John Norreys, maybe.'

Elizabeth jumped as Robert slammed his fist down on the table. 'They do not ask for John Norreys. They want me.'

Elizabeth glowered at him, her jaw tightening. 'Do not presume to raise your voice to me, sir. If I say you will not go, you will not go. I will hear no more about this. Sir Francis, you are to inform Sir John Norreys of my decision.'

She rose, ending the meeting, and left the chamber. Walsingham glanced at Robert and shook his head apologetically. Hatton wiped inky fingers on the tablecloth and said quietly, 'I did not think she would let you go. Leicester, wait.'

Robert had thrown his chair back, ignoring the clatter as it fell over and thudded against the floor. He hurried after the queen.

'Your Majesty,' he shouted as he turned a corner and spied her entourage further ahead. He quickened his pace as Elizabeth halted and turned. 'I must speak with you, Your Majesty.'

'I have said all I mean to, Robin.'

'You must hear me, madam.'

'Must?' she repeated, raising an eyebrow.

'I beg you.'

'Very well.' They walked to her chamber. 'I know what you would say,' she began. 'You can spare yourself the trouble.'

'Madam, I beg you, let me go.'

'I have already spoken on the matter.'

'I mean no disrespect, but I fear you do not fully understand the matter. Let me explain, away from Cecil, so he cannot influence you and I shall give you the clear, unvarnished truth.'

'That will be a first for you. Very well. On with your lecture, sir.'

'No lecture, Bess,' he said tiredly, taking a seat. He pointed towards her Ladies. 'Must they stay?'

She smothered a little smile and told them to leave. 'You never like my Ladies around you, do you?'

'I'm not keen on giving Cecil's spies information. Anyway, whoever you send to the Netherlands will be there as your representative. Do you want a nobody to be your deputy? Who in the Netherlands has heard of Sir John Norreys?'

'He is an able soldier.'

'That, I do not doubt, but he is a knight. I am an earl, thanks to your good graces. An earl who understands their plight and one who sympathises with it, and sees the potential damage to England, a country I love as much as you do.'

'That is quite a speech, Rob,' Elizabeth said, quietly impressed. 'You wish to leave my court?'

'I wish to be of service, Bess.'

'You are of service. Here.'

'I can serve you better there.'

'You would be away for months, perhaps years. I can't have you from me for such a long time.'

He leaned forward anxiously. 'The Netherlands are only a few days' sailing away. I could return at a moment's notice.'

'And leave your men?' she asked sharply.

He smiled at Elizabeth, being as contrary as ever. 'I would obey your orders.' He waited for an answer, but she just sat there, her chin upon her hand. 'For thirty years, I have served you faithfully and will do so until the day I die. But for those thirty years, you have had me tied to your skirts, as if I cannot be trusted away from you. You will have unmanned me, Bess, if you do not send me on this mission.'

'I unman you?'

'I have not been on a battlefield since St Quentin,' he fell back exasperatedly. 'You refused to let me go to Le Havre, and I obeyed you in that.'

'A good thing I did refuse, otherwise it might have been you who was shot and not your brother.'

'My point is I obeyed you in that, to my eternal shame.'

'There have been no other battles for you to fight in,' she said proudly.

'How can I persuade you?' he asked desperately. 'Tell me, how?'

'I will not be bullied,' she shouted, stamping her foot. 'Oh, I have had enough of this. If you so desperately wish to leave me, you can go.'

375

Robert fell to his knees. 'Oh, Bess, you will not regret it, I promise you. Just think of the benefits. I will serve your interests, none other, and I can anticipate your wishes, for I know you so well.'

'I shall hold you to that, Rob. Now, get up. But just one thing. Your wife stays in England. Do not argue with me on this, Rob. You can go to the Netherlands, if you want, but you go alone. I won't have Lettice queening it over there.'

'Very well, Bess,' Robert agreed. If that was her one condition, he could live with it.

'Well, go. No doubt you will want to start making arrangements.' She waved him away. 'Send Essex to me. I could do with some entertainment.'

CHAPTER FIFTY-SIX

He was gone. Elizabeth lay in her bed, her favourite spaniel rolling against her legs, showing his belly, waiting for his accustomed caress. None came. The dog was forgotten, for Robert was gone. Strange, she had not thought she would miss him so. She had other men now, younger and wittier, Raleigh, for example, and Essex. So, why should she miss him so?

He had been gone but three days. She leant over to the table beside the bed and fumbled in its drawer. Her fingers closed around the object she sought. A small oval frame. She smiled at its label: *My lord's portrait*. It was an old picture, of course, painted many years before. When had she last looked at this? Oh, yes, she remembered. It was when James Melville, Mary Stuart's ambassador, had come to court and she had just created Robert the earl of Leicester. What had she said to Melville then? That when Mary Stuart had Robert, she would need the picture, and she had snatched it from his hands. Why had she let him go to war? He could be hurt or killed. She knew she had been unkind, making him cold in the shade of her favour while she preferred his stepson and other handsome young men.

377

But that was only because she was getting old and she did not want to be reminded of it every time she looked at him. And yes, she wanted to make him suffer, as she suffered. Her nights were tormented with thoughts of him and Lettice, and haunted by the ghost of the little boy she had wished dead. That was why she slept so little, demanded so many diversions. And now war, always men pushing her towards war. More deaths on her conscience, more danger for those she loved. Maybe she should recall him? But he would hate her for it, and then she would lose him completely.

God help me, she prayed, *tell me what to do.*

THE NETHERLANDS

The mighty cannons of the port of Flushing boomed and their thunder rolled across the sea, rumbling to the hull of the ship that carried the new Lieutenant General, Robert Dudley. A small boat carried him and his party to the dock, where fireworks erupted high over their heads and the crowds hanging over railings cheered and banged their drums. Robert waved and smiled and wondered if this was how Elizabeth felt when she went out into the streets of London or on progress through the country. Was this what it felt like to be a king?

'Uncle,' Philip hallooed him from the dockside. 'It's good to see you.'

'And you, my boy,' Robert called, taking the hand of a sailor and setting foot on to firm land. 'I didn't expect such a reception.'

'Then you should have done, Uncle,' Philip said. 'The Netherlanders are a sorry people at present, but they have great hopes of you.'

Robert grimaced. 'I feel sure then that they will be disappointed.'

'Why?'

'I'll tell you later. Where do we go from here?'

'To your headquarters for the next two nights. Then you go to Middlebury, Rotterdam, Delft, other towns whose names I have forgotten, ending at the Hague. So, I warn you, Uncle, this will be a tiring fortnight for you. Pageants and entertainments—'

'No more than on one of the queen's progresses, my boy. You must not worry about me.'

'Then I must defy my mother,' Philip laughed.

'Well, you can write to your mother and tell her not to worry about me, either. I'll be fine. I have you with me.'

'You have rather more than me. I understand on that fleet out there,' Philip pointed back to the dock where the English ships floated on the horizon, 'are ten thousand horse and six thousand foot soldiers. Is that right?'

'Sounds right,' Robert nodded, 'and we shall need them.'

'And more besides, I should not wonder,' Philip agreed grimly.

'Well, don't hope for more men. The queen has made it quite clear that she doesn't favour this operation and no doubt she will keep a tight rein on her purse strings.'

Philip moved closer to Robert and asked quietly, 'What are the terms of your commission from the queen?'

Robert shrugged. 'To maintain defences.'

'Uncle,' Philip frowned, 'I have seen the terms of the Netherlanders commission to you. They expect you to perform offensive manoeuvres as well as defensive. I gave them a promise.'

'I know you did, and I'm sorry. But it's not me, it's the queen. What can I do?'

'But when the Netherlanders find out your limits?' Robert patted his arm. 'We'll talk about it later, Phil. Just let me enjoy the moment.'

379

CHAPTER FIFTY-SEVEN

1586

'Uncle, let me call a physician,' Philip said, handing Robert a cup of hot wine.

'He could do nothing.' Robert shook his head, wincing at another stab of pain in his stomach. 'It will be better in the morning.'

'I cannot stand by and see you in pain,' Philip persisted.

'Phil, I thank you for your concern, but it must cease. The last fortnight has been a strain, that is all. Now, come and sit by me.'

'Well, now the pageantry is over, the real work can begin.'

'I have already started,' Robert said, handing Philip a rolled-up sheet of paper. 'That has been given to the commanders to be posted up all over the camp.'

Philip unrolled the paper and read aloud. 'Every man is to attend church services, no swearing or blaspheming, no whores or other camp followers, and under no circumstances are there to be violations of women.' He let out a low whistle. 'That is a tall order, Uncle.'

'I don't think so.'

'Women are considered spoils of war.'

'You think we should allow our army to rape women?' Robert asked, aghast.

'Of course not, Uncle,' Philip assured him hastily. 'I can think of nothing more abhorrent than rape, any disregard for women. But you and I speak of our own station. Such strictures rarely apply to men baser than we. You and I are not the rabble that serve in this army. How can you expect to enforce such a law?'

'By the severest penalty. Any man found violating a woman will be taken and hung immediately. It says there.' He pointed with the tip of a quill to the broadsheet.

'Very well, Uncle.' Philip rolled the sheet back up and stuffed it into his doublet. 'I trust the proclamation will deter any man from testing your punishment.'

'I hope so,' Robert nodded, shifting uncomfortably in his seat. 'Phil, is there something you want to say to me? You seem to have an expectant air about you.'

Philip nodded. 'If we are only to defend the towns we already hold and make no overt gestures of war towards the Spanish, what are you going to do when the Netherlanders demand more?'

'I could tell them the truth, that the queen hopes my presence here will make the Spanish pack up their guns and go home, but then, that would sound ridiculous, wouldn't it?'

'The queen must be made to understand the situation here, Uncle. Is there no one you can send to her to explain?'

'Walsingham will do what he can for me,' Robert said. 'And I have been telling her for months.'

'I fear the queen is ill using you, Uncle,' Philip said, patting Robert's hand. 'Does she know how unwell you are? Sending you here—'

'I asked for this command, Phil. I need it.'

'Even if it makes you ill, and it will do, Uncle, I can see it.'

'I can't expect you to understand,' Robert said kindly. 'You are a young man, and will, no doubt, do great things. My time is nearly up and what have I to show for it? Nothing. No son, you are my heir. No achievements, only a reputation for scandal. I need to achieve something before I die. You say nothing, Phil, I see, you know it's true.'

'I know you think it is true. But I assure you, Uncle, your family knows your worth, even if nobody else does.'

'My New Year's gift to the queen,' Robert said, holding up a necklace of pearls and jewels, a large central diamond flanked by enormous rubies. 'It cost a fortune. Do you think she will like it?'

Philip shrugged, raising an eyebrow at such extravagance. 'You know the queen better than I, Uncle.'

'She will like it. Davison will take it back for me when he leaves tomorrow.'

'Talking of Davison, he's outside with a delegation from the Assembly. They want to see you.'

'But it's Sunday,' Robert protested.

'They know and don't care. Will you see them?'

'Oh, I suppose so, though don't let it go on too long. I want my dinner.'

Philip laughed and threw his arm around Robert's shoulders. 'I thought your wife insisted on you eating less, Uncle.'

'She can insist all she wants, Phil. She is not here.'

They strode out into the main hall to meet the delegation. Six men doffed their black caps and bowed. Then they offered him a crown.

Robert wasn't sure he had heard correctly at first, their accents mangling some of their attempts at English pronunciation, but when he looked at Philip, who wore an undisguised expression of surprise and perplexity, he realised he must have heard correctly. They did not call it sovereignty; they termed it Supreme Governor of the United Provinces, but it amounted to the same thing.

Robert thanked them but told them, as any good subject would have done, that he could not accept without his queen's permission. They pressed him again. There was no time for prevarication, they insisted. Their States were divided without a leader. They wanted him to be their leader. Was it not a generous offer?

'God's Death,' Robert yelled as he strode back into his chamber.

'Uncle, what will you do?' Philip asked, grabbing the door and quickly closing it.

'I don't know,' Robert floundered. 'What are they thinking of, putting me in this position?'

'No doubt they thought it would please you.'

'Elizabeth refused their crown and now they as good as offer it to me.'

'You must write to the queen,' Philip hurried to the table and sorted through paper until he found a clean sheet. He dipped a quill into the inkwell, scattering blobs of ink over the tablecloth. 'Shall I write, Uncle?'

Robert was not listening. He stood before the fire, gazing into the dancing flames. His mind was a whirl. Here on offer was what he had wanted all his life. He had briefly been brother to a king consort, son to a king in all but name, and had come close to marrying two queens. All that had escaped him. And now he was being offered the position of Supreme Governor. Well, all right, it was not king, but it was as good as. He wanted it, and God knew he deserved it. Who but him had campaigned so vigorously for the Netherlanders cause? Who had lost favour, standing and health in the pursuit? Here, these people appreciated him, as he had never been appreciated in England.

Philip questioned him again.

'No, not the queen. Cecil and Walsingham first.'

'What do you want me to write?'

'Tell them of the Netherlanders' offer and how much they understand they are beholden to Her Majesty. Tell them I am waiting to hear of the queen's permission before accepting, but trust that her answer will not take too long, as I am importuned to accept with all haste due to the current deplorable situation here. How does that sound?'

'It sounds very good. I shall give it to Davison and he can take it back to England with him tomorrow.'

No word came from Elizabeth. The offer was made again and again, until the Netherlanders grew impatient and irritated with the delay. Much longer and they would feel insulted, too. Robert did not know that bad weather had delayed Davison in reaching England, so Elizabeth didn't hear about the offer until weeks later. By that time, Robert felt he had to accept, but once accepted, he was not so sure he had done the right thing.

Sir Thomas Heneage arrived at Robert's headquarters, cap in one hand and a letter from the queen in the other. He asked to see Robert immediately. Robert, whose brow had grown moist with the news of his arrival, had him shown into his private chamber, sure that he only brought news of condemnation with him.

'Sir Thomas,' Robert greeted him with a forced smile and took his hand. 'You had an easy journey?'

'I did, my lord. You must forgive me if I dispense with some of the pleasantries. I have a letter from the queen.'

Robert swallowed uneasily as Heneage held out the letter with the queen's seal emblazoned upon it. He took the letter and turned his back to read.

Heneage waited patiently while the earl read. These two had once been rivals. Now, Heneage felt only sympathy for the man who suffered under the queen's love.

Robert wiped his sweaty brow with his handkerchief. Elizabeth insisted he renounce the title.

'My lord?' Heneage enquired.

'I suffer the queen's displeasure,' he said, 'but no doubt you knew that already.'

'I did, my lord. But I can tell you, Cecil has worked on your behalf and has persuaded the queen that a formal resignation of your title will not be necessary, just its relinquishment.'

'That was kind of him,' Robert said. 'I do feel the queen's indignation at me could have been avoided, though.'

'In what way, my lord?'

'Davison,' Robert said. 'If he had told the queen what I told him to say, she would have understood that I had no choice.'

'You feel Davison is to blame?'

'Well, am I to blame?' Robert replied indignantly. 'For myself, I would rather have not been put in such a position. I didn't ask for this title.'

No, but you did not refuse it either, thought Heneage, *and here you are, blaming a poor secretary.*

'My lord, perhaps you should write to the queen herself, put your side to her. I am sure you will be able to placate her. You have her love.'

Robert was not so sure.

. . .

Robert did write, but it was some months before Elizabeth calmed down and stopped berating him in her letters. By April, she was calling him her Sweet Robin once more. He could breathe freely again and return with a focused mind to the business of war.

Months passed, and Robert was too busy to worry about Elizabeth. This glorious mission of his to help the Netherlanders chase the Spanish away was turning out to be the biggest disappointment of his life.

His army was suffering, diminishing daily as soldiers died or deserted. Their pay was not even reaching them but being diverted into the corrupt pockets of Robert's officers, and Elizabeth refused to send more. Robert began paying his remaining men out of his own dwindling coffers and it was a relief when he received a letter from Cecil recalling him to England.

There was a dilemma at court. A decision had to be made whether the troublesome Scottish queen, Mary Stuart, imprisoned but constantly plotting, should live or die. Elizabeth was being difficult, and only Robert, out of all her counsellors, knew how to handle her.

CHAPTER FIFTY-EIGHT

1587

WHITEHALL PALACE

'She has signed it.' Davison showed Robert, Walsingham and Cecil the warrant for the execution of Mary Stuart. 'But she said I was not to show it to the council.'

Walsingham looked at Robert. 'Why sign it, then?'

Robert didn't answer, but took the document from Davison.

'We can do nothing,' Cecil sighed. 'Leicester?'

Robert rubbed his chin. 'She wants Mary Stuart dead, I'm sure of it. She just doesn't want to be the one to give the order.'

'No one else can give it,' Walsingham said irritably. 'The order has to come from her.'

'She's worried about the precedent it will create if we execute an anointed queen,' Robert explained. 'She thinks if it could be done to Mary Stuart, then it could be done to her. And she's always been wary of executing her kin.'

'She's different from her father in that, at least,' Walsingham muttered. 'So, what are we going to do?'

'I say we send it on,' Robert said. Cecil and Walsingham looked at him in surprise. 'If we don't, this damn matter will never be resolved and Mary Stuart will continue to plague us with her plots to take the throne. Don't look at me like that. This is what you brought me back for, isn't it? To persuade the queen to make a decision? Well, I've told her she should execute the Scottish queen and, here, she has signed the warrant. What more do you want?'

'She expressly told me not to show it to you, though, my lord.' Davison reminded him.

Robert, still believing that Davison had failed him with his handling of the sovereignty affair, looked up at him meanly. 'I think I have a deeper understanding of the queen than a mere secretary, Davison. Leave this to us.' He was pleased to see Davison redden before he turned back to Walsingham and Cecil. 'Well, are you going to be cowardly or do as I say?'

Walsingham didn't mind being called names, but he agreed with Robert that they would never be free of Mary Stuart until her head was off. 'Send the warrant to Fotheringhay Castle,' he said. 'Have them perform the deed immediately.'

'Cecil?' Robert raised an eyebrow at him.

'Yes,' Cecil said after a long pause, 'send it.'

'Thank God we've reached an agreement,' Robert said, handing the warrant back to Davison. 'Seal it and send it.'

'And if the queen dislikes what we've done?' Walsingham asked when the door had closed upon Davison.

'Fortunately,' Robert said with a tired smile, 'I'll be back in the Netherlands by the time Mary Stuart's head is off, so whatever Elizabeth thinks of our decision, I won't be here to hear it.'

Robert returned to the Netherlands, and a siege. The Spanish inhabitants of the town, Zutphen, had barricaded themselves in against the Dutch and English forces.

'Uncle,' Philip cried, bursting into Robert's tent and waving a letter. 'General Parma has written to Marshal Verdugo. Our soldiers intercepted the messenger.' He paused to catch his breath. 'Parma intends to re-supply Zutphen. He is sending a convoy, guarded by only six hundred men.' Robert snatched the letter from Philip's hand. 'Six hundred, Uncle. We can take that supply train and end this siege. We have men enough, don't you think?'

'Yes, I think we do,' Robert agreed. 'Tomorrow morning then. early.'

'An ambush, Uncle?' Philip grinned.

Robert smiled back, his first in days. 'An ambush, Phil.'

They woke the next morning to a thick fog, and it pleased them, knowing that the fog would hide them. Then it lifted and Robert and Philip could see the supply train. But it was escorted not by six but by fifteen-hundred horsemen and at least three-thousand foot soldiers. The English position exposed, there was no time to retreat. They had no choice but to press on. Their attack had lost the element of surprise, but it was still quick enough for the English cavalry to charge the Spanish and see them retreat beyond their own pikemen. But it was not enough, for no sooner did the English cavalry pass the pikes than they were driven back by musket fire.

'Leicester.' Norreys pulled his horse alongside Robert's and snatched at the mare's bridle. 'I could do with more men.'

'I can't spare any,' Robert shouted above the noise. 'You shall have to do the best you can with what you have.'

'If I must, I must. But you should look more cheerful, my lord. A mere handful of your men have driven the enemy back three times.'

'That should make me cheerful?' Robert scoffed. 'Yes, they have driven the enemy back three times, and three times have they returned. Get back to your men, Norreys. See if you can conjure a victory out of this debacle.'

Robert stood at the entrance to his tent, the flap batting against his arm, watching as the smoke and dirt of battle passed by him. 'How many men did we lose?' he asked as Norreys joined him.

'Twenty-two foot, no more than thirteen horse.'

'And the Spanish? How many did they lose?'

'Three hundred. Maybe more.'

'Well, that is something,' Robert said bitterly. 'For all your talk of victory earlier, the supply train still got through, the Spanish got their supplies.'

'My lord,' shouted a young boy, skidding to a halt before Robert, his short, dirty-blond hair sticking up in spikes where it was coated in dried mud. 'You are wanted in the surgeon's tent.'

Robert suddenly realised he had not seen Philip since that morning. He hurried to the surgeon's tent, his nostrils tightening at its smell of blood and shit from injured and dying men mingling with the noxious fumes of potions. It was dark inside, only a few lamps swinging from the poles holding up the roof. Beneath one of these stood a rickety table and upon it Philip lay, propped against a soldier who still wore his bloody and battered armour. Philip screamed as the surgeon's probe scraped against his bone, the cry ending in a whimper as he tried to stifle his cry.

Robert staggered forward, shocked and sickened by the sight. 'Phil, what—'

'God Almighty,' Philip cursed, the blasphemy sounding odd in his mouth. He screwed up his face as another bolt of pain seared through his body and he snorted, spittle flying from his mouth to sliver down his front.

'A bullet in the leg,' the surgeon explained, pointing at Philip's left thigh where the flesh was horribly torn. Bright red blood ran down to the table's surface, the skin at the edges of the wound black with thick, dark blood. White bone showed through the redness.

Robert stared at the wound. 'Where was your armour?'

'I didn't put it on. It slowed me down.'

'You foolish boy. Will it mend?' he asked the surgeon.

'I cannot say, my lord,' the surgeon said. 'Only time will tell.'

'You cannot say?' Robert repeated incredulously. 'You will say, damn you, or I shall run you through where you stand.' He pulled his sword from its scabbard and pointed it at the surgeon's chest.

'Uncle.' Philip's shaking hand pushed away the point of the sword. 'You do me no good by killing my doctor. He is a good man. He will do what he can.'

'He better,' Robert growled, sheathing his sword. 'This is my nephew,' he said to the surgeon. 'More, he is my heir and my son. You will take care of him.'

The surgeon nodded uneasily.

'Leave me, Uncle,' Philip tried to smile. 'You must be needed elsewhere. I think I could sleep for a while, if this fellow will only aid me by removing the bullet. Believe me, Uncle, I will be here when you come again.'

Philip's wound did not heal. Some two weeks passed and Philip appeared to be improving, but one morning he had lifted his bedclothes a little and the smell of putrefaction greeted his nostrils. Gangrene had set in, for which there was no cure, save for the amputation of the limb, but the surgeon shook his head and said it was too late even for that.

So Philip, the hope of many, so beloved, so accomplished, died and with him, Robert's dreams of victory. He was sick of the Netherlands. He wanted to go home.

CHAPTER FIFTY-NINE

HAMPTON COURT PALACE

Elizabeth tapped her foot impatiently while the ambassador before her twittered on. She had no idea what he was talking about, for she had stopped listening about ten minutes before, when Hatton had leant over her shoulder and whispered in her ear that Robert had arrived at the palace.

The ambassador finished his sentence and Elizabeth was suddenly aware that he expected her to make some reply.

She smiled gently. 'My good man, now is not the time for such a question.' *Whatever that question was*, she thought. 'We shall talk more another day.'

The ambassador opened his mouth, his brow creasing in confusion. This was not the response he had expected. But Hatton guessed which subject was occupying the queen's mind and he expertly guided the poor man away from the Presence Chamber with an offer of dinner.

Hatton met Robert on the way out. 'Leicester, it's good to see you.'

'And you, Hatton. How is the queen?'

Hatton bit his bottom lip and hung his head to one side, the ambassador at his heels, momentarily forgotten. 'Not so good. The death of Mary Stuart, it... well, it has not been easy, Leicester, that I can tell you.'

'I don't imagine it has, Hatton. I hear Walsingham and Cecil are banished from her presence for their part in it.'

'Yes. For Cecil's part, I think he is almost glad. The queen sets a swift pace, and he has difficulty keeping up these days. I know his wife praises the death of Mary Stuart for that reason alone.' Hatton grinned at him. 'The queen is eager for your return. This fellow here,' he jerked a discreet thumb at the ambassador behind him, 'had no chance at all when I told her you were in the palace. She didn't listen to a word of his speech, poor man.'

Robert smiled gratefully. 'I am just as eager to see her. Good to see you, Hatton. Let's dine tomorrow.'

The warders opened the doors to the Presence Chamber, and as Robert entered, he felt dozens of courtiers' eyes fall upon him. He held himself upright, making a strong effort to ignore a new pain in his right leg as he placed his weight upon it. He paid no attention to the courtiers as he passed them, though he was aware they smiled and inclined their heads to him. He looked only at the woman who seemed years older than when he had left her six months before, the woman who never took her eyes off of him.

Robert stood before her, bent his left knee and suppressed a wince as his right banged against the floor-boards. 'Your Majesty.'

'My Lord,' the thin voice croaked, and he looked up sharply in concern. Elizabeth smiled down at him, and he suddenly knew that everything was going to be all right. She would not hurl abuse at him for his failures, at least not in public. She held her hands out to him and stepped down from the dais, her skirts swishing on the wood. 'I am glad you are back,' she said, pulling him towards her and kissing his cheek.

'I am glad to be back, Bess,' he murmured against her ear.

She drew back, her eyes glinting with tears. 'Come with me, my lord,' and still holding his hand, drew him along behind her to her chamber. Her Ladies moved to follow her, but she shooed them away.

She turned the handle of her Privy Chamber door herself before her warders could do it for her and dragged Robert inside. Before he could utter a word, Elizabeth had thrown her arms around his neck and was crying, great shuddering tears. He held her tight until her tears gradually abated and she pushed him roughly away.

'I do not know why I should be pleased to see you, Rob,' she sniffed. 'You have done me many an ill turn.'

'Oh, Bess, please, don't let us begin like this. I know you have reason to be angry with me, I admit my faults. Is that not enough?'

'I needed you and you weren't here. They tricked me, all of them, those curs Cecil and Walsingham. They killed her, killed her without my consent. I didn't want her dead.'

'But Bess,' he soothed, taking her hand, 'she *is* dead and what is done cannot be undone. Why torment yourself?'

'Because it isn't over. There will be consequences, I know it. I have killed an anointed queen. What is to stop anyone else from doing the same to me?'

'You are well protected and well loved by your people.'

'Maybe that is true, but what of the Spanish? Philip has been waiting for years to attack England and now I have given him the perfect excuse by killing a fellow Catholic. God's Death, Rob, I have killed a saint.'

She began to laugh, a high hysterical laugh that made Robert think of her mother, Anne Boleyn, who was said to have developed a hysteria while waiting for her execution. Without thinking, Robert slapped her cheek, hard.

'For your own good, Bess,' he whispered, his face close to hers. 'Now, I will not have this madness. Mary Stuart is dead. You driving yourself mad is no help, to you or your people. This must stop. I am here now.'

'Then stay here with me,' she pleaded, gesturing to her bed. 'Don't go home to Lettice tonight.'

He hesitated. 'What will everyone think if I stay?'

'To the devil with what everyone thinks,' Elizabeth snapped. 'At my time of life, why should I care for the tongues of gossips?'

'At your time of life, Bess? You are not old. You could dance those young scamps out there under the table every night.'

Elizabeth dismissed all her attendants, and they supped till late, and Robert consumed a vast amount of wine and, for once, Elizabeth did not chide him for it. His head was nodding upon his breast when Elizabeth pulled him to her bed and laid him back on it. He was asleep as soon as his head touched the pillow. She pulled off his boots and threw them on the floor. She stood for a moment looking down at him. This was Robert Dudley, Sweet Bonny Robin, lying bloated and red-faced upon her bed. She laughed to herself. Time was when Robert would have been anything but asleep at such a time.

But time had moved on. She felt herself growing old. She tried to hide the signs with heavy makeup and unnaturally red wigs, but these props could not change her inside. The death of Mary Stuart had heaped even more worries upon her, and she had felt alone, so very alone.

She allowed herself a satisfied smile. She was not alone now. Robert's first night back in England was spent with her, and the husband of Lettice was even now in Elizabeth's bed.

Robert began to snore and, like a mother, Elizabeth pulled the bedclothes over him, tucking them under his chin. For the first time she could remember, she undressed herself, her fingers clumsy with the unfamiliar lacings and hooks. Wearing nothing but her shift, she eased back a section of the bedclothes and curved her thin body around Robert's, covering herself again with the blankets. He moaned groggily as her leg rested upon his and he eased his arm under her body, arcing it around her waist. He did not wake up at all that night and the two of them slept late the following morning.

CHAPTER SIXTY

1588

'We are sorry to say it, but we have a poor opinion of this Spanish Armada and fear some disaster,' Elizabeth said to the council, reading from the letter she held. 'There, gentlemen. Even the Pope has no faith in the Spaniards. Why look you so, Walsingham? Do you doubt the words of your own spies?'

'No, madam,' Walsingham shook his head. 'I do not doubt that the Pope spoke those words, but I do fear he underestimates the power of Spain.'

'Ha,' Elizabeth snorted, pulling a plate of walnuts towards her. 'Drake has seen to the power of Spain. He has destroyed Spanish ships faster than Philip can build them.' She bit down and winced as a pain shot through her cheek. No one noticed and Elizabeth was faintly annoyed. All her counsellors were searching through the documents scattered across the table before them, trying to find some argument among the thousands of words to convince the queen of the danger. 'Cecil and I will settle this matter with Spain. Peaceably.'

'You mean a treaty with Parma, madam?' Robert

asked. 'The peace is a fraud, madam. Parma plays you for a fool.'

Elizabeth's eyes blazed. 'How dare you, I wil—'

'I dare, madam, because next to you, the thing I hold most dear is the safety of this country and its people.' It was a calculated answer, one that all present knew the queen would not argue with.

'Do you dare to say I hold them any less dear?' Elizabeth said, 'I am trying to spare them from another war—'

'Walsingham,' Robert again interrupted her, holding out his hand, 'that letter from Lord Howard.'

Elizabeth watched tight-lipped as Walsingham sifted through his pile of papers, found the letter Robert wanted and handed it to him.

Robert held the paper at arm's length and read aloud. '"There was never, since England was England, such a stratagem and mask made to deceive England as this treaty of peace". You see, madam? Even Admiral Knollys, your own cousin, knows this peace to be false.'

'Indeed?' Elizabeth tapped at her empty wine cup with her fingernail and Hatton poured more wine into it from a jug on the table. 'What else does the Admiral know?'

'Only what is known by us all, madam,' Walsingham answered. 'The Spanish are preparing a fleet for the invasion of England and may be on our shores at any time.'

'Such melodrama, my Moor,' Elizabeth sneered, and Walsingham had to bite his lip. 'I will not tolerate such scaremongering. I want evidence of this armada before I set my people on a course of war. Bring me that evidence, and I may reconsider.'

'Enough, Rob.' Elizabeth took the wine cup from his hand. 'Any more and you shall be asleep and I want you awake. I want to talk to you about your stepson. He wants something to do.'

Robert belched. 'I thought he was busy keeping you amused?'

'Do you mind that?'

'Would it matter if I did?'

'Of course it would,' she said, leaning forward and stroking the swollen blue veins on the back of his hand. 'I wouldn't want you to think you are being replaced.'

'I'm teasing you, Bess. It's all right, I can see the attraction. He's a lively lad.'

Elizabeth grunted. 'Needs bringing down a peg or two.'

'Well, he gets that from his mother.'

Elizabeth gave his foot a gentle kick. 'Anyway, you are getting fat and overworked. I want you to give your stepson the Master of the Horse.'

'That would keep him close to you.'

'You are jealous.'

'Can you blame me?' he cried. 'And I've held the Master of the Horse since the beginning of your reign, Bess. I have made it what it is. You have the best horses of any monarch in Europe and now you want me to hand it over to a boy just out of his swaddling clothes?'

'He's hardly that,' Elizabeth giggled.

Robert was suddenly too tired to argue. 'Oh, give him the Horse, if that is what you want. What have you in store for me?'

'First, tell me what you really think of Spain and do not exaggerate the matter.'

'What I really think is what I said earlier,' he protested. 'The Spanish are planning to attack and at present, we will not be able to put up any kind of defence. It is as simple as that. And remember, you said yourself Philip of Spain now has the perfect excuse to invade.'

Elizabeth nodded unhappily. 'With Mary Stuart dead by my hands. She causes me more trouble dead than alive.'

'Mobilise the fleet, Bess. Walsingham and Drake can provide the evidence you demand. Parma deceives you with talk of peace. Philip is readying his fleet. The Spanish are coming.'

'I suppose I must believe you, as you all say the same thing. Except Cecil, of course.'

'Oh, Cecil is an old woman,' Robert said impatiently.

'What am I then, Rob?' Elizabeth raised an eyebrow.

'Cecil is a good man,' he replied hastily, sidestepping her question, 'but cautious, too much so. He has his eyes on his account books and the treasury. Of course, to prepare for invasion will take money and your treasury will shrink, perhaps desperately so. But if it is a case of an empty treasury or a Spanish-swollen England, I know what course I should take.'

Elizabeth considered for a few minutes. 'You always were most persuasive, Rob. Damn you.'

'Then you will—'

She nodded. 'I shall give the order for war, however much it goes against my conscience.'

'To hell with conscience. What have you to feel guilty about? It is Spain who are the aggressors, not us. And besides, your conscience will feel better when we are celebrating an English victory.'

CHAPTER SIXTY-ONE

Tilbury was damnably cold, and Robert wrapped his fur
cloak tighter about his neck. Once Elizabeth had decided
to see off the Spanish, events progressed at a swift pace.
Orders were sent to Dover and along the coast to prepare
for an invasion, and Robert was despatched to Tilbury
with orders to amass a land army in the event of an incur-
sion into England via the Thames. Elizabeth had promised
him an office to make up for the loss of the Master of the
Horse and she had been as good as her word. Robert had
command of the land army and the grand title of Lieutenant and Captain General of the Queen's Armies and
Companies.

Robert had taken up his command with enthusiasm at
first, but by the time he had set up camp, he had realised
what a burdensome task he had ahead of him. It was like
the Netherlands all over again. So much to do and few officers capable of executing his orders or willing. He had
found some of his officers treating the whole thing as a
joke, disobeying orders and sauntering off to the coast,

where they had behaved like ruffian schoolboys, disdainful of Robert and his position.

For himself, Robert was often sent here and there, trying to raise up companies of men with patriotic speeches, or if those did not work, trying to generate self-interest with talk of rewards. The army was seriously understocked and a great deal of his time was spent trying to find supplies to feed the men.

It took time and much effort, but his army was eventually ready for a visit from the queen.

Elizabeth arrived by a gloriously bedecked and canopied barge escorted by two thousand men. Her entrance was grand, but her land procession was to be intimate. She rode a white horse, herself dazzlingly arrayed in a gown of purest white, a steel corselet and bodice her only concession to the safety concerns of her counsellors. Robert walked on her right, his stepson, Essex, leading her horse on the left. The ranks of men parted as they approached and many dropped to their knees before this woman who appeared, goddess-like, in their midst.

She dropped down lightly from her horse into Robert's arms and he led her by the hand to a makeshift dais from which she was to address her subjects. Robert took up a position to the side and her words flew over his head to the men, who, he noted, looked at their queen with awe. It was easy for a man like Robert, who had been almost daily in the presence of the queen for thirty years, to forget that the ordinary people of England rarely had a chance of seeing their sovereign close up.

Elizabeth was remarkable. Her speech was full of rousing phrases and stirring words. She promised to stay and fight with them if necessary, to lay down her life for her subjects and her country, and they believed her. The cheering was overwhelming as she stepped down, her hand in Robert's, and she smiled warmly at him, basking in her subjects' love. He led her towards the tent where a supper table awaited them and the officers.

'I bid you all, leave us.' Elizabeth said to the officers, and they departed. 'So, Rob, how did I do?'

'You were glorious,' Robert said.

'I was, wasn't I?' Elizabeth laughed and clapped her hands. 'I still love to hear it.'

'You love to hear how wonderful you are?'

'The cheers of my people, you rogue,' she flicked her napkin at him. 'But I do love to hear how wonderful I am as well.'

Robert laughed, then wished he had not, as it seemed to make the pain in his stomach worse.

Elizabeth's eyes narrowed. 'Rob, you are not well.'

'No, Bess,' he admitted, 'I am not. I will be glad when all this is over and I can go to Buxton.'

'The waters there will cure you?'

'They always have before.'

'You eat too much,' Elizabeth said, sinking back into the chair and fidgeting with a cushion.

'As you always tell me,' Robert agreed, wishing Elizabeth would dismiss him, for he was damnably weary and wanted nothing but his bed.

'You cannot stay too long at Buxton, though. I shall need you.'

'If you need me, I will not go.'

'Oh, you fool, of course you must go. But I want you back, sound in mind and body, you hear? You look tired, my love. Go to your bed.'

He smiled gratefully at her. 'Thank you, Bess. My stepson shall escort you to your lodging. Shall I see you in the morning?'

'Yes, Rob. Let us hope the morning will bring good news.'

The morning came, clear and bright, and with it, a muddied, horse-sweat stinking messenger from the coast with the news that the Spanish armada had been defeated. Drums beat, fire beacons blazed, and there was wine and song aplenty throughout the camp at Tilbury. Money was always a concern with the queen and Robert was instructed to break up his army and send his men home as soon as possible to avoid unnecessary expense. This done, he made his way to London.

He stayed only two days, enough time to celebrate and watch his stepson parade the remaining troops, but he was more than ready to make the journey to take the soothing waters at Buxton.

CHAPTER SIXTY-TWO

Robert first went home to Wanstead. The journey had been beset by torrential rain and the road had turned to thick mud. He had pulled up the wooden windows of his coach against the foul weather and now sat huddled in the corner, wrapped in his thickest fur cloak and leaning his aching head against the side of the swaying, rattling coach.

'My lord.' His attendant, Richard Pepper, reached forward and gently shook Robert's knee. 'My lord, we have arrived.'

Robert opened a bleary eye. The coach door opened, and Pepper stepped down, holding out a helping hand. Lettice waited for him at the door, looking bright and younger than her forty-six years. Robert supposed that was the effect of fornicating nightly with Christopher Blount, his Gentleman of the Horse. Robert knew he should care more, run the young scamp through with his sword. Ten, perhaps even five years ago, he would have done, but not now. Now he didn't care, had not the energy to care, and it even gave him a sense of relief. If Lettice was being serviced regularly by Blount, she would not pester him in bed.

'My dear,' he greeted her with a weak smile.

'Robert, you look ill. Are you sure this trip to Buxton is good for you?' She took him by the arm and led him into the hall. 'Perhaps you should just rest here?'

He walked away from her into the main chamber and sank heavily into a cushioned chair. 'If you do not wish to accompany me, Lettice—'

'You are my husband, and I go where you go. If you allow me to, that is,' she added peevishly, settling herself into a chair opposite.

'I just thought you may have reason to want to stay here, that is all.'

'What reason could I have?' she asked sharply, wondering what he knew.

He sighed and said, 'We leave in the morning. I trust I can leave all the packing to you, my dear. You know what I want to take. I am going to bed.'

Lettice kicked the bedclothes back, for the night had turned very warm. 'I suppose you are writing to her.'

'Yes.' Robert sat at a table in the bay window. It was a light evening, and with the aid of a candle, he could just see well enough to write by. He dipped his quill in the ink and continued his letter to Elizabeth.

'You only left her three days ago.'

'She wants to know how I am, Lettice.'

Lettice sighed. She had grown tired of being jealous of the queen. She still loved Robert, but since the death of their son, that love had diminished. She knew it was irrational, but some corner of her mind blamed him for their son's death. If Robert had spent more time with them and less with the queen, maybe their boy would be alive. She shook away the thought, knowing that her eyes would fill with tears if she permitted herself to think of her dead son.

'Come to bed, Rob,' she called gently. 'Leave that damned letter till the morning.'

'I've finished, anyway.' He threw down his quill and snuffed out the candle. He settled himself in the enormous bed gratefully and Lettice curled herself around him.

'Is that better?' she asked.

He grunted. 'Not really, Lettice. I feel like I'm wearing down.'

CORNBURY, OXFORDSHIRE

'Quick,' Lettice shouted to the gaping servants as she clambered from the coach. 'My husband needs to be taken to his bed at once. You,' she pointed at a young girl, 'go to the village. Order the physician to attend to my husband at once. Tell him he is grievously ill.'

Robert cried out in pain as he stumbled to the front door of the lodge. Several pairs of hands gripped his arms and guided him towards the hall. A chair was placed beneath him and he fell into it, clutching at his burning stomach. He heard Lettice barking orders to the servants, then felt himself lifted into the air. Four men had taken hold of the chair and were carrying him up the stairs to his bedchamber.

He must have passed out, for he did not remember being put to bed, yet when he opened his eyes, he was flat on his back with the bedclothes pulled up to his chin. He licked his dry lips.

'Lettice?' he whispered, and from the window, a black shape moved to the side of the bed.

'I'm here,' she said gently, leaning over to stroke his brow.

'The pain—'

'I know, dearest. The doctor is here. He will give you something for the pain.'

'My lady.' The surgeon steered Lettice away from the bedside. 'I have nothing to give him. There is nothing more I can do.'

'Nothing?'

'The earl is dying. It's only a matter of time.'

Lettice looked over the doctor's shoulder at her husband, who was in so much pain, dying before her very eyes. Even now, William Haynes, one of Robert's pages, leant over his master and attempted to place a cup of the doctor's medicine to his lips, but with what little energy Robert had, he swept William's hand aside. William came over to Lettice.

'My lady,' he said softly, 'my lord refuses the medicine. Perhaps you should try?'

Lettice suddenly gripped the doctor's wrist. 'There is something you could do. Your medicine. A larger dose, that would… that would—'

'My lady,' the doctor interrupted, horrified. 'I could not do that.'

'God rot you,' Lettice snarled. 'My husband is in agony and you yourself say that he is dying, that you can do no more for him. So, release him. Let him die, I beg you.'

'No, my lady. For the sake of my immortal soul, I cannot do as you ask.'

Robert slipped in and out of consciousness. When he was awake, he thought of Lettice. He knew she would survive without him. Knew it and was not upset. But then he thought of Elizabeth and was glad that at least someone would mourn him. How would she bear the loss of him? They had been together for more years than some people were married. They had had their arguments, their jealousies, and their separate betrayals. Yet, they had stayed together and loved. What was a marriage if it was not that?

He also thought of his family; not Lettice, not his step-family, but that family he had lost so many years before. Of his mother, of his brothers, but most especially, of his father. He had tried to live his life in a way that would have made his father proud, but he knew he had failed. He had tried for a crown and Elizabeth and Amy's death had defeated him. He had tried to become a great soldier but pride had defeated him. He had tried to continue the Dudley line and death had defeated him. The room darkened still more, and the voices grew fainter.

Robert Dudley closed his weary eyes and died.

CHAPTER SIXTY-THREE

Cecil limped along the Long Gallery, wincing with each step, his gouty left foot a throbbing agony. As he passed the large windows, he looked out into the gardens of the palace and saw courtiers in an unusual state of happiness. He wished he was young enough to feel the same for he knew the jubilation could not last the month.

Or at least, he hoped not. He understood the need to celebrate; a little island had not only withstood but fought off the might of Spain and that didn't happen every day. But the expense! The costs had being going around his head all night and he wondered at the queen's willingness to spend so much. But then, she was happy, and he was pleased to see her so.

He heard feet running up behind him and he turned stiffly.

'My lord.' One of his pages was holding out a letter to him. 'One of Lord Leicester's men just delivered this.'

Cecil took the letter and tried to ease his thumb under the sealed flap but his long walking stick hampered him.

He gave the letter back to the boy and told him to break the seal on the letter. 'Read it, boy.'

The boy read the contents of the letter aloud and then looked up at his master.

Cecil's face had turned grey. He stared out of the window, watching the courtiers as they laughed. 'He gives with one hand, and takes with the other,' he muttered.

'Cecil,' Elizabeth hallooed with a wide smile as the chamber doors opened. 'Sir Francis here was just telling me how the Irish are taking care of the Spaniards.'

Cecil gave a curt nod to the stocky Drake. 'Indeed, madam. You must tell me later, Sir Francis.'

Elizabeth grinned, curling herself into a chair. 'I don't mind hearing the story again.'

'I will hear it later,' Cecil said firmly. 'Sir Francis, would you mind leaving us?'

'Is something wrong, Cecil?' Elizabeth frowned when Drake had gone.

'Yes, madam, something is indeed wrong.' He paused, uncertain how to frame his next sentence. 'I have received news from the countess of Leicester.'

'What news do I want to hear from that woman?'

'Madam,' he said with a deep sigh, 'the earl of Leicester has died.'

Elizabeth stared at him. His heart quickened as her amber eyes widened and darkened to brown. Her throat with its sagging skin tightened.

She rose slowly, her hands gripping the pommels of the chair. 'Robin... dead?'

'He died at Cornbury, on his way to take the waters at Buxton.'

'He wasn't well when he left,' she said falteringly. 'That's it,' she pointed a shaking finger at him. 'Your message got it wrong. He's not dead, he's ill. He will be well again.'

'Madam, there has been no mistake. The countess herself has written this letter.

'You cannot trust that woman!' Elizabeth shrieked. 'She lies. She always lies. Look,' she said suddenly, passing through the open doorway that led to her bedchamber, 'look at this.' She snatched up a letter from a table by the window. She thrust it into his hand and he saw the image on the broken seal, the bear and ragged staff, the earl of Leicester's emblem. 'He wrote to me not a week ago.'

'He died three days ago, madam. I do not lie to you.'

'He can't be,' she cried, shaking her head. 'He wouldn't leave me.'

'He would never have done so willingly.'

Elizabeth looked at him, her face contorting as her tears fell. He smiled sympathetically. Then she sprang at him. Her thin, bony hands pushed him backwards. He almost fell as she forced him from the room. She yanked the doors shut, and he heard the key turning in the lock.

Then he heard a thud against the wood, a sliding sound, sobbing. He knocked lightly, pressing his ear to the door. 'Your Majesty?'

CHAPTER SIXTY-FOUR

She lay on her side on the canopied bed, legs drawn up to her chest. Every now and then, her spare, thin frame would shudder as another sob worked its way up from her chest to be belched out through her aching throat. The greying hair that was never shown to the wide world clung to her skull, bereft of its disguise of copper curls and jewels, which lay on the floor, thrown there after she had ripped it from her head in the first violence of her grief. The false hair had slid across the floorboards, its jewelled pins scattering, coming to rest beneath an oak coffer, like some remnant of a beheading.

The sunlight dipped and darkened, marking the passing hours as it moved from one panelled wall to another. At last, the dazed, staring eyes blinked and moved to the paper that lay on the pillow beside her. Her long fingers reached for it, gripped it in her hand, the broken wax seal digging into her palm. She clutched it against her heart, wishing she could feel his touch upon it.

How could God do this to her? He had given her such a victory, a shining hour, and then blighted it by exacting a heavy payment. For defeating the armada, He had taken

Robin. And left her alone. She screwed up her face as the pain came again. Could He have not taken someone less dear? Hatton, Walsingham? She could even bear the loss of Burghley if only she had Robin still.

She turned over and climbed shakily from the bed, still clutching the letter. She shuffled to her desk, stumbling on the folds of her skirts, and fell into the chair. Reaching for her quill, she wrote 'His Last Letter' on the cream page, threw the pen aside and blew on the ink to dry it.

A simple letter had become a treasure, as precious to her as the jewels that lay in the casket by her bed. She opened its lid and placed the letter inside. As she did so, her fingers brushed against the metal frame of a miniature portrait. She withdrew it, berating herself for leaving it so long since she had looked at it last. Robert looked back at her, a younger Robert than the one who had departed less than a month before to take the waters at Buxton. He had been such a handsome man, she reflected with a wistful smile. A handsome boy too, even at eight years old. That was when they had first become acquainted in the schoolroom they shared. He had been a friend to her from the first.

He never stopped.

ALSO BY LAURA DOWERS

Visit my website - www.lauradowers.com
You can also follow me on:

facebook.com/lauradowersauthor
goodreads.com/lauradowers
amazon.com/author/lauradowers